WEE WILLIAM'S WOMAN

Book Three of The Clan MacDougall Series

SUZAN TISDALE

Targe & Thistle, Inc.

Cover Art: Damonza

Printed in the United States of America

ISBN: **978-0985544348**

I am dedicating this book to my uncle,
Fred Dixon,
who passed away on March 5, 2013.
Fred was one of the most remarkable,
amazing men that I have ever known.
He loved to introduce me as "my niece Suzie, the author," ...
Words cannot begin to express what Fred meant to me
and to those who knew him.
This book is for him.

Don't be sad, we had fun.

For my children because you are amazing and
I love you beyond all measure
For my cousins...never let go of your dreams
For all my aunts and uncles...thanks for being awesome
And for all of my nieces and nephews.

ALSO BY SUZAN TISDALE

The Clan MacDougall Series

Laiden's Daughter

Findley's Lass

Wee William's Woman

McKenna's Honor

The Clan Graham Series

Rowan's Lady

Frederick's Queen

The Mackintoshes and McLarens Series

Ian's Rose

The Bowie Bride

Rodrick the Bold

Brogan's Promise

The Clan McDunnah Series

A Murmur of Providence

A Whisper of Fate

A Breath of Promise

Moirra's Heart Series

Stealing Moirra's Heart

Saving Moirra's Heart

Stand Alone Novels

Isle of the Blessed

Forever Her Champion

The Edge of Forever

Arriving in 2018:

Black Richard's Heart

The Brides of the Clan MacDougall

(A Sweet Series)

Aishlinn

Maggy (arriving 2018)

Nora (arriving 2018)

Coming Soon:

The MacAllens and Randalls

PROLOGUE

LATE WINTER 1345

Winter was unrelenting. It held on to the land as fiercely as a Highland warrior grasped his sword, refusing to let loose its grip and allow spring its turn.

The cold night air bit at the men who sat silently atop their steeds. Watching, waiting, looking for any movement, any sign of life that might stir in the cottage that lay below them. Gray smoke rising slowly from the chimney before disappearing into the moonlit night was the only sign of life coming from within the cottage.

Puffs of white mist blew from the horses' nostrils like steam from a boiling kettle. The nine were draped in heavy furs, broadswords strapped to their backs, swords at their sides, and daggers hidden in various places across their bodies. If by chance anyone was awake at this ungodly hour, the sight of these fierce men would bring a chill of fear to even the bravest man.

Each man had been handpicked by his chief for the special qualities he held, whether it was his fealty, his fierceness, or his ability to enter a place unheard and unseen. 'Twas a simple task they'd been given: sneak in under the cloak of darkness and retrieve hidden treasures so they could be returned to their rightful owner.

The first inkling that things might not go as planned came from the fact that the night was not bathed in darkness as had been hoped. A full moon shone brilliantly, casting the earth in shades of blues, whites, and grays. Had they not been delayed two days by a snowstorm of near biblical proportions, they would have arrived two nights ago when it was certain to have been pitch black.

No worries, the leader of the nine had assured his men. The inhabitants of the cottage were more likely than not fast asleep at this hour. They would proceed with their mission, moon or no.

After studying the land and the cottage a while longer, the leader gave a nod of his head. He and his men proceeded toward the little farm, taking their positions around the perimeter. Two of his stealthiest men headed towards the barn where they dismounted and with the grace and silence of a cat, they entered.

The leader stood with two of his men not far from the entrance of the cottage. They waited patiently, keeping a close eye on the barn as well as the cottage. Everything seemed to be going as planned. But the leader of the band of retrievers would not breathe a sigh of relief until they were far away from these God-forsaken English lands.

He wished he could break down the door of the cottage and slit the throats of the three bastards inside. His chief had shot that idea down, but not before thinking on it for a long moment. The chief had admitted nothing would have brought him greater pleasure than knowing the bastards would not live to see the light of another day. But he could not allow his men to take the chance of being found and taken to the gallows.

Nay, their mission was simple and if all went well, no blood would be shed this night. In a matter of days, should the weather hold, the treasures would be returned and the men handsomely rewarded for their efforts.

Uneasiness began to creep under the leader's skin. The men in the barn were taking too long. Concern began to well in his belly. If the treasures weren't where they should be, he'd have no problem then in busting down the door to the cottage and killing the men inside. He shuddered when he thought of returning empty handed. 'Twas a possibility he did not enjoy. He swore under his breath he'd tear this farm apart until he found what he had come for.

God's teeth! What was taking them so long? He exchanged a look of concern with the two men who sat on horses beside him. Something was wrong. He could feel it in his bones.

After what seemed like hours, his men appeared from the barn and looked across the yard. They held up empty hands as they shrugged their shoulders. Damnation! This was not good, not good at all. He let out a heavy sigh and hung his head.

'Twasn't exactly how he had planned it, but at least now he had the opportunity to bash in the skulls of the three men inside the cottage. The idea of giving those sons of whores their due brought a pleasant tingling sensation to his belly. The night would not be wasted after all.

I

They called him Wee William.

But nothing about the giant man could be considered *wee.* Not his massive height or his arms and legs the size of tree trunks. Not his broad massive chest or his hands that were the size of buckets. And *especially* not his heart nor his honor.

As he sat atop his horse this cold winter night, he thought about the mission he and his eight men were undertaking. They were here to retrieve the treasures left behind by a beautiful young lass who not long ago had captured each of their hearts. Her simple treasures were hidden away on this small farm and he'd not leave without them.

The thought of running his dirk across the throats of the whoresons who inhabited the tiny cottage brought a smile to his face. He'd either bring back the treasures or the bastards' heads in baskets. Either way, he'd not leave this God-forsaken country empty handed.

It was to have been an easy mission, but nothing about it had been easy since they left Castle Gregor more than a sennight ago. They'd been plagued with a lame horse, a blizzard of near biblical proportions, and a bout with a stomach ailment that was almost as fierce as the blizzard. To say the least, the giant's patience had worn thin, and the eight men who traveled with him were growing just as impatient.

Now the two men he'd sent into the barn to retrieve the treasures were quietly walking toward him empty handed. Their footfalls were barely perceptible on the soft, powdery snow. As they approached, Wee William straightened himself in his saddle and cast a frustrated look to the two men who sat atop horses on either side of him. Eager smiles formed on their lips, which brought one to his own.

Now the Highlanders had the opportunity to make right the appalling wrongs that had been done to Aishlinn McEwan. They were just as eager as their leader to seek vengeance on the three men who'd cut off her braid more than two years past. The bastards had made her life a living hell.

Before he could form his next thought, the door to the cottage slowly opened. Yellow candlelight spilled out onto the soft winter snow and a half-asleep young man stood in the doorway, scratching his stomach and yawning. Terror filled the young man's eyes the moment he caught sight of the Highlanders that filled the yard before him. He dropped the candle and heard the flame sizzle in the snow before its light extinguished.

The two men on foot approached the young man with such stealth and speed that he'd no time to react. The young Englishman gasped as the two large Highlanders pressed their swords against his chest. Silently, they backed him into the cottage until his spine pressed against the wall.

Wee William and his men quickly dismounted to follow the others inside. He paused at the threshold and cursed the low doorway. He hated small cottages with low ceilings for 'twas impossible for him to stand completely upright in one.

The warriors inside gave a quick survey of their surroundings. They took note of a man asleep on a pallet in front of the low burning fire, while another slept on the only bed. The room smelled of smoke, bad ale and sweat.

With a frustrated sigh and a shake of his head, Wee William entered the cottage, albeit at an odd angle. His scowl was enough to make the bones of anyone with a half a dose of common sense rattle with fear.

Wee William drew in a quiet breath as he crossed the room in two steps to stand at the foot of the bed. At his barely measurable nod, one of the Highlanders kicked at the sleeping figure on the floor, then bent and pulled him to his feet. Simultaneously, Wee William grabbed the man in the bed and hoisted him up by the collar of his nightshirt, pulling him to his knees.

"What the bloody hell?" the man, startled from his sleep, began to curse. While the other two brothers shook with fear and remained mute, this one, the one that Wee William held, let loose with a slew of curses, demanding the Highlanders explain their presence.

The eldest, Wee William thought with a shake of his head. The one whose throat I look forward to slicing through the most.

As Wee William began to hand the eldest brother over to his man Rowan, he felt a resistance and heard an odd noise. On closer inspection, he saw that a rope tied to the eldest brother's ankle snaked across the bed toward the corner of the room.

With a smile, Rowan grabbed the angry eldest brother by the back of his shirt, twisted his arm behind his back and ordered him to remain still and silent.

"Black Richard!" the giant boomed in the Gaelic, "Light a candle!" His voice thundered through the small cottage and seemed to rattle the thatched roof.

Black Richard made his way to the mantle and lit a candle using the low embers from the fireplace. Glancing at his leader, he held the candle up to see what had captured the man's attention.

The candle cast a sliver of light across the small bed and into the corner. He saw nothing but a small dark shadow. Wee William gave a hard tug on the rope, which was quickly followed by a loud gasp, a gulp, and a slender leg flying into the air before landing on the floor with a loud thump.

Bending one knee onto the bed, which groaned and squeaked its protestations of his massive girth, he reached one large hand into the corner. He groped around in the dark, finding what he believed was an arm and pulled.

Another frightened gasp was heard as a figure was pulled through the air and landed with a thump in the middle of the bed. Black Richard held the candle closer.

It was that moment, as the candlelight flickered across the very frightened face of the most beautiful woman he had ever seen, that was Wee William's undoing.

The most beautiful, pale blue eyes—the color of moonlit snow when he thought of it—stared up at him. Actually 'twas only one eye, for the other was swollen shut. In the soft candlelight he could see a large, purple bruise surrounding her right eye, and another along her chin.

Long, soft tendrils of dark brown hair fell away from her face into a long braid that trailed across a very ample bosom. He could see the fear in her good eye. He could hear it in her breathing as her bosom rose and fell rapidly.

In that tiny moment of time, something began to happen to this giant's heart. 'Twas a rather odd sensation, one he could not ever remember feeling. 'Twas a palpable sensation. It started in his chest before exploding to his fingers and toes. It caught him completely off balance and left him feeling discombobulated and confused.

Blended with that, was a tremendous amount of anger. He didn't have to ask whom it was that left her beautiful face bruised and battered.

"Who are ye?" he finally managed to ask as he pulled his dagger from his belt. Her good eye grew wider as she sucked in a deep breath and held it. The giant shook his head and rolled his eyes in disgust. The fear he saw looking back at him intensified his anger toward the eldest brother. The anticipation of running a blade across his throat increased tenfold.

With a gentle hand that trembled ever so slightly, he lifted the young woman's slender ankle and cut the rope. "Again, I ask ye lass, who ye are?"

She shook her head, still looking quite fearful. "I don't speak the Gaelic," she whispered.

He repeated his question a little louder and this time in English.

"She belongs to me!" the man to whom she'd been tied yelled from behind the giant. "Ye keep yer mouth shut!" He directed his order to the beautiful young woman.

Wee William spun, growled deep in his throat, and lifted the man up by his collar before throwing him across the room. He landed on the table where two warriors grabbed hold of his arms before he could slide onto the floor.

The giant scowled at him before looking back to the young woman. "Are ye his wife?" he asked, his voice deep and menacing. She nodded her head but said nothing.

"Did he do that to ye?" he asked, referring to her blackened eye and bruised face. He knew the answer and only asked it for confirmation's sake. She answered with another affirmative nod of her head.

"You stupid whore! You keep your mouth shut or I'll beat you again!" the idiot shouted, struggling against the two warriors.

In the blink of an eye, the men holding on to him, each withdrew his dirk and held it against the man's throat. "Ye might want to reconsider that, Sassenach," the warrior with the long blonde hair growled at him.

"She's my wife! I have every right to beat her! So go back to the stinkin' land from where you came, you bloody Scottish heathens!"

The swift hand of the blonde headed warrior swung out and landed on the Englishman's nose. Blood spurted and began to run down his upper lip and across the side of his face.

"I hate the English," the warrior told him as he pushed his arm across the fool's chest. "Especially those that beat their women."

"Ye utter another word, ye coward, and I'll rip yer tongue out and feed it to ye through yer arse!" Wee William shouted angrily across his shoulder.

He looked back to the young woman as he sat down on the bed. Suddenly he felt the need to reach out and touch her face with his fingers, but immediately pushed the thought aside. Instead, he gently tugged at the hem of her shift to cover her bare legs. He heard her gasp the moment his hands touched the coarse fabric. Once he removed his hand, she lifted herself up by the elbows and scurried to the far side of the bed. She didn't take her eyes off his as she grabbed the pillow and held it tightly to her chest, as if the pillow could act as a shield.

"Are ye fond of yer husband lass?" he asked in a low, gentle voice, unsure why he'd asked that particular question. A heartbeat later, she slowly shook her head no.

Wee William glanced around the room. The two brothers who had remained quiet during the ordeal were proving to be far smarter than their older brother. Though he'd never had the displeasure of meeting any of them in person, he knew well who each of them were. He'd heard enough stories over the past year to know not a one of them owned either a heart or an ounce of compassion.

He turned back to the lass with the beautiful blue eyes and studied her for several moments. That odd and unsettling feeling was growing by leaps and bounds, and for the life of him, he didn't know what to make of it.

"Does he beat ye often, lass?" he asked quietly. She nodded her head again. His stomach tightened when he saw tears begin to well in her eyes. *Damned bloody Sassenach.*

"Would ye like to become a widow this night?" he could not have explained to anyone why he asked *that* particular question. He supposed it had something to do with the odd sensation that enveloped him. Or mayhap he simply hated men who beat their women. Or it could have been that beautiful face and that pale blue eye, filled with fear, staring up at him. Whatever the reasons, he found himself holding his breath while he waited for her to answer.

She swallowed hard, taking very little time to think on his question. Another nod and a whispered, "Aye," was the answer he hadn't realized he'd been hoping for until he heard her give it.

"They call me Wee William," he told her with a tilt of his head and a wink.

Her response was not what he was accustomed to. She didn't stare at him with mouth agape and ask *why* he was called that when one considered his size and stature.

Nay, this beautiful lass did something he was not accustomed to. Her full lips curved into a slight smile, but 'twas a smile nonetheless, and she offered her hand to him. When he took it in his own and felt her warm skin against his, he knew he was lost. Forever lost, to those soft blue eyes filled to the rim with tears. Lost to that exquisite face, bruises and all. He began to feel as though he had fallen through a deep chasm, but instead of falling hard to the ground, he was floating in the air.

"They call me Nora."

2

Nora. He let the sweet sound of her name roll around in his mind for a moment. He concluded it was, perhaps, the most beautiful sounding of names. *Nora.*

He turned his gaze back to her. *Nora.* There was a special, musical quality to it. *What the bloody hell is happening to me?* He forced a scowl to his face and stood, best that he could considering the very tight quarters, and looked around the room to his men.

"Take them," he said in Gaelic.

"Take them *where?*" Black Richard asked, with a tilt of his head, looking quite perplexed.

"Anywhere. Just take them, kill them, and leave the bodies fer the scavengers."

Every Highlander in the room blinked before casting an astonished look at Wee William.

"Ye canna be serious, Wee William," Rowan said.

"Aye, I am," Wee William answered calmly.

"But Angus said to no' kill anyone. We're to find the treasure—" Rowan began to protest.

Wee William wouldn't allow him to finish. "I ken verra well what

Angus said. But since we canna find the treasure, I'd rather we brought their heads back in baskets." He eyed his friend for a moment.

Rowan and Black Richard cast wearied glances at one another.

The idiot on the table tried to sit up again and began to make demands. "What the bloody hell are you going on about?" he shouted.

Once again, Rowan silenced him with another hard fist to his face. The man fell backwards, his head making a loud thumping noise as it hit the hard wooden table. The man moaned as his head lolled from side to side.

"Wee William," Black Richard began. "I beg ye to reconsider this." He pleaded, uncertain just how serious Wee William was with his order.

Wee William grunted. "Did ye no' hear the lass? She wishes to be a widow this night and *I* wish to see her request granted."

Had he lost his mind? The Highlanders stared at one another for a long moment. Mayhap Wee William only wanted the Englishmen to *think* they were headed to their deaths. Angus had been quite adamant that no lives were to be taken unless it was absolutely necessary.

Believing he wasn't truly serious about killing the three unarmed men, Black Richard and Garret stood on either side of the unconscious, bleeding brother, and lifted him to his feet. His head fell limp against his chest as the two men dragged him out of the cottage.

Tall Thomas and Daniel motioned for the other brothers to follow, which they did, without protest. They did allow them to pull on their boots before ushering them out the door, though 'twas more than any of them deserved. Rowan followed the group out of the cottage and closed the door behind them.

Once the small home was cleared, Wee William turned his attention back to Nora.

She had been quietly watching the events as they played out before her. She couldn't suppress feeling a bit of satisfaction each time the large Highlander hit her husband. It was all she could do to not cry out and beg for them to hit him again.

Deciding good manners barred cheering these strangers on, she remained mute. *Served the fool right,* she thought to herself. When the Highlanders gathered up Horace and his younger brothers, she was left wondering just where they were going and what would happen to them. She was also curious as to what they planned to do with her. She could only pray that they would show her some mercy and leave her unharmed.

"What are they doing with them?" she whispered, afraid to ask what his intentions toward her might be.

Wee William eyed her curiously for a moment. "Did ye no' say ye wished to be a widow this night?" he asked, as if his question would answer hers.

God has a very peculiar way of answering a girl's prayers, she thought to herself. How many prayers had she sent to the good Lord asking for a way out of her marriage? How often over the past months had she prayed God would strike Horace dead?

Of course, she'd meant for his untimely death to come by means of a heart seizure, an apoplexy, or a simple strike of lightning. She'd not once imagined a group of tall, angry, fierce looking Highlanders coming in the dead of night to kill him.

Their actual presence did not surprise her overly much as there were always strange people coming and going. More often than not they were coming to collect money Horace owed them. Her husband was as odd as he was cruel and was constantly getting into trouble of some sort or another.

Mayhap these men were sent to settle a debt on behalf of someone else, for Horace appeared not to recognize them. She wondered exactly who he had angered to the point that they'd send such big men after him.

Shivers of fear coursed over her as she sat staring up at this most strange fellow. Her teeth began to chatter and the lingering question seemed lodged in her throat.

"Are ye cold, lass?" Wee William asked. His voice was deep, and while he was a rather frightening man to look at, there was something odd about his voice. She should have found the sound of it quite frightening. Instead, she found comfort in it.

Nora's brow twisted into a knot of confusion before she realized she was shivering, from fear as much as the cold night air. Before she could answer, the giant lifted the blanket and tucked it under her chin and around her shoulders. She was quite surprised by his kind gesture. Horace would have yelled at her to stop chattering her teeth whereas the giant seemed to care. She thought that more than odd.

Seeing the fear still alight in her eyes and her shivering body, Wee William spoke softly. "Lass, I'll no' harm ye, and neither will me men."

It wasn't simply his words that told her he had no intentions of harming her, for if he had, he certainly wouldn't have cared if she were cold. Something in his hazel eyes told her he spoke the truth.

Her most fervent prayers were being answered this night. 'Twas all she could do at the moment to tamp down the wave of giddiness that bubbled in her heart. She was finally free.

"Have ye a place to go, lass?" Wee William asked her.

In truth, she had no place to call home and no desire to make this one hers. But she did have a mission to tend to, now that Horace and his nasty brothers were on their way to meet their maker. Excited that she was now free and could leave this place and its memories far behind, she flung the blanket off and leapt from the bed.

"Nay, William," she told him excitedly as she rushed to the trunk at the end of the bed. "I've no place to call home, but I do have family I need to get to!"

He was unsure why the thought of her leaving him left a knot in his stomach. But the feeling was there, making him feel foolish. It had to be the blue eyes. He'd always been partial to blue-eyed women.

Nora was mumbling to herself as she quickly pulled her green dress over her head and began lacing it up the front. Once done, out of habit, she went to the spot by the door to retrieve her shoes. Shoes that weren't there. Horace had hidden them to keep her from running away again.

Wee William's eyebrows raised in surprise when he heard her curse and he could not contain the smile that formed on his lips.

Nora went back to the trunk, threw the lid up again and searched inside. A moment later, she pulled out woolens and slammed the lid down. Her mind was racing with all she needed to do as she pulled them on over her cold feet.

Hope for a future without Horace in it had returned and she could barely wait to be out of the cottage. Once she had the woolens on, she set to packing what few possessions she had to her name. She took her good blue dress, the shift she wore in summertime, and the other pair of woolens and tied them up inside her shawl.

She jerked with a start when she heard Wee William chuckle. She tilted her head and looked at him. Small wrinkles had formed around his hazel eyes as he stared at her.

It suddenly occurred to her that she had no idea *why* he was here. "M'lord, forgive me, but why *are* you here?"

The smile left his face as he shook his head.

"Does Horace owe you for a gambling debt?" she asked.

"Nay," Wee William answered as he let out a heavy sigh. "'Tisn't me he owes a debt to, lass."

Nora nodded her head as if she understood. "I see. Then you're mercenaries sent to collect the debt for another?"

Wee William nodded his head. "Aye, 'tis something like that, lass."

"He has no money, and nothing of value left to his name," she told him. "He has gambled everything away."

Wee William let out another sigh. "'Tisn't coin we search for, lass. 'Tis far more valuable than coin, or even gold."

Nora tilted her head slightly as she thought about his statement. What could be more valuable than coin or gold? And who was Horace indebted to that would send Highlanders to English soil in the cold harsh winter?

Clarity dawned and suddenly it all began to make sense. "Aishlinn!" Nora exclaimed as she shot to her feet. "You're here to claim the debt they owe Aishlinn!"

The scowl returned to Wee William's face. "How do ye ken of Aishlinn?"

Nora rolled her eyes at him as if he were daft. "I've known Aishlinn since she was a little girl! Aye, they kept her tucked away most of the time, but I met her a few times." Nora came and stood before him. She was able to look him directly in the eye without straining her neck only because he sat on the bed.

"She was a beautiful young girl. They say she died last summer, that English soldiers killed her in a battle against a group of Scots." Nora rested her hands on her hips as she studied Wee William's face. When it remained unchanged, she knew without question that *that* mayhap, was not the truth.

"She still lives and that is why you're here. You've come for her treasures."

He was so surprised by what she'd just told him that he bolted upright off the bed. His head burst through the thatched roof and sent bits and pieces of it falling onto his shoulders. Cursing, he pulled away the fragments of the roof and drew his head back into the room. Cold air began to fill the room around him.

"What do ye ken of her treasures?" he demanded, bending over to look her in the eye.

For reasons she couldn't fathom, she didn't feel frightened by the sound of his loud voice booming through the cottage. Nor did she flinch in response to the deep lines that had formed across his forehead or the most serious expression on his face. Or the fact that he towered over her, even when he'd bent at the waist to look at her. The urge to giggle at the sight of such a large man with bits of straw sticking out of his hair, looking so utterly serious, stern and perplexed, was too much.

The giggle escaped and her face lit up with a smile, stinging her cheek and blackened eye in the process. Her fingers flew to her lips to suppress it, but the damage was done. The line in Wee William's brow deepened and his lips thinned into a hard line.

She knew she should have been frightened or at the very least concerned about angering him. Had Horace been the one standing there, looking so blasted angry, she would have been running for the hills in terror. She wondered briefly if she hadn't lost her mind.

"M'lord, I do apologize," she murmured before thrusting her hands into the pockets of her dress and pinching her thighs to quell her laughter.

Wee William tilted his head, baffled by her behavior. Mayhap the lass was daft or slow. The fact that she was married to Horace was enough evidence that she might not be well of mind.

"I ask ye again, lass. What do ye ken of Aishlinn's treasures?"

Nora cleared her throat before answering. "I found Aishlinn's things not long after I married Horace. I came across them one afternoon in the barn."

She purposely left out the reason *why* she'd been in the barn, hiding, fearful of her husband and his harsh, cruel, heavy hands. "I knew they must be Aishlinn's, for Horace would have sold them, if they were his. I knew that if Horace found the silver candlesticks or the trinket box, he'd sell them. I didn't know at the time if Aishlinn was dead or alive. But I couldn't let Horace get his dirty hands on her things. So I hid them."

Wee William took a step forward, his eyes alight with surprise and a hint of excitement. "Where are they now, lass?" He felt hopeful and imagined the sheer delight that would come to Aishlinn's eyes when he presented her with her treasures.

'Twas then that Nora's expression changed and she looked rather anxious. She took a deep breath before answering. "I hid them in the cellar."

Wee William's eyes immediately went to the floor and he began looking for the door to the cellar.

"M'lord," Nora whispered, knowing what his eyes searched for. "'Tis under the table."

As Wee William made his way across the room, the door to the cottage opened and Daniel and David walked in. Their presence gave Wee William pause.

"Rowan and the others are takin' the brothers away now, Wee William," Daniel said in Gaelic.

Wee William nodded his head in approval. "Good. Now help me move the table. I ken where Aishlinn's treasures are."

Curious glances flew between the three men before landing on Nora. "How do ye ken?" David asked, surprised by the news.

"The lass," Wee William told him, nodding his head toward Nora. "She came upon them and hid them before Horace could sell them."

She hadn't a clue what they were saying but could assume the discussion involved her for they were all staring at her. She began to grow uneasy.

Wee William seemed kind enough. Still, she had no guarantees as to what his intentions were. Remembering that Horace had been kind to her at one point, until he got what he wanted, brought forth an uneasiness that to spread to her toes. She backed away from them.

"She says the treasures be in the cellar," Wee William said as he moved the table aside and knelt on one knee. His men joined him and together they looked for the door that led to the cellar. It took only a moment before they found the small knothole and Daniel thrust his fingers in and lifted the door.

The three men stared into blackness for a moment before Daniel grabbed a candle, lit it and held it into the opening. A decrepit looking ladder led down into a large hole that was devoid of all light. It was impossible to estimate how deep or wide the cellar was. Even with the candlelight they couldn't see the bottom.

Wee William turned his attention back to Nora who now stood across the room, next to the fireplace. She looked positively terrified. Her good eye was opened wide and she had sucked in her bottom lip. He could see her hands tremble slightly.

Wee William looked at Daniel and David. "Hold the candle," he said as he handed it to Daniel. "I'll go down."

With nod of his head, Wee William twisted around and began lowering himself down the ladder. It creaked and groaned and for a brief moment, he thought it would give out. Cautiously, he stepped down a few more rungs then reached up for the candle before resuming his descent.

The ladder shook and groaned but eventually, Wee William's feet hit dirt. From where he stood, he estimated the hole to be at least ten feet deep and mayhap six feet wide. He held the candle out at arms length to get a better glimpse at his surroundings. Mostly empty shelves lined the walls of the cellar. A few dust covered jars and an old and dingy looking cloth made up the entire contents of the cellar.

Wee William let out a frustrated breath of air and looked around the small space but could find nothing of Aishlinn's treasures.

"Nora!" he called up from the cellar. "Where be the treasures, lass?"

For a long moment there was no response. Finally David spoke. "She says they be behind the ladder," he called down to Wee William.

Wee William took a step toward the ladder and held the candle out, looking for any sign of the treasures. He reached out a hand, but found no shelves or any space where anything could be resting or hidden.

"Nay," Wee William shouted up to his men. "I find nothin' here."

He heard mumbled voices above him as he continued to look.

"She says there be a spot in the wall, behind the ladder, toward the floor," David called down to him. "Ye'll have to look a bit to find a loose stone. Ye'll remove the stone and Aishlinn's treasures be behind it."

Rolling his eyes and cursing under his breath, Wee William bent to his knees. He reached around the ladder, best that he could within the tight confines, and felt for the loose stone. Nothing.

Irritated with wasting time, he shouted. "Send the lass down!"

He could hear a scuffling of feet and a muffled discussion taking place above him. Standing to his full height, he tried to wait patiently for Nora to appear on the ladder.

"I said, send the lass down!" he shouted up to his men.

Some time passed before Daniel replied. "The lass says to tell ye she'd prefer no' to."

Wee William's brow knotted. "What the bloody," he let out an exasperated sigh. "What do ye mean she prefers no' to?"

Daniel cleared his throat before answering. "She prefers no' to go into the cellar."

Wee William shook his head, ran a hand across his forehead and let loose a low grumble. He climbed the ladder until his head popped through the opening and searched for Nora.

She hadn't moved from her spot against the wall.

"Lass," he began. His voice was gruff. "I need yer help. Now, come below and help me find Aishlinn's things!" He hadn't intended to sound so angry, but he had little patience left.

Nora shook her head and pressed her back more firmly against the wall.

"Lass," he said gruffly. "Do no' dally there! Come help me find Aishlinn's things!"

She shook her head again, a bit more vigorously.

Wee William studied her more closely. Though he was a good six or seven feet from her, he could see her trembling and immediately felt guilty for being so short tempered with her.

"Lass, why will ye no' come help me?"

She swallowed hard and seemed to be searching for words. Several long moments passed and Wee William was beginning to think she'd not answer him. Finally, she spoke, her voice cracking. "I do not like it down there."

Her eyes connected with his, silently pleading with him to not push the matter further. 'Twas just a cellar, a place meant to store foods and other necessities. Why on earth was she so frightened?

"Please," she begged, a definitive tremble to her voice.

Wee William held out his hand. "Lass, I need yer help."

Nora swallowed hard again and appeared as if she were fighting some inner battle with herself.

"The stone is in the left corner, behind the ladder. I'm sure ye'll find it," she offered quietly.

Wee William let out a long breath. "Lass, we're wastin' time. Please, now, come help me."

A flash of anger filled her eyes. "No," she told him firmly.

"Why will ye no' come and help me find the blasted stone?" The conversation was going in circles.

Nora stood a bit taller. "I've my reasons."

She'd never been afraid of the dark until the past year. Until she'd married Horace and her life began to fall apart in huge, ugly pieces.

Nora looked into Wee William's face for some sign of trickery or deceit. They'd already told her they were going to kill Horace and his brothers. What was to stop them from leaving her in the cellar? Nay, she did not want to die that way.

"M'lord," she began, "I'd truly prefer not to go into the cellar. Keep looking and I'm sure you'll find Aishlinn's things." The only way she'd go into the cellar was kicking and screaming.

Wee William took a step up the ladder and studied her more closely. He had no doubt she was afraid, mayhap of the dark, or mayhap of being alone in the cellar with him. He felt something tighten in his chest. He didn't want the young woman to fear him.

"Lass, I promise I'll no' harm ye. And if it's the dark ye be afraid of, lass, I've a candle." He stretched his hand out a bit further.

Nora continued to look for some sign that he was being disingenuous. In the beginning of her marriage, Horace had fooled her more times than she could count or cared to admit. Months ago she had promised herself that she'd not let another man make a fool of her.

For inexplicable reasons however, she felt she could trust this giant man and his friends. They were all staring at her, looking perplexed by her refusal to enter the cellar. Their eyes held nothing but patience and concern. There wasn't the disdain or duplicity that she often found looking at Horace or his brothers.

Nora swallowed hard and took a step forward, albeit on very shaky legs. She prayed inwardly that she wasn't being played the fool again. She reasoned that had they wanted her dead they would have taken her along with her husband. They would have killed her already. Or worse.

Wee William let a slight sigh of relief pass through his lips when she approached. Nora knelt and looked him in the eyes.

"Do I have your promise that you'll not leave me below?" she whispered.

His chest tightened again for now he understood the reasons behind her trepidation. She was afraid he'd leave her in the cellar.

"I do so promise, lass." He smiled warmly at her before carefully stepping back down the ladder.

By the time Nora reached the bottom rung, her brow and upper lip were covered in sweat. Not from exertion, but from the undeniable fear that enveloped her. Her throat was tight and had gone completely dry. She paused on the bottom rung and prayed Wee William wouldn't overpower her, race up the ladder and pull it away before she had a chance to react.

After a time, she felt a large hand touch her waist. She took in a deep breath and waited, all the while her hands maintaining a death grip on the rung.

"Lass," Wee William whispered. "I promise I'll no' leave ye."

He would have sworn he could feel the fear emanate from her and hoped that she could hear the sincerity in his voice.

Taking a deep breath, Nora finally took the last step off the ladder and let loose her grip. She rubbed her sweaty palms on her skirts and turned around to face Wee William.

Above stairs, she had appeared small. But in the tight confines of the cellar Wee William could see that she was taller than most women. Even so, compared to Wee William, she was a wee thing. The top of her head barely reached his heart, which was at that very moment, pounding ferociously within his chest.

Trembling still, she looked up and stared into his eyes. "I do not like it down here," she whispered, as if her trembling hands and fear filled eyes weren't evidence enough.

"Then let's hurry and get Aishlinn's things so we may get above stairs," Wee William whispered as he offered her a reassuring smile.

Nora gave a quick nod and spun on her heels. She wiggled her way into the small space behind the ladder and in a matter of moments, had removed the stone, withdrawn a sack, and returned to Wee William.

She started to hand the sack to him, but thought better of it. Clutching it to her chest she eyed him suspiciously. He could not resist the smile that came to his lips. He could have taken that sack from her with very little effort.

"Ye can go first lass," he told her as he nodded toward the ladder.

As if fearing he'd change his mind, Nora quickly raced up the ladder. Moments later when Wee William emerged from the cellar, he found her once again, against the wall, clutching the sack to her bosom.

"I thank ye, Nora, and I'm certain Aishlinn would thank ye as well."

Nora gave a slight nod of her head to him. "I give ye my word, m'lord, that I'll not tell anyone that Aishlinn lives."

Daniel and David chuckled at the title Nora had bestowed upon their friend. Wee William cast them a look of admonition before turning his attention back to Nora. "I be no laird, lass. Just a man."

He came to stand before her and Nora thrust out the hand holding the sack. Wee William took it, but continued to gaze at her face. Inwardly, he hoped that Horace and his brothers would make some grave error in judgment that would give good reason for Rowan to insure they'd not live to see the light of another day.

Wee William's mind was a whirlwind of jumbled thoughts and images of mayhap placing a kiss on the lips of the woman standing before him. He cleared his throat and tried to think of something intelligent to say.

"Where will ye go now, lass?" he asked.

"To retrieve my younger brother and sister from Firth."

Wee William's brow furrowed at the mention of Firth. His good friend, Duncan McEwan had killed Desmond Walcott, the Seventh Earl of Penrith last summer when the man had made the mistake of trying to rape Aishlinn -- a second time. Aye, 'twas good to know that man was dead, but who knew what kind of man had taken his place.

"Firth?" Wee William asked with more than a hint of alarm in his voice.

Nora looked puzzled by his alarmed tone. "Aye, Firth," she answered. "Horace sent my brother and sister there the day after we married." Her good eye filled with sadness and her face fell. It was plainly evident that the memory was not a pleasant one.

Wee William's eye began to twitch. The more he learned of Horace, the more his hatred toward the man intensified. Horace was fond of sending innocent people to Firth. He'd sent his own stepsister, Aishlinn, there with no regard whatsoever to her safety.

"John is two and ten, and Elise is only six. I've not seen them in months." She choked slightly on the tears that threatened.

"I do not know how they fair, William, but I made them a promise that someday, somehow, I'd take them away from there."

Nora took a step forward and placed her hand on Wee William's arm. "I thank you, William, for making me a widow this night." Her lips curved into a warm smile. "Now I can keep that promise!"

The thought of being a widow and retrieving her brother and sister seemed to energize her. She grabbed her cloak from the peg by the door and draped it over her shoulders, then grabbed her bundle of belongings from the bed.

"I will be forever in your debt, William." Craning around Wee

William, she cast a wide smile to Daniel and David. "And to you as well!"

She turned back to Wee William. "Please, extend my thanks and gratitude to your other men as well, William. You and your men were the answers to many prayers and I will never forget any of you!"

Wee William stood dumbfounded before her. She meant to leave, on her own, to retrieve her brother and sister from Firth. 'Twas more evidence that she wasn't of sound mind. How did she intend to go about getting them out of the castle? Did she have any weapons, or plans, or help from someone?

"How do ye intend to get them out of Firth, lass?" Wee William asked as his mind searched for a way to delay her leaving.

"'Tis late and I'm sure all are abed. I've been in the castle several times and I know where they sleep. I'll just quietly creep in and take them."

It took a good amount of energy to suppress the urge to laugh at her naiveté. His men however, didn't possess the same restraint. They snorted at Nora's *plan.* She craned her head around to glare at their rude behavior. It was quite apparent that they weren't impressed with her plan. Nor were they moved by her icy glare of reproach.

Nora added a curt huff before looking back to Wee William. "My thanks to each of you," she said before turning around and opening the door. A gust of virulent wind thrashed into the room. Nora ignored it, lifted up the hood of her cloak and began to step out into the dark winter's night.

"Wait!" Wee William said as he grabbed her by the arm and pulled her back. He was looking at her feet. "Ye have no shoes, lass!"

She cast him a look that said she thought him dimwitted. "Aye, I know I've no shoes, William."

It was Wee William's turn to look at her as if she were daft.

"Horace hid them the last time I ran away. But I care not about my own comfort. I have to hurry to Firth, straight away. Now please, will you kindly remove your hand from my person?"

What was it about the English no' allowin' their women shoes? Wee William wondered silently. He thought back to when Aishlinn had first arrived at Gregor, wearing a tunic and trews meant for a man and no shoes.

There was no doubt as to Nora's sincerity or her intentions. Even if they were a bit naive and ill planned.

"Lass, we canna let ye go with no shoes. And we canna let ye go retrieve yer family without so much as a *sgian dubh*!"

Nora blinked and cocked her head to one side. "What is a-a-" she tried to pronounce the word but fell quite short of it. "Whatever that is you said."

"A *sgian dubh*. A dirk or a knife," he explained. "Ye've no weapons and no shoes. In case ye haven't noticed, it be winter. Ye'll freeze to death before ye even make it to the castle."

Nora shook her head. "I'm well aware of the fact that I've no shoes. I'm also well aware of the time of year."

Daniel and David came to stand nearer Wee William and Nora. With arms crossed over their broad chests and the smiles on their faces, they seemed to be enjoying the conversation that was taking place before them.

"Then ye'll agree, lass, that ye canna go," Wee William smiled.

"I agree to no such thing, William. I *must* go. I told you, I have a promise to keep."

"Yer feet will fall off before yer out of sight of this cottage." He shook his head, bewildered by her obstinacy.

Nora rolled her eyes. "Nay, I plan on taking Benny. I'm sure I'll be quite fine." She started to leave the cottage again, only to have Wee William pull her back in.

He realized she was not going to change her mind. "At least let me saddle yer horse fer ye."

"There isn't a saddle."

His eyes opened wide with surprise. "No saddle?"

Nora shook her head. "Nay. Benny isn't actually a horse."

Daniel and David looked at one another. The young woman was quite perplexing. "Then what is he?" David asked.

Nora cleared her throat and straightened her shoulders. "Benny is the ox Horace uses to plow the fields." It didn't really matter to Nora *what kind* of transportation she had, as long as she could get to Firth before dawn broke. It didn't matter there was no saddle; a blanket would suffice.

"Ye intend to ride an ox?" Daniel asked for clarity's sake.

"Aye, I do," Nora answered tersely.

Wee William took a deep breath in and let it out slowly. "So ye plan to go out in winter's night, with no shoes, no weapons, no provisions, and atop an ox to sneak yer way into a castle to retrieve yer wee brother and sister?"

When he put it that way, it did sound a bit imperfect. Nonetheless, she *had* to get to her brother and sister. She was a widow now, thanks to these fierce Highlanders. She was now free to go wherever she wished and not worry about a husband whose favorite hobby of late seemed to be making her life miserable.

Free though she was, she wasn't about to go anywhere without her family. Nora thrust her chin upward. "Aye, I do."

Broad smiles came to Daniel and David's faces as Wee William looked at them. Nora noticed an exchange of some sort taking place between the three men. 'Twas as if they could read one another's minds.

"I do no' think the lass be a Sassenach, Wee William," Daniel said in English, his eyes sparkling in the candlelight. Nora thought he looked quite mischievous.

Nora knew the term Sassenach was not a compliment but a derogatory term the Scots used in reference to the English. She supposed he meant to compliment her and decided to take it as such. "Why thank you," she paused. "What is your name, sir?"

"I be Daniel," he said with a slight bow at his waist. "This be me brother, David," he said, nodding toward his brother.

Nora could see the family resemblance. Both men were quite tall, though not nearly as tall as Wee William. They looked very imposing in their dark furs. They were quite similar in appearance. Both men had blonde hair that fell past their shoulders. But where David's eyes were green, Daniel's were a very dark blue.

"'Tis my pleasure," Nora said with a curtsey.

Wee William grumbled. He didn't like the way she smiled at his men. For some inexplicable reason he felt jealous. He let out a frustrated grunt. "If yer quite done with the social niceties, may we get back to the issue at hand?"

Nora smiled at Wee William. "Yes, m'lord," she said with a short curtsey. "Again, I thank you for your concern. Now, if you'll please excuse me, I must hurry."

Wee William grabbed her arm again and let loose with a frustrated sigh. "Again, I be no laird, lass, just a man. And, I canna let ye do this alone." He stopped her before she could begin another round of protests. "Ye canna go without shoes, horse, weapons, nor help. Me and me men will be honored to help ye get yer wee ones from Firth, lass."

Nora looked confounded by his offer of assistance. "Why would you do such a thing?"

"Ye kept Aishlinn's things safe, lass. Helpin' ye is the least we could do."

Nora studied each of the men for several long moments. They looked sincere, almost eager to help, and for the life of her, she could not begin to understand why. Nor could she grasp why it was she felt she could trust them.

They were savage looking men. Men who had burst into her home in the middle of the night and taken her husband and brothers-in-law, presumably to their deaths. Why did she feel more comfortable and safe with these men than with her own husband?

How many stories had she heard growing up that told of the savage and barbaric ways of the Scots? Aye they did appear that way, with their long hair, braids, beards, and massive fur-covered bodies. She had been taught that Scots beat their wives and children—and just how *that* differed from the way Englishmen behaved, she had no idea. Yet these men had shown her nothing but a gentle hand and were now offering their help.

Her father had been a good, honorable man who was always one to help those in need. Mayhap she caught a glimpse of him in the eyes of the men standing before her. He had died two years past and not a day went by that she didn't think of him or her mum who passed away in her childbed giving birth to Elise. Her parents had always been her strongest allies. Her heart ached with missing them.

It was the kindness she found in the eyes of these strangers that gave her hope. Hope she thought lost this past year.

Their help *was* needed. Dawn would be breaking across the horizon in a few short hours. She would allow them to help her get John and Elise out of Castle Firth. She could hitch the cart to the ox and use it as a means to get as far away from Firth as possible.

She would find employment with a manor house as a maid or servant of some kind. Mayhap she'd meet a kind man who would want more in a wife than just someone to punish. A man who'd allow her to keep John and Elise.

Her mind made up, she smiled at the men and gave them an approving nod. "I'll accept your kind offer, William. I'll never be able to repay you the kindness you've shown me this night."

Wee William let go the breath he hadn't realized he'd been holding. He was glad she came to her senses. A wee lass such as the one before him did not stand a chance against castle guards, shoes or no. With a broad smile, he scooped her up and headed toward his horse.

When she began to protest that she was quite capable of walking of her own accord, his smile broadened. "I canna let yer feet freeze, lass," he said by way of an explanation for carrying her. His heart thrummed happily as he quietly carried her through the soft snow.

Nora had no way of knowing that at that moment, as the giant Highlander carried her through the cold winter's night, she had just been claimed as Wee William's woman. He had decided at some point in the last few minutes that he would do anything to keep her, even if it meant breaking into an English castle in the middle of the night.

3

Wee William hoisted Nora onto his horse and made sure she was safely seated before unraveling a fur blanket from the back of his saddle. Using his dirk, he cut two strips from the fur then grabbed leather ties from his saddlebags. In short order, he had makeshift-boots wrapped around her feet.

"How do those feel, lass?" Wee William asked as he looked to see that his men were mounted and ready. Though each man held the reins to spare horses, Wee William had a strong desire to keep Nora close to him.

"They're quite warm!" she smiled down at him as she wriggled her toes. "I thank you, kindly."

Wee William pulled himself up to sit behind her and wrapped the remaining fur around her shoulders. As he leaned forward to grab the reins, he caught the faint smell of lilac and for a moment, he thought he might swoon and fall from his horse. Blue-eyed women who smelled of lilacs were dangerous.

Nora gasped as he tapped the flanks of his horse. "Wait!" she exclaimed as the horse moved forward. Wee William quickly pulled rein.

"What?" he asked impatiently.

Nora wriggled around to look at him. "The ox and cart! I'll need them after we get John and Elise. I cannot walk to southern England in this weather."

Wee William smiled and urged his horse forward. "Have ye family in the south?"

"Nay," Nora began.

"Have ye someone there waitin' fer ye?" he asked.

"Nay, but I hope to gain a position in a manner house or a castle, as a scullery maid, or a servant of some other fashion."

"Have ye ever been to southern England lass?"

Nora let out a heavy sigh. "Nay, I haven't." She'd never been more than a few miles from Penrith her entire life. But it mattered not at the moment. Soon she'd be reunited with her brother and sister and they'd be starting their lives over, somewhere far away from the horrible memories of the past year.

"Och! 'Tis a terrible place to raise children. 'Tis filled with all manner of evil, wicked men who'd think nothin' of taking advantage of an innocent young woman such as yerself."

Nora swallowed hard. What did William know of southern England, she wondered aloud.

Wee William chuckled. "I've been there. Only once mind ye, fer it was a den of sin and corruption and evil!" He feigned horror and added a shudder of disgust for good measure. "'Tis a place I wish never to step foot upon again."

Truth be told, Wee William had never been farther south than Northallerton. He preferred keeping his big Scottish feet safely on Scottish soil where the good Lord meant them to be.

He wouldn't be in England now were it not for his chief, Angus McKenna. Retrieving these small treasures was Angus' way of making up for all the years stolen from him and his daughter, Aishlinn. Wee William had taken this mission only as a favor to Angus and to bring a smile to the face of Aishlinn who was now heavy with her first child. Of course Aishlinn had no idea they were here, very few people did.

Nora was so lost in her own worries that she was paying very little attention to Wee William or his men. Could she put much stock in what he was telling her or was his vision of England jaded from all the years their two countries had been at war?

Daniel and David, who now rode on either side of Wee William and Nora, nodded their heads in agreement with Wee William's description of southern England. Of course as far as either of them was concerned, *all* of England was filled with deviants, thieves, and men of ill repute. It could be said that neither man held a good opinion of any Englishmen. Mayhap save for the wee lass that now rode atop Wee William's lap.

"And the woods ye'd travel through along the way?" Wee William said before shaking his head in dismay. "They be filled with highwaymen and reivers, and men who'd think nothin' of harmin' a wee lass such as ye."

She had given no thought to what she might encounter either on her travels south or once she'd arrived at a seemingly safe haven. More than a hint of trepidation began to creep into her heart. How could she not have thought of such things as highwaymen and ne'er-do-wells?

She shook her head at her lack of thinking. In the past year she'd met more men of questionable character than she would have previously thought existed, thanks to Horace. How could she have been so naive as to not give consideration to such things?

Being alone on the roads with her younger siblings, without so much as a knife for protection was something she had not considered. Her only concern these many months had been to get her brother and sister out of Firth and all of them as far away from Horace as possible. The bountiful hope she had felt only moments ago began to dwindle quickly.

"Aye," Daniel interjected. "The *Sassenach* to the south be heartless and cruel, lass. And the highwaymen are notorious for killin' innocents fer the sheer pleasure of it!"

"I heard tell of a band of reivers who killed a man, his wife and their five bairns, just fer the two pigs the family traveled with," David added.

Neither man had known that Wee William's intent was not to terrify the young woman. He only meant to place a few seeds of doubt in her mind so that she'd agree to what he intended to propose. When he saw her fingertips brush away what he assumed were tears, he was quite tempted to knock both men from their horses.

"Daniel! David!" Wee William boomed. "Yer scarin' the lass!"

"What shall I do?" Nora asked to no one in particular. "My only thought has been to get to John and Elise, and take them somewhere safe. I cannot, in good conscience, take them south if 'tis bad as you say! How will I keep them from harm?"

Her mind began to fill with images of ne'er-do-wells, dirty highwaymen, and heartless, lust-crazed men. She began to feel foolish and uncertain.

"Wheesht, lass!" Wee William whispered in her ear. "All be no' lost now. Ye've other options ye might no' have considered."

Nora wiped away another tear, took a deep breath and looked at him over her shoulder. "What other options?" she asked hopefully.

"There is more to this world than England, lass. Much more," Wee William whispered softly.

"Do ye mean I should go to France?" she asked incredulously. "But I cannot speak French, William."

Wee William chuckled at her innocence. "Nay, lass, I dunna mean France." He smiled thoughtfully and gave her waist a slight squeeze with his arms. "Have ye ever thought of going *north*?"

"North? We're already as far north as we can possibly be, William," she said dolefully. "We are just two day's ride from the border." She sighed and shook her head. "I wish to be as far away from *here* as I can possibly get."

By now Horace's and his brothers' bodies were growing cold from their blessed deaths. Still, she had no desire to stay here. Her prospects of making a living here were nonexistent, unless she chose to work at Castle Firth. She would give no consideration to working or living there.

Her chances of finding a husband under the age of fifty were just as bleak. Though he was seven years her senior, Horace had been the most palatable of her choices for a husband. There were only three other available men in her village and each of them were old enough to be her grandfather. Horace's age, along with his promise that he would allow her to keep John and Elise, had been the only reasons she had agreed to marry him.

"Nay, I dunna mean France," he said softly. "Have ye thought of Scotland?

Scotland. The idea had never crossed her mind. Of all the places she had thought of going, if she were ever free from Horace, Scotland was never one of them. Her parents, or more specifically her father, had always spoken ill of the Scots. There wasn't a man or woman in her village that had ever bespoke a kind word toward the people who occupied the land to the north.

From the time she was old enough to talk, she'd been warned about the barbaric Scots. Scotland was filled with strange, angry men who raped, plundered, and murdered their way across the lands.

Again, she had to ask herself why she felt safer with these men, these Highlanders she'd been warned about since she was a babe, than she did with any other since her father had died? It made no sense. By all rights she should be absolutely terrified in their presence. Yet, she felt safer now, with Wee William's arms wrapped around her, than she could remember feeling since her father's passing.

"Ye'll no' find a more beautiful land than ours, lass," David offered.

"Aye, no greener, lusher land and no better people," Daniel said as further enticement.

Of course they would think such a thing. What good man doesn't have a fondness and great love for his own country?

"What if I do not like it there?" she asked. "Would I have your promise that you'd bring us back to England?"

Wee William wasn't about to make such a promise, not if he could help it. "That'll never happen."

"What won't happen?" Nora asked, worried she might not like his answer.

"The chances of ye *no'* likin' Scotland are as far-fetched as Daniel here sproutin' wings and flyin' amongst the birds!" Wee William said, adding a nod for emphasis. *Besides,* he thought to himself, *I do no' plan on lettin' ye go.*

THEY MADE PLANS FOR THE RETRIEVAL OF YOUNG JOHN AND ELISE. Much to Wee William's consternation, he had to admit their options were few. Option one would be to allow Nora and David to slip into the castle, find John and Elise, and extricate them as quickly as possible.

Option two, which was far more to his own liking than the first, involved three hundred Scots hell-bent on revenge against the English, a catapult and flaming oil. Since they had none of the latter at their immediate disposal, and only because they could not wait to get off English lands and back to their motherland, they went with option one.

The decision made, they left their horses tied to a stout tree not too far from the wall of the castle. Nora was insistent that she knew exactly which of the solars the children would be sleeping in and just how to get into the castle. Wee William prayed the plan would be easily implemented for the thought of spending the rest of his life in an English dungeon was not one that he enjoyed.

"OCH!" WEE WILLIAM WHISPERED HARSHLY. "I'D LIKE TO KEEP both me eyes, David!"

"Sorry, Wee William," David whispered back. "Can ye stand a bit taller?" he asked as quietly as he could. "I can almost reach." David's foot had slipped again, the toe of his boot poking into Wee William's eye as he tried to find purchase on the top of Wee William's head.

"Ssshh!" Nora whispered hoarsely at the two of them. "Do ye wish to be caught and thrown in the gallows?"

"Would ye like David to stand on *yer* head, lass?" Wee William shot back. 'Twasn't easy having someone use you for a ladder.

Wee William took a deep breath and tried to stand a bit straighter. He had his hands wrapped tightly around David's calves to keep him from falling and breaking his neck. Wee William stood on his tiptoes to gain the extra inch or two David needed to reach the window ledge.

A moment later, David grabbed the ledge of the window with his fingertips, grunted and pulled himself up. Quickly, he hoisted himself up and onto the wide window ledge. He crossed himself and thanked the good Lord for Wee William's height and strength.

"Ee-God woman!" Wee William groused again as Nora began to scurry up his back so anxious she was to get into the castle and to her brother and sister.

With her snow-encrusted, fur covered feet, 'twas quite difficult to gain any traction. She had started to slip and grabbed Wee William's hair to keep from falling back into the snow.

She shushed him again and began her ascent.

David tested the window and was relieved to find it unbarred. He stretched out on the window ledge, one hand holding the windowsill while the other reached down to grab Nora's arm. After a few futile attempts, Nora growled and thrust herself up to David's open hand. She began to recite the Lord's Prayer as she dangled rather precariously in the air.

"Thy will be done," was as far as she got before David swung her sideways and hoisted her up onto the ledge with him. She landed with a gasp and continued to pray.

"Lass, can ye let go of me beard?" David asked. His voice sounded pained, as if he were trying to keep himself from crying.

Nora hadn't realized she was holding his beard with a death like grip until she opened her eyes. If it were daylight, he'd certainly see her face burn with embarrassment. She realized she would not have made a good soldier or spy, for she was terrified of heights.

"I'm sorry, David," she said in a very hushed and humiliated tone.

"No worries, lass." David let loose a sigh of relief when she finally let go of his beard. He rubbed his jaw for a moment before pushing her upright.

Under different circumstances he might have enjoyed having the lass straddling him as she now did. But fifteen feet off the ground on a window ledge attached to an English castle was not the best place for such things.

David sat up, pushed the window open and Nora slid into the room. David followed quickly behind and gently pulled the window closed. They took a moment to allow their eyes to adjust to the darkness. Soon, Nora began making her way between the pallets in search of her brother.

From one spot to another she slipped in between the snoring, teeth-grinding, dreaming young men until she found her brother. He was asleep on his back with one arm thrown over his forehead. She knew it was John because he'd been sleeping like that since he was a babe.

Ever so quietly, she bent to her knees beside her brother's sleeping form. She was fully prepared for what would happen next for she'd been waking him each morn for years. Nora knew to stay away from the arm that rested comfortably on his forehead. David however, wasn't privy to that information.

When Nora clamped her hand over John's mouth, she made sure to keep her head away from his hand. John was notorious for waking up swinging and he did just that. Bolting upright, he flung out his arm and the back of his hand landed across David's nose.

It was all David could do not to swing back or yell at the lad. Grabbing his nose, cursing under his breath, he grabbed John's hand to keep him from swinging again.

"John!" Nora whispered. "'Tis me Nora. I've come to take you away." She waited a moment for recognition to settle in before removing her hand from his mouth.

In the time it took for a heart to beat once, John's tense shoulders sagged and his eyes filled with relief. "I thought you were Mad George coming to try to bugger me again!"

Nora hadn't a clue what he meant and supposed she had disturbed John's dream. She noticed David flinch as he drew his dirk from his waist and glance around the room.

"Put your shoes on, John!" she whispered.

John did as he was told without question. He donned his shoes and grabbed his cloak that he had draped across the blanket of his pallet. Silently, he followed between his sister and the strange man who was with her.

They paused at the door that led to the young ladies' solar next door. Nora carefully opened it a crack and peeked inside. Thankfully it appeared all its inhabitants were asleep.

Nora turned and motioned to John and David to wait while she slipped into the girl's solar. She knew if any of the women in the solar were roused, they'd not become alarmed at seeing another female figure in the dark. But a young boy and a large Highlander would bring forth enough screaming to wake the dead.

It took less time to find Elise than it had to find John. Elise was in a far corner of the room. Anger swelled when Nora saw her baby sister curled into a tight ball, wearing her cloak, the hood pulled up over her head to help ward off the cold. Could the older women not show some amount of compassion toward such a small girl and at the least offer to let her sleep near the fire?

Nora resisted the urge to scream at these women and, instead, gently nudged Elise awake. Elise's little eyes widened with surprise and delight. When she saw the child draw in a deep breath in preparation of a happy squeal, Nora shushed her by placing a hand across the little girl's mouth.

"Ssshh, Elise!" Nora warned her softly. "We're taking you away this night. John awaits next door. I'm here to take you home, child. Ye mustn't utter a sound or a word until we are far from here, Elise. Do you understand?"

Elise nodded her head vigorously. When Nora removed her hand, Elise held her arms up and beamed a very bright smile. Nora smiled in return before scooping the little girl up into her arms. Nora looked around for the little girl's shoes before realizing she was wearing them, more likely than not to keep her little feet warm. Shaking her head, Nora made a solemn vow that she'd never allow her brother or sister to live in such poor conditions again. Silently they made their way across the room and back to the men's solar where David and John waited.

Together the four of them wound their way back to the window where Wee William and Daniel waited below. Nora whispered into John's ear that two fine gentlemen waited below and to do exactly as they said. John nodded once before he climbed out the window. He cast a glance to the dark figures below before looking back to his sister for some reassurance.

David clasped his arm around John's before lowering him as far as he was able. John squeezed his eyes shut before letting loose and falling. Thankfully, Wee William broke his fall with a grunt. He righted the boy, turned him around and pushed him off toward Daniel.

"Ye go next, lass," David said as he took Elise from Nora's arms. Nora quickly explained to Elise that no matter how frightened she might be, she needed to remain quiet and let the nice man below catch her.

Reluctantly, Elise agreed and allowed David to set her on the ledge before dropping her to Wee William's waiting arms.

'Twas Nora's turn next. Without a word, she grabbed David's arm, swung over the ledge and fell. She hadn't warned Wee William that she was coming, and knocked him backward and onto the ground. His breath was momentarily taken away when he fell onto his back with her knee pressed firmly into his groin.

Without bothering to check if he was still alive, Nora apologized quickly. "My apologies, William," she said as she scurried to her feet and grabbed her sister's hand. Wee William remained prone as David fell away from the window. He landed on his feet before falling forward and landing on Wee William in a heap of grunts and curses.

As his eyes watered from the pain shooting through his loins, Wee William began to doubt his ability to live through this night, or at the least make it out with his manly parts safely intact.

They left Wee William where he lay as they hurried across the lawn toward the wall. It wasn't until Wee William heard the angry barking of dogs that he found both the strength and the wind to move. He rolled to his feet as three mean, growling, snarling dogs rounded the corner at a full run.

The dogs were fast on his heals by the time he made his way through the hidden door and slammed it shut. A moment later, the warning bells sounded and much shouting could be heard coming from within the castle walls.

Nora was handing Elise up to Daniel as John was scrambling up to sit behind David. Wee William threw himself up onto his own horse and raced toward Nora. He leaned over, grabbed her around her waist and lifted her onto his lap before she could even make sense of what was happening.

Bare branches scratched and clawed at them as they raced through the dense forest. Nora clung to Wee William's waist, all the while praying she'd not be jostled off the horse, and that no one in the castle would realize exactly what had happened until they were safely across the border.

No one spoke a word as they tore across the countryside. Nora was amazed that Elise had remained as quiet as she had for the child usually talked incessantly. Mayhap it was the fear that hung over them like a heavy cloak that made the child remain silent.

For now, Nora wouldn't question the reason for the silence. She would instead be glad for it. She knew that once Elise was permitted to speak, the Highlanders would undoubtedly begin to question their offer of help.

'Twas all that Rowan, Black Richard and the others could do to maintain serious expressions and not burst out laughing at the three clumsy and terrified brothers. Horace had been complaining over the less-than-kind treatment he was being given.

For more than an hour he had been trying to convince Rowan and the other Highlanders that he was an earl. Considering the poor conditions of the farm and cottage, a claim at being a member of the aristocracy was laughable.

The Highlanders were on horseback surrounding Horace and his brothers, Donald and Nigel. The Englishmen fell repeatedly, only to be drawn to their feet again by a hard yank on the rope that was tied around each of their waists.

"Ye best calm yerselves, lads," Rowan's voice was low and cool. "Wolves can smell fear from miles away."

Of the three, Nigel seemed the smartest. He thumped the back of Donald's head with the palm of his hand and told him to quiet down for he didn't want the wolves to feast on their dead bodies. He was thoroughly convinced, with a little help from Tall Thomas and Garret, that he'd not be allowed past the gates of Heaven if any of his body parts were missing.

Donald told him to go bugger himself. Horace accused the other two of being cowards for not fighting the Scots off to begin with. Nigel and Donald stared at him in disbelief before telling him he was a fool, through and through.

It appeared to intensify the Englishmen's fears whenever the Highlanders began speaking in the Gaelic and so the language was spoken during most of the trek. They derived great pleasure from the Englishmen's fears.

"I demand to know why you broke into my home!" Horace did not care if his voice carried to the ears of wolves or not. He was incensed. How dare these Scots treat him, an Englishman, in such a barbaric fashion! "I would also like to know where you are taking us and for what purpose!"

Black Richard wasn't as amused with Horace's outbursts as the other Highlanders were. With a slight pull of his reins, he brought his horse up to the back of Horace -- who was not having much luck walking through the snow. With a flick of the reins, Black Richard's horse shoved his nose into Horace's back, nudging him along. Horace let loose with another string of curses.

Outwardly, the Highlanders were unmoved by his tirade. Inwardly, there was not a one of them that didn't wish they could cut out his tongue.

Having had his fill of England and its offspring, Black Richard looked at Rowan and spoke in the Gaelic. "The sun will be comin' up soon," he said with a nod toward the eastern horizon. "Let's leave them now."

Rowan nodded his head in agreement and guided the men into a dense part of the forest. Once he found a place to his liking, he pulled his horse to a stop.

"This is far enough, Sassenachs," Rowan told them. His voice was menacing and laced with disgust.

The light of the waning moon streamed in through the trees, casting an ominous glow on the men and their surroundings. Horace and his brothers stopped and turned their attentions toward Rowan.

"Who has sent you?" Horace asked. "I demand to know what this is about!"

As much as he tried to sound like a man of means, of good breeding and title, Horace fell quite short. Blood had crusted around the indignant man's nose and lips and the collar of his shirt. Though he was quite tempted to run him through with his sword, Rowan resisted the urge.

Rowan ignored Horace's demands and made a few of his own. He directed Tall Thomas to remove the ropes that had been tied to Horace and his brothers. Once Tall Thomas had remounted, Rowan spoke to the Englishmen.

"Hand over yer clothes. We'll let ye keep yer boots."

Horace's eyes opened wide, but it wasn't fear that Rowan saw staring back at him in the moonlight. Try as he might, he wasn't able to put a word to the expression. It unsettled him nonetheless.

"Why do ye want our clothes?" Nigel asked as he began to shiver from the cold night air as it hit his sweaty skin.

"Don't get yer hopes up, Sassenach," Rowan told him. "Hand over yer clothes and we may let ye live. Argue it further and there'll be naught much of ye left fer the wolves."

The three men began undressing. Nigel and Donald were visibly distressed. Their teeth chattered and their bodies shivered. However, Horace's countenance continued to puzzle Rowan. Black Richard picked up on Rowan's discomfort and glanced at Horace.

After removing their clothes, Nigel and Donald slipped their boots back over their feet and stood rubbing their hands over their arms and shifting from one foot to the other.

Horace was nearly motionless save for his heaving chest. Rowan was unbothered by the hateful glower the man gave him.

"The shirt too, Sassenach," Black Richard instructed Horace.

Horace cast an odd look his way before complying. Slowly, he pulled his shirt up and over his head.

Rowan's first impression of Horace had been correct. The evidence was quite clear once his shirt, which had covered him to mid-thigh, was removed. Apparently, Horace was excited. *Physically* excited.

The man stood proudly with his shoulders thrown back, his chin held high, as if he were quite proud of his soft, pale, flabby belly and his protruding male member, small though it was.

Rowan thought it more resembled a large toe than a man's organ. Rowan would have hidden his head in shame were he cursed with such an aberration of nature. No wonder the man was such an evil bastard!

"Turn around," Rowan ordered. Though there was no fear in Horace's eyes, Nigel's and Donald's were filled to tears with it. Shaking from head to toe, the two turned around.

With his eyes closed, Nigel began praying. His lips moved silently while he recited what few prayers he knew. Donald soon joined him. Horace however, remained mute. Until he'd been asked to remove his clothes, he had done nothing but complain and curse at the Scots. Now he looked like a man who anticipated the receipt of some grand and special gift.

"I said *turn around,* Sassenach," Rowan told him calmly.

Horace finally did as ordered, keeping his hands at his sides, breathing deeply in and out through flared nostrils.

Rowan had hoped the man would have ignored his orders or tried something foolish so that he'd have the opportunity to kill him. There was still time for the fool to make a fatal error in judgment, but Rowan doubted the idiot would even try. As far as he was concerned, Horace Crawford was a coward.

Not once in the past hours had the man begged for mercy to be shown to his brothers. He also had not once asked after his wife. His lack of inquiry as to her safety did not go unnoticed by Rowan or any of his men. Were the roles reversed, Rowan was confident that he would have fought to his own death to protect his wife and brothers and at the very least he would have been worried sick over her. But not Horace. It was easy to surmise that the only one that Horace loved was Horace.

"Do no' move until dawn breaks," Rowan spoke to the Englishmen's backs. "We have shown ye more mercy than ye deserve this night, Sassenachs. Do no' tempt yer fate."

Moments later, Rowan and his men broke away and went pounding through the forest, leaving two terrified young men quite literally shaking in their boots. The other man was enraged. He was left naked and humiliated and he swore he would someday exact his vengeance on the Highlanders who had left them for dead.

4

"Again?" Daniel asked incredulously, before sighing heavily and rolling his eyes. Strawberry blonde curls bounced around the little girl's face as she nodded in affirmation.

"But, lass, ye just went not more than three miles back."

"But I has to go!" the child pleaded and wriggled around on the saddle in front of him.

Daniel let loose a frustrated sigh as he pulled rein and wondered what he'd done to anger God in such a manner.

"What is it now?" Wee William barked when he saw Daniel stopping again for what seemed to be the hundredth time in the past hour.

"She has to go. *Again,*" Daniel answered, at a loss for any plausible explanation as to how someone so wee as this child would need to pee as often as she did.

"Again?" Wee William shook his head and stared down at Nora. "I swear there isn't a rock nor a tree that child hasn't went behind in the past six hours!"

"I'm sorry William, I truly am." Nora hoped the smile she offered would somehow soften his growing irritation toward her little sister. She slid down from Wee William's lap and pulled Elise from Daniel's horse and went in search of yet another tree.

As they ambled through the low brush Nora looked for a suitable tree that was far enough away from the men yet close enough that she could keep an eye on them. These constant stops were wearing their already thin patience to a near translucent state.

"Elise! You must really try to not be such a bother!" Nora scolded the small child as they walked behind an old oak tree.

"But I has to go, Nora."

"But do you have to go so frequently?"

"I always has to go when I'm ascared," Elise said solemnly.

"Scared, not *a*-scared," Nora corrected her. She couldn't fault her sister for being frightened for she was just as nervous and just as afraid, but for quite different reasons. "Tell me why you're scared and mayhap we can do something to help you not be so."

"The men," Elise offered. "They're so big!" she spread her arms wide and nearly toppled over in doing so. Nora righted her and bade her to continue.

"And they talk funny, I don't unnerstand what they're saying. And they have lots of big knives!"

Nora resisted her urge to giggle, knowing full well it wouldn't do to embarrass her sister. "They're speaking Gaelic, and if you listen closely you'll find it sounds rather pretty."

Elise's blue eyes stared up in disbelief.

"And those knives are called swords, you know that. You saw father make many of those." Their father had been a blacksmith up until the lung fever took his life. He made everything from pots to broadswords. Elise was only four when he died, so Nora supposed she might not remember much of the blacksmith shop.

"I miss papa." Elise's eyes began to water.

"I miss him too," Nora said as she tried to smooth down the strawberry blonde ringlets. "I miss him every day. But papa wouldn't want us to cry, now. He'd want us to be brave."

"I wanna go home."

Nora let out a heavy sigh. "I would love to go home too, Elise. But I told you, we had to sell the blacksmith shop as well as our home."

The money from the sale of both had barely gotten them through the first year after their father's death. It was one more reason why she had agreed to marry Horace. The fear of starvation and freezing to death will often make a person do things they'd rather not do. There were very few appealing options available for women in such dire straits.

"Can we buy it back?" Elise asked hopefully.

"Nay, we cannot." As appealing as the thought was, it was impossible. Thinking of her father and the life they were leaving behind was bittersweet. Nora had many fond memories of her life in Penrith, her life before Horace Crawford.

A sudden sense of foreboding flooded over her. What if the Highlanders hadn't buried Horace and his brothers well enough? What if a hunter stumbled upon them and realized Nora was missing? Would they assume that she had killed them? She shuddered at the thought and prayed that the scavengers and wolves would get to the bodies first and leave them unrecognizable.

"How did you hurt your eye?" Elise asked rather quietly.

Nora debated between telling the truth and lying. Elise was an innocent six-year-old little girl, far from home, and frightened.

"Did the big men hurt you?"

"Nay!" Nora exclaimed. She took a deep breath before answering. "Do you remember Horace?"

Elise nodded as she scratched the tip of her nose. "He is your husband and he doesn't like me and John."

"No, he was not fond of any of us." Nora took a deep breath and let it out slowly. To say Horace wasn't *fond* of her was an immense understatement. She was certain he despised her.

"So how did you hurt your eye?"

Nora chewed her bottom lip for a moment before answering. "Horace did this to me. But you needn't worry overmuch." Deciding it best to leave out the part about the Highlanders bursting into their home and carrying Horace and his brothers off into the dark winter night, Nora continued calmly. "Neither Horace nor his brothers will be bothering us ever again. They've been sent away and shan't be coming back."

"Did they go to heaven like our mammas?" Elise asked.

"I don't know if the good Lord would see fit to allow men of their kind into Heaven, but that isn't a question for us to ask." For the past few hours, Nora had been quietly contemplating her own admission into Heaven. It was precarious at best.

She was uncertain if her own soul wasn't now damned to hell for all eternity. Had she not answered in the affirmative to Wee William's question those many hours ago, well, Horace would still be alive and she'd still be married to him and not reunited with her brother and sister. Nora had to hold on to the belief that God had sent the Highlanders as her rescuers and not as a test of her commitment to her marriage.

Horace had broken every promise and vow. It didn't make sense to Nora that she should remain steadfast and cheerful while Horace lied, stole, cheated, and beat her. Certainly that wasn't God's plan for her.

"Are you done?" Nora asked impatiently.

Elise nodded and stood. Nora straightened out their skirts and cloaks before taking Elise's hand. "These men you're so frightened of, they've risked much in order to help me get you away from Castle Firth."

"Why did they do that?" Elise asked as her brow twisted into a tiny knot. "And how do you know them?"

Nora sighed, unsure exactly how to answer that question. She pondered it for a moment before smiling. "God sent them to us, Elise. He knew how sad you and John and I were, so He sent these men to help us."

Elise's eyes widened with surprise and excitement. "You mean they're angels?"

"Aye, something like that." Nora knew they were the furthest things from angels as one could get, for they were, after all, Scots. And Highlanders to boot! But thus far, they had shown nothing but kindness toward her and her siblings.

"I thought angels were small and had wings," Elise said, uncertainty claiming her face.

"Angels come in all forms, Elise." Nora gave her tiny hand a slight squeeze.

"Then I shouldn't be afraid of them because they're angels?"

"Aye, you needn't be afraid." Nora smiled down at her sister hoping that she'd be less afraid and now less inclined to need to relieve her bladder every three miles.

They had stopped at the edge of the clearing while Nora re-tied Elise's cloak.

"Do angels kill people, Nora?" Elise asked.

"Nay, they do not," Nora answered, amazed with how a child's mind sometimes worked.

"Then why does that big man have his hands around John's neck?"

NORA'S HEAD NEARLY SPUN FROM HER SHOULDERS WHEN SHE TURNED to see what Elise was referring to. Wee William was holding John by the scruff of his neck!

She raced across the small clearing. Daniel and David were standing on either side of Wee William, who definitely had a firm hold on John's neck while he growled at him.

"William! John!" Nora shouted as she pushed her way through the wall of men. "William! Put him down this instant!" she demanded as she pulled on Wee William's arm.

Wee William loosened his grip slightly but kept his hold on the boy. "Yer brother here needs a lesson in manners, Nora!" he barked at her.

Nora didn't care what the reasons were behind Wee William's attempt at strangling John, she only wished that he would stop. Anger bubbled up as she shouted back. "You put my brother down this instant!" She continued to pull on Wee William's arm but to no avail. "You'll kill him!"

Wee William rolled his eyes and looked down at her. "Lass, if I wanted the little brat dead, he'd already be dead! I mean only to teach him to have some respect!"

"I'll show you no respect, you damned heathen!" John spat out. His face was as red as a beet, not from lack of air but from anger.

Wee William growled back at him. "Listen, ye little shite! Ye better get that temper in check and rethink yer attitude, or I'll no' give a second thought to leavin' ye out here to fend fer yerself!"

"I'd rather fend for myself than be anywhere near a filthy Scot!"

Nora had reached her breaking point. "William, put him down!"

"Why?" he shot back.

"So that I may beat the fool senseless!"

Wee William's expression changed from anger to surprise in the blink of an eye. "What did ye say?" he asked as he loosened his grip.

Nora let out a harsh breath. "I said put him down so that I can beat him senseless!" She would brook no disrespect on her brother's part toward these men who were trying to help them. "Then I shall beat *you* senseless when I'm done!"

Wee William startled and let go of John's shirt. John fell to the ground and landed on his rear end with a thud. "Me?" Wee William asked, more than a tad bewildered by her threat.

"Aye, the both of you!" Nora shouted as she stomped her foot and thrust her fists to her hips. "John!" she said as she looked down at her brother. "I know your opinion of Scots and where it came from."

She thrust her hand toward her brother and glared angrily down at him, stopping him before he could utter one word of protest. "'Tis foolish notions and preconceived opinions such as *that*, that keep our countries constantly at war with one another! These men have risked a great deal to help us and I will *not* have you behaving in such a disrespectful and ill-mannered fashion!"

Nora then turned her wrath toward Wee William who stood with his arms crossed over his chest and smiling as if he approved of the scolding she was giving John.

"And you!" she pierced him in place with a furious glare. His smile left instantly.

"A full grown man! Strangling a defenseless boy who simply doesn't know any better! But *you* should!" She stomped her foot again and shook her head in disgust.

"You do nothing but help inflame those preconceived notions of his by using violence! I'll not have that, sir, no I won't! I'm sure you're used to solving all your problems and disagreements with physical violence, but I will have none of it!"

She began pacing back and forth as exhaustion began to overtake her. She knew she was beginning to ramble, but she didn't care. She was beyond angry with the two of them and put all the blame where it belonged: with Horace. Had he been at all kind and considerate, had he not broken his promises and vows to her, then she'd not be in this situation. May he, at this very moment, be burning in hell for all his sins!

Nora hadn't realized she was speaking her inner thoughts about Horace aloud until she saw the perplexed faces on all those around her. She stopped abruptly as tears filled her eyes. Choking them back she first looked at Wee William then to John. "I expect more out of each of you than *this*!"

Both Wee William and John looked thoroughly remorseful, though still quite angry. Drained from riding nearly nonstop all these many hours, from lack of sleep and food, and freezing to the bone, Nora could no longer hold back her tears. She left the group of them and walked to stand beside Wee William's horse. She held onto the bridle as she let the tears fall.

Elise, ever the dutiful little sister, stuck her tongue out, first at her brother and then at Wee William. With her head held high, she went to console her sister.

ONCE HER TEARS WERE SHED, NORA STRAIGHTENED HER SHOULDERS and pulled Elise in close to her hip.

"Are you better now, Nora?" Elise asked.

"Aye, I am. I'm just very tired. 'Tis been a long night and an even longer day. Do not worry overmuch, Elise. I will be fine."

Elise nodded her head and hugged Nora around her legs, strained her head back to look up at her teary eyed sister. "I love you, Nora."

"And I love you, Elise." Nora wiped her face with her fingertips and winced slightly when she rubbed too hard along her blackened eye. She could see the fear and uncertainty in her little sister's eyes. She could only hope that someday soon, once they'd settle in somewhere, Elise wouldn't be so afraid.

"Lass," Wee William was now standing behind them. His voice was soft and low and sounded sorrowful. "I am sorry fer makin' ye cry. I canna promise I will no' be *tempted* to strangle him again, but I do promise to keep me temper in check."

He would however, have a very long talk with John once they got back to Castle Gregor. He could well understand the lad's low opinion of Scots, for he had, after all, been raised by Englishmen. 'Twas through no fault of his own that the lad behaved in such a poor manner. Most Englishmen did.

Nora took a settling breath before turning around to face him. "I thank you for that, William. And I shall have a very long talk with John regarding his poor manners. If you feel compelled to beat him for his insufferable behavior, I do ask that you allow me to stand in his stead. He's just a boy and he's been through enough these past few years."

Wee William rolled his eyes in disgust. "Lass, I've never laid a hand on a woman in anger in me life. And I've never beat a child, even one as old as yer brother and deservin' of it! There be other ways of correctin' such behavior as young John has shown."

Nora was confused. "Then why did you try to strangle him?"

Wee William laughed. "Lass, I told ye, if I'd wanted him dead, he'd *be* dead. I meant only to scare him a bit, to show him what *could* happen if he continued on with his current attitude. Others might no' be as nice about it as I."

"So your intent was only to scare him?" Nora asked for confirmation's sake. Her head was beginning to feel foggy and a slight pounding was forming behind her right eye.

"Aye, ye see the way of it, lass." Wee William cast a glance over his shoulder to make certain John was far enough away that he could not hear the conversation.

"I'd never beat him, but he does no' need to ken that just yet. A little bit of fear won't hurt the lad. It might help him control that tongue of his."

She was too tired to argue the point any further. While she felt he could have gotten the same results by simply talking to John, man to man, she knew her point would probably be lost on Wee William. And more likely than not on John as well. Men and women tended to handle these types of things in completely different ways.

"Now, what say we have a bit of bread and cheese before we set to ride again?" Wee William looked down at the sweet little girl who was studying him intently, as if he were some foreign object. Her bright blue eyes sparkled in the afternoon sun. "I might even have some dried figs in me bag, little one." He offered a smile and was glad to see her return it. "Do ye like dried figs, lassie?"

"Aye, I do! And I'm very hungry."

Wee William nodded his head as he removed the bag from the back of his saddle. "Then 'tis a feast we shall have, little one."

Nora stood next to the horse as she watched the giant of a man walk away with her little sister. He had managed, somehow, to bring a smile to Elise's face, where only moments ago, Nora had seen fear and distrust. What was it about this man, this huge, hairy creature, that made her feel so safe and at peace? Moments ago she was questioning her decision to go to Scotland with them. Her heart had been filled with doubt over her decision and fear of the future. How on earth had he disarmed her senses so easily?

5

John seemed in slightly better humor once he had eaten. But to say he was at ease or happy would have been an outright lie. Nora, for now, would settle for a silent and contrite younger brother. Elise, ever bright and cheerful, was now rattling on about their time at Firth, a place she hoped she'd never *ever* have to return to.

"They were very mean to us, Nora," Elise explained as she took another dried fig. "That mean man, Mr. Oliver would box John's ears when he didn't move fast enough! And once, he whipped him with a cane until he cried! I tried to stop him, but Mrs. Ellison tossed me in the larder! I didn't like her at all!"

Nora's jaw fell open as she looked at her brother. His eyes were cast to the ground at his feet.

"John, I am so sorry," she told him as she choked back tears of guilt. "I tried to get to you sooner, I did..." her words trailed off with the realization that there was nothing she could do to erase from his memory the past year at Firth, nor anything she could do to alleviate her own guilt.

"What in God's name was the reason behind canin' ye, lad?" Wee William asked, visibly angry.

"I took food from the larder, not for me, but for Elise and the other little ones," John said, as he looked Wee William directly in the eye. "I'd do it again, and take another beating for it too." His voice was firm and unyielding. "So you may label me a thief if you wish, but I've no regrets for what I did."

Wee William, Daniel, and David looked at him with visible admiration, their opinion of the lad increasing a thousand fold at his admission.

"'Tis a good man who does what he can fer his family. An even better man to see an injustice and do what he can to right it," Wee William told him.

He looked at Daniel and David before turning back to John. "We'd have done the same thing, lad, were we in yer position. Tell me, have ye scars from the canin' ye took?"

John's expression changed from pride to confusion and embarrassment. "Aye, a few."

The men nodded their heads approvingly. "'Tis good!" Daniel said. "They'll serve ye well as a reminder of the injustices served on someone weaker than ye, and how ye became a man and stood up fer what was right." He leaned over and squeezed John's shoulder. "Ye did well, lad."

"Aye," David said. "I couldna be more proud of ye if ye were me own brother by blood!"

Nora felt like crying again, for a myriad of reasons. These men were holding no grudge against the boy who not more than half an hour ago had been calling them filthy Scots. Instead, they looked at him with approval and what could only be described as pride. While she felt guilty at not being there to protect her younger brother, she couldn't help but feel proud of him. He had certainly matured and grown in this past year.

"Now, lad," Wee William said as he drew himself to his feet. "How well do ye ride?"

John looked confused. "Ride? Ride what?"

"Why a horse, lad!"

John shook his head. "I've never been on a horse until this day."

The three men looked aghast. "Ye haven't?" David asked.

John stood taller. "Nay, I haven't. If I've anywhere to go, I use my feet to take me."

The men laughed before informing him he'd be riding one of the spare horses. Nora could tell by the look on John's face that he was quite taken aback by how the men were treating him. She knew it wasn't at all what he had expected.

John had yet to ask why the Highlanders were helping and where they were heading. Nora decided to wait until he asked. Mayhap he would grow to trust these men more fully in the days ahead and thereby lessening the shock that was sure to come.

While Daniel and David took over giving John quick instructions on riding, Wee William turned his attention on Nora. She was using the hem of her dress to clean Elise's face. She had scooped up a small amount of snow and let it melt in her hands before using it to scrub the little girl's face.

"That's cold, Nora!" Elise complained as she shivered.

"Aye, I know it is. But we cannot allow you to have a sticky face. It's very un-lady like."

When Nora was satisfied that Elise's face was clean, she took another section of her hem to rub the little cheeks vigorously in order to warm them.

That tingling sensation that William had first felt back at the cottage had returned. As he watched the beautiful woman care for her little sister, he couldn't help but think what a wonderful mother she would someday make. That thought brought forth a warm sensation in his chest, and he found himself wanting to know her better.

Aye, it had been sheer physical attraction that had helped him make the hasty decision to take her back to Scotland in the first place. He couldn't deny it. What with those intense blue eyes, those full lips, and her long, dark hair, what man wouldn't be drawn to such beauty?

But as the hours had passed by, and with her absolute devotion to her family, and the way she handled herself back at Firth, he began to realize it was much more than just her beauty that was drawing him toward her. It was her resolve, her steadfast dedication to her brother and sister, and her quiet inner strength. And that round little bottom as it sat on his lap...his mind began to wander again.

Nora had the sense that someone was watching her. Looking up, she saw Wee William standing near their horse and assumed he meant for her to hurry. She smiled at him as she gave Elise a kiss on the top of her head.

"We're hurrying, William," she told him. "I thought it best to take Elise to a tree *before* we set off again."

Wee William nodded his head and turned away, embarrassed that he'd been caught watching her. He decided it best to double check the straps on his saddle and to insure the bags were securely fastened. It also afforded him more time to get his heart to stop pounding and his mind to quit racing around the lustful thoughts of Nora and her plump derrière.

"WHAT IS HEAVEN LIKE, SIR DANIEL?" ELISE ASKED. DANIEL HAD her wrapped so tightly in warm fur that only her tiny face could be seen from under it.

Daniel had no idea what to make of her question as he'd only half heard it. The child had been chattering on about one thing or another since they'd begun riding again some three hours ago. Her chatter was much preferable than having to stop every other mile in order for her to relieve her bladder. But still, it was beginning to grow tiresome.

David chuckled at the title the little girl had bestowed upon them. No matter how many times they informed her that none of them were knighted and therefore undeserving of such a title, she still insisted on putting the *sir* in front of each of their names.

"Heaven?" Daniel asked. "I imagine 'tis quite a beautiful place, lass."

Elise turned her face as best she could to look up at him. "But you're an angel, Sir Daniel, of course you know what Heaven is like. Or are you not s'posed to tell? Is it a secret?"

David and Wee William let loose with a fit of laughter at hearing Daniel being referred to as an angel. Their laughter woke Nora who had dozed off several miles back.

"An angel? Me?" Daniel asked incredulously.

"Nora says you're angels, all of you. Nora says God sent you down to help us. Nora never tells a lie."

"Mayhap you misunderstood her, lass," Daniel offered.

"Nay!" Elise said firmly. "Nora said you and Sir David and Sir William are angels sent to help us. Nora wouldn't tell such a lie, Sir Daniel!" Elise leaned forward in search of her sister. Upon finding Nora, she became worried that she'd said something she shouldn't have. "It wasn't a secret, was it Nora? You didn't say not to tell that they were angels!"

"Shush, child!" Nora told her from behind a crimson face.

"You didn't lie, did you Nora? You said I shouldn't be afraid of them because they're angels."

Nora let out a sigh of frustration. "Elise, angels come in all forms. Not *all* angels come down from Heaven, but God sends them to help, nonetheless."

Elise chewed on that for a moment. "So they're not from Heaven?"

Nora shook her head. "Nay, not from Heaven, but angels just the same."

"So they haven't seen our mums?" she looked positively deflated by the news.

"Mums?" Wee William asked.

"Me and Nora have the same papa, but different mums. Nora's mum died in childbed just like my mum."

Wee William looked down at the top of Nora's head and his sympathy for her grew. "I'm sorry, lass," he whispered into her hair.

"'Tis all right, William. 'Tis true that my mum died in childbed, giving birth to me. My father married John and Elise's mum when I was about two. She was the woman who raised me, just the same as if I came from her own womb. She was a beautiful, kind woman."

"They're *still* angels, aren't they Nora?" Elise asked hopefully, not ready yet to let the subject be dropped.

Nora cast a glance at the men around her. While they might not believe they were angels, Nora certainly held them in that high regard. She felt a debt of eternal gratitude for these men.

"Aye," Nora said boldly, sitting a bit taller in Wee William's lap. "No matter what they might think, they *are* answers to many prayers. While they may be a bit rough around the edges, they are angels just the same, Elise. So you needn't be afraid of them."

She hoped the men would pick up on her hidden meaning and would realize she had told Elise what she had in order that the child might not be afraid of them.

"I haven't been called an angel since I was a wean, and then 'twas by me grand mum!" David said with a smile.

"We thank ye fer yer compliment, lass," Daniel said with a similar smile.

There was much more Wee William wanted to ask but didn't. He was curious as to how Nora came to be married to such a vile man as Horace Crawford. He left his many questions unasked as they rode along the snow covered countryside.

"Now, to answer yer question about Heaven, lass," Daniel said to Elise. "Aye, I've seen Heaven with me own eyes."

"You have?" Elise asked disbelievingly.

"Aye, lass, I have. Ye see, lass, I like to think of me home as a little Heaven on earth. Ye'll never rest yer eyes on a more beautiful place!"

"Really?" Nora asked, still unsure if she could believe him.

"Aye," David interjected. "Come springtime, the land comes to life, ye see. There'll be more flowers than a man could count in ten lifetimes. And 'tis also when all the animals are born. The sheep call out to one another, the birds twitter about singing their love of their country, and everything just bursts to life."

As the men went on talking about the beauty of their homeland, Nora felt at peace. Much like a child being told a bedtime story, she began to doze off to the soft timbre of the Highlanders voices and within a very short time, she finally succumbed to the exhaustion that had been plaguing her for the past many hours.

"WILL I GET TO SEE YOUR HOME SOMETIME, SIR DANIEL?" ELISE asked sleepily.

"Of course ye will, lass. That be where we be headin' right now."

Elise sat upright at the news and pulled the fur from her head along with the hood of her cloak. Excitedly she looked up at Daniel, her smile beaming. "You're taking us there now? You aren't fibbing are you?"

Daniel chuckled as he returned her smile. The child was positively captivating, with her little ringlets, big blue eyes, and front tooth missing. "I'd never lie to a princess such as ye."

"I'm no princess!" Elise said with a giggle.

"Och! Mayhap not born into a royal family, but a princess just the same," he teased her.

"Sir Daniel, you jest!"

"Nay, I do no' jest," he told her.

Elise rubbed her eyes, forcing herself to remain awake. She was having far too grand a time riding along on the big horse. "So, what is your home called? Does it have a name?"

"Of course it does, lass! It's called Scotland!"

In the timespan of one heartbeat, Elise's smile and bright eyes turned to absolute terror. A heartbeat later, she was shrieking at the top of her lungs, and large teardrops spilled from her eyes.

Nora bolted upright, thinking the child had been injured or had fallen from her horse. The men immediately pulled their horses to a stop, all eyes on the now hysterical child.

"Elise!" Nora called out. "What is wrong? Are you in pain?"

"They're taking us to Scotland!" Elise answered between terrified sobs. "We can't go to Scotland!" she was holding her arms out to Nora. Wee William pulled his horse alongside Daniel's so that Nora could pull the child onto her lap.

"Hush, child! There's nothing to be afraid of!" Nora tried soothing Elise, but to no avail.

Between hysterical sobs, Elise spoke. "They're taking us to Scotland, Nora!" she hiccuped. "Scotland is a bad place! Papa said it was filled with ogres and monsters and the devil lives there!"

The men rolled their eyes and shook their heads in dismay. Nora pulled Elise closer to her breast as she tried to sooth her.

"Elise! Those were just stories, papa told! They're not true, sweetling!"

Elise squeezed her eyes shut and shook her head. "Nay! Papa

wouldn't lie about such things! He said that Scotland was the worst place to ever go and if I ever went there, the earth would swallow me whole and I'd be stuck in Hell with the devil!"

"Elise, calm yourself, please!"

"I wanna go home! I don't wanna go to Scotland! I don't want to be swallowed whole! I don't wanna go to Hell! There are bad, bad men there! And ogres! And Highlanders! And men who steal little girl's ears!"

So it went for a very long while, with Elise in hysterics, John staring at her as if she'd lost her mind and the men looking positively perplexed and at a loss as to how to calm the distraught little girl.

"Elise," Wee William spoke in a calm tone. "Sometimes fathers tell their children stories just to frighten them or to get them to either *do* somethin' or *no'* to do somethin'. I think yer father was just tellin' ye these things because he feared ye'd someday leave him."

Elise looked up at him, her eyes were red from crying and her nose was running. She hiccuped again before asking him if he really, truly believed that.

"Aye, I do, lass! Why, when I was a boy, there was a dangerous bog not far from our home. Me mum worried that I'd go wanderin' off someday and get lost in it. Me da didna like when me mum worried, so he told me a story to keep me close to home."

"A story?" she asked, hiccupping once again.

"Aye, he told me that a scary beast lived in the bog, a beast so ugly, so mean, so vile that if I ever stepped one wee toe on the beast's land, it would not only bite all me toes off, it would turn me to stone!"

"But it wasn't true?"

Wee William smiled at her, lifted the fur that covered Nora, and pulled the child into the warmth. "Nay, child, it wasn't true. It was just a story to keep me from hurtin' myself or bein' lost."

Elise looked at her sister as if to ask if she should believe Wee William's story. Nora smiled down at her before giving her a nod and a kiss to the top of her head. She used the hem of her dress to wipe the child's face clean.

"And do ye know what me da called this terrible beast?" Wee William asked with a twinkle in his eye.

"Nay, what did he call him?"

"An Englishman!" Everyone, but John, joined in Wee William's laughter.

John finally spoke up. "Why did you not tell me where we were going, Nora?" he was making no attempt to mask his anger. His jaw muscles where twitching.

"John, I am sorry that I didn't tell you sooner."

John cut her off. "Were you afraid I couldn't handle being told the right of it? Were you afraid I'd act like a babe and throw a tantrum like Elise just did?"

"No, John, I did not! I thought it best to give you time to get used to-"

He stopped her again. "Nay, you didn't think! You could have at least *asked* me my opinion! I'm not a baby Nora! And 'tis been *I* who has been taking care of Elise for this past year, not *you*. 'Tis been me that's wiped her tears and cared for her when she was sick. 'Tis been *me* that's made sure she had plenty of food and shoes on her feet!"

Nora's eyes flew open. "John! I tried, I tried many times to get to you!"

"I don't believe you!" he spat at her.

Nora was unable to hold her temper in check. She was worn out, hungry, exhausted and cold. John may have gone through hell this past year, but she had been living in her own nightmare.

"Do you think *you're* the only one with scars, John? Do you think I've been living a life of luxury this past year?" her words were biting, angry, and she did not care how incensed she sounded for that is how she felt.

"I've scars too, John! Do you not even care how my eye became blackened, John? Do you not wonder? I've got bruises that you cannot see for my clothes cover them. I've got scars too, from the hands of a man who-" she choked on the tears that seemed to have lodged in her throat. "'Twasn't just you living a nightmare, for I lived my own!"

She wished she could slide from the horse and run, run until she had no breath left in her. She wanted to hide so none would see her guilt, her shame, and her humiliation. She wanted no one's pity at the moment, but that is what she saw in the eyes of Daniel, David and

Wee William. Embarrassed by her own behavior, she turned away and wiped her face with the fur. She hadn't said the things she did to gain any sympathy from them. Her intent had been only to let John know that he hadn't been the only one to suffer.

"I am sorry for my outburst," she whispered.

Wee William had been watching her intently. His heart ached with learning she too had scars and that there were more bruises than those he could see on her face. Silently, he cursed Horace to the bowels of Hell and beyond. A large part of him wanted to hand Nora over to Daniel and David and head back to Penrith to see if Rowan and Black Richard had actually killed the man. If they hadn't, he would do it himself.

"No worries, lass," he whispered. "I think we need to find some shelter for the night." Wee William looked up at the sky. Night was quickly approaching, and from the dark clouds to the north of them, it looked as though more snow was on the way.

John's cracking voice broke through the silence. "Nora," he said softly. "I am sorry."

Nora cleared her throat before speaking. "I know John, and I am too. I am only doing what I must to make certain we can stay together, as a family, and not be torn apart again." She finally looked up at him. "I couldn't bear it again, to lose either one of you."

John's jaw clenched and he took a deep breath in through his nostrils. "I know you are. But are you certain we have no other choice but *Scotland?*" he said it as if the word had a bitter taste simply by speaking it.

"John, we truly have nowhere else to turn. If I could bring our father back, I would. If I could change the past two years, I would. This is the only way I know that we can be together, as a family, and not be torn asunder."

John took another cleansing breath before looking at the stoic faces of the men around him. He had to admit that these men had shown him more kindness in the past several hours than anyone had shown him in the past two years since his father's death. But that didn't mean he had to enjoy their company or the thought of living in

Scotland of all places. He made a solemn vow that he'd go with Nora for now, but he would never call Scotland home. And as soon as he was able, he'd go back to England, where he belonged. With or without his sisters.

6

They had been traveling far too many hours to count but finally arrived on Scottish soil without any signs of English soldiers following. Without Nora and the children, Wee William and his men would have stopped less and rode faster.

Wee William and his men had passed through this wild territory on their journey south two days ago. Now that they were in more familiar territory, Wee William, David and Daniel felt more energized and hopeful. They knew they were not far from the hunting hut they had stumbled upon earlier. God willing, they'd reach it before the snow began to fall.

Apparently, the good Lord was not inclined to allow them a snow free passage. Large, feathery snowflakes began to fall long before they reached their destination. They picked up speed as best they could and veered northeast in search of the place they'd call home for the night.

The sky had just begun to grow dark when they crested the large hill. The small hut was built into the side of the hill. It would be tight quarters, but at least they'd be warm and out of the weather.

David and John saw to the horses, giving them shelter in the small barn. Dusting snow from their furs and clothing, Daniel and Wee William took Nora and Elise into the tiny mud hut. It was one large room, with a small table and two chairs that sat against one wall. Wee William was more than relieved to find a good stack of wood piled against the wall near the brazier.

They set blankets and furs around the brazier. Nora and Elise stayed huddled together, shivering and exhausted while the men started the fire. Within no time, the chill in the air was replaced by gloriously warm heat and the bits of snow that still clung to their clothes began to melt. Little puddles of melted snow dotted the floor.

They ate a simple meal of bannocks, cheese and more dried figs. Nora wouldn't allow Elise to eat too many of the figs for fear they'd spend the following day finding one tree after another.

Once their stomachs were full and their bodies finally began to thaw, John fell asleep sitting up while Elise dozed peacefully on Nora's lap. Wee William took the worn out, sleeping child from Nora and tucked her into a pallet nearby then covered her with a warm fur. Nora gently nudged John and helped him into a spot next to Elise.

Once the children were settled, Nora went back to her spot by the fire. Wee William opened up the fur he had draped around himself and offered her to join him. She eyed him peculiarly for a moment.

A sweet smile came to William's lips. "Lass, yer exhausted beyond words. Come sit by the fire and warm yerself."

She hesitated for a moment before deciding warmth was more important than any required social etiquette. She was, after all, a widow now. Protocol be damned. She was cold.

Nora settled herself in next to Wee William, amazed at the amount of heat his body offered. She wondered for a moment if he didn't have a fever.

Wee William draped the fur around her shoulders and resisted allowing his arm the same good fortune. They sat quietly, staring at the flames in the brazier, lost for a time, in their own thoughts.

"When should we arrive at your home, William?" Nora asked, yawning wide and rubbing her tired eyes.

"It depends on the weather, lass. If we're lucky, I'd say in four days."

Nora nodded and took in a slow, deep, cleansing breath and yawned again. Her eyelids were heavy with fatigue, her rear end sore from hours and hours of riding, and every muscle in her body ached. She stretched her back a bit and winced from a sharp pain that shot down her leg. She didn't know if she would survive four more days on the back of a horse.

"I fear yer not used to being atop a horse any more than yer brother," Wee William said, noting the slight painful expression on her face whenever she moved.

She giggled softly in agreement. "Aye, that is true. Until today, I'd only been on a horse one other time in my life, and that was many years ago and just a short ride. But I'm not complaining! I'm sure I'll get used to it after a time."

She imagined it would take years to get used to it. Riding looked far easier than it actually was. She was determined not to complain or otherwise make their journey north uncomfortable with grievances.

Wee William smiled at her as he retrieved a flask from inside his cloak. He removed the lid before handing it to Nora.

She raised a curious brow. "What is it?" she asked speculatively.

"A wee bit of the chief's best, lass. It'll help ease yer aches and allow ye to sleep."

"And what, pray tell, is the chief's best?" she asked as she stared at the flask.

Daniel and David laughed softly, enjoying the look of uncertainty on Nora's face. "It be the best whiskey in all the land, lass," David told her.

Nora's sleepy eyes widened with more uncertainty. "I've never drank whiskey before," she told them. "I've heard it's quite strong."

"Aye, that it is lass. But it'll cure what ails ye," Wee William said, offering her the flask again.

At home Nora would have brewed tea to help settle her nerves and ease her aches. She doubted these Highlanders were in possession of any of the trappings necessary to make tea.

For a moment, she wondered what Horace would think of her sitting here with all these wild looking men, being treated with kindness and dignity, wrapped up in a fur sitting next to the biggest man she'd ever laid eyes on, while she considered taking a sip of whiskey. She hoped he was rolling around in his grave.

Throwing all caution to the wind, she accepted the offered flask and took a deep drink.

Her eyes watered, her throat burned and constricted, and for a brief moment, she thought her innards had caught fire. She choked and spat while she tried to catch the breath that had been stolen from her.

The men laughed at her, her embarrassment hidden behind the spectacle she was making of herself.

When she finally got her choking under control, she tried to speak, but the words couldn't come. Flames burned her throat. Finally, she managed. "Good Lord! That would etch iron!"

The men chuckled, not so much in agreement, but at her red face and watering eyes.

"But do ye feel better, lass?" Daniel asked with a tinge of hopefulness to his voice.

Nora breathed in through her nose and was about to tell him to go to the devil when she realized the fire had subsided and had turned to calming warmth that spread to her toes. Holding her first impression of the awful liquid at bay, she gave a quick nod of her head before taking another pull at the flask. This time, she was careful to sip it and not drink it as if it were water.

She let out a contented sigh. "Aye, Daniel, I must admit I do feel warmer. And the pain in me back isn't so bad." Nora hadn't realized she had taken on a bit of the Scottish brogue until the men burst out laughing again.

When their laughter finally subsided, Wee William took the flask from her. "Ye don't want to overdo it on yer first round, lass. I think it's best ye try to sleep now."

Nora did not possess the energy to argue. She felt warm, sleepy, and very much at ease and the ache in her muscles was beginning to subside. She bade them all a good night and lay down where she was, taking the fur with her, pulling it away from Wee William.

The last thing she remembered before exhaustion claimed her was the sound of soft chuckles and crackling flames, and the warm sensation of being safe.

As the gentle snowfall turned into a quiet late winter storm, a storm was brewing inside Wee William's heart. He had volunteered to keep first watch and tried to enjoy the quiet that had fallen inside the small hut. He added a few more branches to the brazier and the flames fluttered upwards for a time before settling back down.

Wee William looked around the room. His men were fast asleep, snoring quietly. The children were huddled together under warm furs. Little Elise had the look of a cherub while young John, even in his sleep, looked serious and brooding.

When his eyes fell to Nora, he could not block the sensation that warmed him to his bones. Her long dark tresses were pulled back and disappeared under the dark fur. The warm light of the fire cast an ethereal glow to her beautiful face. Long, dark lashes feathered against skin that had been kissed tenderly by the sun.

As he sat in the quiet of the night, he watched the gentle rise and fall of her shoulders and felt certain he had lost his mind. Quietly, he ran through all the events that had led up to this quiet moment in time. 'Twas those blue eyes of hers, that had been his undoing.

Mayhap if her eyes weren't such a pale blue he would not have been as drawn to her. He tried imagining her with green eyes, or brown, or hazel like his own. As the time passed, he realized it would not have mattered what color they were. In truth, it was what lay *behind* them.

In those first brief moments, back at the cottage, her eyes had stolen his breath away. Aye, one was swollen and black, but the other, the one undamaged by the ugly hands of Horace Crawford, had unraveled his senses. Such a fleeting brief moment it had been, but in that small span of time, he saw fear and terror, and some niggling voice in the back of his mind had said *take that fear away*.

Wee William grunted quietly as he took a deep breath. Aye, he had lost his mind, 'twas no question about it. He was trying to convince himself that it was simply the fact that she needed his help that made him feel so drawn to her.

He was getting older, way past the age when most men were married and filling homes with bairns. In less than two years he would turn thirty. Mayhap his body was telling him it was time to settle down, build a home, take a wife, and make lots of babes.

He had been tempted, years ago, to have that life. Had even gone so far as to propose to a young woman he thought he'd been in love with. However, she had broken his heart and he swore to himself and anyone else that would listen, that he'd never be tempted to make such a mistake again.

Aye, Nora was beautiful. And she was strong, devoted to her family, and kind. A bit naïve perhaps, but with age and experience would come wisdom. She couldn't be much past twenty he reckoned.

But above all else, she was scared. And *that* was his worry, that he was only physically attracted to her out of his strong sense of honor. It was his fervent belief that God had made him as big and strong as He had, so that he could protect those who were weaker.

Was it these things, along with the fact she had been abused by a brutal husband that made her more appealing?

'Twasn't right to try to start a relationship based on those things alone. What, pray tell, would happen once she had gained her own footing, had begun to make a life for herself and her brother and sister? Would he still be drawn to her as he was now, or would she lose some of her appeal? Was he only attracted to her now because she needed him and he had a strong desire to be needed?

Time. That was what was needed. Time to get to know her better. Time to let her start her life anew in the strong embrace of his clan. It might take a while for his clan to adjust to having a Sassenach living amongst them, but eventually, they'd come to like her and accept her as one of their own.

After all, his clan had accepted Aishlinn, almost from the first day she had arrived. While it was true that Aishlinn was a Scot, no one had known that truth for quite some time. Aishlinn had been raised in England. She'd been torn away from the loving embrace of her father, her family, and her clan before she was even born. Torn away by the lies told from the mouth of a madman. The same madman who had fathered Horace Crawford. Wee William supposed the apple didn't fall far from *that* crooked and bent tree.

If his clan had readily accepted Aishlinn, long before any of them knew who she really was -- Angus McKenna's daughter -- then Wee William reckoned they would also show the same kindness to Nora. It might be a bumpy road, but it was a road he was quite willing to travel. Especially if it meant she would no longer be at the mercy of Horace Crawford.

It would help that Nora didn't behave like most of the Sassenach he and his clan were accustomed to. Nora was kind, strong, yet gentle, sweet, and didn't look down her nose at him or his men. Daniel and David were right; she be no Sassenach.

His mind was made up. He'd not shave his beard just yet. He would need to make doubly certain that his feelings for this young lass were sustainable and not just some fleeting fancy. He'd never be able to live with himself if he began to woo her now only to find out later that he had acted too quickly. The thought of bringing one ounce of pain to this beautiful young woman made his chest constrict. Nay, he could never do that to her.

He also doubted that he had the strength to have his feelings trampled and his heart broken again. Nay, he could not survive another heartbreak such as the one he'd suffered through years ago. No woman was worth that. Not even the beautiful one who slept on the floor beside him.

The light of dawn had come far too soon for anyone's liking. The storm had subsided a short time before the sun breached the horizon, casting the early morning earth in shades of brilliant pinks, oranges, yellows and blues. Snow clung to the bare branches of oaks, and padded the dark green needles of the pines.

While they were nearly certain the English wouldn't waste precious resources on two small children, the former Earl of Penrith had proven how insane an Englishman could be. The earl had searched for months for Aishlinn, who had stabbed him while he attempted to rape her. None of the men wanted to risk a repeat of last summer's battle against the English.

The Highlanders' already sparse resources were rapidly dwindling. The men ate very little, which did not go unnoticed by Nora. They were stretching their supplies as far as they could and made certain the children were sufficiently fed.

Other than her father, Nora could not say that she knew of other men who would have made such a sacrifice. She was raised with the belief that the men *always* ate first, then the children, then finally, the women. It was reckoned that the men needed their strength, as they were the ones who did the most physical labor. Her father was the only man she knew, until today, who did not hold that belief. Her heart swelled with growing affection toward these men who were suffering through their own hunger.

David and John readied the horses while Wee William and Daniel brought in wood from the pile near the hut. This would allow the wood time to dry and be ready for the next inhabitants of the tiny mud hut.

Elise insisted upon riding with her Sir Daniel again. Nora knew the little girl was thoroughly enjoying the kind attention he was giving her. It had been two years since the child had any good, strong male influence in her life. The same could be said for John as well as Nora. She could barely remember the last time she was made to feel deserving of anyone's kindness or charity, let alone the feeling of being liked as a person.

Nora only half listened to her little sister who happily chatted away about all manner of things, from faeries to ogres, her time at Castle Firth, her favorite foods, flowers, and colors. Daniel, bless him, was thoughtful enough to listen patiently and only occasionally interjected with his own opinions.

Every so often, Daniel would hand Elise off to John while he and David would break away to scout for any signs of interlopers, the English, or other ne'er-do-wells. It went on like that all throughout the morning.

While Elise asked a million questions, chattered incessantly about nearly every topic under the sun, Nora contemplated the future. Slowly, doubt began to creep in. She prayed she hadn't made a mistake by agreeing to go north instead of south.

When she had made the decision to go to Scotland with Wee William and his men, she had not given much thought to what would happen *afterward.* Her only thought at that time was getting John and Elise as far from Firth and Penrith as she could. But now? She worried about how would she support her family, how would she make a living and where would they live.

She had been so caught up by their offer of help to free her brother and sister, as well as their offer of protection, she hadn't given much thought to anything else. Had she not been so desperate, so anxious to get away from the cottage that held so many bad memories, would she have made a different decision? Had she not been so anxious to get to John and Elise, would she have been able to think more clearly?

The further away they rode from the only home she'd ever known, the more worried she became. While it was true that they couldn't have survived the trip to southern England with nothing more than the clothes on their backs and an ox-driven cart, at least *there* she would feel some semblance of familiarity. She very well could have secured a position in a manor home or a castle or perhaps as a seamstress with a dressmaker shop. That was *if* they had survived the trip.

The more she contemplated her current situation the more frustrated she became. She cursed herself for making such a hasty decision with no thought to the future.

Wee William could sense her unease for she had begun to sit upright. Her fingers worried and rubbed the seam on her cloak.

"Something bothers ye, lass?" he finally asked. His soft yet deep voice startled her.

Nora did not want to seem ungrateful for their help and kindness. How on earth could she tell him she was having second thoughts without seeming ungrateful or immature?

"Ye worry over the future." It was a statement, not a question.

Nora turned abruptly to face him. "How do you know that?"

His lips curled into a warm smile before answering. "Ye wear yer heart on yer sleeve, lass. I suspect I'd be worryin' over it as well, were I wearin' yer shoes."

Nora turned away and shrugged her shoulders. What difference did it make what she worried over? She had made the decision and must follow through with it. They were too far away to turn back now. Besides, she didn't have the heart to ask them to make such a sacrifice. She also worried that if she voiced her concerns they might just leave her and the children here, alone and in the middle of nowhere, without any means of going back. 'Twould serve her right for being so foolish.

Wee William chuckled softly and gave her waist a slight squeeze with his arm. "Lass, 'twould make sense that ye worry over yer future and that ye'd long fer yer homeland. I fear ye worry that ye made a decision in haste when we offered to help ye, am I right?"

Nora wondered how on earth he was able to read her mind! "I worry over all manner of things, William, but it matters not."

"But lass, it does matter, for 'tis yer future we speak of. And that of Elise and John as well. Ye've much weight yer carryin' on yer shoulders, but 'tis a weight ye needn't carry alone."

She was glad she wasn't facing him at the moment because he was unable to see the tears that welled. For a year, she'd been married to a man who cared not about her worries, her concerns, or her self-doubts, for he was the source of them.

She had learned early on never to voice an opinion, a worry, or a fear. Horace's punishments were swift and at times, quite brutal. Nora pressed down the wave of uncertainty and tried to push away the ugly memories.

Her marriage to Horace had been nothing like the marriage she had seen between her parents. Where her parents' marriage had been one of mutual respect, admiration and devotion, Nora's had been the complete opposite. It had been nothing like she had hoped for when she had accepted Horace's proposal.

"Lass, I offer ye me friendship if ye'll take it," Wee William whispered softly.

He, too, had been worrying about her future and was beginning to feel guilty for convincing her to come with them. But only slightly guilty. He knew there had been very little chance that Nora and the children would have survived a trip alone, unescorted, to southern England.

Nora swallowed the tears, unable to look at him. Why was he being so nice? Why did he care what happened to her or to John and Elise? What drove these men to care so kindly for complete strangers when her husband had been so harsh, unforgiving and cruel?

"William," she squeaked out his name, but could not continue. Words were hopelessly lodged in her throat.

"Lass, what worries ye the most?"

She imagined if she started to list all her worries, she would still be listing them long after they arrived wherever it was they were going. Was his concern genuine? Up to this point, neither Wee William nor his men had done anything other than show concern and kindness. "Surely you don't want to hear my worries, William."

"I wouldna have asked if I did no' care," he told her.

Nora let out a heavy sigh. Deciding Wee William would eventually figure out what bothered her, she decided to delay the inevitable. "Very well, then. I worry where we'll live and how I'll support John and Elise. Mayhap not all Scots are as kind and generous as you and your men."

Wee William laughed heartily at her last statement. "'Tis true, not all Scots are as kind and generous as we. There are evil men wherever you go, lass, always remember that." He gave her another gentle squeeze.

"Now, as for where ye'll live, I assumed it was understood that ye'd come to live amongst our clan. They're good and decent people lass. Aye, they might no' be too keen on having another Sassenach livin' among them, but Aishlinn has done much to show them that not *all* English are vile and disgusting. Of course, Aishlinn isn't really *English*."

Nora asked him to clarify what he meant by Aishlinn not being English, for she found his statement quite curious.

"Ye see lass, Aishlinn's mum was Scots. Her mum, Laiden, was to marry Angus, our chief, though he wasn't the chief at that time. Laiden's real da died when she was young and later, *her* mum married an Englishman. Och! If I ever have daughters, I'll teach them never to marry an Englishman!" Wee William shuddered at the thought.

When he felt Nora's shoulders slump with what he assumed was hurt over his remark, he quickly tried to right his insensitive declaration. "My apologies lass. I find English women far more palatable than English *men*."

Nora wasn't sure how to respond. "I can only hope that other Scots will be as *open-minded* as you." She could not say that she blamed him for his opinion for her own countrymen held the same of the Scots.

Wee William's cheeks flushed, but he could not fault her for feeling slightly insulted by his remarks.

"Please, William, tell me more."

Wee William cleared his throat. "Well, Laiden's mum had married the Englishman. He had promised never to take them away from the Highlands, but after a few years, he did just that. Laiden and Isobel were heartbroken at havin' to live so far away from home. They were allowed to visit during the summer months and that is what they did. Laiden grew into a fine, beautiful young woman and she stole Angus' heart, and he hers. When she learned she carried his babe, they made plans to marry upon his return from one of the clan wars that were happenin' at the time. Laiden wanted to see her stepfather, who she had grown to love, even though he be English. So she set out on her own, with only one man as a chaperone, to tell him that she was to be married. That, lass, is when the sadness began."

Wee William paused for a moment to gather his thoughts. Nora's interest was piqued. She turned to look at him. "What sadness? What happened?"

"Well, there was another man who loved Laiden, but no' in a good way. He wanted to possess her only because she was so beautiful. And, her stepfather was a well to do Englishmen. She stood to inherit a good amount of coin on his death. But Broc, he bein' the son of a whore who stole Laiden from Angus, he was too greedy in all manner of things."

Nora interrupted him, her curiosity piqued. "Stole her?" she asked. "How did he steal her?"

Wee William chewed on his tongue for a moment before answering. "Well, he convinced Angus and Laiden that the other was dead. He told Angus that highwaymen had set upon Laiden and he told Laiden that Angus had been killed in the war. She was but seven and ten at the time, alone, her mum long dead, and her stepfather was no' happy that she was with child and unmarried, ye see. So Broc offered his own hand to Laiden so that her child wouldna be born a bastard."

"That's terrible!" Nora exclaimed. "How could anyone do such a thing? Why did they believe Broc?"

"Well, ye see, lass, Broc was Angus' brother. His brother by half, but if ye ask me, no two people were ever more different. They shared the same da, but different mums. Aye, Angus knew of Broc's jealousy and that he wanted Laiden fer his own, but Angus could no' believe that Broc was as evil and full of such hatred as to tell such lies." Wee William however, held no such doubts as to the amount of evil any man was capable of. Kin or no.

Nora wasn't sure how much of Wee William's story was true and how much may have been exaggerated to make the story more dramatic. "Did Laiden agree to marry Broc?"

Wee William nodded his head. "Aye, she did, lass. She married Broc and had her babe, Aishlinn. They stayed in England on Broc's farm. Broc is Horace's da, ye ken, from another woman."

"Nay!" She hadn't made the connection until Wee William pointed it out. "So Horace is only Aishlinn's step-brother," she chewed on that fact for a time. Horace apparently inherited his father's devious ways.

"Poor Aishlinn! And poor Laiden!" Though she could not fathom why she was surprised by what Wee William had just shared with her. She'd been married to Broc Crawford's eldest son for a year. Evidently Horace had inherited his black heart from his father.

"Aye. So Angus fell into the bottle for quite some time after learning his love and his babe were savagely murdered. But Isobel, that be Laiden's sister, she came to help him find his way out of it. And eventually, they married and made a good life together."

"But what of Laiden? How was her life with Broc? Was he good to her?"

"That, I dunna ken fer certain, lass. But I can tell ye how he treated Aishlinn. I think she served as a daily reminder of how much Laiden loved Angus. Aishlinn was just a wee thing when her mum died and Broc refused to let her go to the care of anyone else. I think he feared what would happen if anyone learned the truth, so he kept her hidden away. And the brothers? They were worse than Broc in their treatment of Aishlinn. No lass should ever be treated so harshly."

If anyone understood the kind of poor treatment Horace and his brothers were capable of, it was Nora. Her jaw clenched when she thought back to the last time Horace had beaten her for running away. Aye, her eye might be black and blue, but there were other bruises far worse than those, hidden under her clothes. It wasn't the worst beating he'd ever given her, but it was close.

"I'm glad he's dead."

"What's that lass?" Wee William asked. She had spoken so softly that he wasn't sure he had heard her correctly.

Nora sat a bit taller and turned to look at Wee William directly. "I said I'm glad that Horace is dead. He was a despicable man, William. He was no husband, not by any stretch of the imagination. He acted more a gaoller and I his prisoner, or his possession. I can well imagine the trials he put Aishlinn through." The tears she had fought so hard to keep at bay finally escaped.

"He was no good to anyone, especially women. I will regret until the day I die the day that I agreed to marry him."

Wee William's stomach tightened upon seeing the tears that fell down her cheeks. Guilt assaulted his senses as he battled with his conscience. Should he tell her that there was a chance that Horace still lived, or allow her the peace that came with believing him dead?

He was willing to do anything he could to help her forget Horace and the life she was leaving behind, including lying to her. He couldn't know for certain what Rowan and Black Richard had done with Horace or the brothers. Wee William decided it best to wait until he learned the truth of the matter from them.

"Why did ye marry him, lass, if ye don't mind me askin'."

Nora took a deep breath and wiped the tears away. "'Twas either marry Horace or the old baker." Her choices had not been abundant.

"I've taken care of my family since mum died more than six years ago. Father never remarried and he was in no rush to find me a good husband. After he died, I was able, for a time, to care for John and Elise on my own. But I had to sell his blacksmithing business to do it. I knew the money would not last forever, but I held on as long as I could. Finally, I was left with very few choices. Horace had promised to build a bigger home so that John and Elise could stay with us. He promised we'd be a family."

Nora wiped away more tears using the sleeve of her cloak. The guilt she felt for not being able to protect John and Elise had returned.

"I didn't realize until our wedding night that he had lied to me. By then, it was too late. I tried many times to run away, to get to John and Elise. I was fully determined to walk to the end of the earth if I had to, to get away from Horace. But he found me every time."

Horace had been unapologetic. It wasn't as if they'd had a newlywed quarrel and Nora had run home to the loving bosom of her family. Nay, Horace had hunted her down and literally dragged her back to their cottage. She still bore the scars from that day.

Wee William gently pressed the palm of his hand to her head and brought her to his chest. "Wheesht lass," he whispered as he rested his chin on the top of her head.

Nora buried her face in the warmth of his chest and realized she was feeling better. She was also surprised to find that his beard wasn't scratchy or coarse, but soft and smooth.

Crying helped to purge the guilt and resentment she'd been holding on to. Wee William's kindness was overwhelming yet comforting. As he wrapped his arms around her and patted her back with his hand, she was quite surprised to find her fingers and toes were tingling with a warm sensation that began to spread throughout her body. She didn't quite know what to make of it and assumed it was a combination of gratitude and exhaustion.

"I pledge to ye now, that ye'll never be treated so poorly in the future. I'll no' allow it," Wee William told her as he continued to rub her back.

There was something in the tone of his voice that gave Nora a sense of reassurance. It also told her that he meant to keep his word.

7

Just before noontime, Daniel and David returned to the rest of their group, out of breath and smiling.

"Wee William!" Daniel called out, charging toward their leader.

Wee William pulled rein and turned his horse to face his men.

"Rowan, Black Richard and the others be no' far behind us!" Daniel exclaimed as he pulled his horse to an abrupt stop. "They be less than an hour away."

Whatever news Rowan and Black Richard had, Wee William wanted to receive it away from Nora. He reasoned it made no sense to upset her further. He ordered Daniel and David to make camp while he went to meet with the men he hoped would bear good news.

Rowan and Black Richard smiled when they saw Wee William approaching. The six men picked up speed and raced to meet him.

"Wee William!" Rowan called out. "How be ye this fine day?"

"Well, Rowan," he answered before going straight to the matter at hand. "Be they dead?"

Rowan and Black Richard pulled rein, with the others following suit. "I dunna ken fer certain, Wee William. But 'tis a strong possibility," Rowan offered.

"What do ya mean ye dunna ken?" Wee William asked, his hope rapidly fading. "What happened?"

"We took them several miles south of their home and left them to their own devices," Black Richard said. He sounded amused with what they had done.

Wee William's brow creased with confusion. He had a sneaky suspicion he was not going to like the outcome of Black Richard's tale.

"They either killed each other or froze to death," Black Richard said.

"Angus' orders were no' to kill anyone, unless absolutely necessary," Rowan interjected. "But he said nothin' about leavin' their naked arses to the wolves."

The six men broke out into raucous laughter while Wee William remained puzzled and unable to find any humor in the situation. "Tell me what happened."

Black Richard wiped a tear from his eye, but the rakish smile never left his face. "Well, ye see, Wee William, 'twas like this. We took the bloody bastards several miles from their home, back trackin', goin' in circles fer a time, so that they might not recognize where they be." He was rather proud of what they'd done.

"Aye," Rowan broke in, with his own devilish smile. "All the while the oldest be a rantin' and ravin' that we'd soon regret our transgressions. '*I'm friends with the king!*' he kept sayin', '*I'll have yer heads for treatin' an earl in such a manner!*' On and on he went, as if he were a member of the aristocracy!"

The men started laughing again, but Wee William did not join in the laughter.

"Get to the point," he said calmly, though his insides were anything but.

"The younger two, they were near to tears! They kept tellin' him to be quiet and to quit his belly achin', but he would no' listen to the good advice his brothers were givin' him," Rowan continued.

"Aye," Tall Thomas broke in. "And all the while, Rowan is tellin' them to be quiet for he's certain he hears wolves and mayhap the devil himself roamin' in the woods. They were a quakin' in their boots! I canna be certain, but I think the youngest may have lost control of his bladder!"

More laughter ensued and it began to wear on Wee William's patience. "Lads, we have no' got all day! Tell me what happened to the bloody heathens!"

The men quieted their laughter at the sound of Wee William's booming voice. Rowan wondered why it mattered so much what had happened to the brothers. He cleared his throat before answering. "Well, the short story of it is that we took them deep into some woods, made them strip down to their bare arses and left them there."

Wee William blinked. "That's it? Ye just left them there?" he asked.

Rowan and Black Richard casts puzzled looks to one another. "Aye," Rowan answered as he eyed Wee William suspiciously.

"They were miles from home, Wee William," Black Richard said. "I doubt they could have made it back to their cottage, at least not before their ballocks froze off. At the very least, they've a sore case of frostbite in places no man would want it!" He tried to sound hopeful and was very curious as to why it mattered what happened to the bloody fools.

"Wee William," Rowan said as he fiddled with the reins. "Might I ask *why* it be so important to ken what happened to them? If yer worried that Angus will be angry with our treatment of them—"

"I do no' worry over Angus!" Wee William said impatiently. "The lass thinks she's a widow and I do no' want to have her hope dispelled."

"Och! Ye worry the bastards will return and take their anger out on the poor lass," Rowan said. "I should have thought of that. No' once did Horace ask after his wife. No' once did he plead us to show her or his brothers any mercy. He be a whoreson, let there be no doubt. I am sorry, Wee William, I didna think about what would happen to the lass if they made it back alive." Rowan was suddenly concerned for the young woman's welfare.

"I do no' worry for the lass's safety, for *if* they do make it back alive, they will no' find her there," Wee William told him.

Black Richard and Rowan cast cautious looks to each other again. "What do ye mean?" Black Richard asked.

Wee William shifted in his saddle a bit and scanned the horizon. "The lass be with us."

They eyes of the six men opened wide as they stared at Wee William in disbelief.

"What do ya mean *with us?*" Black Richard asked.

"Exactly what I said. We've brought the lass with us. And her young brother and sister as well."

Wee William saw the glances being exchanged among his men and felt certain he knew what they were thinking.

"'Tis *no'* what yer thinkin'," he told them firmly.

A smile that said he did not believe what Wee William was attempting to declare came to Rowan's lips. "And what exactly do ye believe we're thinkin'?"

Wee William let out a quick breath of air. They hadn't brought back the news he had hoped for and now, he was certain he was in for a good amount of needling.

"The lass had nowhere else to go. Her parents are long dead and she hasn't a coin to her name. I was merely doin' what any good man would do." Wee William's voice was firm and he hoped that would be the end of the discussion.

He wasn't that lucky.

"I see," Rowan said as he nodded his head and looked around at his men. "So 'twas only yer kind heart that made such an offer."

Wee William ignored Rowan's comment. "We're camped not far from here. I suspect Daniel and David have a fire goin'. We'll no' tarry long for the children are hungry and growin' weary of the travelin'."

"Is yer blade sharp, Wee William?" Rowan asked as he sauntered up beside his friend.

"Of course me blade is sharp, 'tis always sharp," Wee William answered.

"And will ye be needin' some help?" Rowan asked with as serious an expression as he could muster.

"Help with what?" Wee William asked as he tapped the flanks of his horse. The men were closing in and he felt suddenly ill at ease.

"With shavin' yer beard, of course."

"What the bloody hell are ye goin' on about?" Wee William was in no mood for teasing and pretended he did not know what Rowan was talking about.

"I reckon if the lass be bonny enough fer ye to want her husband dead, then she be bonny enough fer ye to shave that long, ugly beard of yers." It was getting more difficult for Rowan to keep a straight face.

Wee William cast a sideways glance at Rowan, one that warned him to hold his tongue. But Rowan was not ready yet to give up pestering his friend. There was far too much joy in it.

Rowan turned to the rest of the men. "I wager ten groats now that Wee William shaves his beard within the next fortnight!"

"I give it a sennight!" one of the other men called out.

"I say he shaves it before we arrive home!" called another.

"What happens if she's wooed by another? He'll have shaved his beard for naught."

"I say the lass won't have him!" Tall Thomas yelled from the back of the pack.

All forward motion stopped when Wee William yanked the reins and spun his horse around. There was no mistaking his anger.

"What do ye mean she won't have me?" He sent a piercing glare at Tall Thomas. The words stung and the memories of another bonny lass from long ago came to the forefront of his mind.

Tall Thomas swallowed hard before answering. "'Twas meant in jest, Wee William."

Wee William glared furiously at each man before speaking. "Hear me, and hear me now, lads. I have no intentions of shavin' me beard."

He was not ready yet to admit to anyone that his feelings for Nora were far more than friendly in nature. 'Twas none of their business how he felt or what he thought about her.

Wanting to lighten the mood a bit, Black Richard spoke up. "So ye've no problem if any of us takes a fancy toward the lass?"

Wee William's jaw clenched as he ground his teeth back and forth. Hell would freeze over before he gave these men any further ammunition with which to taunt him with. "The lass is a woman full grown. 'Tisn't up to me who she keeps company with."

A few of the unmarried men, Black Richard included, began to smile hopefully. "So ye dunna care if we court the lass?" Black Richard asked.

Wee William let out an exasperated sigh. "I said, 'tisn't up to me. Just keep in mind the lass has been through much this past year. And we dunna ken if she be a widow or no'. And remember *who* the poor lass was married to! The last thing she needs is ye eejits confusin' her and acting like stags in rut!" He continued to glare at them.

"But I warn ye now, ye dogs. If ye so much as lay an improper hand on the lass, I'll cut yer throats without givin' it a second thought!"

With that, Wee William spun his horse around and left them to ponder his warning. Nora was his responsibility now. He'd do whatever he must to insure her safety. It had nothing to do with any feelings he had for her. He was simply doing what any good man would do.

Before he was out of earshot, the men were making wagers again on not only how soon before Wee William would shave his beard, but what the lass' response to that would be. Depending upon one's point of view, the odds were sorely against Wee William.

THEY MADE CAMP THAT NIGHT WITHIN A SMALL CAVE. NORA HAD slept fitfully, fighting nightmares that she refused divulging the details with anyone, including Wee William. The dreams were always the same -- Horace still lived. He had found her, dragged her back to Penrith and tossed her into the cellar. She would die there, in the dark, damp cellar and her body consumed by wolves and monsters.

The dreams left her feeling afraid and out of sorts. She wondered if she would ever sleep peacefully or dream of happier things.

The further north they rode, the colder the air became. Nora had lost the feeling in her toes and fingers days ago leaving her to wonder if she would ever regain any feeling in them.

Thankfully, at night she was able to curl up under several thick furs and cling to Elise for warmth. It seemed no matter how many furs she wrapped around herself, the cold from the hard ground still seeped in and chilled her to her bones. Nora prayed that it wasn't always this abominably cold and damp. She also prayed that neither Elise nor John would catch their deaths from all their exposure to the biting night air.

During the day, the men vied for Nora's attention and took turns with offers for her to ride with one of them. The men were acting quite strangely. She shrugged their odd behavior off to the fact that they were Highlanders.

Elise refused to ride with anyone other than her Sir Daniel. Nora apologized to the man repeatedly. Daniel would simply smile and say it was his pleasure.

John was not as insolent and angry as he had been in the beginning. Nora could only hope that it meant he was, at the least, coming around to the idea of a brighter future. She knew it would take far more time for him to adjust to their new lives. After all, he was probably just as afraid of it all as she was.

The next night they had camped inside a very dense copse of trees. The men had made a lean-to large enough for Nora, Elise and John to sleep in.

By the third night they were happily on Clan Randolph lands and were given safe haven by a farmer and his wife. While Nora and the children were allowed to sleep in the upper loft of the farmer's tiny home, Wee William and his men slept in the barn.

By the fourth day, Nora's black eye was no longer swollen and puffy. It had turned a very ugly shade of green. However the exhaustion and weariness from traveling left dark circles under her eyes. While she tried to maintain a sunny disposition, she continued to remain quiet. She also did her best to ignore all the attention the men were showing her.

The sun had thankfully made its presence known and began to warm the air and melt the snow. Still, it was not enough to erase the bone-tired weariness or warm Nora's frozen extremities.

The children had seemed far less bothered by all the riding, walking, and living out of doors. Hopefully they would soon arrive at Wee William's home. She wasn't sure how much longer she could stand what Elise happily referred to as their grand adventure.

Wee William's efforts at trying to seem uninterested or unbothered by the way his men were behaving were valiant. It had taken monumental efforts on his part not to crush the skulls of the idiots who were making no good attempts at hiding their motives. For days now, he had sat idly by as he watched his men make utter fools of themselves.

Seven of the nine men were unmarried and unattached. There were bonny lasses back home waiting with giggling anticipation for the return of a few of them. Those men were looking forward to that day as well.

The remaining four, however, had tripped over themselves trying to gain Nora's attention. All of it to Wee William's abject consternation. He wasn't sure if Nora was too naïve, too worried over her future, or too exhausted to notice the men. Either way, she seemed unmoved by their displays of kindness.

Finally, they had reached beloved MacDougall land. They would happily be inside the walls of Castle Gregor soon enough.

They were making camp by a small loch when the foolish men started in again. Wee William's patience had worn to a fine fragile thread. He was doing his level best to hold his tongue and keep his temper in check. But their behavior was grating on his nerves.

"Are ye warm enough, Lady Nora?" Phillip had asked, as he walked toward her carrying a fur.

Nora looked at him as though he were daft. She was sitting next to the fire, bundled from head to toe in three heavy furs.

The men were baffling creatures. She could not understand why they were behaving so oddly. It was all becoming too much.

"I believe three furs should be sufficient, Frederick," she answered as politely as she could.

"I be Phillip, lass." The young man smiled thoughtfully at her. "Frederick is the ugly one with the warts on his neck."

Elise was sitting beside Nora and she giggled at Phillip's insult of Frederick.

"Would ye like more rabbit, Nora?" Daniel asked as he held out a stick holding what remained of the four rabbits they had caught earlier.

It was all she could do not to wretch at the thought of more food. "Nay, Daniel, I've had more than enough. Thank you kindly though."

Daniel looked at Phillip and smiled cheerfully. "Did ye hear that, Phillip? The lass remembers *my* name. I wonder why that is?"

Phillip's face darkened as he cursed at Daniel in their native tongue.

Before Nora knew what was happening, an all-out brawl broke out. Phillip, Daniel, David, and Frederick were rolling around on the ground in front of her. She jumped to her feet and pulled Elise to safety behind a boulder. John refused to budge from his spot by the fire, wholeheartedly enjoying the unseemly display that was taking place before him.

Black Richard and Rowan stood with arms crossed over their chests, next to Wee William. Tall Thomas and Garret stood on either side of them, shaking their heads.

They spoke to one another in Gaelic apparently unbothered by the fight taking place just feet from where they stood.

Nora was appalled. She stomped toward Wee William and pulled on his arm. "Aren't you going to stop them?" she asked, clearly upset with all of them. He gave her a look that questioned her soundness of mind.

Rowan shook his head. "Best to let them fight it out, lass."

Nora let out a sharp breath. "What on earth are they fighting over?"

Black Richard chuckled. "Ye truly have no idea?"

"No, I haven't! 'Tis why I asked the question! Please, make them stop!" The more time she had spent with this band of men, the less she understood them or their odd ways.

The men turned their attentions back to the grunting, cursing bodies that were now one big heap of dirt, sweat, and blood.

Realizing her pleas had fallen on deaf ears, she decided she should at least make an attempt to bring the fracas to a halt. Besides, they were terrifying Elise. The little girl was hiding behind the boulder, her eyes filled to the brim with tears. They couldn't hear her crying over the din of the fighting.

"Gentlemen, please, stop this instant!" Nora yelled, clapping her hands as if she were trying to get a dog out of the garden. "I say stop this instant!" Her pleas went unanswered as well as unnoticed.

She took a step closer to the mass of fighting men so that they might hear her better. "Please, stop this foolishness now!" she yelled.

Phillip had loosened himself from Daniel's grip panting and covered with sweat. His lip was cut and a trickle of blood ran down his chin. He had no idea Nora was but a step away from him. He took a step backward and in the process knocked Nora to the ground. Apparently he hadn't noticed her because he immediately jumped back into the melee.

With great speed, Wee William moved in, scooped Nora up and carried her away just as Frederick went flying through the air and landed on the piece of earth she'd had just occupied.

There could be no doubt with Wee William's level of anger. It was plainly evident by the harsh scowl his face bore. In three strides, he reached the rock, and set Nora upon it.

"Are ye hurt?" he asked, as he looked her over for signs of injury.

"Nay," she muttered, more surprised over the strange expression on Wee William's face than bothered by any injury to her backside.

Wee William let loose a low, furious growl before turning back to his men.

It would later be told that the sound of his deep voice had traveled to the ends of the earth and back in the length of two heartbeats and that the earth shuddered from its boom.

"Enough!" his voice thundered. The men, who only moments ago had been hell-bent on inflicting as much damage on each other as they could, stopped immediately. All eyes turned to Wee William as he stood next to Nora. Elise stopped crying and scurried up the rock to take refuge with her sister. She was far too frightened to cry.

"All of ye, come with me now!" Wee William's eyes blazed with fury as he stomped away from the group of men. Nora could have sworn the earth shook with each step he took. Frozen in place, she was too terrified to move. She shuddered as she pulled Elise tighter to her bosom.

All at once the men were on their feet. Looking rather deflated, as well as nervous, they followed Wee William into the woods. Curious to see what punishment Wee William might inflict upon the young men, Rowan and Black Richard shrugged their shoulders and fell in behind. John was fast on their heels.

Wee William had walked a good distance before he stopped

abruptly and turned to face his men. They all stood frozen in place and waited. John looked as though he was anticipating a good tongue lashing to come from Wee William and he couldn't hide the smile on his face.

"John! Go back and watch over Nora and Elise!" Wee William's voice warned that he'd brook no argument from the boy. John was no fool and decided it best to do as he was told, even though he would have much preferred to stay and listen.

Once John was out of earshot Wee William began. "I have reached the end of me patience! Ye've all been actin' like men who've never laid eyes upon a woman before! Yer behavior is completely unacceptable and I'll have no more of it!"

He began pacing back and forth. At first he thought he'd be able to handle his feelings and emotions while his men bent over backwards to woo Nora. He had nearly choked more than once on his own jealousy. For days, he had remained sullenly quiet while he watched each of these men try to win her affection.

With each smile, each glance, each offer of food, blankets or a walk in the moonlight, his jealousy and anger grew. He could take no more and he certainly would not allow them to fight over her.

He stopped suddenly and turned his attention back to his men. With his feet spread wide, he crossed his arms over his chest and eyed each of them before speaking.

"I claim her as me own," he told them. It was a statement of fact and the tone of his voice warned there would be no argument over it. All eyes grew wide with astonishment and not one could find the strength or courage to speak.

"From this day forward, she is mine. Ye've been warned. If any of ye so much as look at her with even a hint of a smile in yer eyes, I'll run ye through."

He didn't give any of them time to question, needle, tease or otherwise speak. He left them alone and headed back to the camp.

The men stood with mouths agape as they watched Wee William walk away. The day they thought would never come had finally arrived. After a moment, all eyes turned to Rowan. He was the only one smiling.

Without a word, each man begrudgingly walked up to him and each placed five groats in his open palm.

"How did ye ken it?" Black Richard asked as he handed over his own losses.

Rowan smiled as he opened his sporran and dropped the coins in. "'Twas simple, Black Richard. I've seen that look before."

Black Richard's brow furrowed. "What look?"

"Och! Ye canna see the way Wee William looks at the lass?" He clicked his tongue as the last of the coins fell into the pouch that hung at his waist.

Black Richard shook his head. "All I've noticed is that he has looked angry and ill at the same time."

Rowan laughed as he slapped his hand on his friend's back. "Aye, Black Richard. When a man looks that way -- angry and ill -- as well as lost, dazed and confused, ye ken he's a man in love. 'Tis the same look we get when we go into battle, and the same look of a man going to the gallows. He kens that he be lost and he has no idea what to do about it!"

"How did ye know he'd claim her before he shaved his beard?" Black Richard asked.

"That was easy, lad. When he said he didna care if the others wooed the lass, I kent the moment he said it, 'twas a lie. The man is completely besotted with her, though he fights with himself over it. I kent there would be no way he could stomach the others falling over their feet to impress the lass. And the fear in his eyes was verra clear."

Black Richard balked at the notion. "Fear? I've never kent Wee William to be afraid of anything or anyone in his life!"

Rowan laughed again. He gave Black Richard a friendly slap on his back. "Aye, but we've never kent him to be in love before!"

WEE WILLIAM RETURNED TO THE CAMP AND WALKED DIRECTLY TO Nora. She was trying to comfort Elise who was inconsolable.

Nora looked at him, worried and concerned over whatever may have transpired in the woods. She didn't wait for him to reach her or to speak. "She thinks you've killed her Sir Daniel."

Wee William stopped dead in his tracks. Although the thought had crossed his mind more than once these past few days, he'd never really take the lad's life. Nor the lives of any of his friends. But he wasn't above beating them to a bloody pulp.

"Wheesht, lass," Wee William said as he walked toward them. He scooped Elise up and held her close to his chest.

"I didna kill yer Daniel, he's just in a wee bit of trouble for misbehavin' in front of ye ladies."

Elise lifted her head and looked into Wee William's eyes. "Do you promise you didn't hurt him?" she asked between sobs.

A warm, endearing smile came to Wee William's lips and spread to his eyes. "I do so promise, lassie."

Elise wiped her nose on Wee William's shirt before giving him a hug. "Thank you Sir William," she said.

"What lass, do ye be thankin' me fer?" Wee William asked as he patted her little back.

"For not killing my angel. God would have been very upset with you."

Wee William chuckled and gave her another hug. A moment later, Elise was squealing with delight.

"Sir Daniel!" she screamed as she held out her arms for him.

Wee William wondered how long it would be before his hearing returned to the ear in which she had just screamed.

Daniel had been walking into the camp with his head hung low, but the sound of Elise's delightful squeal made him smile. He walked toward them and took the child into his arms.

"Wee William said he didn't kill you!" Elise said as she wrapped her arms around his neck. "I'm very glad that he didn't!"

The look of warmth and kindness that had spread to Wee William's face when he consoled Elise, made Nora's heart swell and with it came an odd fluttering sensation in her stomach. She sat quietly and observed him more closely.

He was indeed a very large man. By rights, she should tremble in his presence. Good sense would dictate, just from his appearance alone, that she should be utterly terrified of him.

That was what flustered her. She was no more afraid of Wee

William than she was of Elise or a newborn kitten. She felt more at ease, safer, and more cared for with him, than she could ever remember feeling.

It was difficult to ascertain if he was handsome or not, what with all the hair and that long beard that reached to his stomach. His eyes? *Those* she could say, without reservation, were...were what, she mused. Not quite beautiful but yet, there was something unusual and appealing about them. There were times when she felt she could easily read his emotions by looking into them. Yet others, when an invisible wall was thrown up, blocking any and all insight into what he may be thinking or feeling.

One by one the men returned to the camp looking physically no worse than when they'd left. However, a detectable silence had fallen over them and none would look Nora in the eye. She wasn't sure if she appreciated the silence or if she should be worried. She wondered what Wee William had said to them.

It soon grew dark and once again they would be sleeping out of doors. Another lean-to was prepared for Nora and the children, yet this time, not one of the men offered to guard her while she slept.

The children fell asleep quickly. Nora lay in the dark, listening to the soft crackle of the fire and the low murmurs of the men whispering in their Gaelic. She wished she could understand the language so that she might know what they were saying. She'd been too distracted, too wrapped up in worrying over her future to try to pick up any of their melodic words.

As she lay there mulling over what she would do once they reached the safe confines of the Scottish castle, Castle Gregor, she heard a grunt come from outside her lean-to. Curiosity getting the better of her, she carefully lifted the fur that served as both wall and door, and peeked outside.

There was Wee William, lying on his back between the lean-to and the fire. His broadsword was resting across his chest. Mayhap, Nora thought, it was his turn to watch over them. Or, she supposed, it was his way of keeping the men from acting so foolishly. Whatever his reasons were for being there, she was grateful.

She felt a sudden urge to scoot across the ground and bury her face in his chest and snuggle up to him. The thought surprised her to the point that she felt her face grow warm from embarrassment. Startled, she quickly dropped the fur for fear the object of her fascination would see her staring at him and read her mind. As she stared up at the darkness, her mind began to wander to all manner of places.

Her mother had died more than six years ago and her father wasn't about to have the kinds of conversations with her that would explain what happened between a man and woman. There had been no other women in her life with whom she felt comfortable enough to ask the many questions she had regarding that topic. Nora had gone into her marriage completely ignorant.

She'd seen sheep mating before, quite by accident of course, and supposed it might be done the same way between a man and a woman. And she had witnessed a cow giving birth and supposed again, that might be how a woman went about it.

Nora seriously doubted the things Horace did to her were the correct way of going about making bairns. It stood to reason, in her mind, that a bairn would go in the same way it came out. If that were the case, Horace had not done it correctly.

Then again, she could have it all wrong and Horace had been right and she really was barren. She had so many questions and lingering doubts and not a soul to turn to to ask. Nearly one and twenty and a widow nonetheless, she felt she was severely lacking in too many areas.

She tried closing her eyes to sleep, but when she did, Wee William's face would pop into her mind. She wondered if his beard would tickle or scratch if she were to kiss him. Would his calloused, strong hands be gentle or harsh if he were to caress her cheek?

Where were these thoughts coming from? Mayhap Horace was right and she was a harlot! He wasn't dead a full sennight yet and here she was having lustful thoughts of a man she'd known just as long!

Mayhap Horace had seen the truth about her and the problems he had with intimacy were truly her fault. Good, virtuous women weren't supposed to think of such things, were they? Mayhap it was *she* who was going to burn in hell for such impure thoughts as the ones skipping happily through her mind.

She crossed herself and began to pray for strength to fight the shameless urges and for forgiveness for her transgressions. She prayed and prayed and prayed for control of her mind, her wanton thoughts, and the sinful images that were jumping around in her brain. Just as she thought she had them under control, and could calmly succumb to exhaustion, she thought of Wee William's bright smile, his hazel eyes, his long beard and she knew she was doomed.

MUCH TO NORA'S MORTIFICATION, SHE WAS FORCED TO RIDE WITH Wee William the following morning. But then, she hadn't really been given a choice in the matter.

When she returned from her morning ablutions, she found that she and Wee William were alone. The others had already left and had taken Elise and John with them. When she inquired as to why the others had left without them, she wasn't sure if she believed Wee William's answer.

"The men are in a hurry to return home," was his curt response from atop his horse.

Seeing she had no choice in the matter, other than walking the rest of the way, she took a deep breath and took his offered hand. He pulled her up to his lap, wrapped the fur around her as he'd done numerous times before, and urged his horse forward.

Why should this time be any different than the other times she had ridden with him? *Something* felt different. Perhaps it had to do with the fact that each time she had closed her eyes to sleep last night, she could only think of Wee William and how a kiss from him might feel.

Feeling tense and a bit embarrassed, she sat ramrod straight, afraid to touch him for fear that he would be able to somehow read her thoughts. It was too embarrassing to think of what his reaction might be if he knew what was tumbling about in her mind.

"What ails ye this mornin', lass?" Wee William asked, after they had ridden for some time.

Nora felt her face flush as she tried to gain control of her stomach. It had plummeted to her toes and back when she heard his voice and his question. "N-nothing ails me, William."

Wee William grunted, a sound she had grown accustomed to these past days. Mayhap it was a noise that all Scots made, for she'd heard that sound come from all the men on numerous occasions.

They were riding through a valley and the sun had not been up for very long. It cast the landscape in brilliant shades of pinks, oranges, and yellows. Nora was glad to see that the snow was still melting, a sure sign that spring was not far away.

"Are ye sure, lass?" Wee William asked, breaking her quiet reverie.

"I assure you, sir, that I am well," she hoped she didn't sound too irritated. It wasn't Wee William's fault that her mind was engulfed with thoughts of kisses and bare skin. She blushed, unable to look at him for fear she'd be tempted to fulfill the fantasies that refused to leave her thoughts.

Wee William grunted again, not believing her for a moment. He had six sisters and he knew that when a woman said *nothing* was the matter, there was usually *something* the matter. He decided to give her some time to sort it out with the belief that eventually, she'd tell him what was bothering her.

It was not long before they caught up with the men and children. As typical, Elise was perched upon Daniel's horse wrapped in fur. The little girl was fast asleep with her head against his chest, a fact that Nora found quite unusual.

Seeing the worry on Nora's face when she noticed Elise fast asleep in his arms, Daniel sent her a warm smile. "She be well, lass. I think our journey has finally caught up with her."

Nora leaned over to take a peek at her sister. Her little nose was red and running, as it had been for days. That in itself was not unusual, considering the cold weather they'd been forced to endure. While fresh air might do a body good, excess exposure to the cold and damp air was never a good thing.

Wishing to ease her worry, Wee William spoke up. "We'll be at Gregor before the sun sets, lass. We'll all feel better then. I believe we could all use a hot bath, warm meal and a nice bed to sink into."

"That sounds heavenly, William," she readily agreed and began to relax.

Mayhap that was all she needed. To be inside, by a warm fire, and away from all the men. More specifically, Wee William. Mayhap these thoughts and odd feelings were merely the result of being surrounded by men for so many days. She concluded that *that* was what had brought the onslaught of lustful feelings and images about. Once she was away from them and surrounded by decent and virtuous women, her thoughts would return to normal.

Nora relaxed with that comforting thought, for she had never aspired to be a wanton woman or a harlot. She wanted to be the righteous woman her father had raised her to be and not like the women she had heard about when no one thought she was listening. The ruined girls who worked as bar wenches or the girls who made their livings by warming a man's bed. She knew she'd not end up like those women for various reasons -- the most important being there wasn't enough gold in all of England to pay her to do what Horace had tried to do.

Elise continued to sleep peacefully while they rode in comfortable silence. They had spilled out of the valley and onto flatter, more open ground before noontime. The land was still blanketed in white but the warmth from the sun was quickly turning it into a heavy, slushy mess.

Though she worried over how Wee William's clan would treat them, Nora decided a roof over their heads was worth any impending ugliness or mistreatment. She was far too cold, tired, and hungry to care. At the moment, her feet were so cold that she could have stuck them in a roaring fire and it would still have taken a week for them to thaw.

The landscape was flat in spots, hilly in others and large black rocks jutted out at random places. Because the ground was far too sloppy and wet they sat upon rocks while they ate a very quick meal. They'd eaten the last of the bread the day before yesterday. Today they finished off the last of the dried beef and cheese. The men promised this would be their last meal out of doors for they would be at Castle Gregor in a few short hours.

Elise ate very little. Nora noticed her sunken eyes and pale skin. The child was not herself and had been sleeping most of the day.

Nora's stomach tightened with worry and unease when she pressed the back of her hand to Elise's forehead. "She's burning up!" she exclaimed. Her eyes immediately went in search of Wee William.

He had been standing with Rowan and Tall Thomas when he heard Nora's worried voice. With a purposeful stride, he reached Nora and Elise in short order. He, too, reached out to feel the child's forehead and cheeks. Her skin was dry and hot, and her pupils were glassy.

"This is all my fault," Nora whispered as she looked up at Wee William.

"Nay, lass!" Wee William argued. If anyone was to blame, it was Horace. Had the man owned an ounce of compassion, well, things would naturally be different.

Nora blamed herself. Had she been a better wife to Horace then he would have allowed her to keep the children. Mayhap, if she had tried harder, been nicer, done things differently. Her mind flittered to and fro to all the "what ifs" and "maybes" and they all circled back to the same place. "What ifs" and "could have beens" weren't important at the moment. Elise was sick and it was Nora's fault.

Wee William looked into Nora's eyes, brimmed with tears of worry as well as exhaustion. He could not stand to see her so distressed.

He stood taller and headed toward the horses. "Mount up!" he called out to his men. "Elise is ill!"

The men did not wait for further instructions. As soon as Wee William's words left his mouth, the men flew into action. They quickly packed away the meal things and were mounted in a matter of moments.

Wee William brought his horse to stand next to the rock where Nora sat cradling Elise in her arms. Nora shifted Elise around with one arm resting under her bottom, the other holding her small head against her shoulder. From atop his horse, Wee William bent slightly and scooped them up and sat them on his lap.

"She'll be well soon enough, Nora," he told her.

For the first time since she met Wee William, she doubted him.

Far too many children died from simple fevers. Malnourishment, cold and damp living conditions and lack of proper care, often made it quite difficult for a child to fight even the simplest of illnesses.

John and Elise had been living in a dank, dark, cold castle for a year. Their living conditions had been squalid and foul. And then they'd been stolen away in the middle of the night and carried halfway across the world, forced to sleep out of doors or in caves, with little more than cheese, dried beef and stale bread for nourishment for days. 'Twas no wonder Elise was ill.

Tears of remorse and self-reproach fell from Nora's eyes. If anything happened to Elise, she would never forgive herself.

8

Humiliation and outrage drove Horace Crawford and kept him warm despite the freezing air and snow. The sun had risen hours before he and his brothers finally made their way back to the cottage. With chattering teeth and frozen skin, they rushed into the cottage and began wrapping themselves in blankets.

Nigel made several attempts at starting a fire. His hands were trembling so much so, that he could not hold the tallow steady. While Nigel battled with the tallow, Donald went to the cupboard in search of the bottle of whiskey. He nearly fell into the opening in the floor that led to the cellar.

Frozen to the bone, angry beyond comprehension, Donald could not speak just yet. He found the whiskey and took a long drink. He made his way around the opening in the floor and across the room to where Horace sat on the bed huddled under the blankets. Donald climbed onto the edge of the bed and held the bottle out.

With shaking hands, Horace took the offered whiskey. He could barely keep the bottle to his lips and had to use both hands to keep from dropping it all together. Streams of whiskey trickled down the sides of his face as he drank greedily. Were he able to speak just yet, he would have been cursing at Nigel to hurry the hell up with the fire.

The three brothers sat clustered together on the bed, each lost in his own thoughts as they drank and stared at the fire Nigel had finally managed. It was quite some time and a full bottle of whiskey later, before any of them began to regain the feeling in their extremities. Exhausted from the long walk home in the snow and cold, the three men fell asleep in front of the warm fire.

Hours later, Nigel and Donald were awakened to the sound of Horace yelling and cursing.

Horace had awakened long before his brothers, still unable to figure out why the Highlanders had come into his home in the middle of the night. He could not begin to fathom why he and his brothers had been taken out into the middle of nowhere and left with no harm done to any of them other than injured pride and frozen skin.

He had gone to the cupboard in search of another bottle of whiskey when he discovered the table had been moved and the door to the cellar opened. Unable still to comprehend why the Highlanders had appeared, the open cellar door caused him more confusion than he wanted. Mayhap they had killed Nora and her body now lay dead in the cellar below. The thought of her dead, frozen corpse brought him nothing but a twinge of delight.

Cautiously, Horace had crept down the ladder and much to his disappointment he did not find his wife dead. But the flicker of the candle he held had shown him something *was* amiss. He moved the ladder to the side and crouched low. That was when he had discovered the stone lying on the ground and a sizable hole in the wall. Curiosity took hold and he warily poked his hand inside it and felt around. Nothing.

He had paced around the cellar for a few moments before the cold air began to seep in. His mind was racing as he made his way back up the ladder. He lowered the door and scooted the table back over it.

Why? What had they wanted? He kept repeating the questions over and over in his mind. What on earth could they have wanted? What had been hidden in the cellar?

And what of Nora? Where the bloody hell was she? He went to the trunk at the end of his bed and saw that her belongings were missing.

Firth. The whore had taken the opportunity to run away again. Ungrateful wench!

Ever so slowly Horace began to piece things together.

Highlanders. He had heard many rumors over the past year that told of his stepsister, Aishlinn, running away to the Highlands. It was also told that the Highlanders she had found refuge with, had killed the former Earl of Penrith. Other rumors said that Aishlinn, too, was dead. He hoped the latter were true. The stupid wench had been far more trouble than she had been worth.

Until that moment, Horace had ignored the rumors. He had brushed them off as stories told by mindless idiots with nothing better to do with their time.

Horace was of the opinion that Aishlinn was a dimwitted fool of a woman, with no more sense than God gave a rock. He could hardly believe she had survived the beating the earl had given her, let alone had the ability to roam around the countryside or to find a home in Scotland.

But the appearance of all those Highlanders now made him seriously doubt his previous thoughts on that subject. It was the only thing that made sense at the moment. Aishlinn still lived.

The more he thought on it, the more he believed it to be true, and the angrier he became. Something had been hidden in the cellar. But what?

It had to be something of great value for he couldn't imagine a group of Highlanders traveling in this weather to burst into his home in the middle of the night for sheer amusement. Aye, they were greedy bastards, every last Scot. Gluttonous fools as well. Nay, *it,* whatever *it* was, had to have been worth a significant amount of coin.

His mind raced at the possibilities. Aishlinn's grandfather *had* been a very wealthy Englishmen, that much he knew from the stories his father, Broc, had told him. Could it be possible that for years, Aishlinn had kept some valuable treasure hidden away? If so, why hadn't she used them to leave long before he'd traded her to Castle Firth?

Aye, it was a very distinct possibility that the stupid girl hadn't realized she owned a treasure or anything of value. Mayhap, she had discussed it with the Scots and discovered the value of it by happenstance. And greedy bastards that they were, they decided to descend upon his home to take it!

Clarity began to bloom. His heart raced as his anger steadily boiled. All these years and untold treasures had been underfoot! By rights, it was *his* treasure. Whatever it was, it belonged to him. He'd put a roof over Aishlinn's head. He had fed her. She owed him.

Before he realized it, he was pacing back and forth, his mind conjuring up all sorts of possibilities as to what had lain under his nose all these years. It couldn't be coin, for even Aishlinn was smart enough to know the value of silver or gold. Nay, it had to be something significant, yet small enough to fit in the hole below. Something so valuable that it would make Highlanders come for it.

The more his mind raced, the angrier he became until he could contain it no longer. He let out a furious yell that jolted his brothers from their sleep.

When he was finished, he was covered in sweat and so furious that his heart pounded in his chest. Something inside him, something dark and menacing, told Horace that he had to do two things.

One, he must find out what the hidden treasure was and two, he must exact his revenge on both Aishlinn and Nora. Aishlinn for being so stupid that she had hidden something of great value from him and Nora for leaving him embarrassed and humiliated.

As his brothers sat quietly watching him, a plan began to form in his mind. No matter what the cost, no matter what trials he must go through, he *would* find the two women who had caused him untold pain. And he would get even with both.

9

Wee William and his men rode like the devil was chasing them to reach Castle Gregor. Not much was said among them, save for the frequent inquiries by the men as to how Elise fared. Daniel and David raced ahead to let their clan know that they had returned, bringing with them people in need of their help.

By the time Wee William, Nora, Elise and the others arrived, the castle was a whirlwind of motion. At the top of the stairs leading up and into the castle, stood Isobel, the chief's wife. Next to her was Mary, the castle's cook and healer. Neither of them looked happy.

Mary, her long white hair pulled away from her face and into a loose bun at the nape of her neck, was wiping her hands on her apron. She studied the group as it came bounding into the courtyard.

"What do ye suppose Wee William has go' himself into?" Mary asked Isobel.

"I canna begin to guess, Mary," Isobel answered as she tucked a loose bit of her black hair behind her ear. "I hope that whatever ails this child, it willna spread to anyone else."

Mary nodded her head in agreement before crossing herself.

Daniel appeared from behind Isobel and Mary, and came running down the stairs and straight to Wee William and Nora. Wee William brought his horse to an abrupt stop. The horse snorted and huffed and shook its head, jangling leather and bit.

Daniel did not wait for Nora or Wee William to dismount before grabbing Elise from Nora's arms and running back into the castle. Mary was right behind him, shouting out orders in Gaelic.

"Take her to Aishlinn's auld room," she told him as they climbed the stairs.

As Wee William helped Nora down, Isobel came to them.

"Wee William!" She did not look the least bit happy to see them as she studied Nora. Her appraisal made Nora feel quite uneasy.

"What the bloody hell is going on?" Isobel asked as Wee William dismounted and handed his horse off to a stable boy.

Nora could not understand what the woman was saying and looked at Wee William for help.

"Isobel," Wee William said in English. "This be Nora Crawford of Penrith."

Isobel recognized the last name and did nothing to disguise her surprise or displeasure. She looked directly at Nora and continued to speak in the Gaelic.

"Crawford? Have ye lost yer mind, Wee William?"

"'Tis no' what ye think, Isobel. She be a Crawford only by marriage."

Isobel glared at Wee William. Angus was *not* going to like this, not at all. Isobel wasn't sure if she really cared how the lass was related to any of the Crawfords. Her thoughts immediately turned to Aishlinn. They'd spent the last year trying to keep her existence a secret, for her own safety as well as the clan's. Now, Wee William brings a Crawford into their midst.

"Why is she here?" Isobel seethed.

"She needs our help, Isobel. She was married to Horace."

"Horace?" She looked Nora up and down. "What do you mean *was?*"

"That be a long story, Isobel. Mayhap we can talk after we see the lass gets a bath, clean clothes and a hot meal?"

Isobel shook her head in disgust. Instinct warned her that she would not like the story behind the young woman's presence.

Nora had been listening, unable to understand *what* they were saying. But Isobel's tone of voice and the angry glances she shot at Nora said plenty; her presence here was not a welcome one.

Wee William had warned Nora that while she would receive his protection as well as his men's, it might take a few days for his clan to warm to having another Sassenach living among them. He had assured her that once they knew the reasons why she was there, his clan would soon warm to the idea. She had prayed these past many days that he was correct and that they would at least be civil and courteous. But the looks this woman was giving her said that would not be the case.

Nora tamped down her disappointment and tried to look as though she did not care what Isobel's opinion of her was. She could remain silent no longer.

"M'lady," Nora said with a short curtsey. "I know our presence here is not welcomed and I apologize for the inconvenience we are causing. You have my word that we will leave as soon as my sister, Elise, is well enough to travel. I ask naught of you or your people other than a warm place for her to recover." She refused to cry or to beg. Her only concern at the moment was Elise's health.

Isobel's expression had changed from anger to curiosity as she studied Nora. The young woman looked gaunt, exhausted, and worried. Though she was covered with mud and muck, she stood with her chin up and her back straight.

Isobel caught a note of pride in the girl, but it wasn't born of arrogance or conceit. Isobel took a deep breath and let it out through her nose. Sympathy for Nora as well as the sick little girl on her way above stairs began to creep in.

"Please forgive me manners, lass. I tend to be overly protective of me family and me clan, as I'm sure ye are of yers."

Nora tilted her head slightly. "Aye, I am. There's naught I wouldn't do for them."

Isobel nodded her head approvingly and turned her attention back to Wee William. "Let's get inside. I've put the babe in Aishlinn's auld room. I'm sure Nora will want to stay with her. Ye all look as though ye could use a hot bath and some clean clothes!"

Wee William's shoulders sagged with relief. He knew that if Isobel was willing to help Nora and her family, then the rest of the clan would soon follow her lead. They trusted Isobel's judgment and guidance. He smiled with the thought that this might end up being easier than he anticipated, until he thought of Angus.

His smile quickly evaporated. How would his chief take this news?

"BLOODY HELL!" ANGUS' DEEP VOICE ECHOED THROUGHOUT THE WAR room. He stood with his palms spread on the top of the table as he glowered at Wee William and the rest of the men who faced him. The clan council sat around the table, waiting in silence while their chief finished his tirade.

"Bloody hell!" he was beginning to repeat himself.

Shaking his head in frustration, Angus pushed himself up and ran a hand through his long blonde hair. He was more than forty now, but no one would guess it from his broad chest and well-muscled arms. The men who surrounded him had witnessed his anger on more than one occasion. Angus let out a deep breath of air and crossed his arms over his chest.

Seventeen years ago when he'd been made chief of Clan MacDougall, he had been honored. While it hadn't always been easy, Angus McKenna had taken his duties and responsibilities seriously and he'd always done what he thought was best for his clan. The safety of his clan, as well as his wife and children, were always at the forefront of any decision he made.

"We pass a decree immediately that does no' allow any unmarried man to cross onto English land!" Angus said through gritted teeth. Fergus, one of the oldest members of the clan and the council, chuckled at Angus' directive. Angus ignored him.

"Every time one of ye goes across that border, ye come back with a woman! And no' just *any* woman! Nay, ye come back with a *Sassenach* woman who threatens the safety of this clan!"

Fergus smiled and chuckled again. "Need I remind ye, Angus, that were it no' for some of these young men, ye'd no' ken about yer own daughter?"

Angus fumed. "I ken that fact very well, Fergus! But that is well beside the point. They brought back the wife of the man who made me daughter's life a livin' hell for her whole life! And they canna even tell me if the man lives or no'."

"Chances are they didna survive the night," Rowan said as he tried to offer some hope. Angus shot him an angry glare that warned him to keep his mouth shut.

"Chances are? Chances are?" Angus seethed. "Aye, 'tis possible that the bastards succumbed to the elements and the wolves still feast on their dead bodies," he feigned calmness as he paced behind the table.

"Aye, 'tis indeed possible." He clasped his hands behind his back and appeared as though he were giving that possibility some weight.

Suddenly he stopped and spun to look at the young men lined against the wall. "'Tis *also* quite possible that the whoresons live and they are on their way to this castle now! What then? Have ye considered that?"

Wee William's jaw was set, his shoulders back with his hand rested on the hilt of his sword. It would be over his dead body that they'd turn Nora over to Horace, *if* he ever showed up to claim her. From what Rowan had told him, the night they took Horace and his brothers away, not once had he inquired as to the safety or wellbeing of his wife. Such a man would not travel far to rescue his wife.

The bruises on Nora's face were all that Wee William needed to confirm his suspicion that Horace Crawford was a coward.

"He'll no' come fer her," Wee William said pointedly.

Angus' brow furrowed into a deep line. "And how can ye be so sure of that?"

"He's a coward and no' once while they were taking him and his brothers away, did he ask after Nora."

"And what be yer point, Wee William?" Angus did not give him time to form an answer. "If Horace be anything like his father, he cares no' fer her as a woman, but only as his possession. 'Tisn't a matter of honor with his ilk. 'Tis a matter of Nora bein' *his*."

"That may well be, Angus. But I doubt that even Horace is fool enough to venture this far into Scotland to retrieve her. He's no' that brave."

"Nay, he may no' be that *brave,* Wee William," Angus said. "But he may be that *stupid.*"

Wee William had not considered that possibility before. Still, it mattered not. Horace could bring a thousand English soldiers with him and it would change nothing. He had grown quite fond of Nora and he wouldn't allow her to go back to the life she'd been living. His honor would not allow Nora or the children to return to England or the life they had been living. He had made a promise.

Angus shook his head, knowing full well that his words fell on deaf ears. Whatever it was about this lass, she had somehow captured the hearts of the men standing before him. There were times when he wished the sense of honor that was instilled into the people of his clan, the sense of right versus wrong, and the innate desire to help the less fortunate, wasn't quite so strong.

There were many nights where he lay in bed at night wishing he had killed Broc years ago. How different his life would be had he not allowed his half-brother to live. Laiden would have lived. Aishlinn would have grown up in the loving bosom of her clan and not suffered as she had, raised by the selfish and cruel Broc and the three idiots he called sons.

The room had gone quiet as Angus and Wee William stood facing one another. Fergus finally pushed himself away from the table and stood, his old bones creaking in the process. He had been watching Wee William rather closely for the past half hour. The young man was determined to keep the young woman and her siblings safe from the man named Horace. Though Fergus had never met Horace, he knew his kind all too well. He could not say that he blamed Wee William or the others for wanting to do what they knew in their hearts to be the right thing.

"There ye have it then," Fergus said, as if it all made perfectly good sense.

Angus looked at him as though he'd become feeble in his old age. "What does that mean, Fergus?"

Fergus chuckled again as he grabbed his walking stick from where it rested against the table. "It means what it means. The lass and her wee sister and brother need our help. And ye ken we will give it to them, just as we would anyone else who came to us fer aid. Bein' angry over it serves no purpose. Ye best decide what to do if ever this Horace Crawford shows up."

"Have ye any suggestions, Fergus?" It was Thomas Gainer that spoke. He was nearly as auld as Fergus, but where Fergus was lanky and gnarled with rheumatism, Thomas Gainer was short and squat, resembling a pickle barrel with arms and legs.

"Aye. Decide where to hide the bloody Sassenach's body. I recommend burying him on Bowie lands. Can't stand the Bowies, ye ken. I doubt anyone will miss the whoreson called Horace Crawford."

All eyes followed Fergus as he left the room, whistling a lively tune.

Mayhap the man *had* grown feeble, Angus supposed, but his words held some merit. Angus looked at the remaining members of his council. None of them argued Fergus' point. They all sat stoic, eyes focused on Angus. Had they objected to Fergus' advice they would have said so. Believing the men agreed with Fergus, Angus turned once again to the young men who stood against the wall.

"I suppose his plan does have some merit," Angus began. The more he thought on it, the less angry he became, and soon, a rather devious smile grew and his eyes lit up. He could not deny the fact that he would enjoy meeting the men who had nearly destroyed his daughter's life.

"Mayhap, if Horace Crawford does decide to do somethin' stupid and come to Scotland, we'll be able to show him a little Highland justice, aye?"

The men at the table burst into laughter. The young men lining the wall -- looking as though they were awaiting their own executions -- let out sighs of relief. Wee William was relieved as well, for he wouldn't have to admit openly that he was developing some very strong feelings toward Nora.

He was quite glad that none of his men had mentioned the fact that he had claimed Nora as his own. Being forced to explain that to the council would have embarrassed him to no end. He would, he supposed, have explained it away as a means of bringing his men under control.

Wee William wondered what he would have done if his men had mentioned what had happened the day before. Would he have been able to renounce his claim on Nora? Taking in a deep breath, he let it out slowly. Nay, he couldn't have done that, at least not with a straight face.

The men in the room broke into smaller groups, discussing everything from suggested improvements to the keep to the weather, and crops they would be planting in a few weeks. They were also excited about the upcoming festival. In a few weeks, hundreds upon hundreds of people would be descending upon Castle Gregor for a summer festival. There was much to prepare for in advance of the arrival of the six clans that would gather in friendship and with the hope of forging more peace between them.

Leaving the men to their discussions, Wee William quit the room and headed up the stairs, telling himself he was going to check on Elise and not her older sister, Nora.

NORA HAD, AT FIRST, DECLINED SEEING TO HER OWN NEED OF A bath, clean clothes and a good meal. Her primary concerns were Elise's health and making certain John was settled in. However, Mary and Isobel had refused to allow Nora to sit with Elise until she had bathed and donned a clean gown. They were quite insistent.

"Lass, ye've been riding with Highlanders for days now and I fear ye've begun to smell like 'em!" Mary had kindly explained. "Now, worry no' over yer sister or yer brother! John is in good care, getting a bath of his own. He's in the men's solar below stairs and I promise as soon as he's clean, we'll feed the lad."

"And ye'll be no use to yer sister in yer current state," Isobel told her as she offered Nora a warm smile. Nora was taken aback by Isobel's expression and kindness. Earlier, she had been convinced that Isobel did not want them here. Seeing her smile so warmly as she fussed over Elise caused her to rethink her previous impression of the woman.

Deciding it would do no good to argue further, for she knew she *did* smell of earth, smoke, sweat, horses, and heaven only knew what else, she accepted their offer. Confident that her sister was in good hands, Nora gave Elise a kiss on her forehead and promised that she would soon return.

Elise's skin was still quite hot to the touch, her eyes still glassy, but she managed a smile before closing her eyes and drifting off to sleep. Isobel promised not to leave her side until Nora returned.

Mary took Nora to the women's solar on the opposite side of the castle. Behind a dressing screen, a tub filled with hot water awaited. Peeling off her dirty clothes and setting them in a pile near the fireplace, Nora stretched her arms and neck for a moment before testing the water with her toe.

She hadn't realized how much she ached or how cold she was until stepped into the tub. The hot water stung, a momentary assault that brought prickly sensations from her toes to her fingers. As she relaxed fully into the water, the heat wrapped her in a cocoon of blissful warmth. It took only a few moments before she began to relax and feel quite sleepy.

Just as she began to doze off, a woman appeared with the offer to help Nora bathe. Nora's cheeks burned with embarrassment, for no one, not even Horace, had ever seen her completely naked before.

The woman, who introduced herself as Eilean, clucked her tongue and rolled her eyes at Nora's enflamed face. "Lass, we all have the same parts! Ye've nothing I've no' seen before."

Nora knew they might well possess the same "parts" as Eilean had put it, but that didn't mean she found any comfort in exposing *hers* to a complete stranger. Nora kept her arms folded across her chest as Eilean scrubbed her hair with lilac scented soap.

Nora was glad that the bruises Horace had left on her more than a week ago had faded and were now barely noticeable. The scars on her wrists, however, were quite obvious. She did her best to keep them hidden. Hopefully Eilean would not notice, and if she did, she not would inquire as to how she obtained them.

Eilean chatted away about one thing or another while she scrubbed Nora clean. Nora was too flummoxed to pay attention to what the woman was talking about. Besides, she spoke in a combination of

English and Gaelic and Nora could understand less than half of what she was saying.

When Eilean was done with the first round of washing, she called for the tub to be emptied and refilled. Nora had been covered with so much muck and grime that she left a murkiness in the bathwater that made her burn with further embarrassment. With so much dirt and grime, she required two tubs of hot water to get clean.

Once Eilean was satisfied with Nora's cleanliness, she helped her don a luxuriously soft white chemise. It had long, full sleeves, and it felt sumptuous against her skin. Over that, Eilean pulled a full skirt made of a beautiful green, blue and yellow woolen plaid. Next, she tugged an overdress of a fine gray fabric, split up the middle so that one could see the lovely underskirt. The overdress was trimmed with a heavy yellow thread that glistened in the candlelight.

Eilean giggled as she laced up the bodice. "Aye, we've the same parts, lass. But ye seem to have been blessed with more on top than I have!"

Nora gulped, burning red yet again and was left feeling stunned and speechless by Eilean's bluntness. Nora knew she was well endowed, but no one had ever commented on that fact before. Nora's embarrassment brought another round of giggles from Eilean.

"Do no' tell me ye never noticed before, lass! Och! I'm sorry I made ye blush, lass. 'Tis me own envy over what the good Lord has given ye, that makes me talk so!"

Envious? Of me? Nora couldn't fathom anyone envying her anything. There wasn't much about herself that she would think anyone would covet or envy. It wasn't until she caught a glimpse of Eilean's own bosom that Nora understood. While Eilean did in fact have what one could consider a healthy bosom, Nora's was *healthier*. She stood a bit straighter and stifled a smile before chastising herself. Pride was one of the seven deadly sins, wasn't it?

Apparently, Eilean was not yet finished dressing Nora. Once she had the bodice tied, she took a large length of the same blue, yellow and green plaid fabric and folded it in half. "Raise yer arms, lass," Eilean directed. Nora dutifully complied, recollecting the fact that she had never worn so many layers of clothing at once. And neither had she worn a gown that showed so much of her bosom!

Eilean draped the plaid over a dark brown leather belt before tying the ensemble around Nora's waist. "'Tis called an arisaid," Eilean explained as she tucked and pulled on the fabric until she was satisfied. "Now, if ye get cold, lass, ye just grab this part of the arisaid and pull it up and over yer shoulders like this."

She demonstrated by pulling part of the fabric out from under the belt and pulling it up and over Nora's shoulders. Nora was glad for the warmth and for the fact that she could cover those parts of her that seemed to be spilling out over the top of her dress.

"And," Eilean said as she began tucking the fabric back under the belt, much to Nora's displeasure. "If ye get a wee too hot, ye just tuck it back!"

"Now, let's see what we can do with that hair." Eilean stood with her hands on her hips and studied Nora closely. "'Tis lovely hair, ye have lass. We could do many things with it, to be certain."

Nora was done being fussed with. "I do thank you Eilean, but I think a braid will suffice. 'Tisn't like I'm trying to impress anyone nor am I going to see the king," Nora offered her a warm smile. "I need to tend to my sister now. I worry over her."

Eilean nodded her head and chewed on her lip. "Aye. Then a simple braid it is." She retrieved a comb and a bit of leather from the table next to the fireplace and set about combing out Nora's long, dark tresses. Though her hair was still damp, it did make braiding it a bit easier. She combed out the knots and with quick and limber fingers, she fashioned Nora's hair into a braid that cascaded down her back where it fell almost to her knees.

By the time Eilean was done, Nora was more than ready to see her sister. Eilean happily escorted Nora out of the women's solar and back down the long and winding corridors to the room where her sister was being cared for.

They had given Nora and the children a room to themselves, for fear that whatever ailed the little girl might be spread to the rest of the clan. It was a beautiful room, with a large bed that sat opposite a massive stone fireplace. Tall windows with heavy green drapes lined the wall that faced east. Between the windows was a table that held little bottles, combs, and a looking glass.

The walls were adorned with large, beautiful, elegant tapestries. Some depicted men hunting, while others had a precisely feminine and romantic flair. Some showed women in beautiful dresses surrounded by tall, broad shouldered men with swords.

Elise was fast asleep, and as promised, Isobel was with her. Isobel sat on a short stool next to the bed and at the moment, she was pressing cool damp cloths to Elise's forehead.

Nora entered the room quietly, her skirts rustling as she walked to stand beside Isobel. "How is she?" Nora asked as she brushed back a few of Elise's strawberry blonde curls.

"She's been asleep since ye left, but she sleeps peacefully. She has started a nasty cough and I fear her illness has settled in her chest."

Nora was glad for Isobel's bluntness. There was no sense in pretending that Elise was fairing any better than she actually was. But still, she wished the news had been better.

"M'lady, I cannot thank you enough for the kindness you and your people are showing us." Nora knew her words didn't quite capture the gratitude that she felt toward these kind people.

"Think nothing of it, Nora. We help those that need it."

"So I have learned, m'lady. But still, I feel compelled to express just how much this means to me. If it weren't for Wee William, and the other men, I would be dead right now. And were it not for you and your gracious help, I do not know what would become of us." Of that, she had no doubt.

Isobel stood and took Nora's hands in her own. "Lass, let's leave Elise to rest and ye can tell me what happened that led ye to us."

Isobel knew that Nora did not want to leave her sister alone and she could not rightly blame her. "Mary will be here in a few moments, with water and tea. Elise will be fine for a little while."

Nora bent and kissed Elise on her forehead, but the child did not stir. Nora's chest constricted when her lips touched Elise's hot skin. "Is there naught we can do for her?" Nora whispered.

"Mary is bringing a tea that will help the fever. And we've herbs that will help with the cough. We'll apply a poultice to her chest that I hope will help the cough. If we've gotten to her in time, she should be well in a week or two."

Two weeks? Nora cringed inwardly at the thought of Elise being this sick for such a long time. The guilt began to creep back into her heart.

Isobel put an arm around her shoulder and led her out of the room. "I can no' promise she will be well, Nora. But I can promise we'll do all that we can for her."

"Thank you, m'lady." Nora choked back her tears and followed Isobel out of the room. They stood just a few steps from the bedchamber and kept the door slightly ajar so they might hear Elise if she needed them.

"Now, tell me, lass," Isobel said as she patted Nora's hand. "How exactly did ye come to be in Wee William's possession?"

Possession? Nora certainly didn't consider herself Wee William's possession. Friend, perhaps. Grateful ward, maybe. But his possession? Nay. Nora supposed Isobel's choice of words had more to do with translating her thoughts from Gaelic to English and decided not to correct her. To do so would be rude.

"I'm not sure where I should begin," Nora said as she chewed on her bottom lip.

Isobel smiled warmly, her deep green eyes twinkling in the light from the torches. "Mayhap ye should begin with how ye came to be married to such a whoreson as Horace Crawford?"

Though she was not used to such harsh language, especially coming from a woman, Nora was growing accustomed to the Scots way of being blunt, to the point, and quite candid. Horace *was* a mean, spiteful man. Nora supposed Isobel's choice of words were as good as any to describe her late husband. Besides, she could not deny that she too had often thought the same of him.

Nora began with how her own mother had died during childbirth and when she was two, her father married Nina, the woman whom Nora would always think of fondly as her mum.

"Nina died in childbed as well, giving birth to Elise. I suppose I've been more of a mother to her than a sister all these years. To John as well."

She went on to further explain that the death of her father had been sudden and she had been ill prepared for it. "I believe my father did not push me into any marriage because he needed me to help care for Elise and John. He died two years ago. By that time, any man worth having was already had, so my choices were very limited. It was either marry the old baker or Horace. I chose Horace." It was a decision she had regretted every day since.

"He had promised me that Elise and John would stay with us. He promised to build a bigger home so that we could all be together. He made many promises, m'lady, and kept none, save for the ones he made *after* we had wed."

Isobel raised a curious eyebrow at Nora's last statement. "What promises were those?"

Nora took a deep breath to steady her nerves. There had never been anyone in her life with whom she could confide in or seek advice from. To finally have someone to share her fears with was a bit frightening and she was not sure how much she should reveal.

"I became inconsolable after he sent John and Elise away. I cried until I threw up. I had never been away from them and I knew how harsh life could be at Firth. I knew it would be a horrible life for both of them. Horace promised to beat me until I became the dutiful wife he demanded."

Isobel did not doubt the threats Horace had made toward Nora. Over the past year, she had learned much about Horace Crawford from Aishlinn's own accounts of her life as his stepsister. There was no reason to think he would treat a wife differently.

"Why did Horace send them away?" Isobel asked.

Embarrassed and humiliated at the memory of why Horace had sent them away, Nora burned red from head to toe. According to Horace, she had no one to blame but herself. Had she been able to do the things he demanded of her, he wouldn't have sent the children away.

He had been furious with her on their wedding night when she cried out in pain and had begged him to stop. The following morning, still quite angry with her, Horace had tossed the children into the ox cart and took them to Firth.

She stumbled for the appropriate words, a way to explain it to

Isobel, but fell short. "Because I failed in my wifely duties."

Isobel looked confused. "What wifely duties would those be?"

Nora looked at the floor. "The private kind, m'lady. The kind that takes place after dark."

Clarity dawned in Isobel's eyes. "I see," she said. "Now, pray tell how did ye fail in that regard?"

Nora cleared her throat and thrust her hands into the pockets of her dress. She pinched her thighs in hopes of controlling the urge to burst into tears.

The whys and wherefores didn't particularly matter as far as Nora was concerned. "I failed him as a wife." She cleared her throat. The topic was not an easy one for her to discuss.

"It was all my fault you see, that he became so angry with me that he sent John and Elise away." The words came rushing out, like water set free from a broken dam. Along with her words came tears. Tears of humiliation, anger, frustration, and sadness.

"Had I been a better wife, had I been able to do what I was supposed to, then he wouldn't have been so angry and he wouldn't have sent them away! Because I failed, John and Elise have lived the past year in fear. Hungry, cold, alone, abused and there is no one to blame but me!"

Isobel wrapped her arms around Nora and pulled her into a warm embrace. "Wheesht lass!" She tried to sooth away Nora's tears. "I ken that Horace blamed *ye* for a problem that any other woman would ken was not *hers* but *his*. Horace was a cruel man, I ken. His problems were his own, no' yers!"

Nora seriously doubted that. Had she not cried out in agony every time he made his attempts to join with her, well, things would have been quite different. She was defective, in so many ways.

"Lass, listen to me." Isobel gave Nora's shoulders a gentle squeeze. "Some men have a verra difficult time with matters of an intimate nature. But most? Most have no problems at all. If yer with the *right* man, the joinin' can be a most delightful experience!"

Nora blinked twice as she stared at Isobel in utter disbelief. How could any women *enjoy* such an act? She felt repulsed and terrified all at once. She had a very difficult time believing that any joy or pleasure could be found in what Horace had wanted so desperately to do with her. Nay, it simply wasn't possible.

"Now, dunna worry yerself over it any more. Ye have the chance to start yer life anew. Mayhap ye can find a man who has no troubles with joinin'. A man who will let ye keep yer brother and sister with ye. There would be plenty of men here, Nora, who would allow you to do just that, I promise ye." She gave Nora another hug before asking her to continue with how she came to be here, at Castle Gregor.

Explaining how she ended up here was much easier. Nora expressed more than once how kind the men had been, how they had done everything in their power to make the journey here as comfortable as possible under the circumstances.

"I owe each of them a lifetime of gratitude. 'Tis a debt to them that I doubt I shall ever be able to repay."

Isobel nodded in full agreement. "Aye, the MacDougall men be a kind, honorable lot. But dunna let them fool ye! They can be stubborn, strong willed men, set in their ways and full of themselves, and with tempers to match. But once ye learn the way to their hearts, they're easy enough to live with. There's no better man to love than a MacDougall. Once he's admitted his love fer his wife and she to him, well, ye can be assured no greater love can be found."

Nora wanted to know what love had to do with marriage but was afraid to ask. Where she came from, marriages were often arranged and love had very little, if anything, to do with it. Aye, she knew her parents loved one another, but that was a rare thing, as her father had told her many times. She supposed if she were to ever marry again, the best she could hope for was mutual respect and admiration. To hope for anything else was preposterous.

THOUGH HE WAS QUITE ANGRY WITH WEE WILLIAM AND THE REST of his men for bringing the Sassenach woman and sick child back to Gregor, Angus McKenna was quite glad that they had been able to find Aishlinn's treasures.

With the coarse burlap sack filled with priceless trinkets in one hand, he knocked on the door to Aishlinn and Duncan's cottage with the other. Angus was looking forward to giving his daughter the only tangible memories left by her mother.

"Da!" Aishlinn greeted him with a bright smile and a warm hug. He never grew weary of her smile and the way her vivid green eyes sparkled when she was happy. There were times, like now, when he still found it difficult to believe that they had found each other after all these years.

"Good day to ye, daughter," he said as he patted her back. "Do ye have a spare moment to spend with a hard, old Highlander?"

Aishlinn's eyes twinkled brighter as she giggled. "That depends on which Highlander you're speaking of," she teased.

Angus smiled and dangled the sack out to his side. "Well, if ye dunna care to have the gifts I bring fer ye..."

Aishlinn sighed heavily. "Da, you really must stop with all the gifts!"

She had chastised him on numerous occasions for what she considered to be frivolity. No matter how many times he tried to explain to her that he had many years of catching up to do, his words often came out awkwardly. He was better at leading his clan, fighting and defending his family and his home, than he was at words of the heart.

"May I come in, lass?"

Aishlinn's smile faded as she took note of the serious tone of his voice and the look on his face. She stepped aside and followed him into the cottage. It was a bit larger than most cottages, perhaps due to the fact that she was the chief's daughter. She also happened to be married to Duncan McEwan, Angus' future successor.

The stone cottage was the only one Aishlinn knew of that boasted real glass in the windows where others used furs to keep out the weather. Angus insisted on the glass and paid for the luxurious expense himself. The little home had stone floors where other cottage floors were made of well-packed dirt.

Last fall, when Angus learned his daughter was with child, he had insisted that Aishlinn and Duncan should move into the main keep. He argued that it was for their own safety, as well as the health and safety of his future grandchild. Kidnapping children and holding them for ransom was as common as heather in the Highlands.

It was in that heated argument that Angus discovered that his daughter had inherited his temper. She adamantly refused to leave the little home that Duncan had built for her. Neither would budge. So Angus did the only sensible thing he could think of at the time; he ordered the original walls that surrounded the keep be enlarged to include Duncan and Aishlinn's home. Construction of the additional walls would be completed in a few short months.

Aishlinn offered Angus a cup of tea, which he politely declined. He sat in the chair at the head of the table as Aishlinn took the seat next to him.

"Da, you look so serious. Is something wrong?"

Angus smiled and laid the bag on the table. "Nay, nothing be the matter, daughter." He played with the edges of the sack for a moment. "Do ye remember the day Duncan brought ye to this cottage?"

A warm smile came to her lips. "Aye, I do. It was such a surprise! I thought he'd gone back to training and I was so upset that he wasn't taking care of himself."

She thought back to that day when her husband had brought her to their little cottage, blindfolded, teasing her about using the blindfold again during a more intimate time. And he had! Her face burned with embarrassment at remembering *that* particular night.

"And do ye remember when Wee William and I talked with you by the fireplace?"

Aishlinn searched her memory and came up short. She shook her head and told him no.

"Ye were happy with yer new home, but ye were missin' something. Some of yer mum's things, such as her candlesticks and trinket box." He smiled thoughtfully at her for a moment and waited.

"Aye! Now I remember," she said. She wondered why he was asking her about that particular moment when she had mentioned how nice it would be to have some of her mother's things in her new home. "Da, 'twas just a passing feeling that day and of no import."

Absentmindedly her hand went to her growing stomach. Her mother had died more than fifteen years ago, but she still thought of her every day. Now that she was married and getting ready to have her first babe, she wished more fervently than ever that her mother was alive to share in all the joy she was feeling.

"Lass, ye wear yer heart on yer sleeve and it is easy to read what yer thinkin'. I suspect ye be thinkin' of yer mum right now, and missin' her."

A faint smile came to her lips. "Aye, that is true, I cannot deny it."

Angus took in a deep breath and let it out slowly. "I ken that I canna bring yer mum back to ye lass, but I *can* give ye something ye hold dear to yer heart."

Carefully he untied the leather string on the burlap and reached inside. He began pulling out each treasure. With each item he placed upon the table, Aishlinn's eyes widened with a mixture of astonishment and joy.

"Da!" she exclaimed. She picked up one of the candlesticks and held it to her chest. Her eyes filled with tears and she jumped from her seat. She wasn't sure if she should scream with glee or cry from surprise and relief. When he was finished, Aishlinn threw her arms around his neck. "I cannot believe ye did this! How did you get them?"

He patted her arm lightly, his anger with Wee William and the others rapidly fading. It was all worth it to see this moment of sheer joy dancing in his daughter's eyes. Angus' heart swelled with pride. "Ye can thank Wee William, Rowan, Black Richard and a few others fer this lass. They went through a bit of excitement to get them."

Her brow furrowed in concern as she took her seat again. "What excitement? Were any of them injured?"

Angus laughed at his daughter's worry. She tended to put the needs and wellbeing of others ahead of her own. "Well now, none of our own was injured."

Aishlinn studied him closely for a moment, her curiosity piqued. "What do you mean, none of our own?"

Angus pushed the trinket box toward Aishlinn. "'Tis nothin' to worry over. Let's just say that Horace and his brothers finally got what they were deservin' of."

"What does that mean?" She may very well have hated her step-brothers for all they had done to her over the years, and she may at one time have wished them all to go to the devil. But that didn't mean she would want any real harm to come to them.

"I dunna want ye to worry over it, Aishlinn." His voice was firm, his jaw set. Not knowing if Horace and his brothers lived still, Angus did not see the need to share what may or may not have happened.

Aishlinn ran her fingers over the top of the pewter trinket box for a few moments. She was afraid to open it for fear the things she knew *should* be in it may have been lost. She eyed her father closely. They may have only known each other for less than a year, but she had learned early on that once Angus McKenna's mind was made up, there was no changing it.

"Are ye goin' to look inside the box, Aishlinn?" he asked her, his voice low and filled with compassion.

She wasn't sure if she wanted to or not. Aye, the box itself was a beautiful piece of pewter craftsmanship. The lid was intricately carved, depicting a woman holding a babe in swaddling clothes. Laiden's step-father, a man Aishlinn had never met, had died before she was born. He had given the box to her mother when she was five and ten.

The box, along with its contents, was a secret, her mother had explained. 'Twas a secret for just the two of them and Aishlinn had managed, after all these years, to keep her word.

The not knowing was unbearable. Taking a deep breath, Aishlinn closed her eyes and carefully lifted the lid.

Angus watched her closely, his lips pursed together as he waited. The joy alight in her eyes and on her face was indescribable. *Aye,* he thought to himself. *It was worth this.*

She bit at her bottom lip as tears began to blur her vision. She sat motionless for a time, as a combination of relief and bittersweet memories washed over her. Delicately, she touched each item as she fought to maintain some semblance of control.

They were silly things, nothing of any true value to anyone but Aishlinn.

There was a lock of Laiden's hair braided with a lock of Aishlinn's. She took it out and held it to her lips as her stomach tightened ever so slightly. No amount of gold or silver in the world would ever be as valuable as these strands of hair tied together with a tiny piece of string.

Aishlinn knew the tiny locks no longer held the scent of her mother. Instead, they smelled of time passed and faded memories. But for a brief moment, she allowed herself to believe that she could detect just the slightest hint of lilac, her mother's favorite flower.

After a few moments, she carefully placed the locks of hair on the table before pulling out a small bundle of dried flowers. Tiny violets, bluebells, and a sprig of lilac, once vibrant with color and life, had turned brown with the passing of time. Aishlinn had picked those flowers the spring after her mother died and had placed them inside the box. Just a little girl at the time, it made her feel more grown up and less afraid knowing she was now in charge of keeping the secret box safe.

Broc didn't know about the box, Laiden had explained. When Aishlinn had asked her mother *why,* Laiden told her that men sometimes didn't understand matters of the heart and often times considered such things to be frivolous. Aishlinn had since learned that not all men were cold-hearted like her stepfather and stepbrothers.

Duncan had proven to her that men could be kind and gentle. While they might not understand why a woman thinks or feels the way she does over some things, men like Duncan appreciated the finer complexities of the opposite sex. Aishlinn's feelings and happiness were all that mattered to him.

A tiny silver band was the next memento to be brought out. Aishlinn held the ring between her index finger and thumb for a few moments, wondering again why her mother held it in such high regard as to place it inside the box. She did not know the story behind the ring; she only knew that her mother treasured it.

Aishlinn placed the ring next to the locks of hair and flowers. There was one last item, one that she had forgotten about, that lay in the bottom of the box. She had never known the importance of that bit of fabric, until she saw it now. *Now,* she knew why it was here, inside the pewter box of secrets.

It was a tiny swatch of MacDougall plaid.

Aishlinn held it up and looked at her father. Angus McKenna -- a tall, braw, courageous, warrior, the leader of more than four hundred clan members -- sat with tears streaming down his face.

Laiden had kept her promise. She never forgot.

10

Nora stayed by Elise's side the remainder of the evening. John argued his desire to stay with her as well, but Nora refused to allow it. She wanted him to stay as far away from Elise as possible so that he wouldn't come down with same ailment. It was only after Daniel and David promised to give him a tour of the castle and the battlements on the morrow that he agreed. Reluctantly, he let Daniel and David take him to the gathering room for the evening meal.

Wee William appeared soon after with a tray filled with all manner of succulent foods. "Ye must eat, to keep yer strength up, Nora."

He put the tray down on the end of the bed and grabbed a chair to sit next to Nora. "I was no' sure what ye'd like, so I brought a bit of everything."

Nora hadn't realized how hungry she was until the aroma of the food hit her nostrils. Her mouth watered instantly and her stomach growled at the sight of the meats, breads, fruits and vegetables.

Wee William balanced the tray on his knees while Nora grabbed a chicken leg and began devouring it. "Thank you, William!" she said in between bites. "This is delicious!"

Wee William chuckled, simply enjoying the passionate way in

which she was eating. She had a chicken leg in one hand and a hunk of bread in the other and was quickly devouring both. Her lips and fingers were covered in grease and she ate without restraint.

He and his men had eaten in similar fashion earlier, for it had been weeks since any of them had eaten a decent meal. He liked the fact that she wasn't pretending not to be hungry, nor was she hell bent on being ladylike. She was famished and wasn't about to pretend otherwise.

In between bites of lamb and potatoes, she thanked him again. "I will forever be in your debt, William," she told him before shoving another bite of potatoes into her mouth. "What you've done for me, for John and Elise," she stopped long enough to take a drink of ale to wash down her food. "I do not know of anyone else who would have done what you have done."

Wee William smiled, fascinated with the passion she was bestowing upon her dinner. "'Twas nothing, lass." He wondered what other things she might attack with similar passion.

"Nay! It *was* very much *something*, William!" She took another gulp of ale and quickly followed up with attacking the leeks. "I don't think you understand."

He remained quiet, enjoying the passionate way she attacked her food. After she finished the leeks, she began to slow down, taking more time to enjoy the actual taste of the food. When she took her first bite of the sweet cake, she closed her eyes slowly and moaned with delight. "Oh, that is soooo good!" She let each word out slowly, and had the very pleased look of a woman experiencing something decadent, nearly sinful. He swallowed hard and breathed in through his nose.

Wee William's mind filled with an image of her repeating those words again, but after a long, languid kiss. Perhaps tucked under a warm fur in their bed in their cottage while a fire burned low in the corner. He'd start with slow, purposeful kisses on her lips, then mayhap take a journey down that enchanting, curvaceous body of hers, letting his lips and his tongue guide the way, while his fingers trailed happily along. Mayhap he would feed her sweet cakes and berries while he delighted in the carnal pleasures that her body could offer.

"William, did you hear me?" Nora's voice broke through his daydream. He startled and sat up a bit taller.

Thank God the tray is on me lap. "No, I'm sorry, me mind was—" he couldn't very well tell her where his mind was. She'd knock him off his chair. "I was thinking of what I must do on the morrow, lass. I apologize. What were ye sayin'?"

Again, he was only half listening. He was making plans to talk to Angus about getting a little plot of land on which to build a wee cottage. *What the hell is wrong with me?* He had never before entertained thoughts of cottages, wives, bairns or parcels of land. Wee William was a warrior. Most women were afraid of him, simply because of his size. Mayhap his unruly hair and beard and scars had something to do with it as well. But Nora? She seemed different. She didn't twitter on incessantly about topics in which he either had no interest or didn't understand. She didn't walk in the opposite direction when he approached. She talked *with* him, not at or about him.

She was bonny, that he could not deny. But he knew that the moment he first laid eyes on her, even if she did have a blackened eye and bruised face.

As she talked, the candlelight bounced off her gray-blue eyes and made them sparkle like stars in the sky. He also took note of her ample bosom and the way the dress hugged her curves. She was quite striking in the gray and yellow dress and the arisaid that hugged her tiny waist. He was having a difficult time concentrating on what she was actually saying.

"So you see, William, you saved me, you saved all of us. Were it not for you, I'd probably be dead and I doubt it would be from natural causes and old age. I think Horace would have eventually killed me."

At the mention of Horace's name, all the pleasant images of Nora evaporated from his mind. *Horace.* Wee William hoped the man was burning in Hell.

"So I have much to thank you for. Most importantly, for making me a widow that night."

Widow? Yes, she still thought she was a widow. Thankfully, no one had told her there was a possibility that *that* wasn't the case. Wee William tried to reason with himself that it was better she did think

Horace dead. How could he tell her otherwise? How could he, in good conscience, take that feeling of safety and hope away from her? He couldn't. *Let her think he is dead, for we do no' really ken the truth of it.*

"Do you think badly of me, William, that I do not mourn the loss of my husband?" She had stopped eating. She had one hand resting on her lap, fidgeting with her napkin, while she held Elise's tiny hand in the other.

"Nay, lass." He couldn't hold that against her. How could you mourn someone who had treated you so poorly?

"I would feel worse pretending, William. To pretend that I care he is dead would be wrong, would it not?" It was one of the many things she'd been contemplating before he had arrived.

"Aye, I believe it would."

Nora nodded her head and brushed away a strand of loose hair from Elise's forehead. She was still burning with fever. Elise began to shiver and her eyes fluttered before opening. "Nora," her voice was scratchy and hoarse. "I am s-so c-cold." A coughing fit quickly began and Nora helped her to sit up, patting her on her back.

"I'll get her another blanket," Wee William offered. His voice was laced with concern and worry.

Nora thanked him as she grabbed a tankard of water from the table beside Elise's bed. Once her coughing quieted, Nora encouraged her to take a drink of water.

"I don't feel good," Elise whispered as she shivered and fought to catch her breath.

"Ssshh, don't talk, now. You need to rest." Nora rubbed her little back and gave her time to settle her lungs.

"I'm glad we're not outside anymore," Elise said as she wiggled her toes under the covers. "Thank you for taking care of me."

"Don't be a goose, of course I'd take care of you."

Elise started coughing again. It was a long, dry cough that made Elise sound like a small barking dog. Nora found it quite unnerving. She did her best to mask her concern.

"I'm glad Horace is dead." Elise coughed again. "'Cause now I get to be with you again."

Nora could not, in good conscience, chastise Elise for speaking her mind on that topic. "Elise, please, don't talk, it makes you cough. You need to rest."

"But I am glad!"

"I am too," Nora whispered. "But we shouldn't say such things aloud and you need to rest." Nora took a clean cloth, dipped it in the bowl of cool water, and began to wash Elise's face and hands. Elise began to shiver again, her little teeth chattered and her breathing sounded labored. Nora set about applying a fresh poultice just as Mary and Isobel had shown her to do earlier.

She had just finished applying fresh cloths over the noxious paste when Wee William returned with not one, but two additional furs. Without a word, he spread the blankets over Elise and tucked them in under her chin.

"Thank you, Sir William," Elise said sleepily and with a slight smile.

"Yer welcome, Princess Elise."

"You know I'm not a princess," Elise said with a yawn.

"And ye ken I'm no knight, lassie," he told her with a smile and a pat on her head.

"You should be," she said as she closed her eyes.

Wee William's warm smile was aimed at Elise, but Nora felt it just the same. "And ye should be a princess." He smoothed her hair away from her face before slowly standing upright. He turned his attention back to Nora.

She sat there, looking at up at him as if she wanted to say something, but hesitated. Instead, gave him an affectionate, warm smile and looked back to Elise. Sometimes words weren't necessary.

NORA STAYED BY ELISE'S SIDE ALL NIGHT, DOZING BETWEEN THE little girl's coughing fits and spiking fevers. She was relieved and thankful to learn that the room had its own privy and therefore she would not be gone too long from Elise's side.

By the time dawn arrived, Nora's shoulders, back and bottom ached from sitting on the stool for so many hours. Elise would wake for only a few minutes at a time. None of the herbs that Isobel had prescribed seemed to be doing anything to help break the fever.

By noon, her cough had turned from dry and hoarse to wet and phlegmy and things had only grown worse from there. John was brought into the room with a fever of his own later that day. Nora's worst fears were coming true; both children were very ill.

A small bed was set next to the larger bed and Elise was moved to that. Nora planted herself between the two beds and did her best to take care of them.

John's fever and cough seemed to be following the same path as Elise's. It started with the high fever and that was followed later by the dry hoarse cough. He too, slept for hours at a time.

It didn't seem possible, but Elise's cough had worsened and soon she was vomiting due to the coughing fits being so severe. Her fever raged on and she began hallucinating at some time past the midnight hour. She cried out for someone to get the fish off her feet. Had it been merely a dream, one might have found some humor in it. But as it was, a heavy pall had fallen over the room.

And so it went for the next several days. Poultices were applied to their chests and they were encouraged to drink the herbal teas. Fevers raged and broke, but for only an hour or two at a time. John's cough changed into the same rattled state as his sister's.

Nora rarely left their sides, and then only to see to the most necessary of her own needs. Isobel and Mary made frequent appearances to bring more herbs and concoctions that they hoped would help the children. She dozed off and on when she was able, sometimes resting her head on the large bed.

In less than a week, both children were so ill with raging fevers and unrelenting coughs, that they were seldom truly awake or aware of their surroundings. Dark circles had formed under their eyes and their skin had taken on a gray pallor that shook Nora to her bones. They were dying and there was naught she could do to help them.

Nora's only sense of comfort was that no one else had yet fallen ill. It was all she could do to not blame herself a hundred times a day for Elise and John's current state. If anyone else had become ill because they were here, she would not have been able to live with herself.

On the morning of the eighth day, the priest was called to their room. Though she was exhausted and tired beyond anything she had ever experienced, Nora became enraged.

"Who called you?" she demanded as she wiped a cold cloth across John's forehead.

"Lass," the young man began in a soothing tone. "I'm no' here to give last rites. I'm here to offer prayer."

Nora studied him closely for a moment. The man couldn't be more than five and twenty. He was tall, broad in the shoulder, and built much like the other Highlander men she had encountered. His light blonde hair was cut close to his scalp and his brown eyes had a peaceful countenance to them. He wore the coarse brown robes of a priest, but they stretched over his muscles. Had she been in a better mood she might have laughed at how odd he appeared. It looked as though he had stolen the robes and was trying to disguise himself.

"I'm Father Michael," he said as he stood at the foot of John's bed. He hadn't taken his eyes from Nora.

Nora wanted nothing to do with the priest at the moment. Priests who appeared when people were ill were bad luck in her mind. It meant death was near. Priests simply pushed the sick toward the inevitable. She bit her tongue to keep from lashing out that he could take his prayers and leave.

"How fare they today?" he asked kindly.

"The same as yesterday and the day before," Nora bit as she rinsed the cloth in the basin. *You cannot have them, not yet.*

"That is good then," he said quietly.

Nora's brow knotted confusion. "What do you mean *that is good then?*"

Father Michael tucked his hands into the sleeves of his robe and smiled. "No change is better than turnin' fer the worst, wouldn't ye agree?" He offered another smile that went unrewarded.

Nora continued to glare at him. He chose to ignore it. "Och, 'twould be far more pleasin' of course, if they would turn fer the better, that I ken."

They stared at each other for a long while. Father Michael refused to wipe the smile from his face and Nora refused to thank him for his presence. It was Nora who finally broke the silence.

"I'll not have you issue last rites, Father. I will not have it."

He cast her another warm smile. It made the corners of his eyes wrinkle ever so slightly. "And I assure ye that I'll no' issue them. They be young, strong children, am I right?"

Yes, yes, they were. Or they were until they spent the last year cooped up inside a dark, damp, dank castle without proper nourishment or clothing. Nora's eyes began to water when she remembered everything John and Elise had told her of their time at Firth. The pain of it stabbed at her heart and made her stomach tighten. If they died, it would be all her fault.

"I failed them," Nora managed to choke out. "They are ill because I couldn't keep them safe." Her shoulders began to shake and she could not hold the tears back any longer. "If they..." she could not say the word aloud, didn't have the strength for it. She wiped her tears away with the backs of her hands. "There will be no one to blame but me."

Father Michael had spoken with Isobel earlier that morning. It had been Isobel who had come to him first, to ask him to please pray for these children. She had told him all that she knew about the circumstances surrounding their arrival at Gregor.

Father Michael nodded his head and pursed his lips together. "I see. So 'twas ye that sent them to live at Firth?"

Nora's eyes grew wide with horror at his suggestion. "Nay! I would never have sent them away!"

Another nod of his head. "That's right. I believe Isobel told me 'twas yer late husband that did that."

Nora blew her nose on a handkerchief and nodded her head.

"But ye were the one who would no' let them come back to yer home, am I right?"

"Nay!" she'd done everything she could to get them out of Firth. "I tried to get them out, I did! But every time I ran away, Horace would find me and..." Her words trailed off. She didn't want to think about the punishments he had meted out.

Father Michael took a step toward Nora. "Lass, none of this is yer fault. I'm sure ye did yer best to help them."

"But I failed every time!" The tears came flooding back as Isobel and Mary walked into the room.

"Nora," Isobel said as she walked to the end of Elise's bed. "Please, take a walk with Father Michael. Mary and I will sit with John and Elise."

"I can't leave them," Nora argued. The guilt she would feel if something happened while she stepped away would have been unbearable.

"Lass, ye need to step out of doors and take up some fresh air," Mary offered from the corner of John's bed. "'Twill do ye good to talk to Father Michael as well. He's a verra good listener, lass."

"But what if John or Elise wake?" Nora did not want to leave them, not even for a moment.

Isobel rubbed her hand along Nora's back and reassured her. "I promise, if either of them wake, we'll come to get ye. Ye'd be surprised how fast Mary can run if she needs to!"

For the first time in days, Nora allowed herself to not only smile, but laugh as well. She found the image of the old, round woman trying to run quite funny.

Nora looked at the three of them. They pleaded silently for her to listen to their advice. Mayhap a bit of fresh air would give her the boost of energy she needed to continue caring for John and Elise. Reluctantly she agreed to take a walk with Father Michael, but not before giving each child a soft kiss and murmuring words of encouragement. She looked back at the children whom she loved more than anything else in the world. Mayhap a bit more prayer would help. It certainly couldn't hurt.

NORA HAD TO ADMIT THAT SHE FELT BETTER AFTER TAKING THE walk with Father Michael. She had been cooped up in the room for more than a week and was happy to find that spring had arrived, bringing with it an abundance of warm air and sunshine. She was glad to see green grass and blue skies but she noticed little else and paid little attention to her surroundings or the goings on as she and Father Michael walked.

As Mary had promised, Father Michael was indeed a very good listener. He said little and only asked an occasional question as Nora explained how she had come to marry Horace, the night when the small army of Highlanders came into her home, and how she ended up at Gregor.

Nora was riddled with guilt, for a variety of reasons. She felt guilty for wishing Horace dead to begin with, for failing as a wife, and for not being able to do more to stop him from sending the children away. She'd already had similar discussions with Isobel and Wee William and they'd done their best to convince her that her current circumstances were not of her own making and that the blame did not rest on her shoulders. The blame belonged solely with Horace.

Nora went on to explain in more detail what married life with Horace had been like. The beatings, the degradation she felt whenever he tried to invoke his husbandly right to join with her, and the numerous times she had tried to run away. Had he been at all kind or patient, she wouldn't have felt compelled to run away. Had he shown even the slightest hint of owning a heart, she would have tried harder to be a better wife. But the constant ridicule, the harsh hands, the lack of decency he'd shown her was too much. Some people were beyond redemption. Father Michael was convinced Horace Crawford was one of those men.

The priest listened and the more he learned of her life, the more compassion and pity he began to feel for her. He knew his role as a priest was not to judge but to help heal wounded souls and to help people on their walk with the Lord. However, he was still a man, and by the time they had taken a third turn around the castle, he was convinced that Nora had been dealt a poor hand. He could not say that he blamed her for wanting out of her marriage or for not mourning the loss of her husband.

"It is a cruel life that many women are sometimes forced to endure," he told her. "Some men forget that their wives are meant to be their partners, no' their property, to do with however they please. I ken some men who treat their cattle and dogs better than they treat their wives. I do not believe that God intended women to be treated thusly, Nora. 'Tisn't God's will for women to suffer so. But men are men and they sometimes do no' heed the word of God."

Nora stopped and turned to look at him. "Do you think God will forgive me?" she asked him.

Father Michael smiled at her. He didn't believe it should be Nora begging the good Lord's forgiveness, but Horace. As a priest, he hoped the man had seen the errors of his ways and accepted Christ as his savior before he died. As a man, however, he hoped the whoreson was burning in hell. It was a fine line he sometimes had to walk, between being a priest and knowing he was a flawed man. That walk was not always an easy one.

"I do, Nora. I believe God kens what is in yer heart, better than I, and mayhap even better than *ye* do." He patted her shoulder and offered her a warm smile. There were large circles under her eyes, brought on, he was sure, by lack of sleep and too much time alone to think. "God kens ye did yer best, lass. I ken it too."

Nora let out a heavy sigh. "Even though I used to wish him dead?" How, she wondered, could God forgive her for such awful thoughts?

Father Michael laughed again. "Aye lass, even though ye wished him dead. Ye ken," took her hand and placed it on the crook of his arm. "The Bible tells us that a man must love his wife as he would himself and God," Father Michael said. "If what ye tell me about Horace's treatment of ye is true—" he stopped her protests before they could start by giving her hand a gentle squeeze. "I do not doubt that what ye tell me is true, Nora. My point is this: Horace did not treat ye in a manner that would make God proud or happy."

Nora had never looked at it from that perspective. If Father Michael was correct, and she had no reason to believe that he wasn't, then Horace was just as much to blame, if not more, for the abysmal failure of their marriage. Had Horace lived, Nora doubted very much that he would agree with anything Father Michael was saying. She would have been forever trapped in a marriage devoid of any kindness or gentleness.

"So what you're telling me is that Horace was not acting in a manner that would please God and I should not blame myself for how *he* behaved."

Father Michael nodded his head, his lips curving into a warm smile. "Aye, that is what I'm tellin' ye. Ye have no control over how anyone behaves, lass. The only one ye can control is yerself."

"And it is not a sin for me to be relieved at his death?" She wanted to make doubly certain she understood him correctly.

"Nay, I do no' believe that to be a sin. I canna say that I blame ye fer feelin' that way. I believe I might be feelin' the same way were I walkin' in yer footsteps."

Nora's shoulders sagged with relief and she let her breath out in a large whoosh. Another thought came to her and she felt nothing wrong in asking Father Michael about it. "Father, had Horace lived, do you think had I asked our priest for an annulment based on what we've just discussed, he would have granted it to me?"

The question was asked for any future need she may have of it. There was no guarantee that she wouldn't end up marrying another man like Horace, for she believed the world was filled with such men. Men who would pretend to be nice, giving, and caring, but once the vows were taken, you saw their true natures.

However, if Wee William and the others were any proof, not all men behaved thusly. So far, not one had given her any inkling that they were pretending to be something other than what they were. Wee William and Daniel had spent much time with her the past sennight, helping her care for Elise and John. They would bring Nora meals and insist she eat. They would sit in quiet solitude, saying little, if anything for it was simply enough to be there for her if she needed something.

There was no guarantee that she would stay here for the rest of her life. Unfortunately, she had no idea what her future held. It might be useful to have such information for the future.

"Mayhap not all priests would look at it with the same perspective that I have, lass. But were ye to have come to me, aye, I would have granted an annulment to ye. Ye were married for a year, were ye no'."

"Aye, just a week past one year," she answered as she fought back a yawn. The fresh air was not energizing her as she had wished. She suddenly felt even more exhausted.

"And he was never able to get ye with child?" he asked, his eyebrows creased as if contemplating something of great importance.

Nora's cheeks flushed with embarrassment. She did not feel comfortable talking with the priest about why she thought she had never become pregnant. "Nay, he was not." There was no lie in her answer.

Father Michael nodded his head and patted her hand again. "Then aye, I would have given ye the annulment. Who is to say which of ye might be barren, but I would suspect that after a year of marriage, a woman should be with child." Teasing her, he went on to ask, "Ye *did* consummate the marriage, did ye no'?"

She could do nothing to hide her discomfort at that topic. He was a man of the cloth for goodness sake. What could he possibly know of such things?

Father Michael threw his head back and laughed heartily at her red face and mortified expression. His laughter did nothing to ease her mortification; in fact, it only made her more uncomfortable.

"Lass, just because I be a man of the cloth, does no' mean that I've no knowledge of what goes on between a man and woman!" His laughter eased into chuckling. "I was no' *always* a priest."

She did not think it possible for her cheeks to burn brighter, but she knew they did with that bit of unsolicited information.

There was something in her silent countenance that made him wonder why she was so embarrassed by his question. Aye, most women would be embarrassed to discuss such things with any man, let alone a priest. But there was something there, under the reddened skin and sorrowful eyes that made him wonder. "Lass, ye *did* consummate yer marriage, didn't ye?"

She mumbled her answer in such a soft tone that he had to repeat his question. Finally, Nora looked up at him, her skin still burning with shame, and answered it again.

"I'm not sure," she whispered.

That was not the answer he expected to hear.

Father Michael had not lived a sheltered life. He'd only taken his vows within the past year. Prior to that, he'd traveled the world and experienced many things. He'd met many people, heard many stories, and had seen as much of the world as anyone of his age could. Not much surprised him about men or how they sometimes behaved. He thoroughly believed that his life experiences helped him to be a better priest in that he could relate to people on a more human level.

But he was ill prepared for the conversation that took place over the next half hour. By the time Nora was done explaining her situation to him, it was all he could do not to stand appalled with his mouth gaping open.

He stared at her for a time. Her eyes were focused on her toes while her fingers were busy with the hem of her arisaid.

He was at a loss for words for several long moments. He was quite certain that *now* he had heard it all and nothing else would ever surprise him. Feeling he needed to offer her some form of comfort, he took a deep breath and placed his hands on her shoulders.

"Nora, ye needn't feel ashamed of what happened. I believe yer late husband was a very flawed man, with problems that not even the Pope could have helped him with. I would have granted ye the annulment on those grounds alone, even if he had never laid a finger to ye or said an unkind word."

She finally looked up at him. He felt she was too exhausted and embarrassed to discuss the matter further. Mayhap he should ask Isobel to have a talk with her regarding the intimacies between husband and wife.

"I'll take ye back to John and Elise now," he told her as he turned her back toward the entrance to the keep.

As they walked along, Nora remained quiet, hoping that everything Father Michael had told her was true. "Thank you, for taking the time to talk with me father."

"Think nothing of it, Nora. If ye ever have need to speak with me again, ye can come see me at the kirk or send fer me."

They walked back to John and Elise's room in silence. Isobel informed them that there was no change in their condition and neither child had wakened during Nora's absence. Father Michael said a prayer that God would give the children the strength they needed to help fight the illness that was plaguing their bodies before he quietly left the room.

As he walked back to the kirk, he prayed for Nora as well. The children would probably not survive beyond another day or two.

11

As he'd done for more than a sennight, Wee William brought a tray to the children's room for Nora along with messages from Aishlinn. Neither Duncan, nor Angus, nor anyone else for that matter, would allow Aishlinn anywhere near the sick children. Aishlinn was less than happy that everyone treated her as though she were made of glass.

Knowing his wife's fondness for going against his wishes, Duncan had threatened to put a guard outside the children's room, and to assign two men to Aishlinn if she did not promise to stay away. Once the children were better and everyone felt comfortable that Nora would not become ill herself, they would allow the two of them to finally meet.

Aishlinn finally agreed as long as someone would keep her informed and would pass her messages on to Nora. The most important one being how thankful she was for Nora keeping her treasures safe. The other being that Aishlinn was praying diligently for them all. She kept three candles lit in the kirk and prayed daily for the children's health as well as Nora's.

Wee William enjoyed the evenings he spent with Nora for they offered quiet time for him to get to know the young woman better.

And the more he learned about her, the more he began to like her. She was a strong woman, a good woman.

Nora had been taking care of her brother and sister for so long that she felt more like their mother than their older sister. While some women might have resented being thrust into the role of mother at such a young age, Nora did not. They were her family, people who loved her unconditionally. The only regret she had was marrying Horace Crawford.

Wee William battled with his conscience each time Nora thanked him for making her a widow. His mind told him he must tell her the truth of what happened that night. If she ever learned the truth, she might not think so highly of him. She would look at him differently, not with pride and gratitude but anger and distrust.

But his heart argued otherwise. Telling her the truth would take away her sense of security and safety. He also worried that if she thought Horace might still be alive she might leave, run even farther north and he might not be able to stop that from happening. He simply could not risk losing her smile or her friendship. He could not risk losing *her*.

The children's fevers had raged on relentlessly and neither child had stirred for two days. Their condition had grown worse. The only way one could tell they still lived was from the heavy wheezing as they fought for each breath they took.

Wee William's heart ached for this small family. To his way of thinking, it did not seem fair that innocent children died while evil men lived. It simply was not fair.

Nora was sitting on the stool between the two beds. She was resting her head in the crook of one arm on the side of John's bed. Her other arm was outstretched, her palm on Elise's chest.

Silently, he set the tray at the end of John's bed. Nora sat upright, her dark, tired, sorrowful eyes looking at first startled, then relieved. "William." Her voice sounded dry and scratchy.

Wee William's first thought was that she was coming down with the children's ailment. The thought made his stomach tighten with worry.

"Nora, when was the last time ye slept?" he asked as he grabbed the chair from beside the fireplace and sat down to face her.

She didn't even pretend to think on it. "The day before my father died was the last time I had a good night's rest." Since then, her sleep had been plagued with worry and more often than not, nightmares. The latter of which worsened after she married Horace.

Wee William let out a heavy sigh. "Lass, ye must try to sleep!" he whispered. "Ye'll be no good to anyone if ye're worn and exhausted. I can stay with the children...."

Nora stopped him with a shake of her head. "Nay, I'll not leave them, William." She tried to rub the tension from her neck while she grabbed the tankard of ale from the tray. "I appreciate your offer though." She took a drink, set the tankard down and stood.

Nora had thought she'd been tired and sore during their ride to Gregor. But today, it seemed every muscle in her body screamed from lack of sleep and the constant worry. Her head felt muddled and fuzzy whenever she stood. She took a deep breath to steady herself.

Wee William jumped to his feet and grabbed her elbow. He recognized the signs of utter exhaustion when he saw them. He'd seen it many times before, on the battlefield when men had gone days without good sleep or food, fighting until they had nothing left to give. Nora had that look about her.

"Nora, I ken ye love yer brother and sister, but lass, ye must get some sleep."

Between Isobel, Mary, Eilean, and the others, she'd reached her breaking point. She'd had enough of people trying to care for her when all she wanted and needed to do was care for her brother and sister.

"Nay!" She scratched out as she tried to focus her eyes. "I will not leave them! I don't need rest! I need them to get well!"

Wee William would not take anything she said at this point as a personal attack. The days and nights of caring for the children were taking their toll. He stood a step away, his hands at his sides, and let her continue.

"What I need is for everyone to leave me the bloody hell alone so I can take care of them! I won't let them die and you can't make me leave them! If I leave, and anything should happen," she could not say it aloud, could not bring herself to admit openly or even in her own heart, that the chances of John and Elise surviving this illness now seemed impossible. Her eyes burned with terrified, grief-stricken tears. Her head hummed and her stomach churned.

"They're all I have left in this world, William," she whispered. Her tongue felt thick, as if it had suddenly grown far too big for her mouth. She swallowed hard as she tried to wipe her tears away. The attempt at lifting her hands seemed unmanageable.

Nora had not noticed the fact that Isobel had come into the room and now stood just a few steps away. She was holding fresh linens and more herbs. "I believe Wee William is right, Nora. Ye do need to rest."

Nora spun and looked at her, the anger quite evident in her eyes. "What is it with all you Scots sneaking up on people like this?" Silent as church mice they seemed. Nora never knew anyone was there until they spoke or appeared in front of her eyes like an apparition.

"And why must you all be so confoundedly kind and beautiful?" she asked, her speech slurred.

Nora realized then that she was not making much sense. Isobel was perhaps one of the kindest women she'd ever met. And her beauty often made Nora feel out of place. It wasn't envy she felt, but something that resembled a strong sense of inadequacy. Mayhap it was the lack of sleep and endless worry that made her feel that way.

The tears she'd been fighting to hold on to came rushing out. She was simply too tired to care anymore about hiding her pain. She had nothing left to give. There were no prayers left, no more bargains to be made with God, no more silent begging and pleading for John and Elise to recover. No more herbs, no more poultices, no more urging them to drink. She could not whisper in their ears again, begging them to fight and to live, simply because she couldn't bear to be without them. Mayhap it was time to let them go, to end their suffering, to finally allow them peace.

She fell into a heap between the beds, her shoulders shaking as she cried. "I'm so sorry that I let you both down."

Wee William could take no more of her anguish. He scooped her up and held her in his arms and whispered comforting words to her.

"Please, I cannot leave them," Nora sobbed into his chest. "I want to be here for them, William. Please, do not make me leave."

Wee William felt as though his heart would shatter into a thousand pieces. Nora's pain and anguish tugged and pulled at his soul. He could no more remove her from this room than he could move a mountain.

"Wheesht lass," he whispered as he softly kissed the top of her head. "We'll stay right here, I promise." He sat down in the chair, adjusting her so that she was more comfortable, wrapping his arms more tightly around her. "We'll sit here, in this chair and we will no' leave until ye ask or until they get better." He kissed the top of her head again.

Isobel placed the clean linens and herbs at the foot of Elise's bed before leaving the room.

"I'm so sorry, William," Nora mumbled into his chest. "I...."

Wee William shushed her again as he rubbed the small of her back with his hand. "Wheesht, lass. Ye needn't speak now. But please, just sleep for at least a little while. I'll hold ye while ye rest."

"I am so very tired, William. And I'm so very afraid that I'll lose them." She could not deny that it felt good to rest her head against his chest, just as she had done on their journey here. She felt safe again.

"I ken that, lass," he whispered. He was afraid too. Afraid that the children would not live much longer and that when death finally came for them, it would destroy Nora's very soul.

Isobel had returned a short time later with a blanket and carefully draped it around Nora's shoulders. Nora cried until she had no more tears left. Wee William held her closely, allowing her to cry, offering soft, and calming words that all would be better.

As she finally succumbed to sleep, Nora could have sworn she heard Elise asking for water. But she was too tired to move. She had lost her mind. Elise's voice was simply the last part of it leaving her.

Isobel let out a gasp of surprise when she heard Elise ask for water. She rushed to the child's side and reflexively put a hand to Elise's forehead. The child was soaked with sweat and her forehead cool to the touch. Isobel poured a cup of water and held it to the little girl's lips.

"It's very hot in here, Lady Isobel." Elise began tossing blankets off and kicking her feet out from under the blankets and furs.

"Praise God," Isobel murmured as she helped Elise drink her fill. "How do ye feel, lass?"

"My head hurts a bit, and I'm very tired," she coughed slightly, covering her mouth with her small fist. Her ringlets of strawberry blonde hair were plastered to her head. "And I'm very hot!"

Isobel took cool cloths and began wiping the child's face, neck and hands. She wasn't ready yet to call the child cured. People often times appeared quite well for a day or two before succumbing to death.

"Let's get ye into a clean nightdress," Isobel said as she pulled the damp nightdress over Elise's head.

"That's better! Thank you Lady Isobel," Elise smiled up at her and pushed herself to sit. She caught a glimpse of something behind Isobel and moved to see.

"Wee William!" Elise exclaimed. "Why are you holding Nora?"

For the first time in a very long time, Wee William found himself completely without words. He held onto Nora, afraid that if he let go, they'd both tumble to the floor.

"And why are you crying?" Elise asked as she scrunched her brows together and pursed her lips.

He hadn't realized he had been crying until she pointed it out. He cleared his throat, sat up a bit taller in the chair and wiped his eyes on his shoulders. "'Tis yer beauty, Princess Elise. Brings tears to a Highlander's eyes." He wasn't exactly lying. It was, perhaps, a beautiful sight to behold. A little girl, who only minutes ago, he was convinced was not long for this world, was now sitting up in her death bed, asking for water and inquiring about his tears.

Elise smiled brightly and even managed a weak giggle. "Sir William! You are silly!"

He could not contain his laughter. He threw his head back and laughed, relieved, and with a happiness that bordered on giddiness. Nora stirred every so slightly, moving her head as if she were trying to bury it into a pillow. Wee William quieted, and winked at Elise. "We best be quiet now, lassie. We dunna want to wake yer sister."

Elise nodded her head. "Why is she so tired?" she whispered.

"She's no' left yer side or yer brother's fer many days, Elise," Isobel told her as she offered her another drink.

"I've been ill, haven't I? And John too?" She searched for John and was relieved to see him asleep in the next bed. "How is John?"

Isobel shushed her and gently guided her to lay back. "Ye needn't worry, lass. John will be well soon, just like ye. He's sleepin' like a good lad."

"I feel like I've been asleep for a very long time." Elise said as she yawned. "And my head hurts. I think I slept too much."

Isobel ran another cool cloth across Elise's face. She glanced over her shoulder at Wee William, who looked as though he'd just been given the greatest of gifts. She had no desire to tell him it was by no means time to celebrate or claim a full recovery. If the child were still awake and improving in a few more days, *then* they would celebrate.

"Wee William," Isobel said to him over her shoulder. "Take Nora into Duncan's old room. Then fetch Mary for me."

He couldn't will his feet to move just yet. He had promised Nora they would remain in this room until she woke or the children's condition changed. Seeing that Elise was awake and Nora was sleeping through all the commotion, he doubted she'd be too upset with him.

He stood and adjusted Nora in his arms. She neither stirred nor protested. He smiled across the room at Elise. "I'll be back soon, lass. Ye do as Isobel bids."

Elise returned his smile with a weaker version of his and nodded her head. "Is Nora ill too?"

Wee William hadn't given that a second thought until now. He prayed that her heavy sleep was from exhaustion and not the illness that had nearly taken Elise.

"Nay, she's just a bit tired from takin' care of ye and yer brother. Now, rest and I'll return soon." With that, he quit the room.

WEE WILLIAM WAS GROWING MORE WORRIED AS THE HOURS PASSED by at an agonizingly slow rate. He had stayed by Nora's side all through the night, touching her forehead every half hour or so to make certain she had no fever. She rarely stirred. Occasionally she would mumble something incoherent, her brow creasing as if she were worried or confused.

Mary and Isobel had tried to assure him that she would be well and that it was simply a matter of being overcome with fatigue and worry. They were convinced that she would have shown other signs of the illness by now. Nora was simply worn out.

The following morn, he decided to take his frustrations out on the training fields. With a solemn promise from both Mary and Isobel, that they would send word the moment Nora woke, he quit her room and headed out of doors. He had a fortnight's worth of frustration built up and he needed a way to release it. For Wee William, there didn't seem a better way to release his frustration and anger than on the fields.

"Ye don' seem yerself today, Wee William," Duncan badgered as he brought his broadsword down hard against Wee William's. Wee William barely had time to respond with an upward thrust of his own broadsword. Had he been paying closer attention, he could have knocked Duncan on his arse more than a half hour ago.

"Could it be yer mind is somewhere else?"

Wee William stood, out of breath, covered in sweat, and quite angry. Duncan was right, his mind was elsewhere, but he refused to admit it. "Nay, I'm just lettin' ye *think* ye've bested me this morn, lad," he panted as he swung his broadsword sideways. Duncan promptly blocked it, spun around and thrust outward. Had it been a real battle, Duncan would have run his sword clean through the arm of his opponent.

"Wee William, I think ye've had enough," Duncan told him as he studied his friend. In all the years they had been training together, Duncan had never bested Wee William. The man was larger and stronger than Duncan, and he possessed an unnerving speed. If Duncan ever were to best the man, he wanted to do it because he was better, not because Wee William's mind was elsewhere.

Wee William growled before calling a halt to the match. Nothing felt right this morning. His mail seemed too small, his sword too heavy, and his mind too muddled. *This is why ye should stay away from the women,* he told himself. *They be far too distractin' and ye'll end up dead.*

The perceptive smile never left Duncan's face. He'd never seen his friend so distracted before and he had a very good suspicion as to its cause. A lovely young lass with long brown hair and pale blue eyes, had stolen Wee William's heart. Duncan recognized the symptoms of a man overwhelmed with feelings he could not understand, for Duncan had suffered the same fate a year ago. Now he was just a few weeks away from becoming a father for the first time.

Duncan slid his broadsword into its sheath and watched Wee William wipe the sweat from his face. He could not hold his laughter in.

Wee William gave him an angry glare. "What be so bloody funny?"

After a few moments, Duncan's laughter quieted enough that he could answer. "Why don' ye just surrender to her, William? I can assure ye, 'tis a battle ye will no' ever win! And the surrender is verra enjoyable."

"What the bloody hell are ye goin' on about? Did my blow to yer head knock somethin' loose?" He pretended not to know what Duncan was referring to. He started across the field toward the table set with tankards of ale and buckets of water. Duncan followed, laughing his way across the field.

"Och! 'Tisn't *what* I refer to, William, but *who,*" he said as he slapped his hand on Wee William's back as they walked side by side.

"I canna say that I blame ye. She is a fetching lass. Isobel says she has a heart of gold too. And a verra strong and loyal disposition."

Wee William shrugged his friend's hand away and continued to ignore him. He was angry with himself for allowing feelings for a woman to interfere with his training or to be noticeable enough that Duncan could take note of them. Nora had somehow managed to seep into his every waking thought, and even his dreams. Such images, feelings, and thoughts would surely sentence him to death if he were ever called to battle before he figured them out.

Aye, he wanted Nora, wanted her more than he could make any sense. His true worry was ending up embarrassed and with his heart broken. He was no more willing to risk being made a fool than he was of Nora learning her dead husband might not be so dead.

He was in no mood to discuss Nora with anyone, let alone Duncan. They reached the table and each man lifted a tankard and filled them with ale from the cask. Wee William tossed back two to Duncan's one.

At least he could still drink the man under the table. *Mayhap*, he thought, *that's what I should do. Get so drunk that I canna think of anything, including Nora.*

As Wee William filled his tankard a third time, one of the boys from the castle came running up to the table. "Wee William!" he called out as he approached.

Wee William's heart seized momentarily, with an overwhelming sense of dread. In an instant, he had convinced himself that Nora had taken a turn for the worse and now fought for her life. "What is it, lad?" he growled, steeling himself for the worst possible news he could imagine.

"Mary sent me," the skinny boy said as he reached the table. "She says to tell ye John is awake and he's askin' fer food!" The boy smiled up at Wee William, pleased he was to be delivering good news.

The scowl never left Wee William's face. Aye, he was glad that John was faring well, but it was the worry over Nora's health that consumed him.

"And what of Nora?" Duncan asked. He had no doubt in his mind now, that his friend's primary and only concern at the moment was Nora. If he hadn't cared about her, Wee William would have had something to say about John's turn for the better.

"She still sleeps," the boy said.

"Thank you, lad," Duncan said before the boy went running back to the keep. Wee William stared off into the distance, distracted with what Duncan could only assume were thoughts of Nora.

"The lass will be fine, William," Duncan offered as he nudged him with his shoulder.

"What?" Wee William hadn't heard him, for his thoughts had indeed been focused on Nora. How long would the woman sleep? It couldn't be good to sleep so long.

By now, a small crowd of men had formed at the table, each grabbing tankards of ale. They stood and watched the exchange between Wee William and Duncan.

"Nora. She'll be fine. I spoke with Isobel earlier. The lass be simply exhausted. She's been through much these past weeks."

Wee William scowled. He took another pull of ale and continued to ignore the topic Duncan seemed unable to let go of.

"So will ye be needin' help to build ye a wee cottage?" One of the men in the crowd asked before ducking behind another man so that Wee William would not know which of them asked the question. The other men chuckled at Wee William's furious glare.

"Och! Mayhap ye could build one next to mine and Aishlinn's!" Duncan laughed.

"Duncan, I warn ye to shut yer mouth now, lad," Wee William ground out.

"William, it be nothin' to be ashamed of! I ken what yer goin' through. Yer fightin' yer feelings fer the woman, and I tell ye it will do ye no good! When I finally admitted how I felt about Aishlinn, why, me life has done nothin' but improve!" Duncan smiled and patted his friend on the back again.

Wee William slammed the empty tankard down and finally noticed that all eyes were on him. He stared back at all of them. His anger boiled. Finally, he could take no more. "Why are ye all starin' at me?" he growled through gritted teeth.

Duncan tried to look serious for a moment, but it was no use. There was too much pleasure to be had from his friend's discomfort. "Well, we're tryin' to imagine what ye'll look like without yer beard."

Everyone laughed, but Wee William. He'd had enough of the needling, the laughter at his expense. In that small moment of time he had made a decision. He wouldn't be shaving his beard for Nora or any other woman for that matter. Aye, he was besotted with her, cared for her, and his body longed for her. But he would not succumb to the feelings no matter how strong they were. He'd done that once before, many years ago, and it had ended miserably.

His anger had reached its breaking point. A low growl began in his belly building until it escaped in a long, guttural, groan. He lifted the table with both hands and tossed it over with little effort. The casks of ale went rolling about, tankards broke, and men went scattering like leaves into the wind. Duncan's eyes grew as wide as trenchers as he watched the rage unfurl. He took two cautious steps backward as Wee William spun, looking for him.

"Now, Wee William," Duncan said, holding his hand up, unable to quash his smile. Aye, Wee William was very much in love, but he was having a harder time dealing with it than most men.

"I've had enough of yer mouth, ye little shite! I will no' be shavin' me beard fer *any* woman! I am merely concerned fer her health!" He took a step forward and Duncan took one back. "I'll no' be buildin' a wee cottage," Wee William said as he took another step. "I'll no be courtin' any woman. I'll no be shavin' me beard and I'll no' be gettin' married!"

"Why the hell no'?" Duncan could not help but ask the question.

"It be none of yer bloody business! All ye need to ken is that I be no' the marryin' sort! Now leave me the bloody hell alone!"

Wee William turned away from Duncan and stomped off toward the loch. Duncan was more than confused as to why Wee William had grown so angry over the friendly needling they'd been doling out. He'd known Wee William for years and had never known him to be unable to take a little needling from time to time. There could be many reasons why Wee William was so angry, but Duncan couldn't think of any that made sense. The woman had gotten to him, that much was certain. But why was Wee William fighting the inevitable? It made no sense.

❧ 12 ❧

Wee William had done his best to stay away from Nora's bedside.

After his argument with Duncan, he had stripped off his battle gear and jumped in the loch for a nice long bath. After that, he had taken a horse out for a very long ride across MacDougall lands and did not return until after the evening meal.

He had tried to concentrate on inane things, such as battles and politics. He recited the alphabet in Gaelic, English, Latin and French. He attempted to add large sums of numbers in his head. He tried to remember faerie tales from his childhood and poetry he'd learned when he was older.

When that didn't work, he thought of his brief stay in France during his fifteenth year. He thought of fishing, hunting bear, and tavern fights. He tried to think of his parents, his six sisters, and his nieces and nephews.

None of it worked. No matter where he tried to focus his mind, it inevitably turned toward two women. The one who had broken his heart years ago and the one who had unknowingly stolen it days ago.

He had been just nine and ten when he'd fallen in love with a beautiful young lass named Ellen. She was a comely thing, only a year younger than he, with long blonde hair and big green eyes. Ellen had laughed at his jokes, seemed to listen intently as he spoke of the dreams he had, and occasionally she let him steal a kiss or two.

His friends had tried to warn him that Ellen was not what she seemed. But Wee William would not listen. He was completely besotted with her.

When the day arrived where he finally marshaled the courage to ask her to marry him, he shook like a leaf in the wind. He had taken her for a lovely picnic on a sunny spring day. She looked beautiful in her green dress, her hair billowing in the breeze. With trembling hands, he began to pour his heart out to her. He loved her and wanted to spend the rest of his life with her.

She laughed in his face. Not at all what he had expected. "Me? Marry ye?" she asked between fits of laughter. "Are ye daft, William?" He could still hear her haughty laughter and to this very day, it still felt like a knife in his heart. "Nay, William, I will no' marry ye. Ye've no money, no trade, no home of yer own!"

Ellen had made no attempt to soften the blows, offered no kind words to make him feel better. Nay, she had pulled his heart out and ground it into the hard earth. "I'll no' end up like me mum, married, bored, havin' one bairn after another and never enough of anything to go around."

He was dumbfounded and felt as though he'd just taken the worst beating of his life, but still, Ellen was not done breaking what little hope he had of recovering. "I doubt ye'll ever find a woman dumb enough to marry ye, William! Look at ye! Yer as big as a barn and as dumb as an ox and no woman would want to have yer bairns fer fear they'd be born the size of a calf!"

She left him there, alone, on the side of the hill. Broken hearted and for the first time in his life, feeling unworthy. He was by no means dumb. Not only could he speak three languages, he could read and write in them as well. Aye, he *was* big, a bit on the skinny side back then. He had put on muscle and weight in the intervening years.

He had not shaved his beard since that day. He had promised himself he'd not shave it ever again.

It had taken time to get over the hurt. Though he no longer felt unworthy, he still carried a few deep seated doubts. He knew that most people took one look at his large stature and girth and immediately assumed he was dumb. They'd hear his thick Scottish brogue and think him uneducated. Women didn't swoon at the sight of him, like they often did with Rowan, Black Richard, and Duncan before he was married. Nay, most women took one look at him and turned in the opposite direction.

Mayhap what Ellen said was true; no woman would have him because they feared their own deaths just by bringing his bairn into the world. It was plausible.

Not long after Ellen broke his heart, he shared his worries with his mother. She had told him such worries were utterly ridiculous. He had been a tiny baby, smaller even than his six sisters. In fact, he'd been such a small baby that they worried over him constantly his first year. He was named after his father, and that was one more reason for the *Wee* before his name.

It wasn't until he was two that he began to grow and to grow rapidly. At age three, he was the size of most six-year-old boys. At age ten, he was taller than his mother. By the time he was two and ten, he was taller than his father and most men that he knew. And he hadn't stopped growing until a few years ago. While he didn't appear chiseled out of stone like most of his friends, he was all muscle and far stronger than anyone he knew.

But there was no guarantee that his children wouldn't be large. He could see a woman worrying over such a thing and he couldn't say it was a worry he could hold against anyone.

And what life, if any, could he offer a woman? He was a warrior. That was all he'd ever done. He had no trade and no land. He was often gone for months at a time, fighting in clan wars, or wars against the English or other invaders. How could he ask a woman to wait for his eventual return when there was no guarantee that he would come back alive and in one piece? This was the only life he knew. And it wasn't enough to offer to anyone.

Aye, he had money saved up, enough that he could afford to build a home and furnish it adequately. Enough even that they could live comfortably for a few years without worry, but afterward? The only thing he was good at was figuring sums in his head and fighting. He wouldn't be able to fight into his auld age.

Nay, it was no life to offer anyone.

No matter how badly he wanted Nora.

Nora. His thoughts always turned back to her. She was beautiful, that he could not deny. But there was so much more to her than outer beauty. She had a giving heart, she was loyal to her family, and wanted nothing more than to give them a better life. What other woman would have tried so many times to escape a bastard like Horace Crawford to rescue younger siblings, knowing full well the consequences if she were caught?

What other woman would put her faith in complete strangers and risk her life to get her family out of England? What other woman was willing to ride for days, braving harsh weather, lack of food and warm clothing, on the word of strangers that life in Scotland was better than life in England?

In the beginning, he had wondered that he cared for her only because she had *needed* someone to care about her. Then, the more time they spent together, especially over these past days, he realized she was someone he could love. And love quite easily.

Nora had a keen sense of humor and she was not afraid to speak her mind. She wanted nothing more in life than to settle into a home and take care of John and Elise. Aye, she did hope to marry again someday and have children of her own.

She had even shared with him what she believed would be the perfect husband when he had asked. "There be no such animal, William. But I'd settle for close. He must be a kind man who will not beat me or the children, a man who will allow me to keep John and Elise." Wee William supposed there was more to her list of requirements in a husband, but they had been interrupted by one of John's horrible coughing spasms. They'd never returned to the subject.

Aye, he could see himself waking up to her sweet face each morn and wrapping her in his arms each night. He could see himself growing auld with her, raising a whole passel of bairns together, somewhere in a wee cottage -- with tall ceilings of course -- mayhap in a glen by a stream.

But it was just a fantasy. One that he knew could never come true. Without a way to support a family, other than by fighting and being gone for months on end, the happy life he envisioned would not last long.

He supposed it was possible to stay with the clan, live amongst them, working side by side with friends. But he had wanted more than that. At least, long ago he had. He'd had dreams of a large home, raising cattle and sheep and horses. Mayhap he could still do that, with Nora by his side. There was a chance he could take the money he saved and buy a parcel of land nearby, build a home, and live out the remainder of his days building up the land, growing crops, making a life of their own.

And so it went, his thoughts going back and forth between what he wanted and what seemed impossible. By the time he found himself heading back to the keep, he had convinced himself that his dreams of a family, of a quiet life, were not in his future. Nora deserved better than he could offer her.

Before he realized it, he had made his way up to Nora's room. She was still sleeping, looking every bit the angel he thought her to be. She lay on her side with the covers pulled up over her shoulder and one hand resting under her cheek.

She looked so much at peace. The dark circles were not quite so pronounced, yet her skin was still pale, due mostly to the fact that she hadn't ventured out of the castle in days. Her dark brown hair spilled over the pillow in soft waves, her thick, dark eyelashes brushed against the tops of her cheeks. Wee William swallowed hard, fought the urge to climb into the bed with her. He let out a slow, quiet breath.

Why could he not stay away from her? Why was he so drawn to this woman? Was she a witch who had cast a spell upon him? An enchantress? Nay. She was simply the most perfect woman he'd ever known.

He wondered what her response would be if he were to ask her to marry him. Would she laugh in his face as Ellen had done? He doubted it. Chances were, he was not her idea of the close to perfect husband she had spoken of. Nay, she'd turn him down, but she'd do it gracefully and with a bit more tact.

There it was, he finally realized: his true fear. He'd ask and she'd say no and he'd spend the rest of his life in utter loneliness and agony. He couldn't bear it. He'd not be able to look her in the eye afterward. He'd rather have her as a friend than not be in her life at all.

It was better not knowing.

It was better to love her from afar than to see pity in her eyes.

13

Nora woke the following morning to the soft sound of someone else's breathing. Her eyes fluttered open and it took a moment for them to adjust to the morning light that filtered in through the tall windows. What she saw next brought a smile to her face.

Wee William.

He was sitting slumped over in a chair next to her bed, with his head on the pillow next to her. He was holding her hand. Admittedly, her first thought was to reach out and touch his cheek to bid him good morning. Mayhap trace her fingers along the scar that ran along the right side of his forehead. Resistance was not easy, but she somehow managed.

After the fog lifted, her thoughts turned to John and Elise. She remembered Wee William promising not to let her go, not to quit the room unless she asked him to. For the life of her, she could not remember making such a request.

She bolted upright. The movement caused her head to swim and jolted Wee William from his sleep. He stared at her for a moment, as if she were not really there.

"John and Elise!" Nora whispered, willing her head to quit spinning.

"Lass, they be fine!" Wee William said as he touched her shoulder.

"You promised!" She said, realizing her throat was dry and she was quite thirsty. It mattered not. She swung her legs over the edge of the bed and tried to stand.

"Nora!" Wee William said, raising his voice only to gain her attention. "I tell ye, they be fine!"

She spun around to look at him and immediately wished she hadn't. Her head felt fuzzy, as though she would teeter over if she moved again. "They need me," she said, wishing for all the world that her throat wasn't so dry.

Wee William stood and grabbed her shoulders. "Lass, I promised I'd no' quit the room unless ye asked me or if they got better."

Nora looked him in the eye, the relieved smile on his face quite evident. It dawned on her that he wouldn't be smiling and wouldn't have broken his promise unless... "Tell me the truth, William! Are they better?"

His beaming smile told her more than words could have. Her heart began to pound, relief washing over her. She flung her arms up and tried to wrap them around his neck, but he was so blasted tall that it was impossible. Wee William chuckled and bent low so that she could embrace him.

"Ye were exhausted, lass. Isobel threatened to skin me alive if I didn't put ye to bed once we saw that Elise was well. John woke yesterday at around noontime. They are both verra well. Elise has got Daniel telling her one story after another and we canna fill John's belly!"

She didn't know if she should laugh or cry so she did both. How long had it been since she'd felt such utter joy? Other than the night they took the children from Firth, it had been many, many years.

Wee William gave her a few moments to pull herself together and finally broke their embrace. "Ye get dressed now lass. I'll let Isobel ken ye be awake. Then I'll take ye to see yer family."

He left the room before she had a chance to thank him.

It was another four days before Isobel declared the

children completely recovered. She'd not allow them out of their rooms for more than an hour at a time, and only to sit quietly in the gardens to take in fresh air. Neither Isobel nor Nora would allow the children do anything that might cause a relapse.

After Isobel's declaration, Aishlinn began pleading a little more loudly for a meeting with Nora. Seeing no harm in finally allowing the two to meet, Aishlinn waited patiently in Isobel's rooms for Nora. When Nora finally arrived, escorted by Isobel, it was not as awkward a meeting as Nora thought it would be. Aishlinn was even more beautiful than Nora remembered. Being heavy with child did not take away from her beauty; it added to it.

Aishlinn stood, breathtakingly beautiful in a gown of dark blue silk, her blonde hair in a fine plait that crowned her head. The morning light streamed in through the tall windows, casting an ethereal glow all around her. She would not stand on pretense and threw all social graces aside and rushed to Nora, embracing her in a very tight hug.

"Thank you!" she exclaimed. "Thank you for keeping my treasures safe!"

Bound together they were, by a past of torment and hell doled out at the hands of Horace Crawford. Nora and Aishlinn became friends in the span of a few heartbeats.

They sat for hours, laughing themselves silly in between sharing horror stories of their time in England. Aishlinn felt that Nora had a much harder time with Horace, for she had been married to him. Nora was convinced it was Aishlinn who had suffered most, for she had spent the first nine and ten years of her life with the fool, whereas Nora's hell had lasted but a year.

"But *you* had to share a bed with him!" Aishlinn blurted out, and immediately felt guilty for it. Nora's cheeks burned with embarrassment and it was all Aishlinn could do to keep from bursting into tears.

"I'm so sorry, Nora! I didn't mean to be so cruel!" Aishlinn begged forgiveness as her eyes filled with tears. "These past weeks, I cannot seem to control my tongue or my tears! I know I don't deserve it, but please, forgive me for being so heartless!"

Nora shook her head and smiled. "You are right, Aishlinn. I *did* have to suffer through *that* with him. So it appears I have won. Count your blessings that you weren't forced to endure *that* part of him." She then burst out laughing, and nearly fell out of her chair.

It surprised Aishlinn that she felt no grief when learning Horace was dead. She did, however, feel a twinge of guilt in learning that Nigel, the youngest of the brothers, had suffered the same fate. Of the three, Nigel was the only one to show he had limits to what he'd go along with or what cruelty he'd allow inflicted upon Aishlinn.

Aishlinn told Nora the story of how she ended up here, at Castle Gregor, how Horace had traded her for two sheep. Aishlinn purposefully left out his other reason for sending her away: he was going to marry a young woman from the village and said the cottage was not big enough for two women. She could only assume that Nora was that woman.

Nora sat still, quietly listening to how the former Earl of Penrith had tried to rape Aishlinn, the beating she took resisting him, and how Baltair had helped her to escape. Aishlinn had often wondered about Baltair and why exactly he had helped her and what had become of him. Nora could not answer the questions regarding the guard, but thought perhaps John or Elise might know.

Aishlinn went on to recount how she had come across Duncan and his men and how they had sworn their fealty to her once they learned she had killed the earl. She told of their journey here, of the kind family who had opened their home to them, and how Rebecca had taken care of the wounds to her back.

"I was so afraid to speak my mind back then," Aishlinn explained. "Every part of my body *hurt,* but I would not say so. I was just so relieved to be away from Firth and from England that I would have endured anything."

"I feel much the same way," Nora admitted. "But I must admit that I do miss my home, and the people I grew up around."

"Aye, I would imagine so. You had a much better upbringing than I, so there is nothing there for me to miss." Aishlinn smiled thoughtfully. "It did not take long for me to make friends here. From the very beginning, everyone has been more kind and generous than I could ever have hoped for. They'll do the same for you, Nora."

Nora agreed. She had not met one person yet who had shown her anything but kindness and generosity. They dispelled all the horror stories she had learned growing up. Nora had not witnessed any of the savagery, the barbaric or archaic ways her father had warned her of.

Aishlinn continued to speak of how much her life had changed, and all for the better. She also went on to tell how she began to fall in love with Duncan.

"As I look back now, I see that he was being honorable, if a bit daft, and he was doing his best to fight how he truly felt in his heart. But, he could only fight it for so long and soon he was courting me!" She smiled in fond remembrance. "And the first time he kissed me? Oh! I could not breathe!" She began fanning herself with her hands as if the room had suddenly grown quite warm.

"Do not ever tell him this, but I still feel the same way," Aishlinn leaned in closer to share more of her secrets. "He makes the roof of my mouth tickle sometimes with his kisses!" Aishlinn giggled, winked and sat back in her chair. "But I will not tell him that. His head is as big as a mountain now. If I were to tell him that he makes my heart pound as though it will leap from my chest? Oh, there would be no living with him then!"

Nora had never felt that way before. She had never been courted, save for Horace, and his kisses had never made her feel the way Aishlinn described. An image of Wee William popped into her head. It made her toes tingle to think of what it might be like if *he* were to kiss her and she still wondered if his beard would scratch her skin. It made her cheeks grow warm to think about it.

Aishlinn paid no attention to Nora's red cheeks and continued on with her story. "The day we learned the Earl was not dead and he had come to Scotland to find me, that was the day Duncan proposed. It was an odd proposal to be sure. He said he wanted to have my bairns!" Aishlinn giggled, shook her head and ran her hand over her belly. She went on with how they had married quickly with no time for flowers or planning a wedding feast. She went on, much to Nora's embarrassment, to describe the joy she felt on her wedding night.

She'd never experienced *that* either! She supposed that the kind of love and adoration that Aishlinn and Duncan felt for one another was a rare thing indeed. A twinge of regret and sadness filled her heart for she was quite certain she'd never be blessed with a husband who would adore her, treasure her, and fight to his death to keep her. Nay, Aishlinn and Duncan's love was the things faerie tales were made of.

Aishlinn went on to tell more of how her life had changed in the past year. She was still learning to read and write and figure sums. Nora admitted to feeling the same kind of wicked excitement as Aishlinn had felt when she first learned that everyone within the Clan MacDougall knew how to read. Nora was overjoyed to learn that soon she and her brother and sister would learn as well. But Aishlinn warned that the Latin was the most difficult. Nora did not care how hard it was. To her way of thinking, having such a skill could only help in securing a better future for her and the children.

And so it went for the remainder of the afternoon. They laughed until they cried, they cried until they laughed. Eilean brought them a tray of tea, bread, cheese and dried fruits. They talked well into the afternoon, enjoying one another's company, oblivious to the rest of the world.

The sun had begun to set when Duncan came to check on his wife.

Were all Highlanders so handsome? Nora had yet to meet a man under the age of seventy that was not handsome, muscular, and large! Duncan was quite remarkable and Nora could very well guess why Aishlinn had fallen in love with him. If he wasn't already married to her new friend, Nora felt she could have gotten lost for a time in those dark blue eyes of his. Or mayhap it was his blonde hair, with the braids at each side of his handsome face. It left Nora feeling ashamed for thinking such thoughts.

"Nora, this is my husband, Duncan McEwan. Duncan, this is Nora." Aishlinn introduced the two of them. Duncan bowed slightly at the waist before taking Nora's hand and brushing a light kiss to the back of it. "So *yer* the Nora I've heard so much about," he said with a smile.

Nora curtsied as she felt a blush come to her face and knew not how to respond to his remark. She resisted the urge to ask exactly whom it was that had been speaking of her. Deep down, she hoped it had been Wee William.

Duncan turned his smile to his wife. "Have ye eaten since the morn, wife?"

Aishlinn rolled her eyes and shook her head. "Have you known me to miss a meal in the past four months? Really, Duncan, I wish you wouldn't worry so!"

Duncan spread his feet apart and crossed his arms over his chest. "I be yer husband and not only is it me duty to worry, it is me right!"

Nora caught the twinkle in his eye as he looked lovingly at his tiny wife with her big belly. Nora had to bite her bottom lip to keep from laughing at Aishlinn's expression of shock and horror. "Your *right?* You do not own me Duncan McEwan! I am your wife, not your possession. You'd best remember that fact."

Duncan chuckled as he wrapped his arms around Aishlinn and drew her in. "Aye, yer right. Ye are me wife. And I'm afraid 'tis ye who possesses me, heart, body and soul. Do no' be angry that I worry. If I didna worry and fuss you'd think I didna love ye anymore!" He pressed a kiss on the top of Aishlinn's head.

"Quit with your romantic ways, Duncan McEwan. 'Tis how I got into my current state!" She tried to push him away but he wouldn't have it.

"I believe it had more to do with a blindfold and a dare, if me memory serves me correct." He taunted her.

Aishlinn's eyes flew open and she stomped her foot down on Duncan's, forcing him to release her.

"Duncan! You must not speak like that in front of people! I swear, you will drive me to madness one of these days!"

She hadn't caused any real damage to his foot, but he would allow her to think she had. "Yer right," he said, trying to look like a chastised child. "Please forgive me, m'lady! I shall spend the rest of me days trying to make up fer all me dastardly ways! I bow before ye, humbled, and it is me fervent desire to do nothing but yer biddin'!"

Nora could no longer contain her laughter. She giggled at the two of them. Duncan pulled his wife in closely for another hug and smiled at Nora. "'Tis the babe she carries that often makes her a bit grumpy. Do no' kick me again wife," he said as he moved his legs away from hers. "Ye love me, ye canna deny it. And ye even love me wickedness."

"Aye, I love you, though sometimes I wonder *why!*" Aishlinn shook her head and rolled her eyes.

Duncan bowed at the waist with a flourish. "Will ye do me the honor of allowing me to escort the two of ye to the evening meal this night?"

"Don't be daft, Duncan. Of course you can," Aishlinn told him as she took his offered arm.

Duncan smiled devilishly at Nora. "Unless there be someone else ye'd want to escort ye?"

Nora felt the burning sensation of embarrassment again, but remained mute. Besides, she hadn't a clue if there would be any hidden meaning to being escorted to dinner by someone and she wanted not to make any errors in social protocol. She decided to err on the side of caution and not name any one individual. "I have been taking my meals in the children's room. Wee William brings us a tray each night."

There was a glint of something in Duncan's eye and a smile on Aishlinn's face. "Does he stay to eat with you?" Aishlinn asked.

"Aye, he does." Nora refused to read anything into Wee William's kind gesture. Aye, she did enjoy those private moments with him. She enjoyed his company, their talks, and his sense of humor. But to think Wee William would have anything other than friendly notions toward her was laughable. He was a handsome, large, kind man. He could have any woman that he chose and Nora was certain that *she* was not the kind of woman a man like him could ever want.

Aishlinn smiled more brightly and looked up at her husband. "Duncan, I've not seen Wee William of late. Pray, tell me, does he still wear his beard?"

"Aye, wife, he does."

Aishlinn nodded and pondered that for a moment. "I see."

Nora looked at the two of them, her curiosity growing.

Duncan took notice of Nora's curious expression. "I can see ye don't understand the importance of Wee William's beard, lass."

"No, m'lord, I do not."

Duncan and Aishlinn cast a glance at one another before Duncan went on to explain it. "Ye see, lass, Wee William has sworn time and again that there isn't a woman in all this world worth shavin' his beard for."

Seeing she was even more confused by his statement, he went on. "So the day he shaves his beard will be the day he's declarin' his love fer a woman. We have wagers with one another as to when that might happen. Though some say 'twill never happen, others among us are a bit more optimistic."

"Wee William is a wonderful man," Aishlinn offered. "You will not find another in all this world who loves children the way he does. You can often find him out of doors, allowing the little ones to climb his shoulders so they can pretend they can reach the stars. Or he'll chase them about, acting like an ogre." Aishlinn gave her husband's arm a gentle squeeze. "He's a good man, Nora. A bit stubborn, just like all Highlanders."

Nora had witnessed the kind side of Wee William. There was a calming influence to him, one that made her sister less afraid. She had also taken note of how he treated John with a firm yet kind hand, which was exactly the kind of influence the boy needed.

Aye, he was a kind, generous, funny, handsome, big man. He could have any woman he wanted. What made her think she stood a chance among all the fine, beautiful Scottish women she had met? She doubted he would be interested in an Englishwoman, with two siblings to look after. Nay, it was too much to hope that a man like him would be interested in a woman like her.

"Aye, he is a fine man, indeed." She wanted nothing more than to change the subject. "I'm not sure how things are done here, but could John and Elise sit with us at the evening meal?"

Taking note that the subject was closed for now, Aishlinn held out her hand to Nora. "Of course they can. It is much different here than in English castles where children are to be seen and not heard. I think you'll be pleasantly surprised by how differently things are done."

Nora gave Aishlinn's hand a gentle squeeze. "I took note of that from the beginning. I could live ten lifetimes and still not be able to repay everyone for the kindness they've shown us. I'm very glad to be here."

Nora did not notice the silent exchange that took place between

Aishlinn and Duncan as they left the study together. She was lost again in her own thoughts and began to plan her future.

Nora needed a husband. Aye, she might not necessarily *want* one, but she knew that she needed one. She did not want to live the rest of her days in the women's solar. She wanted a home, a real home, for John and Elise. A home filled with laughter, love, and kindness.

She was willing to settle for laughter and kindness because she knew love was not an easy thing to acquire. The kind of love she witnessed between Aishlinn and Duncan was so very rare.

She had spent a year praying fervently for a way out of her marriage. Nora felt it would be selfish to ask the Lord for a love she witnessed between Aishlinn and Duncan. Nay, it was enough now that Horace was dead and kind people surrounded her and her brother and sister. Safe, warm, and cared for, and it was more than she had ever asked of God. She'd not risk losing those things by asking for anymore from Him.

✤ 14 ✤

"Ye want me to do what, William?" Father Michael stared at Wee William, uncertain he'd heard the man correctly.

"I need ye to give Nora an annulment but without her knowin' yer doin' it." Wee William told him again for the third time. "I dunna see why ye find it so difficult to understand the request, father."

Father Michael shook his head as if doing so would bring him clarity. It didn't work. "Explain it to me one more time."

Wee William let out a frustrated sigh as he ran his fingers through his hair. He was rapidly losing faith in the young priest. But if explaining it again would bring the man around to his way of thinking, he'd oblige.

"Ye see, father, I've been praying on this fer days now. 'Tis a great guilt I carry with me. I ken Nora thinks her husband be dead, but I've no' guarantee that he *is*. There is a good chance they didna survive that night, what with bein' naked and miles from home and it bein' winter. But, I'd rather no' take the chance that he still be walkin' among the livin'."

"So ye want me to grant her an annulment without her knowledge?" Father Michael asked his voice laced with disbelief.

"Aye!" William smiled. Finally. "Ye've got the right of it. So, will ye do this fer me?"

Father Michael shook his head again and stepped down from the dais of the kirk. He began pacing in front of Wee William, thinking about what the man was asking. He stopped and looked up at the tall Highlander who was looking far more hopeful than Father Michael would have liked.

"William, I would no' be able to just *grant* an annulment. The lass would have to *ask* fer it. And I dunna ken how ye'd get her to ask fer such a thing when she thinks she's a widow."

Wee William ran his hand across his beard. He'd done nothing for the past days but think of a way around his predicament without Nora learning of the very small possibility that her husband might still be alive. He had given her a chance at a better life. Who knew what she'd do if she found out that Horace might still be alive. He'd come to the priest and made his confession, to which Father Michael did nothing to hide his shock.

"I ken the lass has talked with ye, Father Michael. Certainly she's told ye of her life with that whoreson she was married to."

Father Michael cringed at the words Wee William had chosen to describe Horace Crawford. Aye, he agreed with his colorful description, but to use such words in the house of the Lord was unacceptable. "William, remember *where* ye be."

Wee William crossed himself and apologized. "Ye've talked with her, father?"

Father Michael held up his hands to halt Wee William. "Ye ken I canna tell ye what the lass and I spoke of."

Wee William nodded his head and pressed his tongue to his cheek. "Aye, I ken it. Ye canna tell me *what* she said, but certainly ye can tell me if ye discussed her marriage to Horace."

Father Michael stared blankly at Wee William. He knew where the man was headed and wasn't about to be led there.

"I understand ye wantin' to keep her confessions secret. But tell me this, if she *were* to ask for an annulment, do ye think ye could grant it?"

The priest had no idea how Wee William proposed to get Nora to ask that question. "Aye, I would," he answered before quickly adding, "but how on earth do ye plan on getting' her to ask the question when she thinks she be a widow?"

A plan began to form in Wee William's mind. The more he thought on it, the bigger his smile grew. After a few moments, he was positively beaming. His smile sent a chill up and down Father Michael's spine. A beaming Wee William was more frightening than an angry one.

"If I can get her to ask it, will ye grant it?" Wee William asked.

Father Michael was too unnerved by his smile to deny the request. "Aye, I would."

"Good!" Wee William said as he slapped a large hand on the priest's back, nearly knocking him off balance. "I'll return within the hour with the lass. Ye be prepared to grant it."

Father Michael did not doubt the Highlander's tenacity. However, he did have doubts as to how Wee William would go about it. "I'll need time to draw up the annulment documents. Give me two hours."

Wee William slapped his back again, happier than he'd been in weeks. He started to leave, when Father Michael called after him.

"William, am I to assume by yer request that ye have a desire to marry this lass?"

Wee William came to an abrupt halt. He refused to turn around to look at the priest. "Nay, ye needn't assume such a thing. I'm merely doin' it to assuage me guilt. Nothin' else to it."

It was Father Michael's turn to smile. He thought of telling Wee William that God frowned upon liars, but wasn't ready to die this day. Besides, there was the possibility that Wee William wasn't quite ready to admit that he did in fact want to marry the lass. His long beard however, told an entirely different story. He continued to smile as he watched Wee William leave the kirk. Moments later, Father Michael left in a hurry.

He needed to see Fergus Dunbottom about placing a little bet.

"ARE YOU CERTAIN THAT I SHOULDN'T BE BETTER DRESSED FOR SUCH an occasion?" Nora asked Wee William as they headed toward the kirk.

Wee William thought she looked beautiful in anything she wore and today was no exception. The pretty dark blue dress with the arisaid made of MacDougall plaid made her look all the more like a good Scottish woman. With her hair in a simple braid that tumbled over her ample bosom, it was all he could do not to scoop her up and have his way with her. He was thankful that she could not read minds, for he knew she'd slap him silly for all the lustful thoughts bouncing through his.

"Nay, lass, ye look quite bonny this day," he told her as he hurried along the path to the kirk, pulling her along behind him. He was unable to see the way her face blushed or the smile she held at his compliment.

She'd been on her way to speak with Angus when Wee William stopped her. He was rather excited about something and more than once she had to ask him to slow down and to speak in the English. Finally she was able to make out that there was a little ceremony that he and his men wanted to perform, one that would make her an official member of the MacDougall clan.

He went on to further explain that the entire ceremony must be performed in Gaelic or Latin. He'd act as translator between her and the priest. Daniel and David would act as witnesses.

Nora's heart swelled with pride. They wanted her here. *As a member of their clan.* She'd never felt quite so honored in her life. All thoughts of talking with Angus rapidly fell to the wayside.

Happily, she followed along behind Wee William. Her heart was pounding wildly and she wasn't sure if it was because of the excitement she felt at becoming an official member or the way his skin felt as he held her hand.

"'Tis a simple ceremony, but an important one," Wee William explained as he pushed through the door to the kirk.

Father Michael stood at the head of the kirk with Daniel and David waiting on either side of him. They greeted her with warm smiles as Wee William led her to the front of the kirk.

It was a beautiful spring day and sunlight streamed in through the leaded glass windows. Little bits of dust danced in the air. The sound of the birds singing filtered in, along with the distant bleating of newly born lambs. Nora thought it would have been a most perfect day for any ceremony, including the one she was about to participate in.

She smiled happily at all the men and gave each of them a small curtsy. "I am speechless, I truly am," she gushed first at Daniel, then to David. "I feel so very honored to be..."

Wee William stopped her from finishing her sentence. "Lass," he said in a hushed and reverent tone. "We're glad to have ye here as well. But let us begin now, shall we?"

Deciding it was perhaps a far more serious ceremony than she had first imagined, she took on the same reverent expression as Wee William.

Wee William had sent Daniel and David ahead earlier to explain his plan to Father Michael. It was more of a curiosity than anything else that drove the priest to agree. He could barely wait to see how Wee William would get her to utter the words.

"Father," Wee William said as he stood next to Nora and faced the priest. "Ye may begin with the ceremony."

Father Michael wasn't quite sure *what* he was supposed to say or do at this particular time. All that he knew was that he was to speak in Latin and Wee William would act as translator. He cleared his throat and began with a prayer.

"*Hic sponte venis?*" He directed his question to Nora.

"Do ye come here of yer own free will?" Wee William translated.

"Aye, I do," Nora whispered.

"Te delectat hic apud nos?"

"Do ye like it here, among our people?"

"Aye, I do."

"Usquequo sunt tibi nupta Horace?"

Wee William was not sure he wanted to ask any questions regarding Horace, at least not yet. "How long were ye married to Horace?"

Nora looked confused. "Why does that matter?"

"We'll be asking all manner of questions this day lass. We be askin' questions to make certain ye do in fact want to be a member of the clan. We'll be askin' of yer past, yer present and yer future."

It sounded plausible enough. Not knowing anything to the contrary, she answered the priest's question. "A year and a week."

"Erant beatum te in vestri matrimonium?"

"Were ye happy in yer marriage?"

Nora wasn't sure what that had to do with anything, but supposed it had something to do with making sure she had no regrets with her decision to come to Scotland and start her life anew.

"Nay, I was not happy in my marriage to Horace. He was a cruel man, William."

Wee William smiled sympathetically at her before looking to Father Michael.

"Sunt beatum te hic?"

"Are ye happy here, lass?"

Her face lit up with a warm smile. "Aye, William, I most assuredly am." She noticed that Daniel and David gleamed proudly at her answer.

"Do ye have any regrets in comin' here?" He didn't wait for the priest to ask the next question. He was lost in Nora's pale blue eyes.

"No, William, I have no regrets."

"Do ye wish to stay here, among us for all the rest of yer days?" His voice was low and soothing.

"Aye, I do."

Father Michael interjected. "Illa non interrogavit quaestio de adnullacione, William."

Wee William blinked before turning back to the priest. In Gaelic he said, "I ken she hasn't asked the question yet."

The two men looked at each other for a moment before Wee William turned back to Nora. "Lass, we need to ken more of yer life back in England. Do ye miss it?"

"I miss some things, William. I miss the friends that I had there. But nothing else."

"Do ye miss yer cottage?"

Nora's brow knitted into a knot of disgust. "Nay! I do not miss anything about my life with Horace, not even that hovel he called a home! Had I known then, what I know now, I would have done things quite differently. But as it is, I can't change the fact that he is dead."

Wee William looked confused by her statement. "What would ye have done differently?" His stomach tightened into a hard knot, unsure if he wanted to know the answer.

"Well, I would never have married him to begin with!"

Wee William waited for her to expand upon that. When he saw nothing forthcoming, he dared ask another question. "And?"

"And what?"

He rolled his eyes. "Ye said, *to begin with...*"

"Oh!" She'd gotten lost in the soft timbre of his voice for a moment. What was it about this man's voice that was so calming? Giving her head a slight shake, she continued. "Well, I would not have married him had I known he was so cruel. And afterward, when I met the real Horace Crawford, the one with the harsh hands, the cruel mouth, I would have gone to the priest straight away."

Wee William raised an eyebrow. "And done what?"

Nora stood a bit taller, glad that he was holding her hands. "I would have gone to the priest and said, 'Father, I want an annulment. Horace broke all the promises he made before we married. He's cruel, mean, spiteful and I wish to no longer be married to him.'"

Father Michael would never have believed it if he hadn't heard it with his own ears. "*Tute quidam tu forsitan petisses pro an adnullacione?*"

Wee William smiled at the priest before looking back to Nora. "Ye would now, would ye?"

"Aye, I would! You have no idea, William, just how cruel Horace Crawford could be. I am glad he is..."

William stopped her short. "Lass, ye needn't say anything else on that matter."

Nora smiled up at him.

"*Non crediderim fecistis*!" Father Michael exclaimed. He truly could not believe Wee William was able to entice her to utter the words. Daniel and David nudged one another with their shoulders and smiled up at the priest. They had no doubt that, one way or another Wee William would realize his goal.

Nora could not figure out why the priest looked so surprised. "What did he say?" she asked Wee William.

"He says, 'welcome to the clan!'"

SPRING WAS IN FULL FORCE ACROSS THE HIGHLANDS. BLUEBELLS,

daffodils, and buttercups were scattered across the bright spring grass. Newly born lambs walked on unsteady legs alongside their mothers. Countless birds flew about the blue sky. Normally, Aishlinn would have loved how beautiful Scotland looked on this warm and brilliant spring morning. This day however, she was unable to enjoy the splendor.

As Nora and Aishlinn walked along the path toward the castle, Aishlinn nodded toward the lambs in the fields. "It seems every mum can give birth but me!"

Nora smiled as she walked at a snail's pace so that Aishlinn wouldn't feel as though she were holding her back. She knew Aishlinn was growing more frustrated as each day passed without her pains starting.

"I have no doubt, now, Nora," Aishlinn said with labored breaths, "'tis a boy I carry."

Nora looped her arm through Aishlinn's to help her along the path toward the castle. "You will find out soon enough," Nora told her.

Aishlinn grunted. "I should have had this babe a sennight ago!" She paused to catch her breath. Her back ached from all the extra weight she carried and her feet were so swollen it hurt to walk. But Isobel had encouraged her to walk in hopes it would help bring on her labor pains. She was beginning to think the babe would never come.

"Aye," Nora agreed, trying her best to lighten her friend's spirits. "It must be Duncan's *son* you carry, acting just like a true Highlander, taking his own good time."

Aishlinn rubbed her back, let out a long breath and tried to smile. "The day Duncan proposed, he was so nervous, he said '*I want to have yer bairns* -- I wish now that he could!"

Nora could not help but laugh at the image that brought to her mind. "Can you imagine Duncan or Wee William heavy with child?" Nora puffed out her cheeks and stood on her tiptoes, and spoke in a thick Scottish brogue. "Och! I be a Highlander. I can do anythin'! Bravery and honor will ge' me through me pains. And a wee dram of the chief's best will no' hurt!"

Aishlinn laughed until her eyes filled with tears. "Please, Nora! It hurts to laugh!"

While Nora did not envy Aishlinn her discomfort, she did envy

Aishlinn's life with Duncan and the life they created, even though he seemed intent on never leaving his mother's womb.

"Aishlinn, what does it feel like?" The question was out of her mouth before she realized she had even thought it.

Aishlinn rubbed a hand across her stomach and smiled. "'Tis a good feeling most of the time. More the thought of having a babe to hold in my arms is better than actually carrying him around."

Nora looped her arm through Aishlinn's and they began walking again. Nora longed to know what it felt like to have a good husband to share her life with. Aishlinn had everything that Nora wanted: a good husband, a happy life, and a babe on the way.

It wasn't jealousy or envy that Nora felt. It was a sense of longing. Longing to have a life similar to what Aishlinn and Duncan had together.

She wanted a home of her own, one where she could raise John and Elise. But she also wanted to share her life with someone. Someone like Wee William. A good, kind man.

Aishlinn sensed there was more that Nora wanted to ask or say. "Nora, what are you thinking?"

Nora gave a slight shake of her head as if to say her thoughts were of no importance.

"Nora, are we not friends?" Aishlinn asked.

"Of course we are! Don't be silly," Nora said with a smile.

"Then please, tell me what is on your mind. I fear we talk more of my problems and life than we ever do yours."

Nora giggled. "That is because your life is far more exciting and happy a thing to discuss than mine."

"That isn't true, Nora."

"Oh, but it is, Aishlinn. You are the chief's daughter. You're married to a most wonderful man who loves you so very much. You've a quaint home and a babe on the way. You see? Far more exciting and happy than my life."

Aishlinn gave Nora's arm a gentle squeeze. "You need a husband."

Nora laughed aloud at that statement. "Aye, a husband would be a fine thing to have. But I fear that will never happen."

"Why do you fear that? You're a beautiful woman, Nora. And you have so much to offer a man."

"That is very kind of you to say, Aishlinn. But I fear not all women are meant to marry. I tried it once, remember? It was an abysmal failure." Nora did not like thinking about her marriage to Horace and her smile quickly faded at the memories.

"That is because you were married to the wrong man!" Aishlinn exclaimed. "I think you would feel differently if you were married to a kinder man, one with a heart!"

Nora smiled and nodded her head in agreement. "That is probably true. But what man would want to take on a widow and her little brother and sister? That is an awfully large burden to ask any man to bear."

"It isn't a burden when you are doing things together, Nora. It isn't a burden when you are in love."

Nora snorted. "Love? I think love is far too much to hope for. I'd settle for a husband who didn't beat me and would let me keep John and Elise."

"So that is all you want in a man? One who won't beat you? And one who will let you keep your brother and sister?" Aishlinn shook her head and clicked her tongue in dismay. "You deserve more than that, Nora. You need someone who will love you like Duncan loves me."

Nora felt that the love Aishlinn and Duncan shared was a rare and special gift. Aye, she might secretly wish something like that for herself, but knew the probability of ever experiencing such a thing, was as rare as a unicorn.

"What do you think of Wee William, Nora?" Aishlinn asked.

Nora felt her face grow hot and her heart skip a beat at the mention of his name. "What of him?" she asked, hoping her feelings for him were not too obvious.

Aishlinn grinned and cast a sidelong glance at Nora. "He's a very nice man, Nora. He'd make anyone a fine husband."

Nora cleared her throat but remained quiet. She believed that Wee William would make any woman a good husband. He was kind, warm, and generous, but Nora believed he needed a woman with more to offer than what she could.

"You could ask my father to help you find a husband," Aishlinn suggested.

"Find me a husband?" Nora asked incredulously. Did Aishlinn believe she was incapable of finding one of her own accord?

"Aye," Aishlinn answered. "If all you want is a man who will not beat you and allow you to keep John and Elise, then it shouldn't be too difficult a task. I'm sure you could turn away anyone he might suggest, if the man wasn't to your liking."

They had finally reached the keep and paused outside the kitchen door. Nora pondered Aishlinn's suggestion. She had no desire to continue to live in the women's solar. John and Elise needed a home to call their own. They had been through so much in the past year. Mayhap a home of their own would help John to get over his anger and resentment.

Aye, she not only needed a husband, she wanted one as well. She wanted babes of her own someday and she was not getting any younger. Enlisting Angus' help could only help her gain that which she so desperately wanted faster than she could accomplish on her own.

"I think that is an excellent idea, Aishlinn," Nora said.

"YE WANT ME TO DO *WHAT*, LASS?" ANGUS WAS NOT SURE HE HAD heard her correctly the first time.

"I'd like you to help me find a husband," Nora repeated. She was doing her best to sound more enthusiastic than she actually felt about the decision she'd made. She needed a husband.

It was true that she'd been a widow for less than a month. With no discernible skills to offer, she felt she would be better off trying to find a husband than a position with another castle. Besides, she was now an official member of the clan. Certainly that afforded her not only Angus' protection, but his help as well.

More than a sennight had passed since the ceremony in which she'd become an official member of the clan. She could not understand why she was made to swear an oath of secrecy, but she'd made the solemn oath nonetheless. Daniel had explained the oath was necessary to ward off evil spirits. She supposed it was part of Gaelic traditions and superstitions, so she swore the oath.

In the days since the ceremony, some things had changed. She was learning to read, alongside her brother and sister. They were fully recovered and now allowed to play out of doors along with the other children. Elise had no problems making friends. John, however, was a bit slower to warm up to the idea of Scotland being their new and permanent home. Nora could only hope that with time and kindness, he would eventually adjust.

She had moved into the women's solar, along with Elise. Their pallets were side by side and the room was in sharp contrast to the women's solar at Castle Firth. This one was bright, sunny, and warm. The walls were draped in beautiful tapestries; the women were kind and graciously tried to teach Nora and Elise a few words in Gaelic.

But other than that, nothing else had changed. She had noticed that all the men did their best to stay completely away from her. She found that very unsettling and could not fathom why they behaved in such a manner.

Where the women were fun, generous, helpful, the men all acted as though she carried a pox! All save for Wee William, Daniel and David, and the other men that had brought her to Gregor. They were the only men to speak to her.

So here she was, standing before Angus McKenna, asking for his help. She held no idyllic notions that she'd ever find a romance like the one between Aishlinn and Duncan. She needed to think logically about the entire thing. Mayhap, if Angus were to spread the word that she was in fact seeking a husband, the men might treat her differently.

"A husband?" Angus looked positively baffled. "Ye want me to find ye a husband?"

Nora could not understand why her request seemed so foreign to Angus. It wasn't as if she had asked him to pull the moon down from the sky so that she might have a better look at it. For a moment, she began to wonder if she weren't breaking some Scottish social protocol that frowned upon such a request.

"I am sorry, m'lord, if my request is out of order," she demurred.

She had her hands clasped in front of her and prayed he could not see them tremble.

Angus blinked again and looked at his council. Fergus had a peculiar grin to his face, and the other men looked as though they were fighting to keep from laughing. Nora found the entire ordeal very unsettling. She was about to beg for their forgiveness and run from the room when Angus stood up.

"I see. Ye want a husband. Do ye have a particular man in mind?"

Nora shook her head ever so slightly. Truth be told, she'd rather Wee William were the one to offer his hand. But since he'd not shaved his beard or showed any outward signs that he wished to be anything more than friends, she assumed he had no romantic intentions toward her.

"Nay, m'lord. There is no one in particular."

She took note of the glances that were cast between the men on the other side of the table. They whispered to each other in Gaelic and a few of them chuckled. Nora wasn't sure she wished to know what they were saying and decided there was, perhaps, bliss in being ignorant.

"What kind of man do ye seek, lass? What kind of husband do ye wish fer?" Fergus asked.

Nora swallowed hard and gave his question some thought before answering. "Well, m'lord, I'd prefer a man who will not beat me."

Her statement caused a bit of an uproar. There was much growling and scowling. One of the men stood up and said something to her in Gaelic. Though she had no idea what he was saying, there was no mistaking his anger.

Angus ordered them all to be still. "Lads!" he boomed. "Remember, the lass is Sassenach. She comes from a land where men beat their wives far more often than they bathe!"

Nora took offense to his statement. "M'lord, I can assure you that not *all* Englishmen beat their wives! My father never laid an angry finger on my mother."

Angus looked and sounded sincere in his apology. "Fergive me, lass. But we find beating a woman or a child a most disgusting action. Such a deed is not only frowned upon here, 'tis grounds for expulsion. To suggest there be a man among us that would hit a woman, well, 'tis about as likely as yer king voluntarily givin' Scotland her freedom."

Nora regretted the fact that she had insulted the men. However, she did not regret the fact that she wanted to make it abundantly clear that she wanted a kind husband. "I do apologize, m'lord. I meant no disrespect. Please, forgive me. I was married to a very harsh man for more than a year. He thought nothing of beating me, for even the slightest transgression."

She truly disliked admitting that fact openly to this group of strangers. Nora wanted to leave that part of her life far behind her.

"I can understand yer worry lass," Angus voice had softened. "Ye can rest assured that no matter what MacDougall man ye might marry, he will no' lay an angry hand to ye. Ye have me word on that."

Nora thanked him with a smile before continuing on with her list of requirements. "My other requirement would be that he would allow my younger brother and sister to live with us." That would be the only deal breaker she could think of, that would keep her from marrying someone. "And I want his promise in writing, before we're married, that he would allow it." She would not be tricked into marrying another man who would quickly turn John and Elise away.

Angus nodded his head as he crossed his arms over his chest. "I do no' see where that would be a problem. Do ye have any other wishes?"

Aye, I wish for a man who can make the roof of my mouth tickle when he kisses me, she thought to herself. There would be no way she could say those words out loud. "He must be kind and want to have children."

Angus nodded. Thus far, her demands could easily be met by any number of available men. "Anything else?"

Nora could think of several other things she'd wish to find in a husband, but could not put them to voice. "Nay, m'lord. I have nothing else."

"Well, then," Angus said as he rubbed the palms of his hands together. "I shall spread the word that ye be lookin' fer a husband. Yer a bonny lass. I do no' think it will take long to find ye one."

Nora hoped that he was correct and that when the men learned she was seeking a husband, they might begin to treat her differently.

She thanked each of the men and left the room, feeling a bit better than she had when she had first entered.

Fergus was the first man to break out into raucous laughter and was quickly joined by the rest of the men in the room. "How do ye think Wee William will respond to this bit o' news?" he asked Angus.

Angus was not able to answer the question. He was too busy trying to catch his breath. The lass hadn't a clue what her request was going to do to Wee William. "I dunnae! But I wish to be there to see the look on his face!"

"I wonder how many men are brave enough to offer fer her!" Thomas Gainer said with tear filled eyes.

Wee William had come to see the clan council a week ago, asking for a bit of land to call his own. He was quite willing to pay for it. The clan had refused his offer of money and instead gave him a piece of land not far from Aishlinn and Duncan's home, as a reward for his many years of fealty and service to the clan.

When they had inquired as to why he wanted the land, Wee William explained that he was not getting any younger and that he would not always be able to fight as a warrior. He was simply making plans for his auld age. And he was absolutely adamant that it had nothing to do with thoughts of marriage.

The laughter finally began to subside and wagers were placed as to just how many days were left before Wee William shaved his beard. Others placed bets on whether or not Wee William would have an apoplexy at the news.

Angus gave it four days before Wee William shaved his beard, where Fergus gave him a week. "He's too damned stubborn fer his own good, I tell ye. He'll be able to hold out fer a week, but no' a day longer."

Angus called for a messenger to let the men in the clan know that a certain young woman was actively seeking a husband.

"SHE DID WHAT?" WEE WILLIAM'S ANGRY VOICE THUNDERED ACROSS the training fields. Everything came to an abrupt halt. Men began heading toward Wee William and Rowan to learn the source of his anger.

Rowan fought hard to take on a serious demeanor, but he found the look of terror blended with fury on Wee William's face, comical.

"Aye, Wee William. She went to Angus and in front of the whole council, she asked him to help her find a husband." Rowan had to bite his cheek to keep from laughing. "And they agreed to help her."

Wee William glowered at no one in particular. He was furious with...well, with the entire world. He would have sworn, not more than a few moments ago, that he had his feelings for the lass completely under control. Apparently, he had misjudged his heart.

Nay, he could not blame his heart. 'Twas Nora's fault. Somehow, she had managed to cast a spell upon him, had bewitched him in some manner, to make him feel this way. He swallowed hard and considered it.

"What about her mournin' period?" The thought had come to him so quickly, the words spilled out of his mouth before he could rein them back in.

Rowan raised both eyebrows. "Angus says there be no reason for the lass to be in mournin' if she has to lie about her feelings. He said it would be an affront to the good Lord to make her pretend to mourn a loss she welcomed. And ye ken how Angus is about lyin'."

A year. Was it really too much to ask for? He believed that after a year of Nora in mourning, he'd have his feelings for the woman so under control that when or if this day had come, he'd be better able to deal with it. He also knew that the men would have to stay away from her, what with her being a widow and all.

His plans for the next year flittered away like autumn leaves in the wind.

"Don't ye think it's a bit soon fer her to be lookin' fer a husband?" Wee William asked.

Rowan feigned incredulity quite well. "Nay! The lass *needs* a husband. She needs a home fer her brother and sister. She wants bairns of her own, Wee William. She canna live in the castle fer all her days!" He clicked his tongue and shook his head for added emphasis.

If she wanted bairns of her very own, that meant she'd have to join with a man. It was too much to hope for another immaculate conception. His stomach roiled at the thought of someone other than himself giving her that which he could not admit to wanting to give her.

The image of a naked Nora, lying in the arms of any other man, brought forth a rage he had never quite experienced before. Before he realized what had happened, he flipped the trestle table onto its side, the contents spilling to the ground, crushing the casks of ale and tankards in its wake.

The crowd that had formed began to cautiously walk away. Wee William's face was twisted into an ugly scowl. His chest heaved as sweat trickled off his brow.

"If one man so much as blinks at Nora, I will tear him apart, piece by bloody piece and feed the bits to the scavengers!"

There wasn't a man present, or another who would hear of it later, that did not believe every word he said.

Nora could not make sense of it. The men were behaving worse than before she had asked Angus to find her a suitable husband. There was simply no denying it.

Earlier that morning when Mary asked her to help take bread and meat to the men on the training fields, she had happily agreed. On her way to the fields however, two men actually jumped behind the bushes that lined the walkway. One of the stable boys crossed himself, mumbled something in Gaelic, and then raced back into the stable, slamming the door behind him.

By the time she reached the fields she was on the verge of tears. She was not a vain woman, by any stretch of the imagination. However, she did have some pride. She knew she was not an ugly woman. Oh, she might not be as stunning as Isobel, Bree, or Aishlinn. But the way the men were all behaving, one would think she had warts growing on the end of her nose and was missing most of her teeth! It was positively disheartening.

She had, of course, no idea of what had taken place when Wee William learned of her visit with Angus and the clan council. He had let loose with a slew of curses that made even the most hardened men blush. Not only had he tossed the drink table that sat next to the training fields *again,* he had torn it to shreds. Once he was done making sure the table was in fact dead, he began cursing again. He warned any man within ear shot that if they so much as *thought* about offering their hand to Nora, they would suffer a fate worse than the drink table.

The men refused to train with him.

Father Michael tried to speak with him after hearing how he responded to the news. It took more time walking from the kirk to find Wee William than it took to realize he'd made a grave error in judgment. Were he not a man of the cloth, Wee William could have throttled his neck. He told the priest just that.

And still, he had not shaved his beard. He was a complete besotted mess. He had not seen Nora since she had asked for Angus' help. He was too busy trying to kill tables and build his cottage. A cottage he had sworn and be-damned was *not* in preparation for marriage, but for his auld age. And by God, any man who said otherwise was as good as dead. He also reminded them when necessary, of his threat that any man who so much as walked the same path as Nora was as good as dead.

Nora approached the drink table not knowing it was in fact the third such table to be placed in that spot in the past four days. She looked out at the fields and called out to the men. "I've brought you bread and meat!"

Every man, save for Rowan, Black Richard, Daniel, David, and Wee William, turned their backs to her and walked in the opposite direction.

She wished them all to go straight to the devil.

Rowan and Black Richard approached the table first. Were it not for their kind smiles, Nora would have thought she was completely alone in the world. "We thank ye, lass!" Rowan said as he poured ale into tankards.

"Yer a bonny sight this morn," Black Richard offered.

Perhaps she *was* severely lacking in beauty, grace, and intelligence. Mayhap Rowan and his friends were only being kind to her because they pitied her. She tried to smile but was unsuccessful. Daniel and

David's smiles as they approached the table, were quickly replaced with looks of genuine concern.

"What be the matter, lass?" David asked.

Nora swallowed hard and waved their concern away. "It is nothing of import, David. But I do thank you for asking."

"Come now, lassie," Black Richard said. "We can see there be something the matter. Ye do no' carry yer usual bonny smile."

"Oh what does it matter?" she blurted out. "I could be as beautiful as Isobel or Aishlinn and it would not matter in the least! The men here, they all find me atrocious!"

A silent exchange took place between the men, and Nora couldn't help but notice. She was right! They did find her severely lacking. She would never find a husband.

"Lass, the men here do find ye quite bonny. It's just they be a bit afraid," Daniel tried explaining.

"Afraid? Of me?" She thought his statement absurd.

"Mayhap not of ye, but," David's sentence was cut short by a large hand grabbing his shoulder.

"Good day to ye, Nora," Wee William said as he held a death-grip on David's shoulder. It was his way of warning the young man to not utter another word, lest he wanted to lose his arm from the shoulder down. David grimaced and tried to shrug the massive hand from his shoulder. It was immovable.

"Good day, William," Nora replied. She noticed how red David's face had become. "David, are you well?"

He swallowed hard and nodded his head. "Aye," he said through gritted teeth. "Pulled a muscle while sparring with Rowan."

"Mayhap you should have Isobel take a look at it."

"Nay, lass. I'll be well soon enough." He cast a look over his shoulder at Wee William. "I'll just be off to rest it now."

Wee William let David go, giving him a firm slap on the back. "'Tis a verra good idea, lad."

"Thank ye, lass, fer bringing the food. Looks like rain. Mayhap ye should get back to the keep," Wee William said as he filled a tankard with ale. Rowan and Black Richard looked at him as though he'd lost his mind before quickly concealing their concern.

Nora looked up. It was a beautiful spring day, filled with bright sunshine. The brilliant blue sky was dotted with fluffy white clouds. There was not a rain cloud to be seen.

Either Wee William had gone daft or there was a hidden meaning to his message. Nora glanced at the men and realized they all had rather peculiar expressions. She supposed they were merely being kind, not wanting her exposed to more embarrassment such as men jumping into bushes and locking themselves behind doors. Pity, that is what she saw in their eyes.

She couldn't take another moment of it. She spun on her heals and raced back toward the keep. Mayhap she had made a terrible mistake in coming here. Mayhap she should leave and try to find a home amongst another clan, or work at Scottish manor. Something, *anything*, but to remain here another day.

"Yer a damned fool, Wee William," Rowan said when Nora was finally out of earshot. "A complete and utter fool and I be no' afraid to say it to yer face."

He placed himself in front of Wee William and crossed his arms over his chest. Black Richard and Daniel took up rank beside him. Death might be moments away but it mattered not to any of them. Wee William was causing Nora unnecessary pain and anguish, and all because he was too foolish to admit how he felt.

"I'd advise ye no' to say another word, Rowan," Wee William said through gritted teeth.

"I tell no lies, Wee William and ye ken it! Ye canna let that poor girl continue to think the men here find her appearance appalling! 'Tisn't right and 'tisn't fair."

"What the bloody hell are ye talkin' about?" Wee William growled.

Rowan slapped his hand to his head in exasperation. "The men be so terrified ye'll tear them limb from limb that they go out of their way to avoid her. They will no' even bid her good day!"

"And what be yer point?" He wanted them afraid. He wanted them to understand without any doubt that he *would* tear them limb from limb if they took the slightest step out of line. He puffed out his chest, proud that his threats of slow, agonizing and painful deaths to any man who got near Nora were in fact working.

Rowan was quite tempted to pick up the table and beat his friend senseless with it. "Because of *that*, the lass thinks all the men here find her unappealing. Ugly. Unworthy of even a how do ye do."

Regret filled Wee William's heart. He hadn't intended to hurt her feelings. There was nothing that wasn't beautiful about her.

"So ye can see how I come to the conclusion that ye be a fool. The lass is broken hearted and all because ye be a fool and a coward."

Wee William growled. "A coward?" He was furious. "How dare ye call me that!"

"Yer a coward because ye will no' tell the lass how ye feel. Ye want her fer yerself, but are too afraid to say it. And ye will no' let anyone else have her." He took a step toward his foolish friend. "That is why I say yer a coward."

NORA HAD DECIDED TO GO TO AISHLINN'S HOME INSTEAD OF BACK to the keep. She and Aishlinn had become fast friends and a friend was exactly what she needed at the moment. She also did not want to have to explain her tears to anyone in the castle.

She sat now at Aishlinn's table, her sobs finally subsiding. "So you see, Aishlinn, I must leave."

Aishlinn smiled at Nora as she offered yer another handkerchief. "Nay! I tell you the truth, Nora, the men do not find you lacking or unappealing."

Nora blinked a few more tears away. "How can you say that? Men *jump into bushes* when they see me coming. They hide behind closed doors. Please do not try to tell me they're afraid of my stunning beauty!" She snorted, not caring that it was very unladylike gesture, and blew her nose again.

"Nora, you don't quite understand how Highlander men behave. Oh, they're brave, strong, honorable, and quite kind. But dear, not a one of them owns a bit of common sense when it comes to women! Why, you should have seen Duncan the night we had musicians here, and the dance. Why, he nearly had an apoplexy when the other men danced with me!" Aishlinn laughed at the memory. Duncan had been so angry and jealous that night, that his face had turned dark red and he actually growled at a young lad who had the audacity to ask her to dance.

"You are beautiful, Nora. And the men agree, I'm sure of it."

Nora moaned. "Then *why* are they acting this way?"

"I suspect one of the men, and I'm not sure who it might be, has claimed you for his own. Once a Highlander has claimed you, the others back off. It's akin to the biggest bull in the paddock letting it be known that a certain cow is his."

Tears filled Nora's eyes again. "You're saying I'm a cow?" she let her head fall to the table. A cow.

Aishlinn laughed. "Poor choice of words. It's more like a proud peacock strutting around, barking and crying to all who will listen, that he's laying claim to a comely young peahen."

Nora thought long and hard for several moments, trying to piece together what Aishlinn meant. "So, you're saying that one of the men *does* want me, and the other men are staying away out of fear?"

"Aye," Aishlinn said as she patted Nora's hand. "That is exactly what I am saying."

"But who? And why hasn't he told me?"

Aishlinn smiled thoughtfully. "Because, dear, Highlander men do not own a bit of common sense when it comes to women. He may be too afraid, too stubborn, and too stupid yet, to let you know. I'm leaning more toward stupid." She began pouring each of them another cup of tea.

Nora giggled as she was beginning to feel better about the entire situation. "So do I just wait until whoever it is, is ready to let me know his intentions?"

Aishlinn stopped mid-pour. "Nay! Ye could wait years for that to happen!" She shook her head, finished pouring the tea and set the pot down.

"I say we will give it a day or two. If he still has not let you know who he is, then we shall force his hand."

Nora raised an eyebrow. "How will we do that?"

A devilish smile came to Aishlinn's lips. "We'll draw him out and we'll have my father help."

Nora took a sip of tea and admittedly she was beginning to feel better. There was something in Aishlinn's devious smile and twinkling eyes that made Nora quite glad she was on her side.

WEE WILLIAM HAD AMBLED AROUND HIS HOME FOR SOME TIME after Aishlinn left. Sadness enveloped him as he paced around his home. Aye, he would regret not telling Nora how he felt. But the bigger regret would be in telling her and being laughed at. He tried to convince himself that he would rather have the regret of not telling her than the shame of being made a fool again.

Angus was going to pick a husband for Nora this day.

A husband.

A man.

A man who would swear to protect and care for her.

A man who would be blessed with building a life with her.

A man who would be granted the right and the pleasure of waking up to that sweet face of hers each morn.

A man who would be granted the right and the pleasure of kissing her full lips, of running his fingers through those long, dark tresses of hers, of kissing every square inch of that gloriously curvaceous body of hers.

When he thought of any other man enjoying Nora in such a fashion, fury ignited in his gut.

He'd kill the bastard.

15

After bringing Nora in off the ledge on which her esteem and sanity seemed to teeter precariously, Aishlinn shared her suspicions with her husband. He confirmed every one of them. There was only one man in all the clan who could induce such fear into the hearts of other men. Two days had passed since Nora had come to Aishlinn's home and the fool still hadn't admitted how he felt.

So now Aishlinn stood outside Wee William's cottage. She could see him rumbling around inside, for he had yet to hang the door. He was mumbling to himself, and he sounded quite perturbed. Aishlinn supposed someone less courageous, or perhaps less foolish, would have turned and walked away. She was not about to.

He was hammering hooks around the large window on the opposite side of the cottage. They would later be used to hang furs to keep out the cold winter air. He hammered and mumbled away with his back turned from the doorway.

"Wee William!" she said using her most cheerful voice.

He nearly jumped out of his skin. That was not like him to be lost in his own thoughts to the point of distraction. He cursed under his breath as he hit his thumb with the hammer. "Damn!" he shouted as he turned to face her, dropping the hammer to the stone floor. He began shaking his hand as if doing so would somehow make the pain leave at a more rapid pace.

Aishlinn stood a bit taller. She was not as afraid of Wee William as most others were. He was her friend, and she knew he would never do anything to hurt her.

"I'm so very sorry, Wee William!" she said as she entered the cottage. "You haven't a door to knock on yet."

"What are ye doin' here?" He sounded quite gruff, and looked even angrier. This was not how Aishlinn was used to seeing him. He bent down and picked up the hammer and resumed his work.

She tilted her head slightly. "My apologies," she said flatly. "I was merely bringing you a few things for your new home."

"I'm afraid I'm in no mood fer company this day, Aishlinn. Ye can put whatever it is ye brought on the table."

No, this was definitely *not* the Wee William she was used to. Part of her was tempted to give him a good tongue-lashing but she decided that perhaps a more subtle approach would be more effective. Gently, she set her basket on the table.

"Oh!" she cried out, grabbing her stomach.

Wee William spun, dropped the hammer and raced to her. "Good God woman! Do no' tell me it be yer time!" He looked absolutely terrified. That was much better than sullen and angry.

Aishlinn grimaced, and bent over. "Nay, I do not think so," she said breathlessly. "But sometimes, the babe kicks so hard it feels as though he's trying to climb his way out!"

Wee William let out a sigh of relief as he guided her to the bench next to the trestle table. "Sit lass," he told her. "What can I do? Do ye need me to fetch Isobel or Duncan?" His voice was filled with concern. Aishlinn also noted a bit of fear in it. She had to bite her cheek to keep from laughing.

"Nay," she said as she took a deep breath. "Just let me rest a while. I do not want to keep you from your work. I'll just sit here, quietly."

Wee William stood and studied her for a long moment, with his hands on either side of her as if he were afraid she'd keel over at any moment. "Are ye sure lass?"

"Aye, I'm sure. Really, this happens from time to time."

Ever so slowly he began to back away. The thought of Aishlinn giving birth on his kitchen floor nearly made him faint. He sat down on the bench opposite her. She noticed he looked quite pale. It served him right for being so rude.

"Mayhap a spot of tea?" Aishlinn asked him.

Wee William nodded his head. "That sounds good. But I'm afraid I have no' stocked me larder yet. The only thing I have here is a bit of the chief's best and a cask of ale."

Just what every bachelor should have, Aishlinn thought.

"Well, I happen to have brought you some," she said as she lifted the cloth off the basket and pulled out a small tin of tea. "Do you have a kettle?" she asked.

He shook his head. "Nay, lass."

It didn't matter. She was on a mission. "That's quite all right. You can save it for later."

The color was finally beginning to return to his cheeks, the hard lines of his face softening. Aishlinn hoped his mood had improved.

"I'm really sorry to have stopped by unannounced, William. But I've heard what a nice home you're building for your eventual retirement. I simply could not resist. I hope you'll forgive me." She put on her best sweet smile, the one that usually worked best on her father and Duncan. She hoped it would have the same success with Wee William.

He let out a long breath and finally smiled. "Nay, lass. 'Tis quite all right."

"I like the tall ceilings," she offered.

He continued to smile. "Aye, some might take it as a bit ostentatious, but I find me head and low ceilings do no' necessarily get along well."

Aishlinn giggled and patted his hand. "I suppose not," she said as she looked around the room. It was indeed a fine cottage. The floors and walls were made of stone. It boasted a very large fireplace that stood to her immediate left. She assumed it was the mirror image of her own home, the one that Wee William had helped Duncan to build. But she could see from the outside that it was in fact much bigger.

"Could you give me a tour?"

"Aye, I could, if yer sure ye be up to it."

"I am! Really, just a twinge." She would feel no guilt for lying. She was on a mission.

He nodded his head and stood. "Well, ye be in the kitchen and eatin' area right now," he said as he spread his arm out with a flourish.

"Thank you for pointing that out," Aishlinn teased as she walked toward a doorway to her right. "What is in here?" she said, as she walked through it, not waiting for his answer. She was in a small hallway with two doors leading off of it.

She opened one of the doors and stepped inside. There was a small fireplace on the wall that separated the rooms.

"How very nice!" she exclaimed. "You have a study!" She knew very well it was a bedroom, but decided it best to play along for now.

Wee William stood in the hallway, looking rather relieved. "Aye," he said quietly. "A study."

Aishlinn smiled brightly. "Aye, when you are aulder, you'll appreciate a room like this. One filled with books and mementos of your journeys." She slipped back into the hallway and on to the next room.

"My, my, my William! Ye've thought of everything! I would assume this is to be a spare room, for when auld friends visit?"

He nodded his head and ran his tongue around his cheek. "Aye, that is what it is lass."

Aishlinn left that room, closing the door behind her and went back into the kitchen with Wee William following slowly behind her. "'Tis a very nice house William!" She opened the door just off the kitchen.

"Oh! How very nice! Every man should have a large, comfortable bedchamber like this," she said as she entered and stood at the foot of the bed. It sat along the wall, flanked on either side by small tables. On the opposite wall was a large fireplace and placed in front of that were two chairs.

She looked back at the bed. It was indeed quite large, larger than one man would need all to himself. But then again, Wee William was not of average height or build. She supposed he did need a bed of this size.

He was standing in the doorway watching her very closely. He'd grown uncomfortable as she went from room to room. He wasn't certain yet if she had an ulterior motive by coming here. He was in no mood for lectures.

Aishlinn let out a happy sigh. "'Tis a grand home, Wee William. I am sure, when the time comes for you to hang up your sword, you'll be quite happy here."

He remained quiet, waiting for her to begin nagging him like everyone else had been doing of late.

"I do thank you for the tour," she said as she slipped by him and went back into the kitchen.

She looked around the room once again. "Yes, I think you'll be quite happy here. It isn't far from Duncan and me. I do hope our children won't be a bother to you. I mean, later on, when you're ready to retire. You'll be a bachelor after all. I hear that older men like their quiet and solitude. I think you'll have that here, William, yes I do. All this room, the wide-open spaces, the solitude. Do you suspect you might write a book about your life? Your travels, battles, journeys?"

Wee William blinked, cocked his head to one side, and looked very confused. "Lass, what are ye tryin' to get at?"

Aishlinn feigned ignorance. "When you retire. Ye'll be all alone in this great big home. What do you plan to do with all your free time? I would suspect you'd write a book about your life."

He shook his head. "No one would want to read a story about me life, lass." Mayhap pregnancy had addled her mind.

"Oh, I think people would be interested in your story Wee William," she told him softly. "You have much to write about. Battles you fought and won, stories of brawls and fights over lasses, your childhood, your life here."

He listened intently, waiting for the lecture to begin. He could sense she was building up to something and he had a good idea what it was. He remained quiet, deciding to let her broach the subject she was pretending not to want to talk about.

She took a deep breath, drew her shawl around her shoulders and headed for the doorway. "If you did write your story, William, would there be any regrets?"

His brow creased, unsure of what she meant. "Regrets?"

She stood in the doorway, ready to leave. "Aye, regrets. Battles you did not fight, countries you did not visit."

He remained silent.

"Mayhap, mayhap not, I suppose. It would be good to live a long life with no regrets. I have only one, and that is that I was not raised here with my father. But I am very glad to be here, now." She sounded a bit melancholy. "Aye, I suppose everything happens at the right time and for the right reason. Still, I wonder, William. At the end of your life, will you have any regrets?"

He refused to answer her question. Instead, he leaned against the cold mantle of the fireplace and listened. He knew she would eventually get around to speaking of Nora.

"We all know you've sworn there isn't a woman in all the world worth shaving your beard for. But still, I wonder, if at the end of your long, full life of bachelorhood, will you regret not having someone to share it with? Will you regret not professing your love to someone, at least once? Will you regret filling up this big home with books and things, instead of love, children, and laughter?"

Wee William's eyes were focused on the floor. He hadn't given a thought to regrets, until now.

"'Tis a pity, really. You have such a big heart, William. You have so much to offer someone." She took a deep breath and let it out slowly. "Did you know that Angus has called all the men together? They're to meet in the grand gathering room within the hour. He's going to pick a husband for Nora today."

He bolted upright, tried to speak, but fear lodged the words in his throat.

"That really is too bad that he's going to pick someone for her. I know for a fact, that her heart belongs to someone. Someone who has a very special place in my own heart. Whenever she speaks his name, her eyes light up and she smiles. She doesn't realize it though, and that is such a pity. But I suppose she'll make whomever Angus picks, a very good wife. She'll have his bairns, build a life with him, and grow auld with him. But she'll never love him, quite the way she loves you, and that *is* such a pity."

She turned around, took a small step out of the cottage. Over her shoulder, she spoke again. "I hope William, that you do not regret this day. You may return the basket later."

She left him alone then, to think. She hurried along the pathway that led to the castle. Along the way, she prayed that Wee William would come to his senses and that she had somehow gotten through to him. If her words did not work, there was always plan B. But that involved yards and yards of rope, a sleeping potion, and bribing the priest. She prayed it wouldn't come to that.

THE GRAND GATHERING ROOM WAS FILLED TO STANDING ROOM ONLY with single men of all ages gathered at Angus' order. Rowan, Black Richard, Daniel, and David stood together at the front of the room, each craning their necks in hopes that Wee William would soon appear.

Angus sat in a tall chair in the center of the dais, with his wife, Isobel to his left and Nora to his right. His daughters, Aishlinn and Bree, sat directly behind Nora, offering their moral support to the dispirited looking lass. Duncan was pacing in front of him, waiting anxiously for the signal that the man of the hour was approaching.

The clan chief was enjoying himself immensely. He had twenty groats wagered in favor of Wee William appearing and another ten that said he'd fight any man in the room who so much as cast an improper glance toward Nora.

The men had all been informed, much to their relief, that a husband wouldn't actually be chosen for Nora this day. It was all a ruse to get Wee William to finally admit he had feelings for Nora. And if that didn't work, there was always the plan B that Duncan and Rowan had devised. Their money was riding on the implementation of plan B.

Rowan had lost all faith in his friend, convinced he was that Wee William was far too afraid to voluntarily express his desire to marry Nora. He actually looked forward to hogtying the fool and dragging him to the alter. Frankly, Duncan and Black Richard hoped the man wouldn't show for the mere fact that they, too, wanted to see how many ropes it would take to bind Wee William.

The only one in the room not aware of the ruse was Nora. She looked utterly deflated as she sat in her dark green gown, her hair plaited into a long braid. Aishlinn had been so certain that *whoever he was,* as she'd come to referring to the mystery man, who had instilled so much fear into the other men, would be forced to declare for her once he learned that Angus was going to pick someone this day. They'd been in the gathering room for more than half an hour and not one man had yet to step forward.

Elise and John sat at one of the long tables with a group of other children. Whereas Elise was happily chatting away, excited that Nora would soon be receiving a good husband, John was not as thrilled. He was doing his best to adjust to his new life, but Nora felt there was still a part of his heart that longed to return to England.

Nora quietly watched her brother and sister as she waited for this day to finally be done with. Angus had told her that she could turn down any man he might choose for her. While that brought her a good sense of relief, she still felt it necessary to move forward with her decision. If *whoever he is*, did not have the courage to claim her, then so be it.

She had not slept well last night. Her thoughts were consumed with wondering who the mystery man might be and what would happen this day.

Secretly, she held on to the hope that it was Wee William. Her feelings for him had not waned, even though she had not seen him in days. She missed the meals they had taken together when the children were sick. She missed their quiet talks. She missed him.

Whenever he was near, she felt safe and protected. She felt a sense of peace and calmness come over her, but oddly enough, she also felt excited and breathless. Her feelings were a jumbled mess of nonsensical emotions that she could not understand.

Nora's aching heart told her that the mystery man could not be Wee William. He was the bravest, strongest, and most kind man that she had ever known. She was quite confident that had he held any feelings for her he would have voiced them long ago. How could a man as brave and kind as he put her through such an ordeal as this?

Nay, she told herself. Wee William will not be shaving his beard for me.

ANGUS BEGAN TO GROW WORRIED. HE HAD TOO MUCH MONEY riding on this afternoon. Granted, the amount he'd wagered would not break the coffers, but it was the principal of matter. And he hated being wrong.

He cast an anxious look at Duncan who simply shook his head and shrugged his shoulders.

Where in the hell was the fool?

Angus looked at the room full of men and women. His people stood shoulder to shoulder before him and many had taken positions on the walkways on the second and third floors in hopes of witnessing what may be one of the most momentous occasions to take place in this great hall. The longer they waited, the more he, too, began to look forward to hunting the fool down, binding him head to toe in rope, and dragging him to the kirk.

Nora's beautiful face seemed to grow more sorrowful as the long moments passed by. Aishlinn had moved her chair to sit beside her and was now holding her hand.

Angus leaned in to speak with his wife. "Where is the fool?" he asked her impatiently.

Isobel offered him a warm, comforting smile as she patted his hand. "He'll be here," she told him.

Angus sighed heavily. "Always the romantic, ye are," he said.

Her smile brightened. "Do ye no' remember how long it took *ye* to admit yer feelings for me?"

He cleared his throat and sat upright. "'Twasn't *that* long, wife."

Isobel giggled at her husband's embarrassed expression. "'Twas far too long for *my* liking. Ye Highlanders can be a stubborn lot," she said as she turned back to look at the crowd. "But glad I was when ye finally came around."

With the end of his patience reached, he decided to proceed. Mayhap if the lass would turn away all those that he might choose for her, word would reach the obstinate fool and he'd realize what the rest of them knew without question: Nora's heart belonged to Wee William.

Angus cleared his throat again and stood, gaining the attention of most in the room. "We will begin with the proceedings!" His deep voice carried through the room and everyone settled into quiet anticipation.

He cast another wary look at Duncan and received the same response he'd received for more than an hour.

"Black Richard, son of Galen of Lochbraene," Angus called out. "Step forward."

Black Richard smiled and stepped forward to stand in front of Angus. Bending to one knee and bowing his head, he said, "M'laird."

"Black Richard," Angus began. "I present to you, Nora Crawford."

Black Richard stood, nodded his head and stepped toward Nora and smiled. "Lass, how be ye this fine spring day?" He held out his hand.

Nora glanced at Aishlinn, unsure of what she was supposed to do at this point. Aishlinn giggled and whispered in her ear. "Just offer yer hand to him, lass. Then tell Angus if ye accept him."

Nora swallowed hard, and slowly extended her trembling hand to Black Richard. She knew him to be a kind and honorable man. He would make any woman a fine husband. However, when Black Richard took her hand, she did not feel the same rush of excitement that came with Wee William's touch.

I cannot do this! She thought to herself. Her heart screamed for her to grab John and Elise, race from the room, and head back to England. She did not want to accept this man, yet she did not want to hurt his feelings either. Suddenly, she felt decidedly stupid for even thinking it was a good idea for Angus to find her a husband!

Black Richard smiled, gave her a devilish wink, and whispered, "Nay, lass, I be no' the one ye seek."

Nora wasn't sure if she should be relieved or mortified. Had he read her mind? He looked neither wounded nor happy, yet there was a twinkle in his eye, as if he held some secret.

Black Richard nodded his head and stepped away.

"Daniel, son of Floyd, step forward," Angus called the next victim to the front of the room.

Daniel appeared, knelt as Black Richard had, before being introduced to Nora. She thought the introductions unnecessary and bordered on the ridiculous. She'd known these men for weeks, thought of them as friends.

Daniel took her hand and repeated the exact words that Black Richard had said. "Nay lass, I be no' the one ye seek."

Nora stared at him, as confused as she'd ever been in her life.

"Rowan Graham," Angus called out. "Son of Andrew, step forward."

Nora's stomach tightened at the sound of Rowan's name being called. She prayed he wasn't the one. He was beyond handsome and she didn't think she could be married to a man quite as beautiful as him. He made her extremely nervous, especially when he smiled at her.

His teeth were perfect, his hair perfect, not a scar anywhere to be seen on his face. His lips were perfectly full, and she was certain he had long ago perfected the art of kissing and seduction. She doubted she would survive a full hour being his wife, for she'd swoon herself to death. Kind? Yes, he was. Honorable? There was no doubt. Yet, there was something unnerving about him. Mayhap it was his perfection.

He was holding her hand, and she felt the sudden need to find the necessary and relieve her bladder. *Please, good Lord, do not let it be him!*

Those deep brown eyes of his captivated her and when he winked, she felt her stomach tighten further. *Nay, I'd not survive the wedding!*

Lost as she was in her silent prayers and those dark brown eyes of Rowan Graham, she had not heard the murmur that had broken out amongst the throng of people crowded in the room. She was too busy trying to keep her terrified and uneasy stomach from upheaving itself all over the Greek God before her.

She thought she heard someone say Rowan's name, but for the life of her she could not pull her eyes away from his.

"Do ye fancy that hand of yers?"

Rowan cast a devilish smile at Nora, gave her a quick wink, and turned his head to face the voice. "Aye, I do."

"Then kindly remove it from her person."

Nora blinked, finally able to tear her eyes away from Rowan.

Nora bolted to her feet, knocking her chair over in the process. Angus stood, just as surprised, for he had given up all hope. Rowan let loose Nora's hand, stood slowly and turned to look at Wee William.

"Ye shaved yer beard!" Apparently, Angus and Rowan were just as stunned as Nora, for the two of them spoke in unison. That was her same thought. However, her words were temporarily lodged in her throat like a bundle of walnuts.

Her first thought was how her heart stung with a trace of regret, for now she'd never learn if his beard would tickle if he ever took the chance to kiss her.

Her second thoughts bordered on the sinful. How could a man look so completely menacing and magnificent at the same time? Nora had never contemplated what he might look like without all that red-brown hair covering his face and chest. She had looked upon his beard as a permanent part of him, much like his legs and arms. What a glorious surprise had lain hidden all this time!

She took a hard, long look at him, starting at the top of his head. He had cut his hair to just past his shoulders and it was still damp from washing it. He wore two braids on the left side of his face, tied at the end with little bits of leather.

His face was startlingly handsome and it did in fact take her breath away. Long, rich, soft looking eyelashes surrounded his warm, bright hazel eyes. His nose, broken probably more times than he could remember, seemed far less bulbous without the bushy mustache and beard. He had very nice cheekbones and she could see the few places he had nicked himself while shaving his beard. Gloriously full lips that, at the moment, were pursed together in the most serious of expressions.

He was not nearly as heavy looking as she had thought him to be. A white linen tunic was stretched across his fine, massive chest, the arms of which looked as though they had been painted onto his skin! Bulging muscles. Massive muscles.

The tunic showed his narrow hips, and was tucked into a kilt made of MacDougall plaid that hit in the middle of his knees. Rich looking leather boots were stretched around calves that had to have been chiseled from stone.

God-almighty! Had Aishlinn not been standing next to her, holding her up, she would have immediately swooned.

Aye, Rowan Graham was a beautiful man. But Wee William was spectacular.

"I'd like a word with Nora. Alone," Wee William said in a tone that bordered on murderous. Nora thought it went perfectly with the rage-filled stare he was giving Rowan.

"Ye would, would ye?" Rowan asked, crossing his arms over his chest, feet planted apart. "And what if the lass does not wish to speak with ye?"

Wee William pinned Rowan in place with a glare that might have made any other man run screaming like a wee lass. Rowan simply smiled in return.

Somehow Nora had managed to dislodge the walnuts in her throat. "I'll speak with him!" she blurted out.

Wee William growled, grabbed her hand, and stomped away from the dais, out of the gathering room and into a small room the women sometimes used for sewing. He pulled Nora inside and slammed the door behind them.

"Did Rowan Graham ask fer yer hand?" He was pacing back and forth as much as the small room would allow.

"Nay," Nora squeaked. She did not bother to tell Wee William that she would have turned Rowan down had he made such an offer.

Wee William stopped in the center of the room and looked at her. She had her back pressed firmly against the wall and her face held a frightened expression. It brought back the memory of the night back in England, when she had been doing everything she could to keep from joining him in the cellar. A flood of something warm, comforting, and peaceful instantly replaced the rage he had been feeling only a moment before.

They stood looking at one another for a few moments before he finally spoke again.

"I had a speech all planned out in me head. Practiced it for the past hour. And now that I'm here, I find I canna remember a word of it."

Nora raised her eyebrow. "A speech? For me?" She felt a tickle of something in the pit of her stomach.

"Aye," he said, nodding his head and resting his hands on his hips. "I've lots I be wantin' to say to ye."

Nora cleared her throat and tried to appear more in charge of her feelings than she actually was. "Such as?"

He took a deep breath in through his nostrils and let it out very slowly. He was trying to remember the words he wanted to say to her, but he was lost again, in those pale blue eyes of hers.

"William, is there something you wish to say to me?" She hadn't moved, was unable to relax her shoulders, unable to take a step toward him. What she really wanted to ask him was if he had shaved his beard for her, or was there, by some cruel injustice, another woman.

"Aye, lass. There is much I want to say."

"Has it something to do with whom you have shaved your beard for?"

He chuckled slightly and ran his hand across his bare face. "Aye, it does."

Nora felt weak in the knees. Her hands trembled. She decided then to throw all caution aside. "Who is it that has led you to do such a thing?" *If he says a name other than mine, I shall die on this very spot. But not before I scratch her eyes out!* She had no idea where such a thought came from! She had never in her life raised her hand to another human being.

For a brief moment, he thought of toying with her, letting her think it was another woman who had captivated his heart and soul. But she had suffered enough the past fortnight, what with his stubbornness and pigheaded ways. Besides, he was not certain yet how she would respond to the question he was finding more and more difficult to ask.

"Nora," he began. His voice was soft and low, nearly a whisper. "I've no' much to offer a woman. I've no skills or trade with which to buy a woman all those things that they often want, such as silk dresses, and fancy headdresses, and sparkly baubles. I am a warrior. I be gone away more often than I be home. I am by no stretch of the imagination a saint of a man. I am often stubborn and slow to change," he took a step toward her and stopped when he saw that she was trembling.

She was a very bright girl and by now, he assumed, she had figured out it was she for whom he shaved his beard. Mayhap she trembled with dread at the thought of him asking for her hand.

He was about to quit the room when he heard Aishlinn's voice in the back of his mind. *Regrets*. Earlier, he had convinced himself that he would die if Nora turned him away. Now, as he stood here in the tiny room, just inches away from her, he knew deep in his heart, that he would die if he didn't at the very least, tell her how he felt about her.

He took a steadying breath and went on. "Nora, I've no' much to offer a woman."

"You said that," she murmured quietly.

He resisted the urge to growl. "Nora, from the first moment I laid me eyes on ye, I've been a lost man. Ye are in me every wakin' thought and ye invade me dreams. Ye are by far, the most beautiful woman I've ever kent, and no' just on the outside! Ye've a grace, a beauty that comes from within. Ye make me want to be a better man, but I'm having a hard time doin' that because ye have me innards all jumbled up and knotted and I dunnae whether I'm comin' or goin'. I have never felt this way about a woman, ever in me life." He took another breath and fought back the urge to wrap his arms around her and kiss her soundly. "I could no' live another day in this life without tellin' ye that."

Her legs were going to give out she just knew it. He had just spoken the words she had not, until that moment, realized she wanted to hear and now, she could not move, could not speak. She felt like a complete and utter idiot. No man had ever said such sweet, beautiful things to her before and she had no clear idea how she should respond. So she stood there, with her back against the door, clinging to the handle for dear life.

He took a step toward her and reached out his hand as if he wanted to quit the room.

Panic welled up inside her and she refused to let him pass. "That's it?"

He blinked as if to say "what more do ye want". "Aye," he swallowed hard, and he was now very unsure what he should do next.

Nora's eyes widened and he caught a flicker of anger in them. "You drag me in here, say the most beautiful words that no man has ever uttered to me before, and you want to leave?"

He looked positively dumbfounded and lost.

"William, you cannot say such things to a woman and then just walk away!"

He crooked an eyebrow upward. "What would ye have me do now?"

Nora rolled her eyes, ready to give him a good chastisement. "What would *I* have ye do?" she stuttered and fought to find the appropriate words.

Aishlinn was right. Men were stupid beasts. Aye, they were wonderful, kind, sweet, funny, but stupid nonetheless. They could come up with the most amazing plans for buildings, weapons, battle, and inventions. But when it came to the ways of the heart and women? They were as intelligent as a battering ram and just as graceful.

For the first time in her life, Nora growled. It started deep in her belly, bubbled up and escaped her lips and she made no attempt to stop it. She would have to take the lead at this moment, or he'd walk out that door and she'd never see him again. She took a small step away from the door, letting go of the handle. She straightened her shoulders and looked him in the eye. Of course, she had to lean her head back a ways to do so and could only hope the effect was the same.

"William, if you do not kiss me this very instant, I will go back out into that gathering room and ask Rowan Graham for *his* hand in marriage!" Of course she didn't think she actually had the courage to do such a thing, but Wee William did not need to have that bit of information at the moment.

His eyes widened and he scowled down at her. "Ye would no' dare!"

"I do not make idle threats, sir!" She made idle threats with her brother and sister all the time. Such as when she threatened to rip their legs off and beat them about the head when they misbehaved. That was another piece of information William did not need to be privy to at the moment. As angry as she was she felt she could have done that to him and would enjoy it.

They glowered and growled at one another. William's reserve was the first to falter. She looked breathtakingly beautiful with that murderous gleam in her eye and he could no longer resist his urges.

He rushed forward, wrapped his arms around her waist, and pulled her into his chest. He claimed her mouth with his. It wasn't the sweet and tender first kiss he had imagined giving her. Nay, he plundered her mouth, took possession of it, kissed her as if it would be his last act on God's earth.

Nora melted. She could not breathe, could not resist, and her muscles felt as strong as bread dough. When he thrust his tongue into her mouth, she felt as though a bolt of lightning had just pierced her stomach. Her toes and fingers tingled.

And praise be to God, the roof of her mouth tickled!

16

When Wee William and Nora finally returned to the grand gathering room, Nora's lips were swollen from his kisses. Her eyes were red from crying a bucketful of happy tears, and there was a smile on both their faces that would have taken a hammer and chisel to remove.

"Where be Father Michael?" Wee William shouted. Nora giggled.

"And why do we be needin' Father Michael?" Rowan asked from across the room.

Wee William gave him a victorious smile. "Because Nora and I will be gettin' married."

Aishlinn was the first to rush to Nora and hugged her tightly. "Nora, I am so happy for you!" In a matter of moments, women offering congratulations and hearty hugs surrounded Nora.

Elise wiggled her way in between them, squealing with delight. "Nora! Nora!" she called out as she tried to make her way through a sea of full skirts and arisaids.

Nora searched for her sister and smiled as she scooped her up and gave her a tight hug.

"Nora, is it true? Are you really going to marry Sir William?" Elise asked.

"Aye, sister, 'tis true!"

"Is he going to let us live with you?" her little face was filled with worry and concern.

"Aye, Elise, he is. William has built a grand home, and you and John will each have your own room!"

Elise squealed with delight over that bit of news and gave Nora another hug around her neck.

John soon appeared by Nora's side, his face unreadable. His strawberry blonde hair had not been cut in some time, and Nora thought he was beginning to look like a Highlander. She kept that thought to herself as her happiness began to wane slightly. This was the happiest day of her life, yet she worried over John and his reaction to the news.

He stood beside her, his hands thrust deep in his pockets. He shifted from one foot to the other as he stared at the floor.

"John, is there something you wish to say?" Nora asked.

He finally looked up at her. "Are you truly happy Nora?"

"Aye, I am, John. Truly happy."

He shifted on his feet again, looking very uncertain. "Do you love him?"

"Aye, I do."

John nodded his head. "Then I am happy for you."

Nora wrapped her free arm around his shoulders and pulled him in to her bosom. "Thank you John! You'll be glad to know that William has built a grand home for us."

"And we get our own bedchambers, John!" Elise said excitedly.

John remained quiet and wriggled out from Nora's hug. "That will be nice." He offered his first smile in a very long time to his sister before quietly walking away.

The women enclosed around her again, giggling, chattering away, and offering more hugs. Wee William was swept away by a sea of men, all slapping his back and taunting him about his freshly shaved face. He let the good-natured needling go unpunished. He was too damned happy to care what the rest of the world thought about his face. The woman of his dreams had not turned down his proposal.

"So when is the big day?" a woman called out from the crowd.

"As soon as we find Father Michael," Wee William called back to her.

The group of women surrounding Nora all stopped their happy chattering, turned and gave him a murderous glare.

"Ye mean *now?*" Isobel asked, aghast at the notion.

Wee William looked confused. "Aye, now."

"Ye will do no such thing!" Isobel stormed over to him. "We have to get her a proper gown! There is a feast to prepare, cakes to be made! Ye canna just pretend this isn't a momentous day Wee William!"

Mary's cackling laughter could be heard throughout the room. "Isobel!" she called out as she made her way through the crowd. "Isobel, dunna worry it!"

Isobel looked confused. "Of course I will worry it! This is a very special day, Mary. I'll no' have Wee William just rush Nora to the alter without so much as a flower in her hair."

Mary cackled again. "Isobel, when word went out that Angus was going to choose a husband for Nora this day, we all knew Wee William would no' be able to stand the thought. I baked cakes this morn and have three sucklin' pigs a roastin' and two venison on the fire. I've been cookin fer this fer days!"

Isobel looked much relieved. "So all we need is a gown?"

Mary nodded her head. "Aye. There be some dried flowers in the herb room, the lass can carry those. Ye go get her dressed and let us get the room ready for the feast!"

Wee William stood dumbfounded. How had the rest of the world known his heart better than he had? And where was his bride to be?

It took only a moment to find her. Aishlinn, Bree and a handful of other women, who had apparently decided to let him live another day, now that they knew a proper wedding could be held, surrounded her.

Nora. *His* Nora. Very soon, he'd be referring to her as his wife.

She was beaming at him from across the room. Her smile warmed him clear to his toes. He wanted to give her the world, or at least as much of it as he was able. If a proper wedding meant the other women wouldn't hang him by his short hairs, it was worth waiting a few extra minutes.

Someone thrust a cup of whiskey into his hand and wished him luck. A moment later, his soon to be wife was whisked away in a sea of chattering women. His eyes followed her all the way up the stairs, happier than he could ever remember being. It would not be long now, and Nora would be his for all the rest of his days.

A moment later, John was standing in front of Wee William. The boy looked quite serious with his furrowed brow and tightly set jaw.

"Wee William," John said with his shoulders thrown back and his hands fisted at his sides. "Can I have a word with you?"

Wee William nodded his head and led John away from the crowd and into the war room. John stood with his arms across his chest, legs spread apart just as he'd seen the Highlanders do a hundred times in the past months. His deep blue eyes had turned to slits as he studied the giant before him.

"John," Wee William said as he mirrored John's stance.

"Wee William, I know that I am only two and ten and I am nowhere near as big or as strong as you." He was scowling at Wee William as he spoke in the sternest of voices. "But as God is my witness, if you ever do anything to hurt my sister, I will kill you with my bare hands."

Wee William took his threat very seriously. He had given similar speeches to each of the men who had married three of his six sisters. Wee William had meant every word he had said to those men and he knew that John meant the words he just spoke. He knew that he was not the only man to love Nora and hold her in such regard. John loved her, as a brother, and that was something that could never be undone.

"As God is me witness, John, I will die before I let any harm come to yer sister. I swear to ye, that I will never do anything to hurt her in any fashion, either by word, deed or action."

"You will treat her with nothing but respect then?" John asked.

"Aye. And I'll kill any son of a whore that would even think to cause her harm."

John nodded his head as his lips twitched ever so slightly. He believed Wee William. "I'll be watching you, William, and will hold you to your word."

"I love yer sister, John. I swear to ye this day that the marriage she and I will have will be nothing like the one she had with that bastard,

Horace Crawford. I'll never send ye or yer sister away. I'll never raise a hand to any of ye." As an afterthought, he added, "But don't take that to mean that I'll no' hold ye to high standards and will no' expect ye to act as a good lad and a kind young man. Ye'll remember yer manners at all times. And keep in mind, there are worse punishments than a beatin'!" Wee William winked at him.

Wee William could tell by the expression on the boy's face, that his curiosity was piqued, but Wee William chose not to expound upon his playful warning. He winked at John, placed a large hand on his shoulder and led him back to the celebration.

"John," Wee William said as they made their way through the crowd. "I'd like ye to stand with me this day, as my best man."

John's brow furrowed as he looked up at his soon to be brother-in-law. He wasn't sure what a best man was, but it sounded important. "What does a best man do?"

"Well, ye stand as me witness to marryin' yer sister. And ye swear an oath that if anything happens to me, ye make sure she is cared for." He patted John on the back when John cast him a look that said he planned on doing that anyway. "And, ye hold the ring."

'Twas then that Wee William's face went ashen. He began mumbling in Gaelic, crossed himself, and mumbled further.

"What is it Wee William?" John asked, growing very concerned for his future brother-in-law.

Rowan and Black Richard had taken note of Wee William's pale skin, wide eyes, and all around terrified expression. They stepped forward and asked the same question.

"I do no' have a ring!" Wee William finally blurted out in Gaelic.

Rowan and Black Richard crossed themselves before Black Richard handed a cup of whiskey to Wee William.

"This is no' good, Wee William!"

"What isn't good?" John asked, growing more concerned by the moment.

Rowan looked down at the boy. "Wee William does no' have a ring to give yer sister."

John didn't understand why that was so important. "Is that bad?"

All three men turned their eyes toward John and looked at him as though he'd just grown a tail and wings.

"Of course it be bad!" Rowan answered. "Ye have to have a ring to give yer bride. And it must be made of gold. And it must fit her finger perfectly, or 'tis bad luck!"

"Bad luck?" John thought the men were being ridiculous. "Horace never gave her a ring."

"Ye see? And how did that marriage turn out?" Black Richard asked rhetorically. He also looked rather repulsed.

"Ye willna find a Scottish woman in all the world who will marry without a proper fittin' ring!" Rowan explained.

John thought on it for a moment before a chuckle escaped his lips. "But remember, she isn't Scottish! She's English."

The three men looked aghast. "She be no' English anymore, John. No' since she stepped onto Scottish land and William claimed her." Rowan informed him.

"Aye," Black Richard said. "I never thought she acted like a Sassenach to begin with. None of ye do."

John wasn't sure what they meant by *that.* Weeks ago, he'd come to the conclusion that Scots weren't right in their own heads. While he found them all kind and generous, they had such odd ways about them. They took superstition to new heights. The men he'd grown up around did not hold much value to the superstitions like the womenfolk did. But here, things were very different.

John sighed. "Is there time to make her a ring?"

All three eyes were upon him once again.

"They'll be down any moment, John! Nay, there be no time." Rowan said. The boy was daft.

Wee William's mind had been racing, only paying half attention to the conversation going on around him. His mother would kill him if she found out he married without a proper ring. His grandmother would come back from the grave to haunt him. Knowing his grandmother, she'd bring all her family with her. He'd never find a moment's rest.

Angus stepped forward to offer his congratulations and immediately he knew something was wrong. Rowan quickly explained the situation to him. Angus crossed himself, said a prayer, and then thumped Wee William along the side of his head.

"How could ye say ye wanted to marry this day and no' have a ring to give her?"

Wee William already felt miserable and did not appreciate being chastised like a child. "I was no' in me right head, Angus! I be just as surprised as the rest of ye!"

"They say there isn't time to make a proper ring," John told Angus. "The women will be back any moment."

Angus threw his head back and laughed until tears formed in his eyes. "Lads," he said as his laughter began to subside. "Ye've got a bride above stairs in a room filled with me wife, me two daughters, and God only kens who else. I've learned over the years, that a woman will take as much time as she damn well chooses."

Angus had lost five groats on his bet with Thomas Gainer that Wee William would at the very least, beat someone senseless this day. "I'll wager each of ye here, that the women will no' have the bride ready fer two hours."

Wee William decided Angus had been married a very long time and had experience on his side. He refused to take the wager. Two hours? Certainly the smithy could work some magic in that time.

Runners were quickly dispatched to go above stairs with a bit of string to have Nora's finger measured. Rowan found the smithy, who, thankfully, was not too far into his cups to fashion a wedding ring on such short notice.

Even on this most special day, Wee William had to barter with the smithy on the price for the ring. When all was said and done, the ring was going to not only cost Wee William a small fortune, but he was forced to promise he would not kill the smithy when he danced with Nora at the wedding feast.

Engaged less than a half an hour and he'd had one young boy threaten to take his life if he hurt his sister, been thumped in the head by Angus, and had to bargain with the devil to get his bride a ring. Wee William slammed back a tankard of ale and prayed that the marriage itself would be far simpler than anything he experienced thus far this day.

NORA TOOK HIS BREATH AWAY.

Beautiful. Stunning. Brilliant.

It was three hours before she walked down the aisle of the small kirk, her hand resting on Angus' arm. Wee William could not take his eyes away from her.

She looked regal in the silver gossamer gown that twinkled in the waning afternoon light. The dress trailed behind her a good three feet as twinkling bits of silver thread glistened from the ends of the long, draping sleeves, the neckline and the hem.

Shimmering pearls and silver beads were threaded through her long dark hair as it cascaded down her back in waves. A whisper thin veil was attached to her hair and fell away as she walked along the aisle. An icy blue and silver belt hung around her tiny waist. Draped across her chest was the blue, yellow and green MacDougall plaid, held together with a beautiful brooch.

Wee William suddenly wished he had not agreed to a wedding feast. He wanted nothing more at this moment than to say his "I do's" and take her back to their cottage and get Nora out of her dress as quickly as possible. He did not think he could survive the next few hours.

Angus and Nora finally made their way to the front of the kirk. Aishlinn and Elise stood beside her, while John and Rowan stood beside Wee William.

If anyone were to ask him later, exactly what vows he spoke that day, Wee William would have been hard pressed to tell them. He was too enraptured by how beautiful Nora looked to pay much attention to anything else.

When it was finally time to place the tiny gold band on her finger, his hands were shaking so much that he nearly dropped the ring on the floor.

As he slipped the tiny gold band first onto her thumb, then her index finger, then her middle finger, he murmured the words, "*In ainm an althair, mac, agus an taibhse noafa,*" In the name of the father, the son, the holy ghost. On his amen, he placed the ring on the third finger of her left hand.

Father Michael placed a hand on each of their heads and blessed them.

"Ye may now kiss yer bride, William of Dunshire," Father Michael said with a smile.

Wee William placed a hand on Nora's waist and drew her into his chest. He kissed her, a bit more passionately than was probably proper for a church, but he cared not. She was now, finally his.

The crowd inside and outside the church erupted into a loud cheer as they followed Wee William and Nora back to the grand gathering room for the wedding feast.

THE WEDDING FEAST LASTED WELL INTO THE NIGHT. NORA AND Wee William, along with the hundreds of guests, had eaten, drunk, and danced to their hearts content. One toast after another was made wishing them both a long happy life filled with many children.

John's mood had lightened considerably and even he danced a time or two with each of his sisters and a few of the younger lasses. It was a very happy day in deed.

All through the evening, Wee William watched his wife closely. She looked radiant and quite happy. Her cheeks were flushed from all the dancing and never had he seen her smile so much as he did this night. He made a solemn oath that he would spend every day of his life making sure that smile never left her sweet and bonny face.

The hour grew late and the party began to die down. Elise and John would spend the next day or two at the castle while Wee William and his wife enjoyed their wedding night in the home he had built for them.

Nora had been speaking with Aishlinn, Isobel, and Mary when Wee William called for her from across the room. "Wife!"

Nora turned and smiled at him as she bit her bottom lip. She caught the glimmer of playfulness in his eyes as he stood with his hands resting on his hips. As she started to run to him, Isobel held her back.

"Nay lass! Ye don' go a runnin' every time he bellers!" she giggled. "He'll get used to it and expect it from ye all the time! Make *him* wait. He'll come to ye, ye'll see."

The women broke into a fit of giggles before turning serious expressions toward Wee William. The smile left his face. "What be ye tellin' me bride there lassies?" he asked as he crossed the room toward his wife.

The women broke into another round of giggles. "See?" Aishlinn told Nora. "Only let him think he's the master of his castle. Ye'll ken the truth!"

Wee William approached, crossed his arms over his chest and stared at the women. "What are ye tellin' me wife?"

Isobel cleared her throat and tried to look serious. "Nothin' much, Wee William. Just some marital advice."

"What kind?" he asked, raising an eyebrow.

Mary slapped Wee William on his arm. "Now don' ye go fashin' yerself over it, Wee William. We were just telling her to that she must always listen to ye and do as ye tell her."

The women cast knowing glances at one another before breaking into more laughter.

Wee William seriously doubted that these women were telling his wife any such thing but he decided to play along.

"Well then," he said as he scooped Nora up into his arms. She squealed, much to his delight. "If that be the case, we'll be leavin' now!" He raised his eyebrows and cast a wink toward the group of giggling women.

From across the room, Rowan and Black Richard, well into their cups shouted at Wee William. "Do ye ken what yer to do now, Wee William?" "Don't be frightened Wee William! I'm sure yer wife will be gentle with ye!"

Wee William chose to ignore them as he carried his wife out of the gathering room and out of the castle.

Nora's smile warmed his heart. "What are we doing, now William?" she asked.

"We're goin' home, lass," he said as he pressed a kiss to her forehead. "I believe it be time to make the marriage official."

Nora's smile quickly faded. She could only guess, from the devilish look in his eye, that he meant one thing and one thing only: it was time to consummate the marriage. A wave a fear washed over her and she was glad they'd stepped into the black of night, for then, he could not see the utter fear she knew her eyes must hold.

How he found his way from the castle to their cottage in the dark she had no idea. She had hoped he would get lost somewhere along the way, thereby delaying what she knew to be inevitable. But find it, he did.

Their home was not far from the castle. The soft glow of candle light burned from within and the closer they got the more her heart filled with dread and her limbs trembled.

"Yer cold," Wee William said as he felt her shiver in his arms. "Do no' worry, we'll have ye inside where it be warm, soon enough."

Moments later, he pushed open the door to their home, wondering who had hung it because he hadn't done that before he left. It mattered not at the moment as he carried his bride across the threshold and into the light. "I see the womenfolk were here," he said as he looked about the room. Candles were lit along the mantle of the fireplace. Rugs had been placed on the floor, dried lavender, lilac, and heather hung from the rafters. At the moment, he only cared about one room -- their bedchamber.

He crossed the kitchen and opened the door that led into their bedchamber. Thankfully, the womenfolk had adorned the bed with clean sheets, pillows, and warm furs. A low fire crackled in the fireplace, more rugs had been spread across the floor, and more dried flowers were placed about the room.

He turned his attentions toward his wife. She looked positively terrified. "Lass, ye look as though yer scared to death!"

Nora swallowed and tried to pretend she was anything but terrified.

Wee William finally set her on her feet and wrapped his arms around her. "Lass, ye tremble. Are ye cold?"

She shook her head as it rested against his chest. She couldn't answer him.

"Nora, are ye frightened?"

Frightened. Mortified. Nauseous. Scared out of her wits. She remained mute. How on earth could she explain things to him?

Wee William ran a soothing hand up and down her back. He knew a terrified lass when he saw one. "Lass," he said as he pulled her away and lifted her chin with his thumb and forefinger. She kept her gaze averted as she fought back tears.

"If we want our marriage to be a good one, then we must always be honest with one another." He pressed a kiss to her forehead. "Now, ye must tell me what yer thinkin'."

Nora swallowed hard again. She could only hope he was right. She did want their marriage to be successful. She knew a big part of it would be what would be taking place in their marital bed. The last thing she wanted was to upset him or make him regret he married her.

Wee William waited patiently for several long moments. He could see that she was fighting some inner battle and his heart began to feel quite heavy.

"Lass, ye *can* talk to me. I be yer husband after all. We can talk to each other about anything. Now please, tell me what has ye so frightened."

She took a deep breath. She could not put it off any further. "What if," she began, taking another deep breath, "what if I cannot please you in *there*?" she said as she motioned toward the bed.

He wanted to laugh, but resisted that urge. "Lass, the only way ye'll ever *not* please me is if yer no' honest with me. Ye've been pleasin' me since ye threatened to marry Rowan if I did no' kiss ye!"

She finally gained enough courage to look up at him. Lord above, the man was handsome! She looked into his eyes and saw nothing but genuine concern and adoration and that made her feel all the worse. She wanted to be a good wife, in every sense of the word. "But, William," her voice was so quiet he could barely hear her. "I was never able to please Horace in our marital bed, and I worry I've not improved."

It was all he could do to contain himself at the mention of her former husband's name. He never wanted his name spoken in his home, least of all the bedchamber he was going to share with Nora.

His jaw tightened, he counted to ten in four languages before he finally spoke.

"Nora, do ye see that bed there?" he asked, nodding in the direction of the bed. Nora glanced at it before turning to bury her face in his chest again.

"How many people do ye think it holds, lass?"

She looked up at him, the fear returned to her face and she began to tremble as she thought back to the time Horace wanted her to not only share the bed with him, but one of his friends as well. Certainly not all men wanted their wives to do such things! She felt the room begin to spin.

"Lass, that bed has only room for two. Ye and me and no one else."

Her shoulders relaxed and she let out the breath she had been holding and thanked the good Lord above.

"I will no' have ye worryin' over that man. He is no' here, and I am no' him." Wee William could only imagine what hell Horace had put Nora through. He realized it would take some time for her to get over that and be able to trust him.

"I'll no' do anythin' that ye do no' want me to do. We'll take as much time as ye need. We can talk as much as ye need to, Nora." He pressed his lips to her cheek and brushed a tear away with his thumb. "Ye can ask me any question, ye can tell me anything ye wish to. I be yer husband, Nora, and I want nothing more than to make ye happy. Do ye believe me?"

She looked up into his eyes again. There was no anger, no frustration, only adoration and kindness in those hazel eyes of his. How was he able to calm her fears so easily?

Nora cleared her throat, nodded her head and placed her hands on his. "I can ask any question that I want?"

Wee William smiled and nodded his head. "Aye, lass, anything ye want."

She cleared her throat again and took a deep breath. "I do have a few questions," she said. "But I need you to promise you will not laugh at me."

His smile widened. "Nay, lass, I'll no laugh at ye."

"And ye won't get angry with me?" She needed his reassurance.

"On me honor, I'll no' get mad at ye."

She studied him for a moment, praying that he could keep his word.

"Mayhap we should sit down?"

WEE WILLIAM COULD NOT REMEMBER EVER BEING SO ANGRY. IT took every bit of willpower he had not to saddle his horse and head for England. He was not angry with his wife. He was furious with the bastard who had done unthinkable things to her.

If Horace Crawford was not dead, he would kill him. And if he were dead, Wee William would dig up what was left of his body and hack it into pieces before setting it on fire.

They had talked for more than an hour, with Nora blushing with each question and blushing further with each of Wee William's answers. By the time they were done, his face had gone from pale, to red, to purple. It took all that he had to keep his temper in check.

"William?" Nora asked from the edge of the bed. "Are you angry with me?"

"Nay, lass," he said as he draped an arm across her shoulder. "I be no' angry with ye. Ye did no' know the way of it, so how could I be angry with ye?"

Well, she thought to herself, there were plenty of times during her marriage to Horace that he took his anger out on her, though she had nothing to do with whatever it was that was angering him. She didn't think she should share that with Wee William. He looked upset enough as it was. She was growing worried that he might have an apoplexy, for his face was a very deep shade of purple and he kept flexing his jaw back and forth. She wasn't that big of a fool.

"William, did you not say we must be honest with each other if we're to have a good marriage?"

He could not look at her just yet. "Yes, I did."

"So is it only me that has to be honest, or does that include you as well?"

He breathed in through his nose and out through his mouth. She was going to turn his own words on him. "Nay, it goes for both of us."

"Then will you tell me what you're thinking?"

He stood up and walked to the fireplace and added another log to it. He couldn't very well tell her everything he was thinking and feeling at the moment. "I am thinking that I wish I had cut the bastard's throat myself." It wasn't a complete lie.

"William?" she asked in a low voice that trembled. "Did Horace ruin me?" That was in fact her worst fear, now that she had learned that the things Horace had done were wrong.

He spun around to look at her. She was playing with the ends of her belt, her eyes cast to the floor. "If you've changed yer mind, and want an annulment, I'll understand, William."

He went to her then, bent to one knee and took her face in his hands. "Nay, lass, ye be no' ruined and I do no' want an annulment." Nay, what he wanted was to hold her in his arms the rest of the night and reassure her that she was still, in his eyes, the most perfect and beautiful woman he had or would ever know.

"Are you certain?" she asked as she looked at him with tears welling in her eyes. "I would not hold it against you."

He did the thing he had been aching to do for weeks. He lifted her chin and pressed his lips to hers. It was a tender and gentle kiss that made his heart swell with joy when he felt her return it. "Lass," Wee William said softly. "I meant what I said earlier today. I want to spend the rest of me life with ye, and no other. Ye have claimed me heart, me verra soul. I will never want another woman as I want ye."

Nora smiled, happy and relieved for she couldn't see herself with anyone but this gentle giant bent on one knee before her.

"May I ask another question?"

He did not know if his heart could take learning anything else that Horace had done to her. He braced himself and nodded his head. "Aye, ye may."

He saw a twinkle in her eye as she bit her lower lip. "Do you think you could kiss me, like you did in the storage room earlier this day?"

He blew a sigh of relief and pulled her into his chest. "I'll kiss ye any way ye wish."

NORA HAD NO RECOLLECTION OF REMOVING HER DRESS OR HER chemise, but somehow she had lost all items of clothing and now she lay on top of her husband, naked as the day she was born. She remembered tugging William's shirt over his head and throwing it somewhere over her shoulder. His skin felt hot against hers and the soft hair of his chest tickled her skin.

He caressed her with large, warm hands, and she felt both hot and cold at the same time. Every inch of her tingled with excitement and the roof of her mouth tickled again. She did not want his kisses to end. He could kiss her for the next hundred years or so and she'd not grow weary of it.

He was exploring her neck with his lips and tongue as he continued to caress her back. Her stomach fluttered and felt warm. Nay, she had never felt this way before.

"William?" she asked breathlessly.

"Hmm?" he murmured against her neck.

"Your sword," she said.

He was not paying much attention, lost he was in the softness of her skin. "What?" he asked as he nibbled on the other side of her neck.

"Your sword, William. It is poking me in the leg. Could you remove it?"

He quit kissing her and his hands stopped. The bed began to shake and it took a moment for her to realize it was shaking because her husband was trying to hold his laughter in.

"What is so funny?" she asked, wishing he'd go back to kissing her.

"Lass, that no' be me sword."

Was he daft? "Of course it is, I can feel it along my leg."

He could no longer contain his laughter. Nora rolled her eyes before rolling herself off of him. "You see," she began to speak but then realized she had in fact been wrong. That was definitely *not* his sword. Her faced burned with embarrassment and her eyes grew as wide as trenchers. She said the first thing that came to her mind. "It's a tree root!"

Wee William could not speak. He shook with laughter.

He could see her thoughts as they played across her face. She looked both surprised and afraid. He finally managed to speak, "Lass, it be no' *that* big!"

She looked at him as though he had lost his mind. Not that big? Was he insane? Did he really plan to put that, that, that thing where she now knew it properly went?

"Lass, ye needn't worry it," he said as his laughter began to subside. He was beginning to feel a bit guilty for laughing at her. "Certainly ye've seen one of these before."

She shook her head. "Not one that is the size of a tree root! And why is it staring at me?" She buried her face in her hands, mortified beyond imagination, and turned away from her husband. She pulled the sheet around her body. This was not going to go well, she just knew it.

Wee William propped himself up on one elbow. Though he felt guilty for laughing, he could not deny feeling a bit proud. He did not want to terrify his wife to the point of distraction. He wrapped one of the long tendrils of her hair around his finger. "Nora, it will be all right. I promise."

She thought of Horace's tiny-in-comparison male member. He hadn't even been doing it correctly and it had hurt beyond measure. How on earth would this *thing* not hurt as well and with a husband that was going to do it correctly?

Wee William touched her shoulder tenderly with his fingers. "Nora, there are all manner of things we can do, that will no' hurt. We can do those all the night long until ye are ready." He was trying to be as patient as possible with her, but his "tree root" had been waiting far too long. He knew he had to take his time with his wife but it was not going to be easy. She smelled of lavender and lilacs and woman. Her long hair was tousled and tumbling down her beautiful back. The sheet that covered her did little by way of hiding those magnificent breasts of hers. He really had to stop drooling over those, lest she think him insane.

She finally looked at him, doubt awash in her eyes. "Other things?" she dared ask the question. "Such as what?"

A devilish smile came to his lips as he pulled her down onto the bed. He caressed her cheeks with the backs of his fingers very slowly.

Her breath hitched and she closed her eyes. "How about I show ye instead?"

Nora could not think, she could only feel her husband's hands as they caressed her body so tenderly. She felt pleasure in places she did not know she possessed until this night. He'd explained it to her after the first wave of sinfully wicked, unbelievably delicious pleasure had come crashing over her, taking her breath away, making her eyes roll back in her head. She had almost pulled his hair out from his head and flew from the bed.

She apologized to her husband several times, for she hadn't meant to kick him in his eye with her knee the third time he had taken her to heights of ecstasy. But what Wee William had been doing to her, well, she simply held no control over her own extremities. 'Twas his own fault really, and he had no one to blame but himself. But still, she apologized and thanked him. Repeatedly.

By the time she had experienced the fifth wave a pleasure, she was begging him to stop. She needed to breathe and she was certain she was going to die if he didn't cease immediately. The tickling on the roof of her mouth would not cease and her tongue felt thick and swollen. Why he found that so humorous, she could not begin to fathom. There was a decidedly proud tone to his voice.

When he told her that he was going to burst if he didn't get relief of his own, she didn't, at that point, care what he was going to do with that tree root of his. As long as he allowed her to breathe in a more normal fashion and less like a wild boar that had been chased through the woods for days, she did not care.

Normal breathing would not be hers for quite some time. Especially when he began to do things the right way. Aye, at first it did hurt, but it wasn't the kind of pain Horace had inflicted upon her. It was different and lasted only a few moments and was quickly replaced by a new wave of those unique, exciting, thrumming, gratifying pleasures.

Reflexively, driven by instinct, she had squeezed those new muscles she had discovered and it was now Wee William's turn to beg her to stop. She took marvelous pleasure in hearing his heavy panting breaths, the growling in his throat, and the beads of sweat that had begun to form on his forehead.

"Nora, I'll come undone if ye do no' stop!" he hissed into her ear.

"It would serve you right," she murmured in return. "You have undone me five times now!" She wiggled and squeezed again. "It hardly seems fair and I insist you should match me undone for undone."

The low growl in his throat turned to a chuckle and he tried to explain that *that* was not possible, but then she was twisting in pleasure, digging her fingers into his shoulders and holding on for dear life. "Make that six undones!" she said moments later through ragged breaths and clenched teeth.

Never in a thousand years, would Wee William have believed it was possible to feel this way when joined with a woman. It was worth the black eye, the swollen lip, and the scratch marks he was sure she had left on his back. Just as he was beginning to wonder if it were wrong or sinful to take such pride in what he was doing to his wife, his own release arrived.

He could no longer hold back. His wife's machinations of his *tree root* as she had begun to refer to it, along with her rapid, strained breaths, the way she called out his name, over and over again, was all too much. Stars exploded in front of his eyes as warmth enveloped him clear to his toes. For a moment, he thought his soul had left his body and floated high above the earth all the while his blood rushed in his ears, and his heart was either beating too fast to feel or it had stopped altogether, he wasn't sure.

He wondered if he had lost his mind altogether.

NORA LAY WITH HER HEAD RESTING ON WEE WILLIAMS CHEST AND one leg thrown over his. They had slept through dawn breaking over the horizon, in one another's arms, clinging to each other as if they were afraid to let go.

Wee William listened to his wife's steady breathing as she lay peacefully in his arms. She had warned him the night before that she often suffered nightmares and had gone so far as to apologize to him beforehand. As near as he could tell, the nightmares had been kept at bay and he took a good deal of satisfaction in believing it was him -- and his loving of her -- that had kept the bad dreams away.

He liked how she felt curled up next to him. She slept peacefully and did not stir when he gently placed his hand on hers. With a feather light caress, he ran his thumb over her wrist, thinking how wonderful it was going to be to wake up like this every morning for the rest of his days.

Lost in his rumination he continued his gentle caress of her wrist, listening to her breathing, taking great delight in reliving the loving they had shared just hours ago. Several long moments had passed before he realized something was wrong with Nora's wrist. It felt odd. Carefully, he opened his eyes to examine it more closely.

Scars. Thick scars surrounded her wrist. He felt his stomach tighten as his mind raced for an explanation. He had been too busy last night with taking pleasure in loving her to notice any imperfections, big or small, that her body may have held. In Wee William's mind, Nora *was* perfection.

But these scars? They bothered him, tugged at his soul. He knew from experience that the scars had been made by a rope tied too tightly or from struggling to be free of it. He knew without a doubt who the sorry excuse for a human being was that had bound the rope. Horace.

Wee William's heart bled with regret, anger, fury and sorrow. Suddenly he felt guilty that he hadn't been there for Nora. Had he not gone on the journey with Rowan last fall, he would have gone to retrieve Aishlinn's treasures before winter had set in. He would have rescued Nora sooner and thereby cut in half all the hell she had gone through.

He had been lost in his own thoughts, thoughts of retribution should he ever learn the fate of Horace Crawford, and had not noticed that his wife had awakened.

Nora gasped, pulled her arm away from her husband. Certain she was that William would never see her unclothed, for her first husband never had, she had hoped William would never see the scars on her wrists or the ones on her legs.

She pulled away, rolled over and buried her head in her pillow.

Shame, humiliation, and embarrassment engulfed her heart. She did not want to have to explain to him how she came to be scarred. Tears burned her eyes so she closed them tightly, hoping to keep them away.

"Nora," Wee William whispered as he rolled to his side and propped himself up on one elbow.

Her voice was stuck in her throat, along with her heart. She did not want to speak about this with him.

"Nora," he repeated softly. He rested a hand on her hip. "Please, do no turn away." It tore at his heart to have her turn away from him.

"Please, do no' be ashamed of yer scars, lass. I've a few of me own, ye ken."

Nora shook her head slightly. "But yours were earned on the battlefield," she choked out. *Not by heavy hands. Not as a punishment.*

"I think ye earned yers in battle as well, wife." He ran his hand along her hip, attempting to offer what comfort he could.

"Ha!" Nora disagreed. "I'm no warrior, William. I did not earn these fighting on the fields of battle like you."

A soft smile formed on his lips. "Aye, but ye did."

Nora's brows drew together in complete confusion. "You are daft," she told him.

Ever so gently, he encouraged her to roll over to face him. His heart broke when he saw the tears streaming down her face, her eyes closed to him as if she were afraid to look at him.

"Were ye no' fightin' fer yer own freedom lass? Were ye no' fightin' fer the freedom of John and Elise?"

She opened her eyes and looked confused.

Wee William smiled warmly and brushed away the tears with his thumb.

"I wager ye a kiss that I can prove to ye that ye are as fierce as any Highland warrior," he told her.

"You have lost your mind! I am not fierce. I'm not a warrior. I'm just an addle headed woman who could not keep her family safe." Nora shook her head in disbelief.

"Nay!" he said gruffly. "Ye *are* fierce! Ye did everythin' ye could to get John and Elise away from Firth, did ye no'?"

"But I failed every time," she told him with another shake of her head.

"Nay," he said firmly. "Not *every* time."

Nora pondered his words for a moment. "But I had your help the last time. I could not have gotten them away if it weren't for you, and Daniel and David."

"Tell me this," Wee William said, trying another approach. "Had we no' appeared that night, would ye still be trying to get them away from Firth? Would ye no' still be tryin' to get away from Horace?"

"Aye," she answered softly. "I would. I promised them that I would someday get them away or I'd die trying."

The warm smile returned to Wee William's face. "Ye see?" he said. He tapped the end of her nose with the tip of his finger. "That promise ye made is all the proof ye need that ye are a fierce woman, a warrior in her own right. Now, ye owe me a kiss."

Nora's brows knitted together again. "A promise? How does a promise prove such a thing?"

He ignored her question. "How did ye come to have the scars?"

Nora felt her cheeks warm with embarrassment again.

"Do no' be afraid to tell me, lass," Wee William said. "Remember, I be yer husband and I pledged many things to ye last night. One bein' that I'd never judge ye harsh."

Nora took a steadying breath, fighting back the tears and uneasy stomach that came with remembering how she had earned the scars on her wrists.

"I had run away again," she began. "I had waited until Horace and his brothers had left. He had told me they'd be gone for a day or two. Said they were heading to Chesterfield, which is a half-day's ride to the south of us."

She thought back to how difficult it had been to hide her joy at the news. "Horace had beaten me so severely just two months prior for running away. It had taken weeks to completely heal from it. I foolishly believed that I had convinced him that I'd never run away again."

Wee William felt the anger build as Nora spoke.

"So when he said that he and his brothers would be gone, it was all I could do to not scream with joy. I believed that I could make my way to Firth, steal John and Elise away, and be miles from home before he and his brothers returned. I was stupid to believe him." She wiped away a tear and took another breath.

"I waited for nearly two hours before I grabbed my things and left. My heart was pounding so hard in my chest as I made my way down the road. I was running you see, and I did not hear him coming up behind me. I was so happy to be gone that I was not paying any attention to what was going on around me. Horace had been waiting. Somehow, he knew I'd leave again."

Nora cleared her throat and tried in vain to keep her hands from trembling. She could not look at William while she told him what had happened next.

"He fell upon me so quickly that I did not have time to respond. He knocked the air from my lungs. All the while he was screaming at me, calling me a whore, an ungrateful whore. Before I realized what had happened, he had tied a rope around my wrists. He tied the other end to the saddle of his horse and began dragging me back home. Only, he didn't take me directly home. He dragged me through the village first. I tried to walk, to hold my head high, but that only angered him further. He took me to the center of the village, declared me a whore, an adulteress, all manner of awful things. Then he turned around and headed back to the cottage. He was going so fast that I couldn't keep up and he ended up dragging me on my belly and back the three miles back to the cottage."

Wee William's heart felt as though it had been torn in two. By rights, being drug behind a horse in such a manner should have killed her. He remained quiet, listening to his beautiful wife, all the while sending his thanks to God that she had lived.

"I was bloody from head to toe when we got back to the cottage. My wrists burned and bled, the skin torn off them. He left me laying in the yard for a time. I was not able to move for everything hurt so badly. It was worse than the beating I had received before. Worse than all the beatings. It was all I could do to breathe!

"Then he came for me, just before dark. He took me into the cottage and made me go down into the cellar and took the ladder away. He left me there for four days. If it weren't for Nigel sneaking me water and cloths to clean my wounds with, everything would have festered. Had it not been for Nigel tossing scraps of food to me, dropping a flagon of water to drink, I would have died."

She still could not look her husband full on. It hurt too much to remember and even more to speak aloud what had happened. But something had changed, deep within her, she realized after several long moments.

She no longer blamed herself. It wasn't her fault that Horace had done all the things he had done. She realized that it would not have mattered in the least if she had been able to do all the things Horace had wanted her to do. He would have found fault in her, fault enough to justify his cruel and severe treatment of her. Horace had been as flawed an individual as had ever walked the earth.

"I am so very glad he is dead, William. I am so very glad you did come to the cottage that night. I am glad that Rowan killed him and his brothers. I hope the three of them rot in hell for all eternity."

Wee William could not move, could not speak. How could he tell her now that he knew not if Horace lived or died?

Nora finally looked up at her husband only to see that he was staring off at something else, something far away that only he could see. "I owe you my life, William, and so much more. You gave me a second chance at life, you see. You gave me the freedom I had prayed for. You gave me my life back and I shall be forever in your debt."

He turned his gaze toward her then, a most curious expression on his face. 'Twas a look that asked a thousand questions at once, the most important being *did she love him only because he had given her this second chance at a good life?*

Nora managed to smile at him. "Do not worry, William. That isn't the only reason that I love you! Aye, I'll be forever grateful to you, for taking me away from England, from all those horrible memories. It is *you*, the man that you *are*, that I love. It is your strong sense of honor, your wicked sense of humor, and the way you care about those who are less fortunate that makes me love you. It is the way you laugh, the way you care for me, for John and Elise, that makes me love you." A sigh escaped her, along with a few more tears.

"I dare say I don't think there is anything about you that I do not love or admire, William."

He smiled at her and placed a gentle kiss on her forehead. He did not doubt the sincerity of her words or her love. She loved him for who he was as much as for what he had done.

Contentment. For the first time that he could ever recall, Wee William of Dunshire knew what that sentiment that had eluded him all these years truly felt like. 'Twas a most wondrous feeling and one he meant to hold on to.

17

They had remained hidden away from the rest of the world for the next three days, enjoying the happy state of being wedded. While Nora seemed to have recovered nicely from their first evening together as husband and wife, Wee William was walking with a slight limp.

The injury was well and blissfully earned the day before when he and Nora had decided to bless the kitchen table. The table, apparently, was not so inclined and gave out at the most inopportune moment. Thankfully, his wife was uninjured in the melee, for she had been happily perched atop his lap. Had she been under him, it would have most certainly been her death when the table came crashing down. A large bruise and a small gash in the right cheek of his buttocks was his reward for hearing Nora cry out his name in blissful rapture. His bottom would heal. She was worth it.

On the afternoon of the third day, a small group of people approached Wee William and Nora's home. Angus, Isobel, Aishlinn, Duncan, Rowan, Black Richard, and Daniel and David had returned the children. Elise came rushing up to Wee William, squealing with delight, as he was gathering wood for the fire.

"Sir William!" The little girl squealed as she raced to him. "We're home!"

As delighted as he was to see the children and half his clan, he would have liked to have had another few years alone with his wife. He pushed the thought away as quickly as it had arrived, for the smile on Elise's face warmed his heart.

Elise studied his face closely, her little eyes widening with surprise. "Sir William! What happened to your eye?"

He stumbled over his own tongue. There was no way to explain it to the child, so he did the next best thing. He lied.

"Och! This? A faerie came into our home the other night and wanted to have yer room fer her own! I had to fight her off, lass! I saved yer room and warned that no more faeries were welcome here!"

Elise giggled at his story and squeezed him around his neck. "Thank you Sir William," she said before turning quite serious. "I wouldn't want to share my room with a faerie!"

John took his time approaching as he inspected the home with a careful eye. Wee William was pleased to see the look of approval that flashed across John's face.

Nora came bounding out of the house with a look of sheer elation. She pulled Elise from Wee William's arms and spun her around, plastering kisses on the little girl's cheeks. Elise giggled as she wrapped her arms around Nora's neck. "Did you miss us, Nora?" she asked.

"Yes, yes we did!" Nora exclaimed with a bright smile.

John kept his distance for a moment but Nora would not allow him to stay out of her sisterly grasp for long. She put Elise down and wrapped her arms around her young brother. "John!" she said cheerfully. "I've missed you!"

"I'm too old now for you to be hugging on me Nora!" he said, rolling his eyes.

Nora pushed him away but maintained a grip on his shoulders. He was a few inches shorter than she was, so she bent to look him in the eye. "I do not care how old you are or get. I'm your sister and I will hug you whenever I please!" She winked at him, ran her hands through his hair and turned to the large group of people who had approached.

"Good day to you!" she called out to them, the smile never leaving her face.

Wee William had been watching the exchange between his wife and his new brother and sister-in-law. The love Nora felt for them was evidenced in her smile, the way she smothered Elise with kisses, and the way she'd not allowed John to get away without a hug. Wee William's heart swelled with pride, as it had done so many times in the past days. He found himself looking forward to the day Nora gave him children. She would be a very good mother and he knew their home would be full of love and laughter.

Nora went to greet the women, while Wee William made another attempt at gathering wood. The men soon surrounded him, their faces filled with concern and a bit of confusion. Rowan was the first to speak.

"I take it yer wife did no' like yer advances toward her?"

Wee William raised an eyebrow, not knowing what Rowan was referring to. "What are ye talkin' about?"

"Ye've a black eye and I can see where yer lip has been cut. My God, man, what did she hit ye with?"

The concern in Rowan's face was genuine. Wee William's face burned red for a moment before he laughed at his friends. "Though it be none of yer business, lads, me wife did no' spurn me advances, nor did she beat me about the head with a pot!" He cast them a wink before adding another log to his arms.

"Then how did ye get the black eye and the fat lip?"

Elise chose that moment to chime in. "He had to fight a faerie who wanted my room!"

The group of men cast curious looks at one another.

Wee William actually burned deep red with embarrassment. He cleared his throat and lowered his voice to a whisper. "'Tis no' something I could explain in front of the children or the women, lads."

The men eyed him suspiciously for a moment before sudden awareness came to them. There was much clearing of throats, devilish smiles, and winking passed about the small group of men. Wee William was suddenly very glad the children were present for the men would not needle him while they were there. The needling, he knew, was inevitable, but it would wait for a more proper time and place.

AISHLINN WAS MISERABLE. HER BACK ACHED, HER FEET WERE swollen to the point she could barely get her shoes on, and she was not able to sleep comfortably at night. "I do not think I will last another day!" she said as she let out a heavy sigh and stretched her back. "I feel as though I've been with child for ten years!"

Nora smiled as she poured tea into cups. They were sitting in Nora's kitchen and enjoying each other's company. "I'm sure it is positively uncomfortable, Aishlinn. But think about the bonny babe you'll soon be holding in your arms!"

"It better be bonny, after all this kicking and rolling around he's doing in there!" she said playfully as she rubbed her hand over her belly.

"You think it's a boy then?" Nora asked as she took a sip of tea.

"Aye, I do! A stubborn, energetic boy, just like his da. A girl child, I am certain, would *not* be causing her mother this much grief. She'd be a quiet lass, like me."

Nora snorted but immediately pulled her lips inward when Aishlinn glared at her angrily. "You do not find me quiet?"

"Nay, Aishlinn. You're as quiet as a church mouse on a winter's eve."

They looked at one another for a moment before Aishlinn burst out laughing. "Even I know I'm not *that* quiet!"

After the giggling subsided, Aishlinn asked the question she'd been dying to ask for days. "So, Nora, how do you like being married to Wee William?"

Nora's lips curved into a very bright smile. "He's a very good husband! He is so kind and patient with John and Elise."

Aishlinn nodded her head and sipped on her tea. "I did not doubt that he would be anything but good to you and the children," she said. "How is his eye?"

Nora burned red from head to toe. She was hoping no one would ask how her husband came to have not one, but two black eyes. "Um," she stammered, trying to find the right words. She and Aishlinn had become such good friends that Nora felt she could talk to her about anything. "Well, it really was entirely his own fault."

Aishlinn sat forward in her chair with great anticipation. Duncan had refused to tell her how the black eyes came to pass. "How exactly was it his fault?"

Nora cleared her throat and took another sip of tea. "Well, you see, he has this thing he does to undo me."

Aishlinn raised an eyebrow. "*Undo* you?"

Nora nodded her head and looked at Aishlinn as if she should readily know to what she was referring. "You *know. Undo* me." When she saw that understanding on Aishlinn's part was not immediately forthcoming she went on to explain it. "It's this thing he does. With his tongue," she continued to blush and stumble over her words. "It undoes me."

Aishlinn searched her mind for the term undone and then, it suddenly dawned on her what Nora was speaking of. She could not help but laugh, for she herself had some close to blackening Duncan's eye the first time he'd sprung *that* little surprise on her.

"But you needn't worry over any more black eyes on my husband," Nora offered with a sly smile.

"No? Why?" Aishlinn could barely contain her excitement.

"Well, you see, he came up with a rather inventive way of keeping my feet in place."

Aishlinn's eyes grew wide with curiosity while her mind raced, wondering what on earth she meant.

Seeing her friend's curiosity piqued, Nora leaned in. "You see, he made these scarves out of silk,"

Just as Nora was beginning to explain the proper applications of the scarves, Elise came crashing through the front door, with John following on her heals.

"Aishlinn!" she shouted as her eyes fell on Aishlinn's large belly. "You haven't had the babe yet?" she asked looking disappointed.

Nora admonished her for her poor manners. "You do *not* come crashing into the house, Elise!"

"I'm sorry, Nora," Elise said as she climbed up on the bench with John taking a seat next to her.

Aishlinn willed her burning face back to its natural color before answering Elise's question. "Nay, Elise. I've not had my babe yet. It won't be long now."

Elise nodded her head as if she understood. "They take a long time to make, don't they?"

Nora and Aishlinn laughed and agreed.

Elise was apparently done talking about babies. "Do you have any biscuits left, Nora? John said that if we asked very nicely we might have one."

Nora shook her head and rolled her eyes. "The both of you are incorrigible." She stood and went to the shelf where she kept the biscuits. There were only four left! *William*, she said his name as though it were a curse. She could not keep the tin completely filled for more than a few hours. His appetite was as large as he. With her back thankfully turned, she smiled and bit her lip. *Aye,* he had very large appetites for things other than biscuits!

She composed herself and brought the biscuits to the table. She gave one each to Elise and John and the remaining two to Aishlinn, a fact that did not go unnoticed by Elise. "Why does Aishlinn get two?" Elise asked, taking a bite of her biscuit.

"One for her, one for the babe. Now don't be rude."

MARRIED LIFE, IN ITSELF, WAS A WONDROUS THING AS FAR AS WEE William was concerned. His love for Nora grew with each passing day. In his eyes, she was perfection.

It was the children that were making his head pound.

Elise questioned everything. Why must we sleep at night and not the day? Why are you shaving? How do whiskers grow? Why don't women have whiskers? Why can't I sleep in bed with you and Nora? How do seeds turn into apples? How did Aishlinn get the baby in her belly? Will Nora get a baby too?

His favorite question in the past week from the curious child was why did he and Nora sleep without any clothes on. He nearly choked on his breakfast when she asked that particular question.

Wee William was finding it rather difficult to find time alone with his wife during the day. With the children waking at the crack of dawn, all the chores that needed to be done around their home, taking them to their morning lessons with Isobel, and Nora working in the castle in the afternoons, there was little time or energy left at the end of the day for making bairns. Still, he relished that time of the day, when he would climb into bed with his wife and hold her closely. He had been given heaven on earth and he would cherish these small moments all the rest of his days.

As he donned his tunic and trews, someone began knocking loudly at the cottage door. Soon his home was filled with excited voices. Wee William raced into the kitchen only to find Duncan standing next to the table. Nora was smiling as she pulled her shawl from the hook.

"William!" Elise squealed with delight as she sat breaking her fast. "Aishlinn's is having her babe!"

No wonder Duncan looked as though he were about to pass out.

"Isobel has asked that I help her, William," Nora explained as she blew him a kiss. "I've never helped deliver a babe before, but I think I should get along well enough." Nora tried to sound far more excited about the prospect of helping deliver a babe than she actually felt. Truthfully, the thought terrified her to no end. But she had promised Aishlinn she would be there when the time finally arrived.

Wee William smiled down at his wife and grabbed her in his arms before she could leave. "Ye'll no' be getting' away without a proper kiss, wife," he murmured into Nora's ear. "It could be hours before I see ye again."

Nora giggled and stood on her tiptoes and waited for him to bend toward her. He gave her a proper kiss that left her momentarily breathless. Elise giggled and John grunted, much like the Highlander men he'd been surrounded by.

"John," Nora said as she tried to regain her composure. "Please, keep Elise out of trouble while I'm gone. If ye need anything, just come to Aishlinn's cottage, but *knock* before you enter!"

Nora laughed when she finally turned her attention away from her husband. Duncan hadn't moved from his spot by the table and he looked just as pale as when he had first arrived.

"Duncan! For heaven's sake, you best sit before you faint!" she told him as she headed for the door. "William, I think you might want to keep Duncan away from his wife for a time."

Wee William crossed the room, laughing at his friend. He took his arm and helped him to sit at the table.

"Are you ill?" Elise asked.

Duncan could only shake his head.

"He's just a bit unsettled, Elise. This be his first babe," Wee William tried to explain. Duncan hadn't said a word. His eyes were focused on something that only he could see and his skin seemed to grow paler by the moment. Wee William hoped that if he and Nora were blessed with babes of their own, that he wouldn't come apart like Duncan was doing.

"John," Wee William said. "Take Elise to the keep and ask Bree or Eilean to watch over her."

"But I don't want to go to the keep. I want to help Aishlinn have her babe," Elise protested.

Wee William chuckled. "Nay, lass, ye be a wee bit young yet to help. Now do as yer told, or I'll make ye help Auld Phillip in the stables for the next sennight."

Elise wrinkled up her nose. "But the stables smell funny," she told him.

"Aye, and if ye do no' want to be smellin' funny yerself, ye'll do as yer told. Now go, with John to the keep."

Elise let out a heavy sigh. "Will I be able to help when I'm older?"

"If ye do as yer told and mind yer manners, aye," Wee William said as he stood up from the table. "Now *go.*"

John nodded and stood, staring questionably at Duncan. "Are you sure he'll be well?"

"Aye," Wee William nodded.

"Come Elise," John said as he held his hand out. "Mayhap Mary has some sweet cakes for us."

Wee William knew he had to get Duncan's mind off his wife. The poor man looked positively lost at the moment.

"John!" Wee William called out, as an idea to keep Duncan busy had quickly formed in his mind.

John stopped in the doorway and waited patiently.

Wee William studied the lad closely for a moment. The boy had gained weight over the past weeks and he was growing taller. His attitude had improved as well and Wee William knew that with the right guidance, John could grow to be a fine man and warrior.

"After ye take Elise to the keep, meet Duncan and me on the training fields."

John's brow twisted into a knot of confusion. Children were not allowed anywhere near the training fields, at least not while the men occupied it. Not only was it dangerous for the children but it caused too much of a distraction for the men training.

"The training fields?" John asked.

"Aye," Wee William smiled. "I believe it be time fer ye to learn how to use a sword. And I think Duncan be just the man to teach ye."

John looked even more confused. "Him? I doubt he could tell you his own name at the moment."

Wee William chuckled as he patted Duncan on the arm. "Aye, but we need to keep his mind off his wife at the moment. And there be no better way to keep a Highlander occupied than either by fightin' or drinkin'. And ye be too young to help with the latter!" Wee William knew there was yet a third way to keep a Highlander occupied, but John was a bit young yet to share that with him.

"So is it just for today that you want me to learn?" John asked.

"Nay, I think it's time ye started trainin' to be a warrior. Ye'll be three and ten soon, won't ye?"

John swallowed hard. "Aye, I will."

"Then it be time."

John was not sure at the moment if he even *wanted* to learn how to fight. He had no desire to go into battle or to fight in wars. Wee William sensed the boy's reluctance.

"Lad, ye want to ken how to defend yer family, don' ye?"

John's shoulders relaxed a bit at that thought. He supposed it would be useful to learn how to protect his family, if such an event was ever necessary. "Aye, I do."

"Good," Wee William smiled thoughtfully. "Now off with ye!"

Once John had closed the door behind them, Wee William turned his attention back to Duncan. Wee William had never seen a more terrified looking warrior in his life. Wee William shook his head in disbelief thinking it was a poor sight indeed to see his friend so bewildered that he could not move or speak.

"Duncan!" Wee William said gruffly as he slapped Duncan on the back. "Ye need to snap out of it, lad!"

Duncan blinked twice before looking at Wee William. "Women die in childbed, Wee William," Duncan said quietly. "I canna stand the thought of losin' Aishlinn, or me babe."

Wee William gave him a nod of understanding, believing he too would have that same worry were their roles reversed. "I've met yer wife, Duncan. She be a feisty, determined young lass," he offered consolingly. "Why, if it were a battle between Aishlinn and the devil himself, I'd place me wagers on Aishlinn every time."

Duncan chuckled slightly. Aye, his wife *was* a determined woman. But things sometimes happened that were beyond anyone's control. His wife, at that very moment, was lying in their bed attempting to bring forth the life the two of them had created. She was going up against nature, not the devil.

Wee William sighed, shook his head and slapped Duncan's back again. "What say we walk by yer cottage and ye can see how yer wife fairs? Then we'll keep ourselves busy with training me brother-in-law on proper sword fightin'."

Duncan nodded and stood, the wood bench creaking as he scooted it away. "But if she needs me, Wee William, I'll stay by her side. She's such a tiny thing, ye ken that as well as I."

"Again," Wee William said as he led Duncan out of doors. "She's a determined lass."

"Aye, that may well be true. But she's such a wee thing! And she never asks fer much. And she never complains when she's in pain or no' feelin' well."

The air was warm this fine spring morning, but neither man paid much attention to the beautiful surroundings as they walked down the path that led to Duncan and Aishlinn's home.

"I remember the journey here," Duncan said moments later. "Aishlinn had taken such a beatin' from that bastard earl. There were times when I thought she'd no' survive beyond another hour, let alone another day. And not once did she complain. Not once did she say that she hurt, when I knew in fact she did."

Wee William remained quiet as they walked along, allowing his friend to reminisce.

"I think I began to fall in love with her then, on our journey here to Gregor. I think 'twas her quiet and reserved manner and her inner strength that drew me to her." Duncan said as his lips began to form a slight smile.

Highlanders seldom, if ever, shared their innermost feelings with another Highlander. He supposed, however, that Wee William could very well understand how it might feel to love someone more than you loved your next breath.

Wee William remained quiet. He imagined that Duncan felt very much the same way about Aishlinn, as he did about Nora.

"I worry that if something *is* wrong, she'll no' say anything to Isobel. She'll keep her pain to herself, as she so often does, Wee William."

'Twas then, as they were just steps away from Duncan's home, that they heard the most awful of screams. Wee William thought it sounded like a selkie screeching from the sea! Both men paused, looked at each other with wide eyes, and then ran for the cottage.

Duncan pushed the door open causing it to slam against the wall. His heart was pounding in his chest, as he was quite certain the scream had come from his wife. He rushed to the doorway to their bedchamber and came to an abrupt halt. As he stood in the doorway, with Wee William peering in over his shoulder, Duncan felt the air rush from his lungs and his legs turn to jelly.

There was his sweet, beautiful, kind wife, naked, covered in sweat, and squatting over the birthing chair. Isobel and Nora were crouched on either side of her, giving her words of encouragement. Nora was wiping Aishlinn's brow with a wet cloth and Isobel was rubbing her lower back.

"I swear, if that whoreson even thinks about doin' this to me again,

I'll cut his ballocks off with a dull knife!" Aishlinn said through gritted teeth and gulps for air.

Isobel had promised Duncan it would be hours before Aishlinn delivered her babe. *First babes always take the longest,* Isobel had assured him. *Go about yer day and we'll send fer ye when 'tis all over and done.* That was little more than an hour ago. Now she was sitting on the birthing chair!

"What the bloody hell," Duncan whispered.

Isobel and Nora finally took notice of his and Wee William's presence. Isobel looked more perturbed at seeing the two of them standing in the doorway than she looked concerned over Aishlinn. Isobel shot Duncan a look that warned him to be quiet else his wife would direct her wrath directly at him.

"Yer doin' fine, Aishlinn," Nora soothed as she ran the cloth across Aishlinn's forehead.

"This is all *his* fault!" Aishlinn spat between waves of pain. "Damned Highlanders and their want of pleasing their women and having a hundred bairns! I'd like to see *him* try to squeeze a babe out of his damned manhood!"

Duncan had forgotten about Wee William until he heard the man chuckling behind him. Duncan spun and began pushing Wee William out of the room. "Ye canna see me wife in such a state!" Duncan whispered harshly as they walked toward the table. Duncan's face was red with anger. "Ye will do well to ferget what ye just saw and heard, William!"

Wee William smiled down at his friend. "Do no' worrit, lad. I could no' see a thing from where I was standin'."

It was a full out lie, for he had been peeking into the room over Duncan's shoulder. He had also heard every word Aishlinn had said. Now was not the appropriate time to needle his friend. Duncan looked mad enough to draw his sword and chop Wee William's head off.

"Isobel said we had hours before Aishlinn had her babe!" Duncan said as he ran a hand through his hair. "This canna be good!" He began pacing around the room, worry etched into his brow.

Wee William had as much experience with the birthing process as

Duncan, therefore he had no words of consolation to offer his friend. Mayhap silence was best.

"Mayhap we should step outside," Wee William offered after another deep, blood-curdling scream came from Duncan's bedchamber. The sound of Aishlinn's screams set Wee William's nerves on edge. He had never witnessed a birth before. The thought of Aishlinn in so much pain made his stomach tighten. Mayhap Duncan was right to worry. If it were Nora in that chair, Wee William knew he'd have the same anxiety.

Duncan shot an angry glare Wee William's way. "I think we could hear her screamin' all the way to England!" he whispered angrily. Guilt washed over Duncan and it was all he could do to remain standing. Aishlinn was right; it was his fault that she was in such agony and pain.

"That may well be true," Wee William said in a low voice. "But mayhap bein' a bit further away from it will help ye." *And it certainly would no' hurt me!*

"Help me?" Duncan stopped pacing and looked at Wee William. "God, man! 'Tisn't me that needs the help! 'Tis me wife! Can ye no' hear how much this hurts her?"

Wee William reckoned all of Scotland could hear, but did not voice his opinion. "I ken she be in pain, Duncan. Mayhap if ye went in with her, that would help soothe the lass." He thought it an excellent idea. But the look of abject fear that filled Duncan's eyes said he did not agree.

"Are ye mad?" Duncan asked as he resumed his pacing. "*Ye* heard her! She's ready to cut me manhood off with a dull knife!"

Just as Wee William was about to suggest that they leave again, another blood curdling scream and a slew of curses came crashing out of the bedchamber. Wee William blushed. He did not know that women even *knew* such words, let alone had the audacity to speak them! He supposed it wasn't audacity so much as sheer, unadulterated pain that made the lass speak so.

He then heard Nora's laughter filter out of the bedchamber. Wee William and Duncan looked at one another, each of them confused, but Wee William was blushing to his toes. Did his wife find the dirty language Aishlinn spoke, amusing? His wife was every bit the lady that

Aishlinn was. How could she have found humor in such words? Embarrassed over his wife's apparent amusement with Aishlinn's harsh language, Wee William made a mental note to speak to her later, about the appropriateness of laughing at such a time.

In the next instant, the beautiful, precious, and loud cry of Duncan's first babe, along with more laughter from the women, came filtering into the kitchen. Wee William and Duncan stared blankly at one another for a moment before wide, braw smiles came to their faces.

Both men began pacing back and forth, amazed, excited, and eagerly anticipating word from the next room. It seemed as though an hour had passed before Nora stepped into the kitchen with Duncan's babe in swaddling clothes. Wee William's heart skipped a beat when he saw her sweet smile and the tears of joy in her eyes.

Nora stepped toward Duncan and placed the babe into his trembling arms. He could not find the wherewithal to speak at the moment. He wanted to ask after his wife, how she fared, but he was too caught up in the blissful moment of holding his tiny babe for the first time.

"He is a beautiful, strong boy," Nora whispered softly as she placed a gentle kiss on the babe's bald little head.

Duncan's smile increased as he looked at Nora. "A boy?" He was momentarily stunned by the news. He had convinced himself that 'twas a girl child his wife carried, for Aishlinn had gone nearly a fortnight past the time the babe had been expected. Only a girl child would make a man wait longer than necessary.

"Aye, a son," Nora said. "And Aishlinn is doing very well. Isobel is helping her to settle into the bed. You can see her soon."

Duncan turned toward Wee William, his eyes filled with joyful tears, the smile never leaving his face. "Wee William!" Duncan whispered in awe. "I have a *son!*"

Nora went to her husband and wrapped her arms around his waist. Wee William pressed a kiss onto the top of her head as he wrapped his arms around her. They stood together, watching Duncan as he gently rocked his son in his arms. The babe was sucking on his little fist, his eyes closed as he slept peacefully in his father's arms.

"He's a big lad, isn't he?" Duncan asked to no one in particular. "He's handsome too!"

Wee William chuckled slightly. "He must take after his mum then!"

Duncan ignored the insult, unable to take his eyes of his wee bairn. After several long, quiet moments, Isobel appeared and informed Duncan that his wife would like to see him now. Duncan looked very much like a man heading to the gallows as he first cast a look of dread at Wee William before stepping into the bedchamber.

"I thought 'twould be hours before the babe was here," Wee William murmured to his wife.

"'Twas our thinkin' as well," Isobel answered as she went about heating water for tea. "But in hindsight, it only seems it went quickly. I did no' ken until I arrived earlier that Aishlinn has been having pains in her back for two days. She didna tell anyone for she didna realize they were birthing pains."

Isobel stoked the fire until flames began to rise upward. "Aishlinn be a verra strong young woman. Until the babe was ready to come, she did no' so much as utter a sound."

Wee William chuckled slightly. "Aye, but then, the words that came out of that bonny lass's mouth? I never heard such cursin' in all me days!"

Isobel shot him a look of chastisement. "'Tis no' an easy thing to do, Wee William!" Isobel said as she grabbed cups from the cupboard.

"I be sorry, Isobel. I meant no disrespect. 'Twas a surprise to hear *her,* of all people, using such language."

Isobel smiled as she set the cups on the table. "Aye, I was a bit surprised meself!"

"I was as well!" Nora said. "Everything about it surprised me. I've never helped deliver a babe before. Aishlinn made it look very easy until it was time to actually push him out!" She shuddered involuntarily at the memory of her dear friend in so much pain. Nora had not realized just how agonizing birthing could be. She could only hope that if and when her time came, it wouldn't be quite as bad as what Aishlinn had gone through!

Isobel giggled. "Aye, fer some women, the pushin' is the easy part, fer others, 'tis the worst. Each woman is different, ye ken."

Wee William looked down at his wife and studied her for a moment. She looked as though she were thinking hard on something. He would wait until they were alone to ask what she was thinking of.

"Nora," Isobel said. "Ye did a fine job with Aishlinn. Ye were verra comfortin' to her, and ye asked the right questions. Mayhap, ye'd like to help me again?"

Nora's eyes widened with surprise. "You mean, with another birthing?"

"Aye, I do. I believe ye would do well as a midwife. Ye have a good head on yer shoulders. Ye were verra calm when the time came. I ken ye were probably verra nervous and a bit scared, but ye hid it well."

Nora thought on it for a long moment. She'd never thought about becoming a midwife, so she wasn't sure if it was the correct calling for her or not. Mayhap if she did help Isobel with a few more births, she might be better equipped with making the right decision.

She worried however, about being away from William and the children. They'd only been married for a short time. Mayhap her husband would not want to be sharing time with his wife with anyone. He may also not want to be saddled with John and Elise for long periods of time. But Nora *had* liked helping Isobel and she was glad she had been there for Aishlinn.

Had it been Horace standing next to her, Nora would have refused as soon as the offer had been made. She knew Horace would never have allowed her to help in the first place, let alone allow her the chance to do it again. Nora had never truly been his wife, she'd merely been something else that he owned. It made her feel quite ill at ease whenever thoughts of Horace came to her mind. She knew she should not ever compare Horace to Wee William, for there truly was no comparison. However, it was often difficult not to do just that. In each and every comparison, Wee William won out.

It had not been so very long ago that she had felt her life ruined, beyond repair, beyond hope. Before Wee William and his men entered her cottage that fateful night, she had begun to believe Horace's words. She had started to believe that mayhap she was unworthy, stupid, and weak. Mayhap she was a flawed, inferior, defective woman. Mayhap she didn't deserve any amount of happiness.

But Wee William had shown her otherwise.

She owed him so very much. Owed him her own life, and the lives of her brother and sister.

Nora watched Isobel closely for a moment. Certainly it should be considered an honor to be asked to help her again. Mayhap Isobel saw something in Nora that she could not see for herself.

"Mayhap if I did help you a time or two, I could make a better decision, Isobel. I am very flattered that you would ask," Nora said. She looked up at her husband. "But I would not want to go against my husband's wishes. If he does not want me to do this, then I shan't."

The last thing she wanted was friction between herself and William. He was such a good man, in so many ways. There was not a day that went by that she didn't learn something new about him, something that endeared him to her all the more. Nora felt she owed him a lifetime of gratitude and peace for all he had done for her. She could no more go against his wishes than she could fly. If her husband did not wish for her to assist Isobel again, then so be it. Nora would not argue with him over it.

Isobel nodded her head as she glanced at Wee William. "What say ye, Wee William? Would ye be against yer wife learnin' how to help women in such a manner?"

Wee William didn't have to think on it for long. He would much rather his wife help women deliver their bairns over how Aishlinn had wanted to help the women of their clan. Aishlinn wanted to teach the women on the proper usage of bows and arrows, for battle as well as hunting.

When Wee William had first witnessed with his own eyes the lass's good aim, he'd been both surprised and in awe. She was as good as any of the clan's archers when it came right down to it. But battle was no place for any woman to be. Nay, birthing bairns, weaving, sewing, those were the rightful places of a woman.

He knew not to voice his opinion on the subject of a woman's rightful place in front of Isobel or his wife. He'd keep his thoughts to himself for now.

"Aye, I think Nora would do well as a midwife," he said as he hugged his wife. "And as long as it be something Nora *wishes* to do, I see no problem with it."

Nora blinked. *As long as she wanted to.* Excitement, relief, and gratitude exploded into a wide smile as she stared, surprised, at her husband. He was allowing *her* to make the decision. The warm smile he held, the twinkle in his eyes, the way his warm hand felt as it rested on her waist told her more than words ever could.

He believed in her.

He truly loved her.

Suddenly, Nora was overwhelmed with the need to be alone with her husband. Weeks ago, it would have been very difficult for her to express to him just what she was thinking or feeling. Wee William had changed all that. He allowed her to think and feel, whatever it was she might be thinking or feeling at the moment. He never berated her, never scolded or yelled at her. William was the most patient, kind man she had ever known.

Wee William cherished her.

He adored her.

He truly loved her.

"William," Nora asked as she continued to smile at him.

"Aye, lass?"

"Where be Elise and John?"

Wee William recognized the gleam of love in his wife's eyes. He'd seen that look countless times over the past two weeks. That look took his breath away and he knew what *that* particular look meant.

"They be at the keep," he said. He swallowed hard, wanting very much to scoop his wife into his arms and rush her back to their home. The children were at the keep, safe and sound. He could take his sweet time loving his wife.

Nora's eyes twinkled again. Wee William did his best to suppress the urgent need building in his loins.

"Good," she whispered. "How long do you think John will be able to keep Elise out of trouble?"

With the look his wife was giving him, he'd have been quite happy to run to the keep and tie John and Elise to the nearest tree, if it meant having some time alone with his wife. Aye, he could trust John to do his best to keep Elise out of trouble, but not for long. The little sprite had a way of driving her brother crazy. Wee William wasn't certain if trouble found Elise or if Elise sought it out. Poor John.

John.

"John!" Wee William exclaimed as he slapped his hand to his forehead. He had forgotten the boy!

Nora gave her husband a puzzled look. "What of John?" she asked.

Wee William growled. When he had made the promise to teach John the proper use of a sword, he had done so believing he had hours to spend keeping Duncan busy. And with his wife busy helping Aishlinn, there would be no need to tell her about the training. He stared at his wife for a moment. Should he lie or tell the truth? He was certain she would not agree to allow her young brother to train with a bunch of Highlanders. Nora protected her brother and sister as fiercely as a mother bear protected her cubs.

When he looked into his wife's eyes, he knew he must tell her the truth. He braced himself mentally for what he was certain would be a severe tongue lashing.

"I promised to teach the lad to use a sword. 'Twas a promise meant to keep Duncan busy, fer he was so worried over Aishlinn! And I ken ye think the lad be too young, but I was seven when I began me trainin'! He's a good lad, Nora, and I think it be time to teach him to defend himself and his family!"

His words had spilled out so rapidly that Nora could barely keep up. While she hadn't caught every word, she understood most of what he said.

Her heart swelled with pride and love for her husband. It mattered not that he hadn't discussed it with her first, for she knew eventually he would have confessed. And John wouldn't have been able to keep such a thing secret for long. Besides, Elise would have found out and there were not many secrets the little girl was able to keep.

Nora turned to face her husband, who was, at the moment, looking very unsure and a bit afraid of what her response would be. She bit the inside of her lip to keep from laughing at him.

"You mean to train John?" she asked, pretending confusion.

Wee William nodded his head and took a step backward.

"You think a boy of two and ten is ready for such training?" she asked, crossing her arms over her chest.

Wee William nodded his head again and took another step back toward the door. He realized he had never seen his wife angry before. He thought back to a feisty young woman named Maggy Boyle and *her* propensity for throwing anything within reach. He prayed his wife did not hold such a temper as that, but scanned the room for anything that might be within her reach. He cast a glance over his shoulder at the door. He could be out the door before his wife could get to anything to be used as a weapon, save for the chair she now stood next to.

He wasn't prepared for her response. Nora ran to him and flung herself at him, wrapping her arms around his neck. Did she mean to strangle him?

"William!" Nora exclaimed as she began planting kisses on his cheek. "Thank you!"

Wee William stood dumbfounded. Why was she thanking him?

"I think this is just what John needs, to help him feel he belongs here!" Nora said excitedly as she hugged her husband tightly. "I have been so worried about him, William!"

Wee William returned her embrace. His wife had not voiced her worry over John, but he knew that she was concerned over John's adjustment to life in Scotland.

"It has been so hard for him to make friends, William," Nora whispered into his ear. "Mayhap if he is allowed to spend more time with you, and your men, he might start to feel like he belongs. He might learn to see in all of you, what I see in all of you." Nora fought back the urge to cry.

Wee William squeezed her again before setting her down on her feet. "And what it is that you see in us?"

Nora smiled. "Honorable men and women. Good, decent people who are giving, kind, and funny!" Of course, her list of all the good qualities William and his people possessed was much longer than that.

Wee William nodded his head in agreement. "So ye be no' angry that I made the decision without speakin' to ye first?"

A wicked smile came to her lips then. She couldn't very well let him think she was perfectly fine with him making such important decisions without her. "Oh, I am angry with you, William. But my happiness that you want to include John in things, my happiness that he might someday be accepted as one of you far outweighs my anger."

"We have accepted him, Nora," Wee William replied. "John simply canna see it fer he's too angry and missin' his home. It canna be easy fer him to be taken from all he loved and held dear to his heart. It will take time, but I believe that someday, he'll come to realize that home is wherever his *heart* is."

Nora could no more contain her tears than she could hold onto a star. She melted into her husband's arms, thankful beyond words that God had brought him into her life. She would love him always and he, her.

After a few moments, she dried her tears and hugged him again.

"You should not keep John waiting, then, William," she told him. "I'll stay and speak with Isobel, and help Aishlinn where I can. I'll meet you at home later."

Wee William hugged her again before leaving the cottage. As he walked along the path toward the keep, he could not help but feel elated, joyous, and utterly content. He reckoned that he must have done something truly spectacular in another life, for he could not fathom what he'd done in this one to deserve a wife like Nora.

18

The meeting of the seven clans was held at the beginning of summertime. The event was disguised as a festival and games, and only a handful of people knew secret meetings would take place between the clan chiefs.

MacDougalls, McKees, and McDunnahs had been living in relative harmony for decades. The gathering was put forth in hopes of bringing the Grahams, Lindsays, Carruthers, and Randolphs into the fold in a more permanent fashion. While the latter clans were not sworn enemies of the MacDougalls, McKees or McDunnahs, neither had they sworn oaths of fealty in times of need or troubles.

Over the course of the next fortnight, games would be held, feasts eaten, music enjoyed, and much good whiskey drunk. And God willing, an unbreakable bond would be forged between the seven clans.

By the time the last of the clans arrived, more than two thousand men, women, and children were gathered in and around Castle Gregor. The clan chiefs, along with their wives and children, were given fine rooms within Castle Gregor, while their soldiers and people camped out of doors. The hills surrounding Gregor were dotted with tents, wagons, and horses, as far as the eye could see. Flags and banners bearing the colors and crests of each clan waved in the breeze. If one didn't know aforehand, one might think an attack was imminent.

It was very late at night, with most of the inhabitants of the castle fast asleep, save for those assigned the night posts, and the chiefs of the seven clans. The chiefs met in secrecy in Angus' war room. Windows had been drawn shut, the heavy drapes pulled taut to keep sound from carrying too far.

No guards stood outside the door. No pages or squires waited patiently in the background to bring ale or food. No lieutenants, no men-at-arms, no seconds-in-command were present.

Just seven men.

Men who wanted peace. Men who wanted nothing more than for their children or grandchildren to grow up without knowing war, famine, or tyranny.

Each man held his own personal reasons for attending.

Angus sat at the head of the table, with Nial McKee and Caelen McDunnah on either side of him. Seamus Lindsay, Andrew Graham, Douglas Carruthers, and James Randolph, chiefs of their respective clans, were the only other people in attendance. It was the fourth such meeting held over the course of three long years and Angus prayed this would be the meeting where they would finally unite.

"We're stronger as a whole, than as individuals," Angus told the men. "If we unite as Scots, we stand a much better chance against the English or anyone else who decides to invade."

"And what guarantee do we have that none of ye will come against the Randolphs?" James Randolph asked, unable to mask his apprehension.

James Randolph was of the same age as Angus and the two looked quite similar in appearance, with their long blonde hair and substantial builds. But that was where their similarities ended. Where Angus held on to the fervent belief that not all men were devious by nature, James Randolph was far too pessimistic. Perhaps it was due to the fact that James Randolph had entered into truce accords before only to see them broken before the ink on the parchment had dried. "We've no guarantee that the six of ye would no' form an alliance to take *our* lands."

"Ye'd have me word on it, James," Angus told him. He did not take James' question as an insult. Were Angus in the same position as the Randolphs, he'd have the same suspicions and concerns.

"Bah!" James said with a shake of his head. "Yer word? Aye, ye may give us yer word today and we could shake on it and take an oath in blood, but it does no' mean ye won't change yer mind when a better offer comes along."

Angus held his temper in check. "Have any of ye ever ken me to go back on me word?" he asked quietly. "Have any of ye ever ken me to break an oath?"

Angus' reputation as it pertained to his word and his bond, was above reproach and he knew the men surrounding him were well aware of that fact. He'd not allow James Randolph to bait him into an argument over it. They weren't here to discuss his honor, they were here to hopefully forge an alliance.

"Nay," Caelen McDunnah finally spoke. "There be very few men in this world whose word I'd accept above yers, Angus." He directed his statement directly toward James Randolph. "In fact, I canna think of one other I could enter into an agreement with, with just the shake of a hand. Yer word is yer bond, but I be no' so sure I could say the same about anyone else in this room."

Caelen McDunnah did not care if he had insulted the Randolph chief or anyone else. Where Angus' reputation as an honorable, honest man preceded him, Caelen's reputation was not quite as stellar. Aye, he was a man who kept his word, just as Angus did. But Caelen was known as a hell raising, skirt-chasing son of a whore. He was an anomaly of sorts. While men could trust him to keep his word, it wasn't always easy obtaining it.

"Are ye suggestin' Caelen McDunnah, that *I* am no' to be trusted?" James Randolph asked as he leaned forward in his chair. He did nothing to hide his anger.

"Nay," Caelen answered with an air of nonchalance. "I be statin' the fact that of all the men in this room, Angus be the only one I'd trust with me life. I canna say the same fer the rest of ye fer I do no' ken ye as well as I ken Angus." Caelen draped an arm over the back of his chair. "I've ken Angus all me life. He and me father were of like minds. I consider him a true friend, and I canna say that about many people."

"I believe none of us here question Angus' word," Andrew Graham interjected. His deep voice rumbled softly through the room. "I believe James has a right to be concerned. He's made some questionable alliances in the past and he wants no' to make the same mistakes again."

James Randolph bolted to his feet. "Are ye implyin' that I be a poor judge of character, Graham?"

"Nay," Andrew replied coolly. "I be sayin' ye've made alliances in the past with people ye thought ye could trust, such as the Bowie Clan, and it's left a foul taste in yer mouth. No one here can blame ye fer bein' concerned."

Each man knew what Andrew spoke of. Nearly twenty years ago, the Randolph had believed he could form an alliance with Donnel Bowie. The agreement was broken less than a year later when the Bowies attacked the Randolphs from within. The battle waged for more than a month and when all was said and done, the Randolphs had won, but at the cost of countless lives. James Randolph was still trying to rebuild his keep and replace the warriors he had lost.

Douglas Carruthers finally spoke. "James, we ken yer concern and canna blame ye," he leaned forward in his chair and held his palms up. "We all can agree on three things this day."

James slowly sat back into his chair but his angry scowl remained.

"What be those things?" Seamus Lindsay asked after a long moment.

Douglas looked at each of the men before speaking. "One, we can all agree that Angus McKenna is a man of his word. Two, we can all agree that each of us has made alliances in the past that we have lived to regret."

The men waited patiently for Douglas to list the third item.

"And three?" Seamus asked impatiently.

A smile began to form on Douglas' lips. "And three, we all can agree we hate the English."

None would argue his last point.

"Angus," Douglas said with a nod of his head in Angus' direction. "Ye have my full support on this accord. The Clan Carruthers will be proud to call ye brethren."

Angus gave a slight smile in Douglas' direction. Clan Carruthers was not as large a clan as the MacDougall Clan, but their lands bordered MacDougall lands to the north. They would be a very important ally, especially if Carrick Bowie, the son of Donnell Bowie, proved to be a man of his word. He'd recently made a very public promise to behead each of the men currently present in the war room. He wanted their lands, their homes, and their coin. Carrick Bowie was not a man to ignore and none of the men here this day would take his threats lightly.

Angus had previously received the full support of the clans McDunnah, McKee, and Graham. He could only hope that Douglas Carruthers' pledge to join them would be enough to nudge James Randolph in the right direction.

Each of the men looked patiently at James Randolph. He was as pessimistic as they came and Angus knew 'twould not be easy to gain his support.

"What say ye, James Randolph?" Andrew Graham asked with a raised brow. Andrew Graham understood the importance of having the Randolphs as allies as much as any man in the room understood.

The realization of just how important the Randolph Clan was to the agreement and future of the other clans seemed to hit James Randolph like a bolt of lightning. Each man could see that things were finally beginning to click with the cynical clan chief as he tried to hide the wry smile that came to his face. Pretending to be as indifferent and blasé as he could manage, James Randolph cleared his throat and leaned back in his chair.

"I would have to agree with Douglas and the rest of ye. We would make fine allies..." James said as his voice trailed off leaving something unsaid.

Carruthers was growing impatient with the Randolph chief. "And?"

James twisted his lips as if he were contemplating something of great significance then let out a short breath. "The rest of ye are all bigger clans than mine, I'll give ye that. I ken it be what me lands can offer the six of ye that make ye want Clan Randolph to join with ye. I want reassurance that none will try to stab us in the back when an opportunity arises."

"I kindly ask ye to stop makin' yer snide remarks as to our honor, Randolph. 'Tis startin' to rub me the wrong way and if ye say such a thing again, I'll run ye through meself," Carruthers told him pointedly.

Under different circumstances, James Randolph would have taken umbrage with the Carruthers threat. However he had far bigger fish to catch at the moment.

"We have put it in writing, Randolph," Caelen began. He was growing more irritated with James Randolph as the moments passed.

"Aye, but ye ken as well as I that there be times in life when a written promise is no more valuable than the parchment it be written on. I want something far more tangible than a slip of parchment with signatures on it." James Randolph was doing his best to hide his growing excitement. Where he may have fooled some of the men in the room, Angus and Caelen were aware of his sudden shift in attitude. The way James Randolph was twisting his lip and drumming his fingers on the table showed the man was excited about something.

"Quit beatin' around the bush, Randolph and get to what it is ye want," Caelen said, not caring to hide his frustration.

James Randolph cleared his throat again, stared directly at Angus, and then appeared to steal himself for the impending wrath of Angus. "I want a marriage between Bree McKenna and me eldest son, Gillon."

Seamus Lindsay, Douglas Carruthers, Nial McKee, and Andrew Graham laughed boisterously at Randolph's demand. They knew well that Angus McKenna was as against arranged marriages as he was opposed to the English. The only men not laughing were Angus, Caelen, and James Randolph.

"Ye've got a set of ballocks on ye, Randolph!" Nial McKee laughed as he slapped his leg with the palm of his hand. Up to this point, he'd been sitting quietly studying every man in the room. "Anyone who kens Angus McKenna kens he'd never offer any of his daughters as something to seal a bargain with." Nial wiped the tears from his face as his laughter finally began to subside.

"Nay," Nial continued. "Angus believes in letting his children choose their own wives or husbands, Randolph. Me thinks ye'll have to find another way to get yer reassurance of our allegiance."

The fact that Nial had taken a liking to the young Bree McKenna was beside the point. Nial was seven years older than she and he assumed he'd need to wait another year or two before asking Angus' permission to court the girl. He had been dropping hints to Angus ever since the lass turned seven and ten near Hogmanay time. Thus far, Angus had done nothing but grunt and threaten to disembowel him if he made any attempts at wooing his youngest daughter. They were threats that Nial took quite seriously, at least for now.

"Nial be right," Caelen finally spoke. "Ye best find an alternative, Randolph." Caelen didn't hold the same romantic inclinations toward Bree McKenna that Nial and many other young men did. He was more an older brother or uncle to the young girl.

He'd met Gillon Randolph before and hadn't been too impressed with the lad. Aye, he was young, a good fighter, and seemed to have a good head on his shoulders. But there was something about the boy that Caelen hadn't realized he didn't care for until the suggestion of Bree marrying him was brought up.

"While I appreciate yer help, lads," Angus said after letting loose with a long sigh, "I would like to hear *why* James Randolph thinks this would be a good match."

Caelen and Nial nearly choked on their own surprise. They cast each other curious looks that said neither of them could believe Angus was actually considering the proposal.

"Me son is a good man," Randolph began.

Caelen snorted and Nial coughed into his hand. Randolph ignored them and continued. "Me son is a good man, a bit young perhaps, but he'll make a fine chief someday. He's a bit on the quiet side, I'll give ye that. But he's a thinker. When he's quiet, ye ken he be studying and thinkin' the situation over. He be no' one to make rash decisions. He's a man that can be trusted."

Angus studied James Randolph for a moment. Aye, Randolph might be the most pessimistic man that Angus had ever had the displeasure of meeting, but he was an honest man. Angus had only met

Gillon on a handful of occasions over the years. Due to the boy's relatively young age of ten and nine, Angus had yet to develop a full opinion of him. Only time would tell, but for now, he could consider Gillon a young man of good character. Even if there was something a bit off about the lad. Mayhap it was lack of experience or his shy and awkward ways.

Like all men, James Randolph loved his son. But he was also an honest man. Angus supposed his daughter could do far worse for a husband than Gillon Randolph. He knew Nial McKee was growing quite fond of Bree but he also knew that Bree had absolutely no interest in Nial. She thought him far too immature and full of himself, or at least that was what she had told her father on more than one occasion. But who truly knew what was in the secret parts of a young girl's heart?

"As every man here kens," Angus finally spoke. "I do no' trade me children like some trade their cattle or sheep. I let me children decide who 'tis they want to marry."

Andrew Graham interjected. "But good sometimes comes from such arranged marriages." Graham's visit to Castle Gregor was twofold. He was here for the summit, which was a very important event. But he was also here to re-introduce his son to his betrothed. Rowan had not seen the little lass in more than twelve years. Kate Carruthers had been a wee lass of five when Andrew entered into the agreement with Douglas Carruthers, to join the clans through the marriage of their children.

"Aye," Angus conceded though he knew that there were also times when no good came of such arrangements. He'd witnessed that first hand through his own parents' marriage. "But 'tis neither here nor there. Bree has the right to choose who she wishes to marry."

Though James Randolph did not necessarily agree with Angus' view of arranged marriages, he could understand Angus' reluctance. While he would have preferred Angus agreeing outright to his proposal, James also knew not all hope was lost. "So if yer daughter were to agree to such an arrangement, ye'd no' be against it?" James asked for clarification sake.

Angus realized then that he'd made an error in judgment on the tenacity of James Randolph. He now found himself in a very uncomfortable position. Angus had not turned down the idea of his daughter marrying Gillon Randolph in its entirety. If he were to say as much now, James Randolph could very well walk away from the bargaining table and there would be little hope of forming an alliance. He could not allow James Randolph to see how uncomfortable the idea made him feel.

"*If* my daughter *wanted* to marry yer son, I would no' object to it at this point," Angus said. "However, it is my right, as her da, to say aye or nay to anyone she might choose. I would no' allow her to marry a man who could no' support her, or a man of questionable character, or a man of loose morals."

James Randolph let the veiled insult pass, as he had been less than kind in his remarks about the potential for backstabbing. "Aye, a lass should expect no less from her da," he agreed.

So the two fathers sat, each studying the other.

Caelen McDunnah and Nial McKee watched in utter dismay at the exchange that was taking place, neither believing they'd just heard Angus McKenna potentially agreeing to an odd match between James Randolph's son and Bree McKenna.

"But I'll no' have any pressure put on me daughter, James Randolph. If yer son wishes to court her, and she is agreeable to such, then I'll allow it." Angus finally spoke.

James Randolph smiled, very much pleased with the turn of events.

"But," Angus said, his voice firm, stern, and unyielding. "I have conditions."

The smile slowly faded from Randolph's face. "And what conditions would those be, Angus?"

"I want yer promise to join us. Whether or no' me daughter is agreeable to be courted by yer son. I'll no' have all our fates restin' in the hands of a lass of seven and ten," Angus explained as he shifted in his chair. "'Tis a courtin' I'm agreein' to and nothin' more. If me daughter has no interest in marryin' yer son, then that will be the end of that and there will be no hard feelings between us. Ye'll still sign the accord."

James Randolph felt that no girl in her right mind would turn down an offer of either courting or marrying his son. Gillon was a handsome young man who would someday inherit the Randolph lands and title of chief of his clan. Gillon was a good catch by anyone's standards. And if by some chance Bree McKenna turned down any offers his son would make, then it would be her loss and not Gillon's.

James also believed that no fine, upstanding young woman who loved her clan would say no if she learned that the potential for extended peace lay in her answer. Once she learned how much was at stake, she couldn't possibly say no.

"Aye, I'll agree to that," James said with a nod of his head.

"And," Angus continued. "No one is to tell her that we had this discussion. I'll no' have my daughter thinkin' that the hopes fer peace lies solely at her feet, fer that be no' the case. The hope fer peace lies with each of us, and us alone."

James Randolph was beginning to wonder if Angus could not read minds. Angus may have thought he had just taken away Randolph's biggest bargaining chip, appealing to the lass's sense of honor and duty. Angus had said no one was to tell her they had held this discussion. He said nothing about telling her about the potential for peace. While his son was a fine young man, James Randolph couldn't be certain that his son's good looks would alone win the girl's affections.

"So be it then," James finally agreed.

"So 'tis agreed then," Seamus Lindsay asked Randolph. "Ye'll sign the agreement, with or without Bree McKenna agreein' to marry yer son?"

"Aye, I do so agree, Seamus."

Seamus, Andrew, and Douglas all breathed small sighs of relief. This day had been far too long in arriving. However, neither Nial nor Caelen were pleased with the turn of events. Nial's jaw clenched tightly while the scowl on Caelen's face deepened. The two men remained quiet, each deciding to wait until the meeting was over to talk with Angus.

Over the course of the next hour, quill was set to parchment as Angus scratched out the peace agreement that would bring the seven clans together. Each man stood one at a time to sign his own name and in doing so, pledged on his honor to come to the aid of any of the other clans in the event of war between Scotland and England, or anyone else that would do any of them or their people harm.

Just before the sun rose in the east, the chiefs each shared a drink of fine whiskey. Peace, they prayed, would be long lasting.

19

Nial McKee and Caelen McDunnah were as opposite as two men could be.

Though Nial was shorter than most, he was strong as an ox. He wore his brown hair cut close to his scalp and there seemed to always be a twinkle in his gray blue eyes. Nial was a lighthearted man, free with a smile and a bawdy joke. He preferred to use his brains and good humor as the means to an end. But should the need arise he was never afraid to use his brawn. Nial was as good on a battlefield as he was in a war room.

Caelen McDunnah was a very imposing figure. Tall, built like a wall made of stone, Caelen wore his black hair long, well past his shoulders. Unlike Nial, he did not wear his heart on his sleeve. And none who knew him could ever remember seeing a twinkle in his mud-brown eyes—unless he was about to run a sword through someone's gut.

Caelen loved to fight. It was oft said that should he become bored or too long away from battle, he'd start an argument or disagreement for the sole purpose of using his fists or broadsword. Fighting amused him.

While the two men may have disagreed on many things, there was one topic on which they could agree: There was something *off* about

Gillon Randolph. Something about the young lad, something they could not quite put their finger on, that made each of them unable to trust him. What that *something* was, neither could explain to Angus. Therefore Angus was convinced it was simple jealousy that turned their heads and made them act like fools.

The two men had done their best to convince Angus to change his mind as it pertained to Gillon Randolph courting the young, innocent Bree. As far as they were concerned, it was the first bad decision they'd ever known Angus McKenna to make. They felt as though Angus was sending Bree into the proverbial lion's den.

"Ye act as though ye think me daughter does no' have the good sense God gave a goat!" Angus told them, shaking his head. "Bree is a good judge of character, lads. If there is something no' quite right about Gillon Randolph, Bree will see it."

"But she be so young, Angus!" Nial exclaimed. "She does no' have any experience with courtin' or the way of men."

Nial had known Bree for more than a decade. He had watched her grow from a wiry little girl into a bonny young lass. Aye, she was a feisty thing, so full of life, energy, and sweetness. Bree would make any man proud to call her wife. The thought of Gillon Randolph having that honor gnawed at his gut. Bree was too good for the likes of him.

"Nial, I'll thank ye kindly to remember yer place." Angus scowled at him, his ire growing with the man's insistence that he had erred in his judgment.

Nial would not back down. This was far too important to leave it alone and see where things might lead. Bree was too important to him. "Aye, Angus, I do ken me place. I *am* chief of me own clan. And I have called ye friend for many a year. 'Tis why I be speakin' me mind this day."

Angus studied him closely for a long moment. "If we're speakin' blunt then, I'll say me peace. I think yer jealous that I'd allow Bree to be courted by any man that be no' *ye*."

Nial's jaw twitched. "I make no secret that I be fond of yer daughter, Angus. She is a bonny lass. Aye, I would no' mind courtin' her meself, but ye've made it abundantly clear ye want no such thing. 'Tis yer right as her da. But I tell ye this, Gillon Randolph is the wrong man fer yer daughter!"

Caelen could take no more of the arguing. He had been standing silently in the corner listening to Angus and Nial go back and forth for more than half an hour.

"I think yer both as daft as the day is long." He spoke softly as he stepped toward the table.

Anger flashed in Nial's eyes, but only for a fleeting moment. Angus was angry as well, but he made no attempt to hide it.

Caelen turned his attention toward Nial as he walked around the table and stood near the door. "We all ken how ye feel about Bree. And no one can blame ye, fer she is a bonny lass. I still say she be a bit young fer the likes of ye, but 'tis no' my place to decide such things."

Nial's jaw continued to twitch. Angus remained silent, watching Caelen with a scrutinizing glare.

"Angus, I think ye be so determined to be *right* that ye canna see nor hear what we be tryin' to tell ye about Gillon Randolph," Caelen said as he placed his hands on the table and leaned over to look his friend directly in the eye.

"Yer so determined to have the seven clans join in peace that yer willin' to set aside the good advice we be givin' ye. I tell ye this as a friend to ye and to yer wife and yer family. Ye ken that I think of Bree as a sister and ye ken well that I've no romantic inclinations toward yer daughter. 'Tis only Bree's safety and happiness that concerns me."

Caelen paused for a moment, letting Angus and Nial think over what he had said. "I ken ye trust Bree's judgment, but I believe Nial is right. The lass has no experience in matters of the heart and she's only kent honorable men such as ye and those of yer clan. She has no experience with men who are no' as inclined to be kind and gentle. I warn ye this now," Caelen stood upright, with his shoulders back. "Ye be makin' a grave mistake in allowin' this."

What Caelen did not tell his good friend was that he and Nial would be watching Gillon Randolph very closely over the next days. If the lad did anything to hurt Bree, there would be no one on this earth who could stop either one of them from seeking retribution.

20

Rowan Graham had known for weeks that his father, and most likely his mother, would be attending the festival and games at Castle Gregor. *Knowing* it did not make things any easier.

It wasn't that Andrew Graham was a mean man. On the contrary, Andrew Graham was one of the most noble and honorable men that Rowan had ever known. That was the problem. If you made a promise, you kept it. You put your clan first, above all else.

And if your father happened to arrange a marriage for you at the ripe old age of ten and one? Well, you swallowed your pride and accepted your fate, like a man, like a warrior, like a good Scot. No matter how homely and gangly the five-year old girl you were betrothed to might have been.

It was his mother that annoyed him to no end. Enndolynn Graham was a force of nature. Aye, she was a kind woman to most people. Where his father may have been more lenient and ready to shrug off most of Rowan's antics as a young boy, his mother was not quite so inclined.

Growing up, he had received many more thumps on his head and spankings from his mother than from his father. He had no doubt that his mother loved him. However, she was a woman who took her role as mother and wife of a clan chief very seriously.

She was convinced that she was doing God's will in making sure her children grew up strong, independent, and moral. Rowan was certain her favorite biblical passage was "spare the rod, spoil the child" for she would oft recite it while warming his rear end with a stick, a strap, or her hand.

The thought of having to spend more than a few minutes with the woman set his teeth on edge.

Rowan had been told of his parents' arrival late in the morning. The games would not start until the morrow so he had been on the training fields with the other MacDougall men when a runner had been sent for him. His presence in the gathering room was immediately demanded. Knowing it was a command and not a request, he instinctively knew his mother was with his father and it had been her who had sent the young boy to find him.

Andrew would have sent word to join them when he was done with his morning training session. His mother wouldn't have cared if he were in a battle for his life, in the middle of his wedding night, or on his deathbed. Patience could not be counted as one of her virtues.

The command caught Black Richard's attention. With his curiosity piqued by the way Rowan's face paled when he'd received the command, Black Richard could not resist the urge to accompany Rowan to the gathering room. Black Richard had never met Enndolynn Graham but he'd heard much about her over the years.

He reckoned, as they walked toward the castle, that only two entities on this earth frightened Rowan: Satan and Enndolynn Graham. From the way Rowan muttered and cursed under his breath, his sagging shoulders, and colorless face, Black Richard supposed his friend would have preferred to be heading toward a meeting with Satan.

Covered in sweat and grime from their sparring on the field, Rowan and Black Richard walked the long hallway that led to the gathering room. As they rounded the corner, Angus' laughter filtered out into the hallway.

Though the morning meal had been cleared away hours ago, the trestle tables were set again. Breads, cheeses, meats, fruits and ale had been spread out. Laird Andrew Graham sat at the long high table with Angus, apparently amused at something Angus had just told him.

Rowan breathed a sigh of relief when he saw his mother was not in attendance. He felt like a man given the reprieve from a death sentence. He'd live a few minutes more.

Rowan knew, unequivocally, that his father was here for more than just the festival and games. Andrew had sent a letter weeks ago, informing Rowan that the time had finally come when he would meet his betrothed again.

His mother sent her own message informing him that if he did not set a wedding date before the end of the games, she would beat him within an inch of his life. She was not pleased that he had been delaying the inevitable for three years. She would give him no more time.

Rowan weighed his options. He could flee, like a coward, head north and never be seen or heard from again. But that would be shirking his responsibilities as eldest son. His father would hunt him down like a wild animal and run him through. You did *not* break your word. You did not run and hide like a coward. And after his death, his mother would filet him like a freshly caught fish. There would be nothing left of him for the living to bury or the scavengers to feast upon.

"Rowan!"

Black Richard took note of Rowan's clenched jaw and the tiny beads of sweat that had begun to form on his forehead. He had the look of a man heading to the gallows and it was all Black Richard could do to contain his amusement.

Rowan walked toward the table and did indeed feel like a man being led to the gallows. For that was what he thought of marriage: 'twas a death sentence. Especially when you were betrothed to a quiet, mousy, homely girl.

Andrew Graham stepped from behind the table with a broad smile and met Rowan halfway. Before Rowan could react, his father, a man built like a fortress wall and just as strong and formidable, wrapped him in a tight hug.

"'Tis good to see you, son!" Andrew's deep voice was like a barrel rolling across a room full of logs—deep, rumbling, and a bit overwhelming.

"'Tis good to see you as well, father," Rowan managed to speak, though it was quite difficult with his father's strong arms wrapped around him so tightly. 'Twas also a bit difficult to breathe.

Andrew Graham pulled away, but kept his hands on his son's shoulders. The two of them stood appraising each other, for it had been six years since they'd last laid eyes on one another. Rowan took note that his father's dark hair now held strands of gray. There were lines on his forehead and around his still bright eyes. He'd aged, but he had aged well.

"Ye look well, father," Rowan told him.

"And ye've grown into a fine man! But I kent that ye would, fer ye take after me and not yer mother."

Rowan cringed inwardly. His mother reminded him of a berserker -- sweet and quiet one moment, but let her get the scent of fear? An involuntary shudder washed over him. He'd rather fight Satan than argue with his mother. Satan could be beaten, his mother, not likely.

"Angus has been tellin' me how well ye've done here, lad. It does a father's heart good to ken his son has acquired good fightin' skills as well as a good head fer strategy. Ye do a father proud, lad!" He slapped Rowan's back and led him toward the table.

"I'm sure ye can guess why we're here, this day, lad," Andrew asked as they stood next to the table. Angus was smiling down at him from the high table, looking as though he were enjoying himself immensely. Rowan's gut tightened and he turned back to his father.

His father was never one to beat around the bush. Rowan swallowed hard. He could feel the imaginary hangman's noose being draped around his neck. "Aye," he answered, at a loss for anything else intelligent to say.

"Good! The wedding will take place at Castle Áit na Síochána within a fortnight after we return from the festival and games." Rowan thought fondly whenever the name of his birthplace was mentioned. The castle was aptly named *Place of Peace,* after Rowan's great-grandfather settled there in the late thirteenth century. Legend had it that when Torcadall Graham and his brethren made their way out of the dark and dense forest that bordered to the north, a sense of peace came over each man, woman and child. They knew they'd found their home.

Apparently, Rowan would not be allowed to choose the date of his own death. His mind raced for a way out of the betrothal. Other than literally dying, he could not think of any.

"Rowan!"

His stomach lurched when he heard the sound of his mother's voice calling his name.

Rowan turned to see a group of women heading toward him, his mother front and center. Enndolynn Graham looked regal and elegant, as always. Her blonde hair was plaited around her head and covered with a whisper soft veil. She wore a dress of crimson silk and he thought the color quite befitting considering she could verbally castrate him in the blink of an eye.

"Mother," Rowan said as he walked toward her. She had the look of a very pleased woman who had just received a fine gift. Smiling, she wrapped Rowan in a warm embrace.

"Rowan," she smiled at him. "It is good to see ye."

"And ye as well, mother," he said when they broke their embrace.

She offered him a very slight smile that said she knew her son was lying. "I've not received any letters from you in quite some time, Rowan," she admonished him.

"Please forgive me," Rowan said. "I have been verra busy of late."

She eyed him up and down, quirked an eyebrow that said she didn't appreciate his falsehood. "Too busy to send a letter to yer own mother? I think no'." She took a step closer and leaned in to whisper to him. "I think ye be avoidin' the inevitable. Verra unbecoming a warrior."

His ballocks contracted and he swallowed hard. Suddenly, the thought of running like a coward didn't seem such a bad idea. At least he could keep possession of his manhood. Cowardice had to be better than emasculation.

She gave him no time to respond. "Because ye refused to come home when summoned, we were forced to come to retrieve you. I trust yer father has informed ye that the date has been set fer yer weddin'?"

Hanging was more like it. "Aye," he said. "He's told me."

"Good," she said. Her knowing smile never left her face.

"And ye are prepared to do yer duty to yer family?" she asked, her voice dripping with false warmth and curiosity.

For a fleeting moment, Rowan thought of telling his mother than he'd been wounded in battle and had been left impotent. Knowing she'd find it neither amusing, nor important, he merely nodded his head and said, "Aye." A promise had been made years ago and Rowan would not be allowed to worm his way out of it.

Enndolynn studied him for a brief moment before turning to face one of the women behind her. "Rowan, I am sure ye remember yer betrothed?" she said as she bowed her head and waved a hand toward the group.

His mother knew damned well he wouldn't know Kate Carruthers if she came up and slapped him. His eyes scanned over the group. He was looking for a gangly, homely lass with red-blonde locks and dull green eyes. Most of the lasses were of the same height and average build. One was a bit on the heavy side, but comely none-the-less. It mattered not which one of these lasses was Kate Carruthers. A hanging was a hanging was a hanging.

The lasses giggled, gave a short curtsey and then slowly turned their heads toward the back of their group. Standing at the rear was a young and quite bonny lass. Surely, this could not be his betrothed? He suddenly felt quite the idiot, for he was quite certain his betrothed would still be the gangly and unbecoming lass with dull green eyes that he remembered from his youth.

But something drew him to the young woman standing so quietly at the rear of the crowd of women. He tilted his head and searched her face for recognition. There *was* something familiar about the green eyes that were staring back at him, but that was where his recognition ended. He had been fully prepared to see a taller version of the five-year-old Kate Carruthers, not the bonny lass standing before him.

Nay, the lass standing before him was quite beautiful. Her long blonde hair, with streaks of red and gold, fell in soft waves over her shoulders. A simple, whisper soft veil of ice blue fell from the back of her head. The lass wore an exquisite gown of the deepest blue that fit over her curves quite nicely. Nay, this could not be *her*.

The young woman stepped forward and took Enndolynn's offered hand.

"Kate," Enndolynn said, her voice as smooth as silk. "I believe it has been some time since ye've seen Rowan."

Kate's smiled demurely as Enndolynn placed her hand in Rowan's. The young woman curtsied elegantly then stood. "M'laird," she murmured, looking nearly as frightened as Rowan felt. Rowan could feel her fingers tremble slightly as they rested in his hand.

"M'lady," Rowan said, brushing a light kiss across her trembling fingers. He found it quite difficult to take his eyes from hers. Mayhap marriage to a bonny creature such as this would not be so bad.

"Rowan," Enndolynn began. "Kate has been under my tutelage fer the past year now."

Rowan felt his stomach tighten. A year with his mother? The lass had surely been to hell and back.

"I won't hold that against her, mother," Rowan said as he gave Kate a wink. He took note of the confusion that flashed in the girl's bright eyes before she pulled her bottom lip in between her teeth as if to suppress a question. Mayhap not too much damage had been done. He couldn't imagine being married to someone like his mother.

Kate's mother had assured her that if she won Enndolynn Graham's approval, then she would surely win Rowan's. That had been Kate's primary goal this past year, for she did not want to be trapped in a marriage with a man who could not respect her, or worse yet, one who hated her because she could not get along with his mother.

Enndolynn had told Kate countless times over the past year, that Rowan Graham was in fact, a mamma's boy. There was nothing that he would not do for her, so strong was their bond and their love of one another.

Kate hadn't been biting her tongue, holding her temper in check, and acting like a meek and mild lass for the past year to have it all cast aside now. Certain she was that if she did anything to earn Enndolynn's disapproval, her son Rowan's equal disapproval was sure to follow. That was the last thing she wanted.

But the tension between Rowan and his mother was palpable. It certainly did not feel like undying love and devotion between mother and son.

"Do no' be so boorish," Enndolynn admonished him.

Oftentimes it was best to simply ignore his mother. "M'lady," Rowan said as he turned his back to his mother. He placed Kate's hand on his arm and led her away from the group. "How was yer journey?"

Kate flashed a look of surprise at Rowan, and a look of uncertainty toward Enndolynn before being led away. She swallowed hard and cast another look at Enndolynn before answering. "Long and rather treacherous," she whispered.

Rowan's heart felt less heavy than it had only moments ago. He detected a note of humor in her answer and it brought a smile to his face. "When ye say treacherous, are ye referring to the roads ye traveled, or something far more dangerous?"

Kate blushed and focused her eyes on the floor. It would not be polite to tell him the truth, that his mother, while a kind woman in general, tended to be overbearing and strong minded. After her first few days under Enndolynn's care, Kate had found herself praying several times a day that Enndolynn's son would take after his father. She could not imagine being married to someone with Enndolynn's sharp tongue or her less than friendly disposition.

Rowan chuckled and his smile broadened. "Ye have me deepest apologies lass."

Kate furrowed her brow and glanced up at him. "Apologies?"

"Aye," Rowan nodded as he led her out of the gathering room and down the hall that led to the out of doors. "Ye've been forced to live with the force of nature that is me mother fer a year. That ye've survived without killin' her or takin' yer own life or runnin' away, speaks well of yer strength of character. I do no' know many other women who could survive more than a few days alone with her."

His statement, while true, made very little sense. Hadn't Enndolynn told her time and time again that Rowan very nearly worshipped the ground she trod upon? Hadn't the woman assured her that theirs was a bond that could not be broken? That Rowan loved and adored his mother incomparably?

For someone who supposedly loved his mother so devoutly, he certainly did not show it. Mayhap he was only trying to impress Kate with a strong outward countenance.

"I feel ye want to agree, but are afraid to," Rowan said as they walked down the stairs and into the bright sunlight. "Ye needn't be afraid of speakin' yer mind with me, lass. I appreciate honesty and forthrightness in a woman."

Worry began to etch its way across Kate's brow. Mayhap this was a test. Mayhap Rowan wanted to know if she held his mother in the same high regard as Kate had been repeatedly told that he did. The risk at the moment was great and it made her feel very uneasy. If she spoke the truth and told him what she really thought of his mother, then there was a very good chance that he'd break the betrothal.

Kate could not take that risk. She'd been betrothed to this man for more than twelve years. It would bring far too much shame to her family to have the betrothal broken, to have her turned away within a few short moments of meeting her future husband again. Nay, she could not risk that.

"I believe yer mum to be a kind woman, m'laird." It wasn't a full out lie. As long as Enndolynn was getting her way, she was kind.

Rowan threw his head back and laughed heartily. Under different circumstances Kate might have liked the sound of his laughter. A sense of dread washed over her for she did not know *why* he laughed. Did he find her statement humorous? Was he a bit daft or mad?

Rowan brought their slow walk to a stop and turned to face her. Kate was staring at the floor and she was biting her lip again. Gently, he lifted her chin with his forefinger so that he could look at her beautiful face.

"Kate, I have a feeling there is much ye want to say but fear sayin' it, as it pertains to me mum," he said softly. She kept her eyes closed and continued to chew on her lip.

Rowan did not want a wife who was afraid to speak her mind nor did he want one who was fearful of him or his mother. His heart skipped a beat or two at that particular thought.

"Kate, ye need never be afraid to speak yer mind. I be no' a cruel man. I make ye a promise now, that I will never hold yer opinions against ye. I will always be honest and I expect no less from ye."

Kate took a deep breath before daring to look up at him. She tried to read his face, to see if his eyes bespoke the truth or if his words were meant as another test of her convictions. Och! How she wished she knew him better! And it did not help that he was so confoundedly handsome. His sparkling eyes made it difficult to concentrate, to form intelligent thoughts.

Rowan felt overwhelmed with a strong urge to kiss this woman who, less than a quarter of an hour ago he had dreaded meeting. He pushed the urge aside and let his hand fall away from her face for he could see the sense of uncertainty in her eyes.

"Ye fear I test ye," he told her. "And I fear it is because of the year ye've spent with me mum."

He watched as she swallowed and drew her lip in between her teeth and resisted the urge to chuckle. "Aye, that is it, isn't it?"

Rowan shook his head, placed her hand on his arm and continued their walk. "Me mum is good at testing a man's patience. I reckon she be the same with women."

They continued to walk in silence with no apparent destination in mind.

After several long moments, Rowan spoke again. "Since ye be a bit afraid to speak yer mind, I shall try to guess what has transpired over the past year." A smile played at his lips as he pretended to think strongly on it for a time.

"I ken me mum well, lass. It can't have been an easy year ye've spent with her. I'm sure she told ye what a bastard I can be. That I be a neglectful son, ill-tempered and short on patience. So ye fear I'd make the same kind of neglectful, ill-tempered husband."

Kate's eyes flew open with surprise and she stopped dead in her tracks.

"Nay!" she protested. "Yer mum never said such things!"

Rowan raised his brow. He was as confused by her protest as he was pleased by it. He'd finally managed to see a spark of life in the lass and was quite glad for it.

"Pray, tell me, what *did* me mum say of me?"

"She said ye were kind and gentle, m'laird. She said the two of ye have an unparalleled bond, that there is naught ye'd no' do fer her, just to see her happy. Yer mum had nothing but verra kind things to say about ye, m'laird, I swear it!" Her words came so rapidly that Rowan was not certain he had heard her correctly.

"Me mum said I was kind and gentle?" he asked her, beyond perplexed. His mother would never have said such a thing to his face.

Kate nodded her head. "Aye, m'laird. She had nothin' but kind things to say of ye."

"And she said she and *I* have a bond? That there is naught I would no' do fer her?"

"Aye, m'laird," Kate said breathlessly. "She said ye were a true mamma's boy!"

Kate hadn't meant it as an insult. She had meant only to reassure Rowan that his mother held him in the highest esteem. Kate pulled her lip in again when she saw his shoulders begin to shake. At first, she thought Rowan was angry. Then that full, rich laugh of his finally escaped.

He laughed to the point he had tears in his eyes. Kate began to question his mental stability.

"So," he began after the laughter began to subside. "This is why ye be afraid to tell me true, what yer opinion of me mum is! Ye be afraid of the *bond* she and I share!"

Rowan shook his head and continued to smile down at Kate. She trembled, even more confused than she was moments ago.

"Lass," Rowan said. "I be no mamma's son! The relationship I have with me mum is precarious at best. To say it's a bond that canna be broken is no' necessarily the truth. Aye, I love me mum. But she be no' the kind, adoring woman she's made ye to believe. I'm afraid she has no' been as honest with ye as ye think she has.

Kate twisted her lips inward again and tried not to laugh aloud. Enndolynn had duped her into believing she could not have Rowan's affections unless she had hers. Kate appreciated honesty in a man. But she refused to agree out loud with Rowan's keen observation of his mother. She decided it would behoove her to put her best foot forward and not voice her own opinions as yet. While Rowan may very well think his mother a she-devil, it did not mean he would not be offended should someone else voice that opinion.

Erring on the side of caution, Kate merely smiled and continued to look straight ahead. To look him full on was far too dangerous. Rowan Graham was perhaps the most beautiful man she'd ever laid eyes upon. His thick dark hair, tied at the nape of his neck, she imagined would feel like silk. His deep, dark brown eyes were captivating and just as dangerous to look at as his full lips.

There was something in his smile that warned Kate not to allow herself to be left alone with him for more than a few heartbeats. At least, not until they were married. Then and only then, would she allow herself to be lost in his beautiful brown eyes.

"I believe I hear yer mother calling fer us," Kate whispered.

Rowan raised an eyebrow as he cast a sidelong look toward Kate. "Then we should continue *away* from her."

21

Bree McKenna could not believe her ears. Mayhap her father had suffered an injury to his head recently, while training. Or, it could be his age, for she knew he wasn't getting any younger. Bree blinked, tilted her head and stared up at her father.

"What?" she asked him again, for she still wasn't certain she had heard him correctly the first three times.

Angus sighed heavily and ran a hand through his hair. "Bree, I've told ye three times now. What is it that ye do no' understand, lass?"

Bree had a long list of things she didn't understand, but that list had increased tenfold in the moments since her father had come to her room. Her da was giving Gillon Randolph permission to court her. What she could not fathom was *why*.

Aye, her da had given her much freedom over the years, far more freedom that most young ladies were accustomed to. As a very little girl, he had allowed her to run and play with the lads. He had fashioned a sword out of wood for her when she was but six years old. Her da had taught her to defend herself, had taught her how to wield a sword and how to ride a horse.

He had given her the freedom to run about the castle, to dance with the lads who were her friends. He had given her the freedom to choose her own husband when that day came.

However he had *never* given permission for her to be formally courted by any lad, not even those she had known her entire life.

And now he stood before her, telling her he was giving this stranger named Gillon Randolph permission to court her. If, in fact, that was something she wished to happen.

"Ye've never given any lad permission to court me," she told him as she pushed away from her dressing table.

"'Tis because none have been brave enough to ask fer the right," Angus told her.

Bree knew this to be true. The lads she knew, the lads she had grown up with, while they might be brave warriors in the making, not a one was brave enough yet to ask Angus McKenna permission to court her. Truth be told, there wasn't any one of them in particular who she would have wanted to court her. But still, most of the girls her age were already married and working on creating their own families. Bree, at the ripe old age of seven and ten, was beginning to feel like an old maid.

"I have never met this Gillon Randolph," Bree said as she tried to steady her hands. For the life of her, she could not figure out why she was trembling. "Why does he wish to court me?"

Angus smiled as he walked toward her. "I believe he caught sight of ye in the courtyard and was captivated by yer beauty," he told her as he placed a hand on her shoulder.

Bree was not simple minded. Aye, she was a free spirit, laughed easily, and enjoyed life. For those who did not know her well, they might mistake her for a simple minded young lass without the intelligence God gave a goat. For the first time in her life she wondered if her father thought the same of her and believed her unable to see through the lie he had just told.

Deciding it best not to contradict her father, she merely quirked an eyebrow. "He did, did he?"

"Aye, at least that is what his da tells me," Angus said as he gave her shoulder a gentle squeeze.

Bree crossed her arms over her chest. "So this Gillon Randolph did no' come to ye himself, but sent his da to ask?"

"What does it matter how I came to know he wants to court ye?" Angus asked as he turned away.

Bree thought on it for a moment before responding. "I suppose it does no' matter."

Angus had suddenly grown quite interested in the tapestry that hung on the wall next to the fireplace. "So, do ye wish to let him court ye or no?" he finally asked.

She knew instinctively that there was something her father was holding back. Something he did not want her to know. She decided to play along, but only so that she might learn what her father's secret was. "I'll allow it on one condition," she said softly.

"And what might that condition be?"

Bree took a few steps toward her father. "That I do no' have to marry him if I do no' want to."

She could see her father's shoulders relax and a moment later he turned to face her again. "I've told ye since ye were a babe in swaddlin' clothes that I'd never force ye to marry a man ye did no' want to marry. That still holds true, Bree. 'Tis just a courtin' the lad be askin' fer."

Bree nodded her head and stood a bit taller. One way or another, she would learn why this courting was so important to him. "So be it then. When do I meet this man?"

Angus studied her for a moment. No man could be more proud of his children than he. Bree was like him in so many ways -- strong of character, smart as a whip, and not afraid to speak her mind. There were times, however, that he wished she was not as beautiful as her mother. With her dark hair and bright green eyes, it was only through brute strength and threat of death that he had kept the lads away from her. Guilt played with his heart, for he felt as though he were throwing her to the lions. But knowing his daughter was at times a force to be reckoned with, he was certain she could hold her own against any man.

"Yer mum and I will introduce the two of ye at the evenin' meal. We've musicians here fer the festival and games, so there will be a dance this night as well."

"Good. I look forward to meetin' the man brave enough to ask to court me." While something gnawed at the back of her mind that said there was much more to this than her father was telling, she couldn't quite quash her excitement. Mayhap it was nothing more than fear of the unknown that played with her nerves. Mayhap this was all as innocent as her da was attempting to make it.

"I'm verra proud of ye, Bree," Angus said as he wrapped her in a warm embrace. "'Tis an honor to be yer father."

Bree returned his embrace. She tried to shake the sense of trepidation by trying to convince herself that her father would never do anything to put her in harm's way.

"YE KEN I'VE NO DESIRE TO MARRY ANY TIME SOON, SO I DO NO' understand the need to court this lass." Gillon Randolph did not like the idea of being forced to court someone he'd never laid eyes on. But his father was insistent. And if there was anything that Gillon had learned in his life, it was that when James Randolph set his mind to something, he held on to it with a death like grip. Even if the man was far too soft and weak in Gillon's eyes, he could respect his father's stubbornness.

Gillon stood in the middle of the chamber room his father had been given for the duration of their stay at Gregor. It was late in the day and all Gillon wished for at the moment was to leave his father. The festival had begun and there were many young lasses below stairs and out of doors. Lasses he intended to woo and a few that he thought might be willing to come warm his bed after the evening meal.

"Do no' be a fool, Gillon!" James barked at him. "I've seen the lass, and she *is* a bonny thing!"

Gillon didn't care how bonny Bree McKenna was. He had plans, plans that did not include a wife or children, at least not for a very long time. There were things he wanted to do, to see, to experience, before settling down into a state of so-called wedded bliss.

The MacDougalls were a large, strong clan and it was better to have them on his side than against it. The alliance the Randolphs had formed with the Bowies and the treachery that ensued had left a bitter taste in the young man's mouth. He would much prefer to re-build his clan on his own. Aye, it would take years to get back all they had lost due to his father's mistake. Gillon's pride told him 'twould be better to rebuild on their own than to risk another alliance. But his father could not and would not be swayed.

"Ye *will* do this, Gillon. Ye will court this lass and ye'll win her heart," James Randolph demanded. He was unable mask the frustration he felt toward his son. "Ye will be the chief and laird of our clan someday, Gillon. Ye'll take yer rightful place upon me death. I do this fer ye, son, and fer the future of our clan."

"Then *ye* court her!" The words were out before he could pull them back in.

James shot to his feet and unable to check his anger, he lashed out. He slapped Gillon across his face with the back of his hand. There was too much at stake to allow his son to behave with such disrespect and insolence.

Gillon was more surprised than physically hurt by his father's hand. His father rarely lashed out at anyone, at least not with his hands. He thought his father's even temper and gentleness a sign of weakness. That in turn made it very difficult for Gillon to hold any true respect for the man.

"That will be the last time ye ever hit me da," Gillon said as he took a deep breath and stood taller. "I warn ye now that next time, I'll no' show ye the respect of yer position."

James regretted very little in his life. Since the day he became the chief of his clan some two and twenty years past, after the death of his own father, every decision James had made revolved around what was best for his people. He had seldom made a decision in his life that did not take into account how it would affect his people and their futures.

It was no different when he learned twenty years ago that his wife carried another man's babe. He could not hold her accountable or guilty, for the babe had not been conceived from a lust-filled affair. It had been far worse than that. James had spent every day since, trying to make up for what had happened to her.

There were however, times, little moments, like this one, where he regretted claiming Gillon as his own son. Gillon had been a beautiful boy, but as he grew older, he began to display his blood father's disposition and ill temper. Much to James' dismay, Gillon often chose to take the darker paths of life, instead of doing what was honorable or right.

"Be careful what threats ye make, Gillon," James seethed. He tried to pull back the anger but it was not easy when his son refused to see reason.

James knew his son had a mean streak. Mayhap if the lad had a wife with the brightness of spirit and level of intelligence that Bree McKenna possessed, Gillon might turn his life around. Mayhap all he needed was a good woman, like Bree, to help soften his heart. That had been the main reason James had asked Angus to allow his son to court Bree.

"Yer goin' to court Bree McKenna," James said. "Yer goin' to court her, woo her, and win her heart. There be too much at stake fer all of us, Gillon. We *need* this alliance with the MacDougalls. Bree is a fine lass and she'll make ye a fine wife."

Gillon made a decision then to do everything in his power to have the bonny Bree McKenna hate the very ground he walked on, if for no other reason than it would surely drive his father mad. Bree could be the most beautiful, kind, smart, and generous woman on the planet. It would matter not. Come hell or high water, he'd get the lass to hate him, thereby stopping any chance at a union between the two clans.

"As ye bid, da. I'll court Bree McKenna," Gillon told his father as he held his head high. *But I'll make ye rue the day ye ever asked this of me.*

BREE WAS RETURNING FROM VISITING HER BEAUTIFUL NEW NEPHEW, Connell McEwan, named after Duncan's father. Though Connell the first had died not long after Bree was born, she was certain that had he lived, he would have been very proud of his namesake. He was a strong, healthy boy and his parents could not be more happy or proud.

As Bree walked through the kitchen, she returned the hellos given by the kitchen staff. Her mind was elsewhere and she paid little attention to anything as she walked into the grand gathering room and up the stairs toward her room. They'd be serving the evening meal within an hour and she had yet to change her dress and style her hair.

She had been unable to shake the feeling that her father had been less than truthful with her earlier. After her meeting with her da, Bree had gone to discuss the situation with her mum. Isobel had insisted it was just nerves at finally being allowed to have a young man court her. Isobel felt fairly certain there was no more to it than that. Angus would never do anything to put any of his children in harm's way.

So that was that. Gillon Randolph would be allowed to sit next to her at the high table for the evening meal. Bree did not relish the thought of being put on display in such a manner and she knew her friends would tease her relentlessly over it.

But it was just a courting.

It was merely a way for two people to get to know one another.

Certainly nothing more would come of it.

There was a very strong possibility that Gillon Randolph might not like her at all. He might not care for her outspokenness. He might not care for her blunt honesty or her quickness to laugh. Gillon might be one of those very serious men who didn't enjoy life as much as she did. She couldn't see herself with a man like that.

Nay, she'd need a man who would appreciate her honesty, her sincerity. He would need to appreciate her for who she *was* and not just her outer appearance.

Bree was no fool. She'd been told more times than she could ever hope to count, that she was as beautiful as her mother. When she was younger, she couldn't quite see what others saw. But as she grew older, even she could see the similarities between herself and her mum.

Both owned the same dark hair and bright green eyes. Like her mother, she had a straight nose that was neither too long nor too short. Bree's jaw was a bit squarer than her mothers, but considered fine and feminine nonetheless. And like her mother, she'd been blessed with an ample bosom. She recognized that fact only from the way she'd catch her male friends staring at it, all slack jawed and drooling. Fools. There was more to a woman than pretty teeth and an ample chest!

Bree wanted a man who would appreciate *who* she was inside. He'd need to appreciate her intelligence, her cheerfulness, and all the things that made Bree, Bree.

She would need a man who would not expect her to change to suit him. Nay, any man that would ever win her heart would have to allow her to be true to herself.

The man who would steal her heart would need to be just as honest and blunt as she. He would also need to be kind and gentle with all things. He must also possess as much honor as her father and the other men of her clan.

It would help as well if he were easy to look at. He needn't be dangerously handsome for Bree knew that true beauty came from within. As long as his face was not covered in warts and his eyes were not crossed, she imagined she could be completely happy with an average looking young man. As long as he possessed a good heart, a kind yet amiable disposition, and good teeth, looks did not matter. Bree never put much belief in vanity but she did feel it quite well and good to have *some* standards when it came to choosing a husband.

Lost as she was in her own thoughts, Bree was paying no attention at all to where she might be walking or what she might be walking into. As she rounded the corner that led to her sleeping chamber, she walked into what she could only assume at that moment was a wall. Apparently, this particular wall had arms for they reached out and grabbed her before she could fall to the floor.

The wall possessed *very* strong arms. Warm, delightful, bare arms with so many muscles, they looked as though they would burst through the skin! As she fought to catch her breath, with her head resting against a most firm, warm chest, she could hear the pounding of his heart. Lord almighty! She imagined the beating of her heart matched the wall's beat for beat.

"Lass!" a deep, rumbling voice finally spoke. "Are ye well?"

Bree swallowed hard before nodding her head. She imagined she could stay here, wrapped up in the muscly arms for forever and a day and never tire of it.

What on earth had come over her? Panic began to set in, for she'd never felt so discombobulated in her life!

"Are ye sure?" the deep voice asked.

It took a moment or two longer than she would have wished in order to find her voice. "Aye, I am." 'Twas a full out lie, but the wall needn't know that at the moment.

The arms pushed her gently away from his chest, holding her at arm's length. After a time, she managed to open her eyes to see the face that belonged to all those muscles.

She noticed his eyes first. They twinkled. Whether from the torch-light or devilishness, she was not certain. She'd seen those eyes before, many times. But never had she seen a twinkle, a sparkle like what she now witnessed. Sweet danger and a promise of something unknown, yet quite delightfully wicked, stared back at her.

He possessed a most handsome face. A dangerously handsome face. But it was his smile, bright and full of the devil that made her legs feel weak and her heart to pound ferociously in her chest. There was a full-ness to his lips that she'd never seen before. Lips she was certain, had been designed by God for the sole purpose of kissing. Long, languid kisses. Kisses that would take her breath away if she'd allow it.

Embarrassment crashed over her from the top of her head to the tips of her toes. Like a bird flushed from a bush, she said not a word, but took flight down the hallway and straight to her room. Slamming the door behind her, she clung to the latch and rested her hot cheeks against the cool wood.

As she stood, trying to steady the thrumming of her heart and her breathing, her mind raced in too many different directions at once. It left her feeling very light headed and not at all herself. What the devil had come over her?

Oh, this canna be good! she thought to herself as she began to pace around her room.

She was to meet a young man in less than an hour's time, a young man who had expressed a desire to court her. And now here she was, pacing in her room like a wild animal locked in a cage, unable to steady her trembling fingers, unable to get the wicked thoughts from her mind, unable yet to erase the image of the soft, gray-blue eyes and bright smile.

This is no' at all like me! I do no' fall victim to a handsome face! I do no' act foolish nor do I swoon at the mere presence of a bright smile!

Quickly, she set about trying to find the reason behind why she was behaving so oddly. The courting. That had to be it. She'd never been courted before. Her nerves felt raw because she was entering into new territory. It was the excitement of the unknown that made her act so foolishly. There was simply no other explanation!

She was afraid of meeting the stranger named Gillon Randolph. The young man who had apparently seen her about, had asked after her, and now had the desire to court her. His desire rested solely on some physical attraction. At first, she had resented the fact that it was her face that caused Gillon Randolph to want to court her.

And now, here she was, pacing nervously about her room, acting as though she'd never seen a handsome face before. Behaving like her friend Ellen, who was so easily swayed by a handsome face or a bright smile!

Gillon Randolph. This was all *his* fault. Had he never asked to court her, then her mind would not be all twisted and confused.

And she would not be thinking of those full, beautiful lips pressing against her own. Nor would she want to feel those broad hands caressing her face or her back. And she wouldn't be wondering about the sweet surprise the gray-blue eyes had seemed to hold.

To the devil with ye, Gillon Randolph!

ISOBEL HAD COME TO HELP BREE READY HERSELF FOR THE EVENING meal. They chose a dark green damask gown trimmed in gold thread. Isobel plaited Bree's hair into a crown around her head with a long braid dangling down her back. She attached a simple white veil to the top of Bree's crown and smiled in satisfaction.

"Ye'll take his breath away fer certain, Bree!" Isobel giggled when she saw Bree burn crimson. "Don't fash yerself Bree! He is sure to admire yer heart as well as yer bonny face."

Bree wondered silently how her mother always seemed to know what she was thinking.

"I've done some askin' around, Bree," Isobel said as she straightened Bree's veil. "I'm told Gillon Randolph is a handsome lad. He's a bit quiet, they tell me. He's the eldest son of James Randolph and he'll be chief of their clan someday."

Bree's mind was otherwise engaged, thinking back to the wall of muscles and twinkling eyes that had caught her off guard earlier. She sighed heavily as she only half listened to her mother talk of Gillon's qualities.

Isobel grew silent and studied her daughter for several moments. "Lass, what bothers ye?"

Bree shook her head. Her mother would not understand how confused she was feeling at the moment and all because of a pair of gray-blue eyes and sinfully full lips that had seemed to have taken her mind as prisoner.

"Do ye worry he'll no' like ye?" Isobel asked.

"Nay, mum, I do no'."

A warm smile came to Isobel's face. "Ye worry ye'll no' like *him,*" Isobel said as she smoothed non-existent wrinkles from her yellow gown of silk.

Bree closed her eyes and took a deep breath. Aye, that was one of the many things that worried her heart and mind. Mayhap she should tell her mother the truth.

"Och! Bree! Ye needn't worry it much. 'Tis just a courtin'. No one is askin' ye to marry the lad!" Isobel said as she gave a gentle squeeze to Bree's arms.

Bree realized that her mother was correct. She would meet this Gillon Randolph, be polite and gracious, but when the night was done she would pull her parents aside and tell them the truth. She couldn't possibly care for Gillon Randolph. Not now. Not ever.

For her heart had mysteriously and unequivocally fallen for someone else. He was someone she'd known most of her life. Someone she had always looked upon as a brother, a friend, and a guardian.

Until this afternoon, she had never taken notice of his broad shoulders, his strong, muscled arms, or his full lips. She had never noticed how his eyes twinkled or the wicked secret that his lips quietly promised. He'd always been there, like her family, ready to tease or offer a shoulder. Why hadn't she noticed him in such a manner before this day?

But something had happened today, something that was both strange and wonderful and frightening at the same time. Bree could not begin to make sense of it, let alone begin to explain it to anyone else.

Bree lifted her chin, pushed her shoulders back, and nodded to her mum. "Yer right. I worry over nothing. 'Tis just a dinner and nothin' more than that," she said with a smile.

Isobel took Bree's hands into her own and gave them a gentle squeeze. "Now ye have the right of it, lass!"

Admittedly, Bree did feel better. She would get through the evening meal then confess her true heart to her mum and da later. Tonight however, she had to keep the promise that she had made to her da, to allow this Gillon Randolph a chance. Believing no harm could come from it, Bree smiled and gave her mother a hug.

"What harm can one meal do?" Bree asked aloud as Isobel led her from the bedchamber. "'Tisn't like I have to marry the lad!"

BREE FELT AS THOUGH HER VERY SOUL HAD BEEN SUCKED FROM HER body. Never had she felt so alone, so disheartened or disillusioned. It was to have been a simple meal and nothing more. Now she stood before her father and mother, grief stricken and heart broken. And it was all Gillon Randolph's fault.

Why had she agreed to his invitation to walk with him after the meal? Had she simply said no thank you, then none of this would be happening. She wouldn't feel as though her heart had been ripped from her chest and trampled on by a hundred horses.

Had she declined Gillon's invitation, she would at this very moment, be telling her parents the truth instead of the lie that somehow managed to find its way through her lips.

"Bree, are ye certain?" Angus asked her with a scrutinizing glare. He looked as hurt as Bree felt.

"Aye, I am," she answered in a low whisper.

"But ye've just met the lad! How can ye wish to marry him?" Angus tried to add some softness to his voice but it was very difficult. This was his youngest child, his beautiful, sweet Bree.

To tell her father the whole truth would have brought him nothing more than shame. She could not do that to him.

"He's a kind young man, da. He'll make a good husband." She nearly choked on that lie as well. Gillon Randolph would most assuredly *not* make her a good husband. But she had no choice in the matter. She had to do this. She had to do it for the sake of her father's pride as well as the future of her clan.

Bree clasped her hands together to keep anyone from noticing how they trembled. She could not look at her father, or her mother right now. She did not doubt that her mother would be able to see the shame she felt and Bree felt she did not have the strength to deal with it right now.

She was sacrificing herself for the good of the clan, nothing more. She had to do this.

"Bree," Isobel finally spoke. She was sitting in a chair in front of Angus' desk. "Tell me what is in yer *heart* lass. Do ye love Gillon?"

Love Gillon? Nay. Not now, not ever. But she could not admit that to her mother, or to anyone else. For the first time in her life, Bree lied to her mother. "Aye," she said, still unable to look Isobel in the eye.

Isobel's sigh told Bree she did not believe her. But what was she to do? Tell her mother the truth? Nay, it would devastate Isobel to learn the truth of the matter.

Bree could not and would not tell either of her parents that she had learned the truth behind the gathering of the seven clans. She could not tell them that she knew a marriage between she and Gillon Randolph was the only way of bringing peace among the seven.

Angus had always promised that she could choose her own husband, that he would never force a marriage on any of his children. They were all free to pick a spouse of their own liking. But war between the clans was imminent.

Gillon had enlightened her to the truth of it all last night. He had been honest and told her that he no more wanted a marriage with her than she with him. However, he felt he owed a duty to his own clan to agree to such a union and he felt Bree should know the full meaning behind the courting. Ultimately, the decision would be left up to her to marry him or not. But if she denied his offer, war would ensue, and the peaceful life she had been living would be no longer.

How could she say no? How could she in good conscience deny her clan peace? How could she, in good conscience, say no with the knowledge that if any lives were lost they were lost because of that one little word? The fate of so many people, people that she adored and loved, lay at her feet. She could not deny them the peace that they deserved.

And she could not risk the death of the man who had inexplicably won her heart in the hallway just yesterday afternoon. Bree could not put his life in jeopardy.

"Bree, leave us now. Let yer father and me talk fer a time before we give ye our decision," Isobel stood and laid a hand on Bree's shoulder.

"Is it no' my decision to make, mum?" Bree asked.

"To a certain extent, it is lass. But the final say rests with yer da and me. Now, go on with ye. Wait for me in yer chamber."

Bree took a deep breath before leaving the room.

She thought back to her own words the night before. *What harm could one meal do?* Apparently, far more than she could ever have imagined.

22

Word of Bree's impending engagement spread through the keep like wildfire. To say the people were shocked and surprised would have been a tremendous understatement. To say Caelen and Nial were beside themselves with frustration and disgust was just as grand an understatement.

"This is all Angus' fault!" Nial seethed as he paced back and forth in front of the stables.

Caelen sat on the ground nearby and kept his anger hidden, at least for now.

"How could Bree agree to such a thing?" Nial asked, not expecting an answer.

"We've time to stop it," Caelen said rather flatly as he pulled a dagger from his belt. The morning sunshine glinted off the cold steel and brought a slight smile to Caelen's lips.

Nial ran a hand through his hair, his insides all a jumbled mess. "What could she possibly see in the lad?"

"I never much liked the boy and I like his da even less," Caelen said as he ran his thumb along the blade.

"There be something wrong with that lad, I can feel it in me bones!" Nial shook his head and continued to pace.

"I wonder if the lad can fight?" Caelen asked to no one in particular.

"Bree canna ken what she is doin', there can be no other explanation."

"I do no' think he can fight. 'Twould be easy enough to run me blade across his throat. He'd be none the wiser fer it."

"This is why women should no' be allowed to choose their own husbands, fer they do no' always think with clear heads." Nial spat at the ground and continued to shake his head.

"I could kill him easily enough, 'twould no' even break into a sweat." Caelen's smile broadened at the thought.

"She's far too good fer the little snot!" Nial continued to rant.

"I could blame the Bowie clan fer I have a bit of their plaid saved fer such an occasion." Caelen chuckled at the devious plan running through his mind.

"He'll ruin her. He'll try to break her spirit! And 'tis her spirit that makes her so, so..." Nial searched for the right word. "Her spirit is what makes her so bonny!"

"I suppose I should kill the da as well. I do no' trust him. James Randolph is just as odd as his son."

"We must go to Angus and protest this. We must get him to see that Bree be making the biggest mistake of her life."

There were two different conversations taking place, but the intent of each man was the same. They had to stop Bree from marrying Gillon Randolph. Either by reasoning with Angus or by killing the young man. At the moment, it mattered little to either man how they might stop the wedding, so long as it was stopped.

Nial stopped and looked down at Caelen. "So ye agree then?" he asked.

Caelen sheathed his dagger and pulled himself to his feet. "Aye, I do."

Nial nodded his head and breathed a sigh of relief. "Do ye think Bree will forgive us fer stoppin' this?"

"Mayhap no' at first. But eventually she will see the right of it," Caelen said as he patted Nial on the shoulder.

"I would no' care so much, her gettin' married, if she'd chosen a lad more likable," Nial offered.

"True," Caelen agreed. "There are many more suitable men fer Bree. Far more honorable men."

"Aye, and eventually she'll see we were right and did this only fer her benefit," Nial said as he began walking toward the keep.

Caelen agreed with a firm slap to Nial's back. "Aye!" he said with a broad smile. "She'll no grieve long, I'm certain."

Nial assumed Caelen meant that Bree would grieve over the loss of a wedding and not a life.

GILLON HAD BEEN SO ANGRY WITH HIS FATHER THAT HE HAD SPENT the better part of the evening trying to figure out a way to get even. As luck would have it, Bree was easier to mold than he had anticipated.

He stood now, alone on the top floor of the tall north tower. It was very late and a light mist hung in the warm summer night air. He could see the many small fires still burning in the camps that dotted the horizon and laughed in amusement at the false security those below him felt.

None had an inkling or suspicion as to all the secret meetings taking place while they slept peacefully, in utter ignorance. His own father was included among those ranks.

His thoughts turned to Bree McKenna. He did not care for the lass' cheerful disposition or her easy smile. Her only saving grace was that she was a beautiful young woman, curvaceous, and untouched by another man's hands. The fact that she had little interest in or knowledge of clan politics only played to Gillon's favor.

It had been easy enough to convince her that the only way to have peace amongst the clans was for them to marry. The fact that he stressed to her his lack of interest or want in such a betrothal was of great benefit to him. Letting her know he was just as against such a union had only helped matters.

'Twas only after he told her that his desire was for them to eventually forge a genuine, honest bond out of respect for one another, did she finally agree to his proposal. Bree's heart, honor, and love of clan would not only be her downfall, it would also lead to the downfalls of others.

Bree was as unsuspecting a lass as he'd ever encountered. It hadn't taken much work on his part to convince her, to get her to see that the fate of seven clans rested entirely upon her shoulders. Had she not been so confoundedly honorable or possessed such a good heart, his words would have fallen on deaf ears.

His father had been extraordinarily surprised as well as pleased to learn that Gillon had successfully convinced the girl to marry him. James hadn't asked outright what Gillon had done to turn the lass' head so and in such a quick manner, for he had been far too happy with the news.

Gillon had known the truth for quite some time now. James Randolph was not his blood father. It wasn't James Randolph's blood that ran through his veins. Nay, he was not weak like the man who claimed to be his father.

As a younger boy, Gillon had always suspected something was wrong with his mother as well as with the man who called him son. It wasn't until his mother's death three years ago that he learned the truth of his conception, the truth of his mother's whoring ways.

At first he had mourned her death, had missed her terribly. Then a man—a man Gillon felt an immediate connection to, a connection he'd never felt with James Randolph—stepped from the dark shadows and told Gillon the truth.

His mother had been quite the whore in her younger days and Gillon had been born the result of her inability to keep her legs together whenever James was away. There was much doubt as to who fathered his four sisters. Who knew if any of them belonged to James or to some other man?

Gillon didn't much care, for soon, they'd all bow at his feet. Everyone in his clan would. Everyone in attendance at the festival and games would bow before him. All of Scotland would.

Gillon paced, growing impatient as the moments passed by, as he waited for his blood father to appear. He tried to quell his growing anger and frustration by thinking of his future. Within a year's time, all of Scotland would know his name and people would quake with fear at the mere mention of it. It was his destiny and he would not be denied.

He knew he could not wait for James to die of natural causes. Nay, James Randolph was far too healthy a man to hope he would die soon. So Gillon would take matters into his own hands to insure that all he'd been working for these past few years would come to fruition.

Gillon looked forward to James' death with great anticipation. He could hardly wait for the moment when he would tell James Randolph that he knew the truth. That he knew James had lied to him all these years.

He would tell him as he lay dying, a painful, agonizing death. James Randolph's last images on earth would be of Gillon and his *real* father. James' last thoughts would be filled with regret as well as fear. For in his last moments on earth, he would know that Gillon would no longer be denied that to which he was entitled. No longer would he look at Gillon with shame. Nay, his eyes would be filled with fear. Fear in knowing that all that James had tried to quash twenty years ago, was born again and that more than one man's destiny would finally be filled.

Oh, how he relished the thought of confronting him, of letting him know he knew, that he knew all of it. That James had stolen everything he owned, had taken it from Gillon's blood father out of spite and jealousy. James Randolph, by rights, should never have been the chief of Clan Randolph. He had no right to it, by birth or by law.

To the world, James Randolph appeared to be an honorable, honest man. People looked up to him, they admired him, and they believed and trusted him. When the rest of Scotland learned that James was no better than a common thief, that he had killed the true heir and the rightful chief of Clan Randolph for his own selfish pursuits, they'd no longer hold him in such high esteem. They'd spit every time the name James Randolph was mentioned.

A smile formed on Gillon's lips when he thought about that moment. Revenge would be his and it would come very soon.

His hand immediately went to the hilt of his sword when he heard the latch on the door being lifted. Even though only one man knew he was waiting in the tower, one couldn't be too careful. The door pushed open ever so quietly and a moment later a shadow stepped into the room. Gillon smiled and let loose a sigh of relief.

"Da," he said happily as the man walked toward him.

"Son," the shadow whispered. "I hear the lass has agreed to marry ye."

Gillon nodded his head and smiled. "Aye, she has. It did no' take much to convince her."

The shadow crossed the room to look out the narrow window. He stood silently for a time before speaking over his shoulder. "'Ye've done good, son. I be verra proud of ye. Our plan is falling into place verra nicely. The lass is a bonus, to be certain. We need to have ye married as soon as possible of course."

Gillon didn't understand the need to marry quickly and asked his father to explain.

"Ye will give James the poison only after ye marry Bree McKenna. After he's dead and we tell the world the truth, Angus will be so worried fer his daughter's safety that he'll agree to anything."

Sudden awareness dawned in Gillon's eyes. He had not thought of how the marriage would affect Angus McKenna. He'd only been concerned with the thought of bedding the virginal Bree and the eventual death of her inane happy spirit.

"Angus has no' yet agreed to the union, da," Gillon informed him.

"But he will. Ye need to work on Bree. If she is insistent that ye marry soon, she'll be able to convince her da of it with that bonny smile of hers. Fathers can seldom say no to their children."

Gillon didn't think that necessarily true, for James had often told him no. But then, he wasn't really James Randolph's son to begin with, so that may have played a part in how he treated Gillon.

23

Angus McKenna could never be mistaken for a foolish nor stupid man. From the moment Bree came to him asking permission to marry Gillon Randolph, he knew something had gone horribly awry. He had agreed only to Gillon courting his youngest daughter as a means of showing James Randolph that his intentions toward the Randolph clan were good. He hadn't meant for his daughter to be swept away by Gillon.

Isobel agreed with Angus' instincts that Bree was being less than genuine and honest with them. He was glad his wife had also seen through their daughter's lie. They both knew that Bree didn't care for Gillon any more than they believed she'd fallen in love with the little bastard.

Something more was afoot and it did not take long to determine what had happened. James Randolph had broken his promise not to tell Bree the true reasons behind Gillon courting her. It was the only plausible explanation for her sudden interest in marriage.

Thus, Angus called another private meeting, this time, with only a handful of men. Men that he trusted and whose council he put good store in.

Duncan sat to Angus' right, with Wee William to his left. Rowan and Black Richard sat on either side of them. Directly across from Angus sat Nial McKee, Caelen McDunnah, and Findley McKenna.

Findley, Angus' nephew by blood, was now a laird of a vast estate in the eastern part of Scotland, a day's ride from Stirling Castle and more than a week's travel from Castle Gregor. Findley and his new family had arrived just that morning to participate in the festival and games. He hadn't been included in the meeting of the seven clans for several reasons, the primary one being he'd sworn his fealty to Angus years ago. He swore it again just a few short months ago, after Angus and the others in attendance had helped him to free Maggy Boyle from Malcolm Buchannan. Findley had married Maggy not long after and together they were raising her five sons and rebuilding her estate.

These were the men Angus trusted, not only with his own life, but the lives of his wife and children.

"So, ye think James Randolph broke his word to ye?" Wee William asked.

Angus studied him for a moment. It had been more than a month since Wee William had shaved his face and married Nora. Angus didn't think he'd ever get used to seeing Wee William without all that hair and his long beard.

"Aye, I do."

"But why would he do such a thing?" Wee William asked. "He had already signed the agreement. What good could come of tellin' Bree?"

"I do no' think it was James," Nial offered up. "I think 'twas Gillon. I told ye from the start I did no' trust the little bastard."

"We all ken how ye feel about Gillon, Nial," Angus said gruffly.

"I feel the same," Caelen said. "The lad is no' to be trusted."

Angus let out a frustrated breath. "It matters no' *which* of them told her. The point is, she's insistin' on marryin' the boy, and she'll no confess the truth."

Low burning embers crackled softly as each man sat in stony silence. There was not a man in the room who did not hold a special place in his heart for Bree. They would do whatever they could to either change her mind or protect her from making the biggest mistake of her life.

Nial worked his jaw back and forth. The more he thought of Bree marrying Gillon, the more enraged he became. She was too beautiful, too sweet, and far too innocent to understand the consequences of marrying Gillon Randolph. Bree deserved a far better man for a husband than the young lad who made the hair on the back of Nial's neck stand on edge each time he was in his presence.

"So will ye allow her to marry him?" Nial asked. He'd already made up his mind that if Angus agreed to the union, he'd kill Gillon before the boy had time to rejoice at the news.

"Nay, I shall no' allow it. I do no' like the little shite any more than ye do," Angus told him.

Nial breathed a barely perceptible sigh of relief as he cast a look at Caelen. For a brief moment, Caelen looked let down by the news. Nial supposed the man was disappointed that he'd not get the chance to take Gillon Randolph's life.

"So why are we here, Angus?" Findley asked. He had been sitting quietly, with his chin resting on his fingers and his index finger near his temple.

Angus took a deep breath in, held it for a moment before releasing it slowly. "I fear there is somethin' amiss. Somethin' I can't quite put me finger to. It warns me we've a traitor in our midst."

The men looked at each other. Wee William sat forward in his chair. "A traitor? Among the MacDougall clan?" It was not easy for Wee William to believe one of their own would turn against them.

"Nay, not among our clan, Wee William," Angus said as he leaned back in his chair. "I fear it be one of the seven who signed the agreement of peace."

Nial and Caelen looked to one another. Something silent passed between them and it did not go unnoticed by Angus.

"I do no' believe it be either of *ye,* lads," Angus said. His voice was low and steady. "Elst I would no' have ye here this night."

Rowan had been listening intently. There was no way on God's earth that Angus could believe that his father, Andrew Graham, was a traitor. But his lack of presence in the meeting gave Rowan pause. "Do you think me father a traitor?" he asked, a knot forming in the pit of his stomach.

Angus shook his head. "Nay, I do no'. But I fear we must be verra careful from this point forward. The fewer people who are aware of my suspicions, the better off we'll be. Yer da is no more a traitor than I."

Angus' statement did nothing to make Rowan feel better. "If ye do no' consider me da a traitor, then why is he no' here?"

"Rowan, do no' be offended!" Angus barked at him. "I've already spoken privately with yer da, he's well aware of me suspicions. He agreed to no' attend. No one will suspect anything unusual in the seven of us meeting."

Rowan sat back in his seat, glad to know that Angus had already discussed his concerns with Andrew.

"So who do ye think it be?" Wee William asked as he shrugged first one shoulder, then the other, to work out the kinks in his neck. He was tired and sorely missing his wife.

"I prefer to keep that to meself fer now," Angus said. Before anyone could protest, he explained his thinking to them.

"I do no' want me own suspicions to keep any of ye from seein' somethin' that I canna see. There be a good chance I'm wrong. I do no' want me own suspicions cloudin' yer good judgments. If I'm right, then I ken I haven't lost too much of me senses with me auld age," he smiled at the men.

Findley, Wee William and Duncan chuckled softly. The other men were in far more serious moods. "And if I be wrong, I trust ye'll bring it to me attention one way or another."

"So what is the plan then, Angus?" Duncan asked.

"Bree will no' tell me the truth. James and Gillon Randolph are anxiously awaiting me decision. I fear that if I say nay, without good cause, James will do somethin' stupid and back out of the agreement. So," Angus said as he looked at both Duncan and Wee William, "I want to enlist yer wives to help."

Wee William and Duncan looked at one another before turning back to Angus.

"I fear Bree willna talk to me or her mum on this. She may however, speak to yer wives. Aishlinn be her sister and Nora a good friend. Mayhap the two of them can find out *why* Bree is insistin' on marryin' Gillon. While they do that, I'll tell James that I'll give me answer in five days, before we call an end to the festival. That should buy us time to learn if there is truly a traitor among us or no'."

The men agreed that it was a good plan to start with. Each man would be keeping a close eye on Bree as well as looking for anything out of the ordinary as it pertained to the other chiefs who had signed the peace agreement.

NIAL FELT BETTER KNOWING THAT BREE WOULD NOT BE MARRYING Gillon. Aye, he knew he had no chance of his own in gaining Angus' approval at courting her himself. Although Angus never gave Nial any real reasons for being against such a match, Nial assumed it was because he was nearly seven years older than Bree. He also suspected that his life of debauchery and drinking had just as much to do with it as anything else. Nay, more likely than not, Angus felt his daughter could do much better than Nial.

Bree was, after all, Angus' youngest daughter, and more precious to him than breathing. She was a beautiful, sweet, funny lass with a good heart and high spiritedness that one seldom found in women. Those were the qualities that drew Nial to her to begin with.

As Nial left the war room to head above stairs to his own chamber, he reflected on his own life. Like Bree, Nial had a love of life. But where Bree's zealousness of life tended to lean toward things such as riding horses, kissing wee bairns, and far more feminine pursuits, Nial's interests had leaned more toward debauchery and sinful delights.

He had been made chief of his clan -- much to his own surprise and anguish—just three years past. He had been the second son and had never believed he would someday be the leader of his clan. But when his father and older brother were both killed in battle, the responsibility fell to him.

Prior to their deaths, Nial had lived a rather spoiled life, coming and going and doing as he pleased without a care in the world. He would often be gone from home for months at a time, working his way across Scotland in a frenzy of bar wenches, drink, and gambling.

Nial made his way through the dark corridor of the third floor and into his chamber. He stripped off his tunic and trews and climbed into his bed and tried to shrug off the sense of loneliness that had settled over him these past few months.

Had he known he would have been made chief of his clan, he wouldn't have wasted so much time lingering between the sheets with one prostitute after another. He would not have drunk or gambled so much. Instead, he would have listened to his father's good advice, grown up and behaved in a far more honorable manner. He would have spent more time learning from his father than traipsing across the country tossing back whiskey and lifting skirts.

For three years now, he had done his best to make up for lost time and lack of wisdom. Nial maintained the same council of men that his father had relied so heavily upon. He also relied on Caelen McDunnah's good sense, even though it was often hidden behind a dark and brooding facade and his love of fighting.

Nial knew there was far more to his friend than what he let the rest of the world see. Hidden behind the mask of shadows was a man in deep mourning. Caelen's wife had died in childbed five years past. He had never quite gotten over the loss and Nial doubted that he ever would. Caelen had loved her more than he had ever loved anyone or anything. She had been the love of his life. When she died, she took Caelen's heart with her, along with a huge part of his soul.

Prior to becoming chief of his clan, Nial would never have put much stock in love, at least not the kind of love he'd witnessed between Caelen and Fiona.

Physical love, Nial knew from far too much experience, could be purchased for a few groats.

Real love, the kind you felt clear to your bones, was not so easily obtained. He reasoned that not everyone could be blessed with that kind of adoration or devotion. But he was willing to settle for something close to it.

As often happened when he mused on the subject of love and adoration, his mind turned toward Bree McKenna. Aye, she was young, that he could not deny. But most lasses her age were already married with one or two babes.

Bree was different.

It wasn't just a physical attraction that he felt toward her. Aye, she was beautiful, there was no denying that fact. But there was so much more to Bree than her long, dark hair and bright green eyes. She never played dumb or coy. She was not afraid to speak her mind nor was she afraid to smile when the mood struck her. Nor was she afraid to give a man a piece of her mind if she thought him deserving of it. She was a lady, but not so much so that she worried over getting her hands dirty or was afraid to ride a horse astride.

Nial rolled onto his back and stared up at the dark ceiling. The sun would be up in a few hours and there was much to do. Try as he might, his thoughts kept returning to Bree.

He knew, beyond a shadow of a doubt, that Bree thought of him more as a brother or uncle. There was no hope in that ever changing, no matter how much he wished it. What was he to do? He was tired of being alone. He did want someone to share his life with, a fine woman who would help him build his clan, a bonny lass who would happily bear his children.

While Bree was exactly the woman he wished to hold that position, deep down, he knew she deserved better. She was deserving of someone closer to her own age, someone without his history of whoring and drinking. She deserved a better man, one who could give her more than just his heart.

Aye, his clan was growing and his lands were finally beginning to prosper. But it would be years before Clan McKee would be able to boast the same successes and prosperity that Clan MacDougall currently held. He could not ask Bree to sacrifice and go without for the next ten or twenty years, just so he could wake up to her sweet smile each morn.

In his mind, he had settled it: he would begin to look elsewhere for a wife and put all thoughts of Bree McKenna away.

His heart, however, was an entirely different matter.

NORA DIDN'T KNOW IF SHE SHOULD BE PROUD OR TERRIFIED. PROUD that Angus trusted her enough to get to the bottom of why Bree was insisting on marrying Gillon Randolph or terrified of failing. She felt a combination of both and mayhap that was why she felt so uneasy and worried.

Together Nora and Aishlinn sat at Aishlinn's kitchen table across from Bree. The babe slept peacefully in his cradle near the fire. Nora didn't know Bree well, but even she could tell the poor girl was heartbroken.

"Bree," Nora said as she played with her cup of tea. She was not sure how to get Bree to open up, so she decided to speak to her as if it were Elise sitting across from her. "Are you excited about soon becoming a married woman?"

Bree was absentmindedly running a finger along her cup "Aye, I suppose so." Her forlorn expression told Nora the opposite.

"Do you worry over it? Over being a wife, I mean."

Bree shook her head no.

Nora and Aishlinn looked at one another. Neither of them believed her. She *was* worried over something and it was up to them to figure out what.

Aishlinn decided to take a more direct approach. "Do you love this boy? Love him with all your heart? It is the rest of your life we're talking about, Bree."

Bree's eyes began to water as she continued to stare blankly at her cup.

"Bree," Nora said as she gently placed her hand on Bree's. "I can tell you, from personal experience, that if you do not love this boy, love him with all your heart, you will never be happy. My first marriage was all the proof anyone needs that if you marry the wrong person for the wrong reasons, you will never be happy."

Bree swiped away a tear and took a deep breath. "Many marriages start out with neither party knowin' the other. But over time, they grow a fondness fer each other."

That was all the evidence that Aishlinn needed. "Did Gillon Randolph tell ye that the only way for peace to happen between the clans is for you to marry him?"

Bree shrugged her shoulders as if that fact was of no importance.

"He lied," Aishlinn said bluntly.

Bree looked up then, a line of confusion creasing her brow. "Why would he lie over such a thing as that?"

Connell began to fuss and whimper. Aishlinn went to his cradle and carefully lifted him into her arms. "Who knows why men do what they do, Bree," Aishlinn answered as she sat down at the table and gently rocked the babe. "But I tell you this, the boy has lied to you."

"Mayhap the boy himself is confused on the matter," Nora interjected. "Mayhap he is only telling Bree what he himself has been told." She could only hope she was correct. Otherwise, something far more sinister was taking place and that thought made her stomach turn.

"That is a possibility. But either way, she cannot marry the boy," Aishlinn said as Connell began to cry loudly. She opened the front of her dress and offered the babe her breast. He quieted instantly as he latched on rather greedily.

"But what if what he says is true?" Bree asked as she watched her nephew. "What if there is more to everything than the two of ye ken?"

"Bree," Nora began, "Gillon's father has already signed the peace agreement."

Bree was growing frustrated as well as angry. She knew she should put her faith and trust in her family, but she worried over what Gillon had told her. *An agreement is sometimes not worth the parchment it is written upon.* What if he told the truth?

Nora and Aishlinn sensed there was more that Bree was not telling them.

"Bree, what has Gillon told you?" Nora asked softly.

Bree was not sure how much she should tell anyone, least of all Nora and Aishlinn. Gillon had warned her that if she divulged all of what he had told her, war would be immediate. Men would die. Her heart tightened at the thought of losing her father, her brothers, or the man she was falling hopelessly in love with.

"Bree, has Angus ever done anything that made you doubt or distrust him?" Nora asked.

Bree gave a little shake of her head. "Nay, he hasn't."

"Then why can you not trust him now? What has happened that makes you doubt that your father will keep you safe?"

The words slowly tumbled out, along with the tears she'd been trying to hold at bay. "People will die if I don't marry Gillon! If we don't join our two clans together, lives will be lost!"

Nora stood quickly and came around the table. She sat next to Bree and cradled her in her bosom. Patting her back, she tried to soothe away the poor girl's worries.

"You'll save more lives by telling us the truth now, Bree. Marrying Gillon will not stop any bloodshed. In fact, it will cause more." Aishlinn frowned, not out of anger toward Bree, but toward Gillon.

He had put the weight of the world on her shoulders with nothing but lies. She knew her sister's love for her people was the only thing driving her to marry Gillon. It wasn't love that led her. It was fear. It was a love and fear that Aishlinn was all too familiar with.

Last year Aishlinn had made the terrible mistake of believing that the only way to stop the English from wiping out her clan was to turn herself over to the Earl of Penrith. That decision nearly cost Duncan his life. Had she put more faith in her father and the men of her clan, more lives would have been saved that day than lost. She would carry the guilt over that decision with her every day for the rest of her life.

Bree was beginning to feel as though she had been stuffed into a tiny room and the more people talked to her the smaller the room became. It was becoming more and more difficult to keep everything straight in her mind. It was also becoming more difficult to ignore the feelings she had for a certain Highlander.

What if what Nora and Aishlinn told her was true? What if Gillon had lied? If she married him, she would be giving up any chance at a happy future with a man she genuinely cared for.

"Why would Gillon lie to me?" she asked to no one in particular.

Aishlinn took in a deep breath and glanced at Nora. Highlanders and their ways with romance continued to baffle Nora. While Nora could never understand why a man might lie about something, she knew all too well just what some men were capable of.

"Bree," Nora said as she gave her another hug. "There are so many good, kind men in your clan. They're all honorable and honest. Why Gillon lied is not nearly as important as knowing that he did. Please, Bree, do not make the same mistake with Gillon that I made with Horace."

Bree studied Nora's face for a moment. "Was it really that bad with Horace?"

Nora took a deep breath. She felt she was not gaining any ground by speaking. Mayhap *showing* the girl what a man could do might have a better impact. Nora slowly pulled up the sleeves of her dress and showed Bree the scars on her wrists.

"Would you like to see the ones on my back?" Nora asked.

"Or mine?" Aishlinn offered solemnly.

Bree remembered the condition of Aishlinn's back when she had first arrived more than a year ago. She didn't need to see the scars these men had left on the bodies of these kind, beautiful women. It was in that brief moment that clarity dawned and she knew without a doubt, what she must do.

NORA COULD FEEL HER HUSBAND STARING AT HER FROM ACROSS THE courtyard and it brought glorious goose bumps to her skin. She thought it odd, yet exhilarating, to think William capable of making her skin tingle with excitement with only a glance. Married nearly two months now, she no longer worried about being prim and proper, at least not where her husband was concerned. William was quite happy with her free spiritedness, especially when they were alone.

Nora stood in the courtyard enjoying the company of Aishlinn, Bree, Isobel and Maggy. They were remarking at how much Connell resembled his father and how big he was growing. Isobel was a very proud grandmother and believed Connell to be the most beautiful babe she'd ever seen, next to her own of course.

Although she'd only known Maggy but a few days, Nora liked her. Maggy was blunt and honest, yet in a way that wasn't rude. She simply said what was on her mind. It was a trait Nora was beginning to admire and hoped to one day acquire.

The courtyard was very crowded and hundreds of people were milling about waiting for the next round of games to begin. Although similar festivals were held all across England, Nora had never had the opportunity to experience one herself. She enjoyed the jesters and acrobats, the bards and musicians, but most of all she enjoyed watching her husband as he wrestled and battled with one friendly opponent after another.

Elise and John soon joined them, happily munching on sweet cakes that Mary had given them. Elise was her usual cheerful and chatty self. Nora didn't worry much about Elise fitting in for the child had such an outgoing personality and seemed to make friends wherever she went. Nay, she worried less about Elise but more over John.

The first few weeks had been the most difficult for him. However, he seemed to be doing much better since Wee William had taken over the role of both father figure and older brother. The two had begun to form a friendship that Nora thanked God for each day.

She was glad to see that John was smiling and seemed to be enjoying the festivities. He was growing into a fine young man. The changes she was seeing in him of late, brought forth a great sense of pride. Wee William had remarked on more than one occasion that John was doing quite well with his sword work.

"Nora," John said as he chewed the last bite of his sweet cake. "Will you be watching me later?"

Nora had no idea what John was talking about and voiced her confusion. She took immediate notice of his attempt at appearing as nonchalant as he could.

"Has Wee William not told you then?"

"Told me what?" Nora asked as she wiped crumbs from Elise's face.

"I'll be in a challenge later today. I'll be going up against one of the McKee boys."

Nora blinked before her brow drew into a hard line of confusion blended with anger. "You're what?" she asked, with more than a hint of disbelief to her voice.

Somewhere in the past weeks, John had acquired that wry, *do-no'-worry-yer-pretty-little-head-over-it-lass* smile that Wee William often threw her way. That blasted smile had disarmed her on countless occasions. It was a smile she had grown to love seeing on her husband.

But now her younger brother was attempting to use that smile to disarm her into not worrying over this battle that had been planned without her knowledge.

"Nora, we'll be usin' wooden swords. And we'll both be in pads and mail, so ye needn't fash yerself."

Not only had he acquired the smile, he was also acquiring a Scottish brogue. She'd have none of it. "Do not try to flash that smile at me, young man," she told him through gritted teeth. "And since when do you not only act like a Highlander, but you speak like one? What happened to hating Scots? What happened to *I'll go home with or without you?*"

John laughed as he rested his palm on the hilt of his wooden sword. Wee William had warned him that Nora would respond thusly, so John had been completely prepared for it. John couldn't help but laugh, for Wee William had even foretold what Nora would say. His brother-in-law was a very smart man.

"Am I not allowed to change my mind?" John asked as he shifted his weight from one foot to the other. "I thought you wanted me to try to fit in here. I thought you wanted me to think of this place as my home?" He tried to look broken-hearted and forlorn. Wee William had told him that when a smile didn't work to try looking sad and hurt.

Nora pursed her lips together and thrust her hands on her hips. Apparently her husband was doing more than just training John in swordplay. Her husband was teaching him how to beguile her with either a smile or a frown. She rolled her eyes and looked to the women standing next to her. One look and Nora could tell they thought the same as she: John was attempting to play with her feelings.

"Och, Nora!" Maggy interjected. "Do no' fash yerself, lass! John looks as though he can take care of himself. He's a fine lookin' lad."

Aishlinn cast a knowing look at Nora before agreeing. "I'm sure he's learned much these past weeks, especially with Wee William training him."

"Aye, Wee William is verra good with a sword," Maggy said. She knew from personal experience that Wee William was a fine warrior. She also knew well that he was full of the devil, but she marked that as one of his finer qualities.

"Which McKee lad are ye goin' up against?" Maggy asked.

John sighed heavily before looking up at her. "Thomas McKee," John answered.

Maggy gave a whistle of surprise. "Thomas McKee, ye say?"

"Aye," John answered. He wasn't sure why she looked so surprised. It instantly made him feel uneasy.

Maggy thought on it for a moment before nodding her head. "He's a good warrior in the makin'. He's got a wee bit more experience than ye, but do no' let that be a worry, lad. He won't kill ye."

John swallowed nervously. Wee William had assured him that the lad he was going up against was the same size and age as himself, and with the same experience level. Mayhap Wee William was wrong.

"I ken the McKee lad well!" Isobel said with a smile. "He's been wielding a sword since the day he could walk. All the McKee lads are trained that way. 'Tis why Angus enjoys havin' them as allies." She turned her attention toward Maggy then. "Ye weren't here for the festival last year. Thomas McKee won, going up against lads older and bigger than he."

Maggy nodded her head in agreement. "Aye, Findley told me of it. Andrew McDunnah's parents are quite grateful that the lad didna die from the broken arm Thomas McKee gave him."

Suddenly, the women had forgotten John was even there. They huddled around talking excitedly about Thomas McKee's skills on the field.

"I'm sure Wee William has his reasons for putting John up against Thomas McKee," Aishlinn offered.

Nora finally stepped into the conversation. "Aye, I'm sure you are right, Aishlinn. William would never do anything to put John in harm's way. I'm sure the padding and mail will keep him safe."

"Aye, it will keep him safe enough. Mayhap ye should ask William to put extra padding on John's arms?" Isobel said as she turned her back to John.

"That might not be a bad idea. I'm sure William trusts in John's abilities, or he wouldn't put him up against such an experienced lad," Nora said as she pulled her lips inward.

"I'm sure yer right," Maggy said. "Why else would Wee William put John up against the likes of Thomas McKee? John's been a good lad, hasn't he?"

"To a certain extent he has. But we did get off to a rather rocky start. John was not at all pleased with my decision to move to Scotland. But I'm sure William harbors no resentment toward John now. I mean that was months ago."

John was growing more and more uneasy. Self-doubt began to creep in as he began to second-guess Wee William's motives.

"Wee William isn't one to harbor a grudge for long," Aishlinn said. "I seriously doubt he wants to get even with John for all the horrible things he said about Scots and Highlanders on your journey here."

"I agree," Nora said as she cast a sideways glance toward John. He was growing a bit pale and looked rather worried. She thought it served him right. "Nay, Wee William has his reasons for doing this, but I doubt any of them are meant to hurt John."

Isobel peeked over Maggy's shoulders and had to bite her tongue to keep from laughing at John. "I believe yer right, Nora. Nay, John must be a very fine swordsman for Wee William to make such a decision. The lad must have a natural talent that none of us are aware of."

Nora could see John growing more worried as he listened in on their conversation. She began to feel guilty. It wasn't that she was against him sparring with some other young lad in a contest. It was simply the fact that the decision had been made without her. That and the fact that John tried to use tactics he could only have learned at the hands of her husband to gain her approval.

She wanted John to succeed here. She wanted him to feel like he belonged and if learning to be a fine warrior was something he enjoyed, she would not keep him from it. Even if it did make her heart heavy with worry.

Nora broke away from the group of women and placed a hand on John's shoulder. "John," she said softly. "We've been having a bit of fun at your expense. I'm sure Wee William has made the right decision on who you should spar against this day."

John looked up and Nora could see the self-doubt etched in his face.

"I was upset that you tried to sway me with that smile you learned from William," she gave his shoulder a slight squeeze. "If you had simply come to me and talked to me honestly about what you wanted to do, I would not have tried to stop you. You've learned how to smile and frown from my husband. Apparently, he doesn't understand the importance of being honest and he's taught you to be disingenuous. I'll not have that. If there is something you want to do, just come to me and we'll discuss it. Do not try to ply me with a smile, a twinkle in your eyes, or a frown. Just talk to me."

John sighed with relief as well as regret. He'd been caught and he felt guilty for it. Although in his defense, he was simply doing what Wee William had told him to do. Still, deep down, he knew Nora was right.

"I'm sorry, Nora," he told her, wishing all the while he could just slip away. Sparring didn't seem quite so important or fun anymore. Neither did trying to play with his sister's feelings.

"I do not hold you as accountable as I hold my husband, John. Trust me, he is in far more trouble than you," she told him with a smile. "Now, tell me, just how good with a sword are you?"

Truthfully, John was no longer certain. "Well, according to Wee William, I'm quite good. He says I have a natural talent for it."

Nora smiled at him as she ran a hand across his head. "Now *that* I do believe."

John raised a doubtful eyebrow at her. "Why?"

"You might not know this, but our father was *very* good with a sword when he was younger. He spent time as a soldier, but he gave it up when he married your mother. You get that natural talent from him. Besides, while my husband might be full of the devil most of the time, he isn't so stupid as to put you in harm's way. He knows that I'd kill him if anything happened to you."

The smile returned to John's face. He did not doubt his sister's sincerity.

"Now, you'll not worry about it any further. I will watch you spar this day and I'll be cheering you on. But keep in mind that if you get hurt, I'll throttle your neck!"

His spirits were lifted so much so that he allowed Nora to give him a hug without protesting.

24

If Horace Crawford had believed in any kind of god, benevolent or otherwise, he would have given the credit for his good fortune to him. But as it was, Horace Crawford believed in God as much as he believed in faeries and ghosts -- not one bit.

There was no heaven, there was no hell, and there certainly was no all-knowing, all-powerful, almighty God who had a hand in anything. Horace Crawford looked to no one but himself for those things that he craved, desired, or needed. And he sure as hell would not give credit to God for blessing him with the good fortune that lay before him at the moment.

He had found her.

Or rather, both *hers*.

There they were: Nora and Aishlinn. The women who had betrayed him, the women who had stolen from him. Standing together, laughing and giggling like the whores that they were. Aishlinn held someone's babe in her arms while she and Nora twittered and oohed and ahhed over it as if it held great importance to them.

He doubted it belonged to the older woman who stood next to Aishlinn or the redhead that stood next Nora. The dark haired woman looked too old to birth a bairn and the redhead was most definitely pregnant. The babe must belong to someone else.

Horace didn't give a care who the babe belonged to. If he had to kill it in order to get to these women, he would. One less filthy Scot to have to worry over.

Horace had left England just two days after the Highlanders had stormed into his home. He had sold everything he owned, including the little farm, in order to purchase horses and supplies for himself and for each of his brothers. He had visited the current Earl of Penrith and forged a bargain of sorts with him.

Horace had been able to convince the man that he knew exactly where Aishlinn was and that he would be returning her in short order to finally face the justice she deserved for stabbing his brother. Horace asked for very little in return. He wanted only to keep whatever it was that Aishlinn had stolen. And he wanted to be certain his wife would be punished severely for her transgressions.

The Earl of Penrith readily agreed. While he hadn't been particularly close with his brother, the thought of avenging his death was appealing. Perversion ran in their family and none of the males were immune to it.

Horace had been traveling all over this God-forsaken Scottish soil for weeks, searching for the giant. It had been quite easy to learn the giant's name, for it had been told to him time and time again. The answer was always the same; there wasn't a man as big as Wee William of Dunshire in all of Scotland.

Aye, the land was crawling with big, hairy men. But none as big as *him,* this man whose name was spoken with more than a hint of awe and wonder. The way people talked, Wee William was legendary, a man above men. They spoke of him as though he were some kind of pagan god. The man was known for his prowess in battle just as much as he was known for his size. The more Horace learned of the man, the more he hated him.

And now, here he stood, on the land of the so-called proud Clan MacDougall. He was so close to Aishlinn and Nora that it made his hands tingle with excitement. Revenge would be his before this day was over.

The two women were so wrapped up in themselves that Horace and his two brothers went unnoticed by either of them. It also worked to their advantage that the land was filled with hundreds upon hundreds of people. It was easy to get lost in a crowd this size. It also did not hurt that the two feckless women were so engaged with the babe that they paid little attention to anything else around them.

Neither Horace nor his brothers had shaved in weeks. They'd also traded their English farmer clothing in for tunics, trews, and plaids to help them better blend in with the rest of the Highlanders. No one seemed to notice that they did not belong and that gave Horace a great sense of security.

He and his brothers kept a safe distance as they followed Nora, Aishlinn, John and Elise and the other women away from the keep and toward the fields. Horace had no interest in anything other than how he would get Nora and Aishlinn away from these people. As much as he would have liked to have simply marched up to them and taken them away at knifepoint, he was not that incredibly stupid. He knew he would take less than ten steps before one of the Highlanders would step in.

He would stay in the background, silently watching until he felt comfortable enough to take them. Hopefully he'd not have long to wait.

NORA WATCHED WITH A SIGNIFICANT AMOUNT OF PRIDE AS HER husband took to the fields. Aye, she was upset with him that he hadn't come to her to discuss John's sparring later, but decided it was a conversation best saved for later. She didn't want her husband going out onto the fields with his mind elsewhere.

She thought her husband looked magnificent in his battle gear, and the sight of him, dressed in his pads, mail and hauberk. It brought splendid tingles of excitement to her skin. Though he was covered head to toe, she could see the steely resolve in his eyes.

Wee William looked around the crowd for his wife. He was unsure if he wanted her there or not. Though they fought with dull swords, the possibility of injury was still great. He knew she'd worry herself into a frenzy if anything happened to him. He found he rather liked that thought, that if anything were to happen to him, she'd worry and fuss. Although he felt guilty for thinking such a thing, the thought warmed his heart.

But it was the pride he would see in her eyes and the smile on her face when he bested his opponent that energized him. He finally found her, standing with Aishlinn, Isobel, Maggy, and the children. Six months ago, if anyone had told him he would be filled with pride as well as want of a woman, like he felt at that very moment, he would have laughed at them.

Smiling, he sauntered over to his wife, and without speaking a word, he pulled her into his chest and kissed her in front of God and everyone. He no longer cared what anyone would think of him. All he cared about was his wife and the love she showed him.

The kiss lasted far longer than was proper, but again, he cared not for social propriety. He took great pride in watching his wife trying to catch her breath when he let loose his hold on her. He leaned in and whispered into her ear.

"Wife, what boon shall ye give me when I best me opponent?"

Nora licked her lips and giggled. She stood taller on her tiptoes so that she could whisper her answer.

Wee William could feel himself burning red from head to toe. His wife, God love her, was becoming more and more brazen the longer they were married. He couldn't imagine her giving him such an answer as she just did, only a few short months ago.

His lips curved into a warm smile as he kissed her again, this time on her forehead. "Yer becoming a wanton woman and I like that about ye, wife!"

Nora returned his smile and blushed. "If I'm a wanton, it's because you're full of the devil and made me this way."

He supposed that was true, therefore he did not argue the point. He gave her a wink and a smile and started to walk away. Elise stopped him.

"William!" she called out to him.

He turned back to her and bent on one knee. "Yes, lass?"

"You won't get hurt will you?" She looked genuinely worried and it made him chuckle.

"Nay, lass, I will no' get hurt."

"And you won't kill the man, will you?"

Wee William chuckled again and patted her on her head. "Nay, lass, I'll no' be killin' anyone this day. I told ye, we're just pretending to battle, to see who is the better warrior."

Elise looked relieved. "I say you'll win then, because no one is as big as you!"

"Aye, 'tis more than size a man needs to be a good warrior, lass. But I must go now. I'll explain it to ye later."

Elise smiled and wished him good luck as he stood and entered the circle. Wee William's first opponent of the day would be Philip Douglas of the Randolph clan. Philip was three and twenty and a good warrior. A head shorter than Wee William and not nearly as heavy or well muscled, the lad had speed and leanness on his side.

It was nigh impossible to find an opponent who was as close to Wee William in size or weight or in experience and abilities. He had not been defeated either in training or on the battlefield in nearly ten years. Anyone who had never seen Wee William fight or train, might be led to believe he could be defeated simply because he was so big. Philip Douglas was not so ignorant. He had been fighting against Wee William in three festivals to date and he knew there was a very good chance he'd not win again this day. Still, it was all in fun and he had to at least try.

The match was called to a start and both men circled each other for a few moments, swords drawn and at the ready as they sized up one another. Philip was the first to swing his sword, to which Wee William answered by blocking it with his own.

Philip believed he might have a chance at beating Wee William if he were to wear the man down. Believing a man of such size would, hopefully, wear down easily, Philip took his time with small thrusts and jabs.

This was not Wee William's first games. It took only a few moments to understand Philip's intention. There were other fights to be won at these games and Wee William wanted to take his wife home so that she could make good on her promised boon. He debated momentarily on whether he should at least make it appear as though it was a battle well fought or end it quickly.

As they spun around the circle, he caught a glimpse of his wife. He could read her face as easily as he could read a book. She was attempting to look as though she was not worried about him, but he could still see her apprehension. He decided to end the match quickly.

In the span of three heartbeats, Wee William answered Philip's upward sword thrust by blocking it with his own. He followed through with his left arm coming down hard on the back of Philip's head, which sent Philip to his knees. A heartbeat later, Wee William had the young man on his back and his dagger a hair's breadth away from the young man's throat. It was an easy win, but a win nonetheless.

The crowd erupted in a combination of applause and cheers and disappointment. Wee William knew they would have preferred a much longer and more challenging match, but the day was still early. There would be far better men to fight as the day wore on.

As Wee William helped Philip to his feet and dusted the man off, he looked to the crowd again for his wife. He found her still standing next to Aishlinn, but the look on Nora's face wasn't one of pride or adoration. Nora's face was as white as a sheet and she looked as though she had just witnessed a most horrific sight. He watched in a state of confusion as Nora stared at something across the ring.

Wee William's heart seized as he watched his beautiful wife fall to the ground.

25

Bree had decided earlier in the day that she must find out *why* Gillon had lied to her. No matter that Nora and Aishlinn had told her, that the why of his lies was not as important as the lie itself, Bree had to know. If there was something nefarious going on, something that would put her family and her clan in jeopardy, she had to know what it was.

So she set about to find out. In hindsight she questioned her plan of extracting information. Mayhap it would have been better to tell someone what her intentions had been. Mayhap she should have gone to her father and told him what Gillon had told her. Mayhap she shouldn't have gone to Gillon and told him her own little lie in hopes of learning more.

For if she had done any of those things, she would not now be sitting atop a horse with her hands bound and her heart racing with fear. She would not be Gillon's prisoner and heading toward Randolph lands.

As it stood, no one knew where she was or what had happened. There wouldn't be hordes of MacDougall warriors in fast pursuit, at least not yet. Nay, she was going to have to rely on her own wits and instincts if she were to get out of this alive.

Doubt over her wits and instincts had taken hold however. Bree was no longer certain if she should rely on them further. It had been her instincts that had gotten her into the mess to begin with. She battled with the doubt and fear as they rode through MacDougall lands.

When she caught Gillon looking at her as though she were a piece of venison, her resolve to get out of this predicament alive began to return. Nay, she'd not let Gillon Randolph get away with this, not with any of it.

She returned his devious smile with one of her own. *Ye can go straight to hell, Gillon Randolph.*

WEE WILLIAM RUSHED TO HIS WIFE'S SIDE, PUSHING PEOPLE OUT OF his way as he knelt to the ground. He could not fathom why she had looked so terrified just before she collapsed to the ground.

He lifted her head into his arms. "Nora!" His voice was laced with worry, dread, confusion, and fear. "Nora!"

Isobel knelt on the other side of Wee William and began to look for signs of wounds or other trauma. "What the bloody hell happened?" she demanded to no one in particular. The crowd around them murmured they did not know.

Wee William touched Nora's forehead. It felt clammy and cold.

"Get her to the keep," Isobel ordered as she stood.

Wee William scooped his wife up and raced toward the keep. He paid no attention to what anyone was telling him as his mind raced with a thousand reasons as to why Nora had fainted. His mind flashed back to when Elise and John were ill. He knew in his heart that he could not bear the thought of Nora being as sick as the children had been.

With his wife in his arms, he bounded up the stairs of the keep and directly to Aishlinn's former bedchamber. Gently, as if she were made of glass, he laid Nora on the bed. His eyes scanned her limp body for any indication as to what would have caused her to faint. There was no blood, no signs of a wound of any kind.

Her skin was still cold, her forehead and hands damp. Wee William drew a blanket up and covered her with it as he spoke to her in soft, hushed and worried tones.

"Nora, please wake up," he pleaded with her.

She did not stir.

Tears of worry filled his eyes as quickly as the terrifying scenarios that played out in his mind.

He held her hand and pressed a kiss to the back of it while he pleaded quietly with her to open her eyes, to say something, to please not leave him.

Wee William could not say how much time passed before Isobel and Mary entered the room. Mary carried in a bowl of water while Isobel held linens in her arms. In very little time, they set about placing damp clothes on her forehead and began to examine her again.

Wee William's head fell to rest near Nora's. He was rubbing the back of her hand as he prayed silently that she would be well. Mayhap she had just become too hot in the afternoon sun. Or perhaps she had been far more worried over watching him spar than he realized.

Isobel had loosened the ties on Nora's dress while Mary had removed her boots. Wee William paid no attention.

A short time later, Nora began to mumble and opened her eyes. She looked about the room, confused as to how she had come to be there.

"William," Nora scratched out when she saw him at her side.

Wee William sat up with a start and the look of relief on his face was undeniable.

"Nora!" he cried out. He breathed a very heavy sigh of relief. "You scared the bloody hell out of me!"

The foggy cloud began to lift as she began to remember. Her heart felt heavy as the image of Horace came to the forefront.

"Horace," she said.

Wee William looked positively confused. Why would she be thinking of him?

Nora tried to sit, but the wave of nausea roiled in her belly. She swallowed it down and hoped she would not throw up. She closed her eyes and waited for the wave to pass. "I saw Horace," she whispered.

Wee William shook his head. Nay, it was impossible. Wee William had spent weeks convincing himself that if Horace Crawford had lived, he was too selfish and too big a coward to come to Scotland to retrieve his wife.

"Nay, lass," Wee William said, trying to sound far more confident than he actually felt at the moment. A voice niggled at the back of his mind that warned him he might be about to lose everything he loved in this world if what Nora said was true. He pushed the thought away. He could not lose Nora.

"Mayhap you were just overly hot from the afternoon sun. Mayhap it was just someone who looked like Horace," Wee William said. He was trying to convince both of them.

"Nay! I know what I saw, William!" Nora argued. To her very core she knew it was him, the man who had hurt her in so many possible ways. What she could not figure out was *how*. How had he lived? Rowan and Black Richard and the others had taken Horace and his brothers away, to kill them, to make her a widow. Wee William had told her as much.

It was Duncan's voice that Wee William heard next.

"Nora speaks the truth," Duncan said as he stepped into the room. "Aishlinn saw him as well."

Wee William spun and looked at Duncan. Wee William felt as though his entire world was falling apart. He would have to be honest with his wife now. He could only pray that she would understand that he had done all that he had done because he loved her.

"Is Aishlinn well?" Isobel asked as she came to Duncan's side.

"Aye, she's in your room with the babe and Angus," Duncan answered. His eyes were glued to Wee William.

"How could they still be alive?" Nora asked worriedly as she looked to her husband for answers.

Wee William stood then and let go of his wife's hand. His heart felt lodged in his throat.

"William," Nora said softly as she carefully sat up. "What is it that you're not telling me?"

Wee William walked to the window. He did not see the crowds, the banners, or the children playing. He did not hear the sounds of laughter and music that floated up and into the room. All he saw in his mind was the image of a very angry and hurt Nora packing her things and leaving him.

"Lass," Duncan began quietly. "Ye must ken that what we did, we did fer ye and Aishlinn."

Nora turned her gaze to Duncan. "What do you mean?"

Duncan continued to look at Wee William's back as he answered Nora's query. "The men were under strict orders no' to kill anyone. Rowan and Black Richard, they took Horace and his brothers far away from the farm. With no clothes or furs to keep the three of them warm, Rowan assumed the bastards would freeze to death. No one thought they'd find their way home let alone survive the night."

The wave of nausea returned and Nora felt dizzy again. Her mind was a jumbled mess of thoughts. Why would Wee William have lied about killing Horace?

Wee William turned away from the window and looked at his wife.

"Why did you lie?" Nora asked him. "Why did you ask me if I wanted to be a widow? Why did you let me believe Horace and his brothers were dead?"

"I saw the fear in yer eyes that night, Nora. I saw what the bastard had done to yer face. I canna explain to ye why I even asked ye that question. I just kent that I could no' allow such a wee, bonny lass as ye to remain with a man who treated women with such contempt and hatred."

Nora's head continued to spin and race. She was still married to Horace. She had never been a widow. *I'm married to two men at once!* The thought made her feel all the more like throwing up.

"Ye made me an adulteress!" she yelled at Wee William. "Ye made me a whore, a bigamist, and adulteress!"

Wee William rushed to her side and tried to hold her hands. She refused him, could not look at him.

"Nay, Nora! Ye must believe me. Ye be none of those things!"

"How can you say that? I was not a widow when I married you!"

"Nay, ye weren't," Wee William said.

"You lied, William." Nora's voice had turned to ice. Her heart was shattering inside and the pieces felt like tiny knives cutting at her soul.

Wee William stood upright. Deep down he knew the day would

come when he'd have to tell her the truth. He had hoped it would not have been for another thirty or forty years.

"Yes, I lied to ye then. I lied to protect ye."

"Protect me from what? From Horace?" Nora spat at him.

"Aye! From Horace and from the fear that man had put into ye! To help ye gain a new life, to help ye to be rid of him and all the bad memories! I did it fer ye, Nora."

She shook her head. "Nay, you did it for your own selfish reasons! You could have told me, from the beginning or every time after when I thanked you for making me a widow. You could have told me the truth. I'm not a weak woman, William. I could have dealt with the truth."

"Nay, ye be no weak woman, I ken that. But yer *my* woman."

Nora wished that she could have stood up to slap him, but the dizziness and nausea prohibited it.

"I'm your woman no longer," she seethed. "Get out. Get out and do not come back!"

She could not have hurt him more had she run a sword through his heart. "If ye'll let me explain,"

Nora cut him off. "I do not wish to hear more of your lies, William. Please, leave me now." *Leave me now before I change my mind.*

Nora did not doubt that Wee William loved her. She would never question that. But she did not know if she had the strength or courage to stay with him, knowing he often lied or at the least, skirted the truth. It mattered not at the moment that he proclaimed that he had lied to protect her. The reasons why he lied were not as important as the fact he had lied. Had she not just told Bree the very same thing? And if he would lie about something as important as this, what else would he lie about? She doubted if she could trust him again.

"Nora," Wee William said as he lowered his voice. He had to get her to see reason, to understand why he had done all that he had done. "I am sorry. Ye must ken the why of it."

"No, I don't William. I don't need to know the why of it. I only know that I cannot trust you. You married me knowing full well that I was still married to Horace."

Wee William let loose a frustrated breath. "Nay, ye were no' still married to him. I had yer marriage to Horace annulled."

Nora's brow furrowed with confusion. "How on earth could you have gotten my marriage to Horace annulled without my knowledge or consent?"

The initiation ceremony had seemed like such a good idea at the time. It had been the only way to assuage his guilt over not telling her the truth. At the time, he felt rather proud of his plan. Now, when he looked into his wife's eyes and saw the pain and sorrow he had caused, he no longer felt so proud.

"Do ye remember the initiation ceremony?" he asked.

It took only a moment for her to replay that day in her mind and another moment for her to figure it out. All the questions about Horace. All that she had said about what she would have done if she could have done it. It all made perfectly good sense now.

She was beyond angry, she was furious. "How many other lies have you told me? Wait! Do not answer that for I do not want to know!" She was shouting at him now and did not care one bit who might hear her.

She wanted nothing more than to be left alone. Nora was never one to wallow in self-pity, but this was beyond the pale. Thinking was nearly impossible with him still in the room, pleading with her, looking so forlorn and lost. *Well,* she thought to herself, *it serves him right for lying, for not believing in her enough to tell her the truth of it.*

"Please, William, leave me be for now. I need time to think."

It took every ounce of willpower he owned not the sink to his knees and beg her forgiveness. His heart screamed for the chance to have her listen to him, to allow him to explain his actions. He studied her face for several long moments. The pain, the hurt, was all too apparent. Mayhap if he gave her some time to think things through and for the anger to subside, he might stand a better chance at explaining it to her.

Duncan walked to Wee William and placed a hand on his shoulder to guide him from the room. He whispered to Wee William, "She needs some time to think, Wee William. Do not fash yourself over it much. Aishlinn is just as angry with *me* as Nora is with ye."

He knew Duncan was trying to make him feel better, but it wasn't working. Suddenly it dawned on Wee William that if both Nora and

Aishlinn had seen Horace and his brothers, then there was a very strong chance that the two of them were in grave danger.

Casting another look at his wife, who lay in the bed with tears brimming in those beautiful eyes, Wee William relented. "I'll leave ye now, Nora. All that I ask is that ye ken me heart. I love ye, more than I love anything else in this world."

Nora responded by turning away from him. He could only pray that time would help to heal this chasm he'd put between them. He imagined that the one thing that could help him most now, was to find Horace Crawford and finally do what he should have done months ago. Kill the whoreson.

WEE WILLIAM AND DUNCAN STOOD IN THE HALLWAY OUTSIDE OF Nora's temporary chambers, trying to decide the best plan of action. Few people knew what Horace Crawford or his brothers looked like. Wee William was relieved to know that John and Elise were tucked safely away in Isobel's chambers. They would stay in the keep until Horace and his brothers were found.

As they made plans, Nial and Caelen appeared, and neither of them looked very happy.

"What be the matter?" Duncan asked as the two men approached.

"Bree is missing!" Nial said. He looked positively beside himself with worry. "We've been looking all the afternoon fer her and she is nowhere to be found."

Duncan and Wee William cast curious looks to one another.

"And Gillon Randolph is missing as well," Caelen put forth.

Wee William could not think of a time in all the years that he had known both Caelen and Nial that he had ever seen the two of them this angry or worried. It left a cold feeling in the pit of his stomach.

"Have ye told Angus?" Wee William asked.

"Aye," Nial answered. "He's putting together a search party for them now. One of the Carruthers' men believes he saw Gillon and Bree leaving before the noon meal, riding out on horseback together. If they went out for a leisurely ride, they should have been back by now."

Wee William ran a hand through his hair and let out a whoosh of air. There was too much happening at once. His primary concern at the moment was the safety of his wife and her brother and sister. He had to find Horace Crawford before he worried over anything else.

"Angus wants the two of ye to join us in findin' Bree," Caelen told them.

Wee William needed no time to answer. "Nay," he said harshly. "I need to be with me wife now. I canna leave her while that bastard still breathes."

"What bastard is that?" Caelen asked.

Duncan answered for his friend. "Someone from both Aishlinn and Nora's pasts. He's Aishlinn's step-brother and Nora's former husband."

Caelen's brow quirked upward. "Former husband?"

"Aye," Wee William answered gruffly. "*Former* husband. Her marriage was annulled not long ago. But he's back and I can only imagine that he seeks revenge."

Nial was just as confused as Caelen. "Revenge fer what?"

"Fer takin' her out of England I suppose," Wee William offered.

Caelen was growing frustrated. "Very well then, we can deal with that whoreson after we deal with Bree."

Duncan nodded his head in agreement. "I agree. If Bree has run off with Gillon, we must stop them before they do anything stupid. We can keep our wives safe, here in the keep, Wee William." Duncan turned his attention back to Wee William. "We will put Daniel and David in charge of the search for Horace. They ken what he and his brothers look like."

Wee William thought long and hard. His wife needed him, but at the moment, she was too angry to even be in the same room with him, let alone have a thoughtful conversation. Bree was young and innocent and there was no telling why she had left with Gillon or why they had yet to return. If his instincts could be trusted, then Bree was in serious trouble. He could not imagine her leaving with Gillon voluntarily. And if she had, the foolish girl was in way over her head. He did not trust Gillon Randolph any more than the men who now stood before him did.

"They've got at least a four hour head start on us," Caelen told them. “I canna believe Bree would have left on her own without tellin’ anyone. I think Gillon has taken her against her wishes.”

As much as he hated the thought of leaving his wife at the moment, Wee William knew he must do what he could to help find Bree. Nora, he reckoned, would be safely tucked away in the keep. They would put guards on her and the children as well as Aishlinn. There would be no way anyone would let Horace near any of them.

“Fine,” Wee William said, frustrated with the entire situation. “Let us get Bree and get back here so that I can deal with me wife.”

He started toward his wife’s room when Duncan stopped him. “Nay, Wee William. I’ll tell yer wife and ye’ll go tell mine. Neither of them wants much to do with us at the moment. Aishlinn is far less likely to bash ye over the head than me.”

Believing Duncan’s assessment of the situation to be more than accurate, he agreed.

“Give us a few moments lads,” Wee William said as he headed down the hallway toward Isobel’s chambers. “Tell Angus we’ll be below stairs shortly.”

26

Wee William was going to kill him. David was certain of it.

He had only stepped away from Nora's door long enough to relieve his bladder. When he returned he found the door to her room slightly ajar. At first he was not alarmed to find that Nora was not in her room. He had assumed she had stepped down the hall to see Elise and John. The alarm bells in his head did not go off until he found that neither Elise nor John had seen her.

By the time he had searched the keep from top to bottom only to come up empty handed, his life began to flash before his eyes. He wasn't ready to die yet, but die he would if he did not find Nora.

"Wee William is going to kill me!" He was declaring this fact to his brother Daniel, as they were heading out of the castle.

"Aye," Daniel agreed. "It has been nice havin' ye as me brother all these years." He was fully prepared to say his goodbyes to his brother. He too had no doubt that Wee William would kill David the moment he learned his wife was missing.

"Where the bloody hell could she be?" David seethed as they made their way through the crowds of people enjoying the festival.

"It makes no sense," Daniel offered. "She kens that we have no' yet located Horace. Why would she leave the damned keep?"

David had no answer, just a heavy sense of his own impending death should they not find her.

NORA WAS FURIOUS. SHE SET OFF TO DO THAT WHICH SHOULD HAVE been done months ago. *If my current husband cannot kill my former, then I'll do it myself,* she thought as she made her way around a group of people assembled to watch a man juggling two knives and an apple.

She had the sgian dubh tucked safely inside the pocket of her dress and was currently making her way through all the people who were enjoying the festival. They were all oblivious to her or what she hoped was about to happen.

She spotted Nigel first. He was standing at the end of the stables looking as nervous as Nora felt, with his eyes darting from one place to another. Nora followed his gaze to Donald who stood at the other end of the stables.

Good, she thought. Where there is one Crawford brother, the other is not far away.

Nora wrapped her fingers around her sgian dubh, noting how sweaty her hands were and cursing herself for being so nervous. She convinced herself that she was doing the right thing in seeking out Horace, to kill him before he had a chance to kill her or harm anyone else.

For a fleeting moment, she wondered if God would forgive her for what she was about to do, then decided it no longer mattered. The world without Horace Crawford would be a much safer place.

She continued to scan the throngs of people hoping and praying that she would find Horace before he found her. There were so many people milling about that it made her task all the more difficult. But she refused to be disheartened. Neither would she let the mere thought of Horace Crawford terrify her to the point that she threw up.

Nay, she was going to finally be free of him. She was a woman on a mission. A mission to rid the world of the cruel, perverse, uncaring man. She cared not what Wee William, Angus, Aishlinn or anyone else thought of her when they learned she had killed the man who was the bane of her existence. She was willing to risk hanging or imprisonment, even banishment, if she could save just one other woman from the likes of Horace.

Whatever punishment lay in her future would be worth that one moment when she saw the life fade from his eyes. She'd be Horace Crawford's widow if it was the last thing she did.

Nora began to grow uneasy, for she had walked through the courtyard and grounds twice now, and had not found Horace anywhere. Nigel and Donald hadn't moved from their posts at the stables. She continued to clutch the tiny dagger as she headed back toward the keep. He had to be here, somewhere. He would not have left without his brothers.

Nora paused next to a stand where a woman was selling her woven wares. As she stood, nervously looking through the crowd for Horace, she felt something small, sharp and pointy press against the small of her back.

"Are you looking for someone in particular, whore?" a voice whispered in her ear as a hand grabbed her arm and squeezed it.

She felt her knees buckle, but held on.

"Aye," she swallowed, doing her best to hide the fear that came with the sound of his voice and his touch. "I was looking for you, you stinking bastard." She prayed she sounded fierce, like a Highlander, like a woman who could take care of herself.

Horace made a tisk tisking sound as he pressed the knife more firmly against the small of her back. "You sound like a bloody Scot when you talk that way, Nora. Very unbecoming."

She wanted nothing more than the take her sgian dubh and thrust it firmly into his throat, but his hand gripped tightly around the arm that held it. Her mind raced for a way out of her current predicament but fell quite short. He'd stab her before she had a chance to do anything.

"Do you wish for John and Elise to live?" Horace asked as he leaned in more closely to her ear. The feel of his hot breath on her skin made her flesh crawl and the nausea to return to her stomach. Fear pricked her skin at the mention of John and Elise. She would die before she let him harm either of them.

It would be worth the sacrifice. She knew that John and Elise were both tucked safely away in Isobel's chambers. She also knew Horace was not stupid enough to try to get to them. For now, she would let him think she was frightened. She wanted to know *why* on earth he was here.

"I know well that they are here and inside the keep. It would not take much to send Donald up to them. Donald's had his eye on Elise for a time. Of course, I keep telling him he needs to wait until she is older before he takes her as his own wife. I think one and ten is old enough. What say you?"

Her stomach roiled at the thought of Donald Crawford laying his hands on Elise. If she had to kill both Horace and Donald to stop that from happening, she would.

"If Donald lays one finger on Elise, I'll kill him with my bare hands." She didn't need to *hope* she sounded fierce. She was startled at just how fierce and determined she sounded.

Her words angered Horace. He squeezed his hand more tightly around her arm. "I'm going to kill you, Nora. You know that. One way or another, you'll die. But first, I want what was stolen from me."

"What are you talking about? I stole nothing from you." She wondered briefly if he hadn't lost his mind.

"I found the hole in the cellar, you stupid bitch! I know something was hidden there. I know it had to be something of great value, or else those stinking Highlanders would not have traveled so far to steal it from me. Now, where is it?"

Nora could not contain her laughter. It escaped before she had the thought to rein it in. She stopped laughing however, the moment he yanked on her arm and pressed the knife so hard against her back, that she felt it rend a tear in her dress. Horace was not in the mood for laughter.

"The treasure they took was more valuable than gold," Nora bated him. "The value is something that you will never understand, Horace."

"Quit speaking in riddles and tell me what they took and where it is!" he seethed.

Nora took a deep breath before answering. "The treasures? Nothing more than candlesticks and a trinket box, you fool! The only one who values them is Aishlinn. The Highlanders came to get them for *her,* because they care about her. They love her. And that is what you'll never understand, Horace, that love means more than all the gold or silver in the world."

For a moment, Horace felt as though the earth had been pulled from under his feet. He simply could not fathom anyone traveling such a distance and going to so much trouble for mere baubles and trinkets.

"You lie, Nora!"

Nora shook her head. "Nay, Horace, I tell you the truth. They were Laiden's candlesticks and her trinket box that I kept hidden in the cellar. In case the rumors about Aishlinn had been false. And to keep you from selling them." Nora knew Horace would never understand such things as love, loyalty, or kindness. His heart, she reckoned, was too black to let even a glimmer of light into it.

His heart began to beat faster. "I do not believe you."

"That is because you cannot understand it. Not everyone is filled with greed or malice or hatred like you, Horace. I tell you the truth. There are countless treasures in our lives and none of them have a thing to do with gold or silver or coin."

If he had not feared being killed within moments, he would have stuck his knife through Nora's back and left her to die. There were far too many people around them to get away with killing her here. Large beads of sweat began to form on his brow while his heart pounded with hatred and fury.

"Horace, I've told you the truth of it, I swear on the lives of Elise and John that I have," Nora told him.

There was no doubt in his mind that Nora spoke the truth. He had sold his farm and everything he had left to his name, and for what? Candlesticks and a trinket box. Memories and baubles. The kinds of things that only a woman would hold dear or priceless.

The fault he would lay at the feet of Nora and Aishlinn, and women in general. Were it not for women, the world would be a far simpler place. He imagined a world where only men roamed above it and women were held below only to be used for breeding purposes. His life would be so much simpler and far better if he could live it without women.

He could feel Nora trembling with fear. Her fear acted as a balm to his wounded pride. Nay, he might not have found the treasure of gold he had come for. Nora might think him incapable of understanding the value of things other than coin and gold but she would be wrong. While she found value in those things he despised the most—love, memories, and kindness—he found value in far darker and more painful pursuits.

"Horace, let me go now and be on your way. You'll find nothing but your own death if you try to bring harm to any of us here."

It was Horace's turn to laugh. "Do you think I am daft? I know the moment I let you go, you'll cry out and I'll be dead before I can reach the gate." He looked toward Nigel and Donald and motioned them to come to him. "Nay, *wife,* I think not."

An overwhelming sense of dread washed over Nora. Horace was insane and there was no telling what his plans for her were. "Please, Horace, I'll tell no one you were here, if you'll just let me go." *But the moment your back is turned, I'll run my knife through it again and again until you breathe no more.*

Nigel and Donald approached. Nora thought both men looked apprehensive.

"Nigel," Horace said. "You will stay behind until we are safely beyond these grounds. If Nora makes any attempt at escape or to cry for help, you know what to do."

Nigel looked as though he had swallowed something quite bitter. "You cannot be serious Horace." His voice was unsteady.

"I am quite serious. Make your way into the castle. Watch through the windows. If Nora does anything to call attention to us, you will kill both John and Elise."

Nora felt her heart fall from her chest. It had been quite easy for her to leave her own room unnoticed. What if those men watching John and Elise were as lax in their duties as David had been? She could not risk the possibility that Nigel would be able to find a way to get to the children. In an instant, she made the decision to allow Horace to take her away from the keep. Once they were out of Nigel's line of vision, she would make her escape.

She remained mute as her fingers continued to tremble with fear. She took slow, deep breaths to keep from throwing up. This was not going as she had planned, but she refused to give up hope. Soon, she told herself, soon she would have the opportunity to run her dagger through his chest. She simply needed to remain calm. As long as she kept her wits about her, she would be able to extricate herself from the situation.

Horace pulled her into his side as if they were long lost friends. He leaned in and whispered in her ear. "Nora, we'll be leaving this place now. I advise you to remain quiet if you wish no harm to come to those brats of yours."

Nora could only allow him to lead her away on shaky legs. With each step she took away from the keep, she became more fearful. What if she could not get her dagger out of her pocket in time? What if the first thrust did not harm him enough to allow her to run away? What if no one noticed her missing until it was too late?

She began to wish she had begged Wee William to stay with her, to work things out. But she had been far too angry with him for lying. She still was not convinced that her marriage to Horace had been properly annulled. What if what Father Michael had done was not enough in the eyes of God or the law? What if she really were married to two men at once?

As they walked away from the keep, her mind raced in far too many directions at once. She worried over the safety of John and Elise as well as Aishlinn and her babe. What if Horace killed her and returned to kill Aishlinn? She could not risk trying to escape just yet. She had to get Horace and his brothers away from the keep, away from those that she loved before she could take the chance to kill him.

She was furious with Wee William for not being honest. She knew he had meant well, but had he been honest, then mayhap she could have prevented this. How, she could not think at the moment, but certainly she could have been better prepared.

Soon, they were walking through the gate. Her mind was a blur of thoughts and worries, her heart heavy with fear and a longing for Wee William. Mayhap he would return soon and realize what had happened. Nora knew without question that her husband would come for her. Her only worry was that he'd not find her in time.

David felt an overwhelming sense of anger and dread when he finally caught a glimpse of Nora. He had been looking out the window from the second floor of the keep when he saw her pass through the gate.

By the time he made it down the stairs and out of doors she was gone.

He found Daniel just outside the keep.

"Horace has her," David said to his brother as he ran inside the stables. "I saw one only of the brothers with them." David went to a stall at the far end of the stable and led his horse, a beautiful bay gelding out of his stall.

"The third could still be here or mayhap he awaits with horses beyond the keep," Daniel offered as he watched his brother hastily saddle his horse.

"Ye try to find the other brother. Check on Aishlinn and the children and double their guards. No strangers are to enter Isobel's rooms," he said, checking the straps of his saddle.

"Send someone to find Phillip, Garret, and anyone else ye can find to help. I'm going after Nora." David led the horse out of the stables as he gave more directions.

Daniel wasted no time with questions as David mounted his horse and fled on a search for Nora.

Daniel grabbed any able-bodied man he could find as he hurried back to the keep. He gave orders as he made his way inside and up to Isobel's rooms. Though he was relieved to see that two MacDougall men stood outside the room where Aishlinn and the children had been secured, he'd not breathe a sigh of relief until he saw them with his own eyes.

Without knocking, he flung open the door.

"Thanks be to God!" he whispered as his eyes landed on Isobel. She was sitting at one of the long tables with John and Elise. Aishlinn sat near the window feeding the babe.

Overcome with relief, he let loose a breath and ran a hand across his face. He would have to explain the situation to Isobel and Aishlinn and he did not relish the thought. Isobel would be furious, but not nearly as furious as Wee William was going to be.

"M'lady," Daniel said before clearing his throat. "We need to talk."

THE SEARCH PARTY FROM CASTLE GREGOR HAD NO DIFFICULTY following the tracks left behind by Gillon Randolph and his men. That fact bothered Nial. If *he* had taken Bree he would have made sure no one could have followed them. Either Gillon Randolph was stupid or he *wanted* to be followed.

When they had left the keep a few short hours ago, James Randolph had insisted on riding with them. He swore he had no idea what either his son or Bree were up to, but admitted to Angus that he was worried. Gillon had left with Bree along with fifteen Randolph men. Whatever they were up to, James swore he had no part in it. Much to Nial's dismay, Angus apparently believed him.

Nial felt more comfortable knowing they had seventy-five men to Gillon's small band of sixteen. The lad would realize, albeit a bit too late, that he had made several errors in judgment. The first one being the tenacity and ferocity of Clan MacDougall men, especially as it pertained to protecting Clan MacDougall women. He would also learn that Angus McKenna was a force of nature in his own right.

The sun was beginning to set and night would soon be upon them. Since learning of Bree's disappearance, Nial's heart had been pounding with dread and worry. He had been cursing, sometimes silently, sometimes openly, since learning she was with Gillon. He swore that when he got his hands on Gillon, he'd slice the bastard's throat.

Doubt lingered as to whether or not Bree left willingly or if she was taken. If she had left of her own accord, what on earth had been her reasons? He could not imagine her doing this, not after what happened last summer with Aishlinn. Nay, Nial could not believe she'd gone willingly.

As they rode east, following those all-too-easy-to-follow tracks, Nial allowed his mind to wander to the different methods of torture he would inflict on Gillon. The thought of feeding the little bastard's lower intestines to the wolves -- while he still lived and was forced to watch -- was rather appealing.

That method of torture had been Caelen's idea. Nial was glad to have Caelen as an ally. Knowing what he did about Caelen, to have him as an enemy was not something he wanted to experience. Nay, 'twas definitely in his favor to have the man as his friend.

Nial finally realized they were heading south. Randolph lands lay to the east of MacDougall lands.

"Where do ye suppose the little shite's headed?" Wee William asked as he rode alongside Nial and Caelen.

"Who knows, Wee William," Caelen answered. "But the lad's a fool if he thinks he can lose us."

Nial knew he'd go to the ends of the earth if he had to in order to find Bree. Gillon Randolph could try whatever tactic he desired. Nial would not be stopped.

Before long, night had descended across the lands and it made following Gillon's tracks next to impossible. They led through a very thick and dense forest. With night upon them they could no longer follow them.

"When I get me hands on this little bastard," Wee William groused as he dismounted, "I'll kill him!" He wanted to get back to his wife and to killing Horace Crawford once and for all.

"Ye can have what's left of him when I'm finished," Nial said from beside his own horse. At the moment, he was far too angry to eat. Instead, he pulled a flask of whiskey from his saddle and took a long, hard drink.

"I think the line should form behind Angus," Caelen offered as he motioned toward their chief with a nod of his head.

Angus was standing in a small clearing with James Randolph, Rowan, and Andrew Graham. None of the men was happy, but Angus was nearly beside himself with anger.

Wee William, Caelen and Nial unsaddled their horses and tied them to a rope draped between the trees. Anger, resentment, and fury hung in the air as thick as smoke. The only things that tempered any of them were the thoughts of what they would do to Gillon Randolph when they finally got their hands on him.

Angus sent ten men to scout ahead and around the forest. If they were able to pick up Gillon's trail, they would return immediately and pick up where they left off.

Wee William was too furious to sit and far too worried about his wife to rest. He worried that Nora would never forgive him and worried that Horace would not be found. The happy family life he had begun to cherish was being torn apart. His heart heavy with guilt and dread he paced around the small clearing.

"Yer worried about yer wife," Duncan said as he joined Wee William. "I worry over Aishlinn and our babe too. But I trust in those we left behind that no harm will come to either of them."

Wee William knew that Duncan meant to help assuage his fears but it did not help. "What if Nora canna forgive me fer lyin'?" he asked.

Duncan took a deep breath and looked up at the night sky while he thought on the question for a few moments. "Nora loves ye, Wee William. There is no doubt of that. It may take some time, but she'll forgive ye."

Wee William could only pray that Duncan was correct. He felt sick with worry that the trust he'd been able to gain from Nora, the love that they had shared these past months, would never be rekindled. He had lied, but he had damned good reasons for doing so. Or so he told himself. He hadn't done it for selfish reasons. He'd done it for her, to keep her from ever being afraid again. The lies he had told, he told because he loved her and wanted to protect her.

Though his reasons were noble, he doubted Nora would see it that way. A lie was a lie, plain and simple.

If he had to spend a lifetime to gain her forgiveness or regain her love and trust, he would. Living a life without her in it was too difficult to imagine.

APPARENTLY, GILLON RANDOLPH WAS UNACCUSTOMED TO WOMEN who armed themselves. For had he been accustomed to such things he would have searched Bree thoroughly before taking her away from Castle Gregor.

His imprudence and arrogance would lead to his downfall, Bree thought quietly, if not his death.

They had ridden east for several hours before turning south. Over hills, through valleys, and dense forests, they traveled without stopping, even long after the sun had set.

Early on, Bree had taken note that neither Gillon nor his men made any attempt at covering their tracks. It wasn't until they had spilled out of the forest that Bree learned why they were not being more careful at not being found. Leaving good clear tracks for the MacDougall men to follow was all a part of Gillon's plan. In two days' time, they would be safely ensconced on Bowie lands. And as soon as the MacDougall men crossed onto those lands, they would be ambushed by at least one hundred Bowie men.

It was not peace that Gillon sought, but war.

The only question Bree had was *why*.

Why did Gillon want war when peace was within reach? Her only conclusion was that he was evil incarnate and insane. That combination could prove deadly if one wasn't careful.

Although she was exhausted and wanted nothing more than to sleep, her instincts told her to remain as alert and vigilant as possible. Not only did her own life depend on it, so did the lives of countless others. Knowing that others could die if she were not careful gave Bree a sense of determination and will.

As she fought to remain awake, she thought of her mother and father. Bree sent a silent promise to them on the night breeze. She would die before she let any harm come to her family or those that she loved. Making that solemn promise to herself somehow made her feel closer to her father than she thought possible. Suddenly, she realized what her father had meant and mayhap how he had felt on those occasions he had made similar promises.

To fight to your own death was not an empty promise lightly made. They were not words spoken to gain attention or to appear bigger or stronger. They were words spoken from the heart.

Bree knew without a doubt that her father would look for her. Nothing would stop him from finding her. Certainly they had realized by now that she was missing. She felt better believing that her father would find her, one way or another.

27

Bree's resolve and strength had faded, replaced by exhaustion. Gillon had refused to stop and continued to push them southward. As the hours wore on, it began to be too much work to keep her eyes open or her instincts on full alert. She finally succumbed and rested her head against the neck of her horse.

Hours had passed by before Gillon finally brought them to a stop. Bree was rousted from sleep by someone yanking her from her horse. She hadn't had time to react before she fell on her rump with a thud. She cursed under her breath as she tried to stand.

"Be careful with the wench, ye fool!" Gillon laughed from atop his horse. "That be me future wife yer treatin' so unkindly."

Bree was not as amused as Gillon and was quite tempted to remove the sgian dubh from her boot and send it hurling straight at his heart. But her hands were still bound and her fingers shook from lack of food and sleep. She did not want to risk missing for they might then think to search her for more weapons.

She struggled to her feet, dusted the dirt from her dress with her hands and looked at her surroundings while she stretched her weary bones. She had no idea if they were on Bowie lands yet but did not dare make an inquiry.

Gillon came to stand directly behind her and he placed his hands on either side of her waist. Bree tamped down the revulsion that came with his touch, but could not steady her breathing.

"The men are makin' us a tent to rest in fer the night," he whispered in her ear.

There were a thousand things she wanted to say to him but did not put them to voice. She doubted he would take it kindly if she were to knee him in the groin and warn him to keep his filthy hands off her. Bree was no fool.

"But I doubt we'll get much rest," Gillon said as he pressed a kiss against her neck.

The grogginess and longing for sleep left her immediately. The hair on her neck stood at full attention as her stomach tightened. She knew full well what his intentions were and she'd have no part in it. She'd cut off his man parts before she allowed them anywhere near her person.

Gillon left her to stand alone next to her horse, with her hands still bound and fear slowly creeping in.

Please, da, she prayed quietly, please get here soon.

NORA'S PLAN TO KILL HORACE HAD FAILED MISERABLY. HE HAD searched her before he set her atop the horse and had found her sgian dubh. Without it, she knew she was defenseless, but she was not without hope. In her heart she knew that William would eventually come for her. Hopefully, this time he would kill Horace, even if Angus ordered him not to. That was, if he ever came for her.

The further they rode away from Dunshire, the more Nora doubted a timely rescue. As the hours turned into days, she began to believe no one would come for her. Mayhap they believed she had left voluntarily or worse yet, William was injured or killed while trying to save Bree. The thought of William dying left her feeling as though someone had reached into her chest and grabbed her heart with his fist, squeezing it until it barely beat. It made her ill and on more than one occasion she retched from atop her mount. Horace would not even allow her the decency of water to clean her mouth or face.

Though she had been angry with William, she had not wished any harm to come to him. She still loved him, no matter if there was a possibility that she was still married to Horace. As far as she was concerned, Wee William was her husband and she would love him to her dying day. That day might arrive sooner than she wanted if no one came for her.

They had ridden across Scotland at breakneck speeds, rarely stopping, and never resting for more than an hour at a time. Donald worried over the fact that Nigel had not yet caught up with them.

"He can take care of himself," Horace told him.

"What if they caught him?" Donald worried, growing more apprehensive as the hours passed.

"Then you should pray they cut his tongue out before he had the chance to tell them where we're going."

"He's your brother for the sake of Christ!" Donald shouted as they rode fast, heading for Firth. "Do you not care for anyone but yourself?"

Nora knew Donald's question to be rhetorical. A complete stranger would be able to answer that question within moments of meeting Horace. His selfishness knew no end.

It was early morning when they reached the outskirts of Firth. Horace brought them to a stop and pulled Nora from her horse.

"Do you remember the last time I brought you to Firth?" he asked as he bound her hands with rope.

How could she forget when she had scars on her wrists to remind her? Humiliation set in, no matter how hard she tried to stop it. He was going to drag her through Firth again. This time he would probably declare to all within earshot that Nora was a bigamist, a whore who had married another man, a Scot no less, while still married to Horace. What terrified her most was the belief that he would take her back to the cottage and throw her in the cellar again. This time she knew she would not make it out alive. He would leave her there to die. Nigel would not be there to drop down bread or water.

Nora truly did not care what the people of Firth thought of her. She knew the truth.

"Had you been a better wife to me Nora, I wouldn't have to punish you so harshly," Horace said pulling on the rope. It rubbed against her existing scars, sending raw sensations up to her neck.

"Had you been a better husband, I could have been a better wife," Nora shot back.

The back of his hand hit hard across her cheek, but she remained on her feet. Her mouth began to bleed from where her teeth cut into her cheek. She spat on the ground, her steely resolve returning full force.

It didn't matter anymore what she said or did, she was helpless to stop him. She decided to finally tell him what she thought of him. "You are a selfish, perverted man, Horace Crawford, and I know there is a special place in hell for you."

Horace yanked on the rope again before climbing back onto his horse. "Aye, but you'll get there before me."

She could see the fury in his eyes and knew her death was inevitable.

As he pulled her along the road to Firth, she could only think of John, Elise and Wee William. She prayed that William would continue to raise the children, that he would not send them back to England. If anything had happened to him, she prayed that Aishlinn and Duncan would keep her brother and sister. Aishlinn was her friend and she would know what to do with John and Elise. It did make her feel better knowing that Aishlinn would care for them, that she would not let anything happen to them.

She fell and scraped her knees and hands as Horace hurried her along. He yanked her to her feet, looking pleased with her inability to keep up. Nora wished she could wipe that hateful sneer from his lips.

Donald said nothing, his face filled with anger as he rode behind Nora. Part of her wished that Horace would just kill her and be done with it. But nay, he would have to humiliate her first. That was where he gained his pleasure, in the suffering and degradation of others.

They were halfway to Firth when Horace called out to Donald. "Ride ahead and tell the sheriff I have an adulteress and a whore of a wife I wish to punish."

Donald mumbled something indiscernible as he kicked his horse into a full run. Nora hoped his horse would toss him and break his neck before he made his way to the village.

Nora fell several more times before they reached the center of

Firth. They passed vendors and villagers, people Nora had known most of her life. Not one lifted a finger to help. Had they been Highlanders or MacDougalls, Nora knew many of them would have intervened. Either they were too afraid of Horace or they simply did not care what was happening to her. She never missed Scotland as much as she did as she walked by these people.

Donald seemed both irritated and disgusted as he waited with the sheriff outside his office. Apparently the sheriff had not missed too many meals, and if he by chance were to miss one, he could have feasted off the bits of food that clung to his dirty tunic. Short, squat and grubby, he held a leg of mutton in one hand and a hunk of bread in the other.

The sheriff appeared perplexed as he watched Horace pull Nora toward him. When she was but a few steps away from Donald and the sheriff, Horace yanked her off her feet with a strong pull of the rope. Obviously the sheriff was unmoved by Horace's mistreatment of Nora for his only response was to take a bite of mutton as he watched the spectacle taking place before him.

Nora fell forward, the dirt and tiny rocks digging into her knees and knuckles. Her wrists burned and her hands were swollen from the tight bond of the rope. She was covered with dirt, grime, sweat, and vomit and imagined she must look like a wild animal.

A small crowd of villagers had begun to form around them. Not much excitement ever happened in this small village. A man dragging his wife through the street brought forth a good deal of curiosity.

"What the bloody hell are you doin' Horace Crawford?" the sheriff asked.

"I want my wife punished. She's an adulteress and a bigamist. She ran off weeks ago and married a filthy Scot."

The sheriff looked at Nora. "Is that true?"

Nora pushed herself to her feet and held her head high. "Nay, it isn't." She began to argue that their marriage had been annulled—at least by Scottish standards, but Horace yanked on the rope again. This time however, Nora was better prepared. She planted her feet firmly and with what little strength she had left, she pulled back on the rope.

Her actions inflamed Horace and he pulled again, this time with more effort and anger. She fell face first in the dirt.

"She's a liar as well. Donald can vouch that I speak the truth."

The sheriff turned to Donald who leaned against the doorway of the sheriff's office with his arms folded across his chest. Donald's disgusted expression was easily read.

"Well?" the sheriff asked.

Donald answered with a shrug of his shoulders, as if he didn't give a damn about anything.

Nora assumed Donald's silence was his way of avoiding outright lying to the sheriff. His reticence proved Nora's opinion correct. Donald was just as much a coward as Horace. Though she had not expected him to come to her defense, his silence still irked her. Silently, she wished them all to go to the devil.

The sheriff harrumphed before taking another bite of his mutton. He stared at Nora as he wiped the grease onto the sleeve of his shirt. He studied her quietly for a moment before looking up at Horace.

"'Tis your right as her husband to have her punished for her misdeeds. How do you want to do it?"

The evil sneer that Nora had come to loathe resurfaced on Horace's face. "The hole," he said as he glared at Nora.

Nora could contain neither her shock nor her fear. A gasp passed through her lips and she suddenly felt nauseous all over again.

The hole was a deep, dark place that sat near the center of the village. It was a place where criminals, thieves and ne'er-do-wells were sometimes put as a means of punishment. A set of wooden planks covered the hole where the accused would be left in almost complete darkness. How long the guilty stayed was dependent upon the nature of the crime or the discretion of the sheriff. Seldom, if ever, did the sheriff show mercy.

"Horace, please," Nora began to plead with him. She would have received more sympathy and compassion from a stone.

"You heard the sheriff. 'Tis my right as your husband to choose your punishment." Horace pulled on the rope again and began to lead her toward the hole.

In England, criminals were afforded more rights than a wife. All a husband need do was accuse his wife of some offense. It mattered not if he told the truth or lied. A wife was considered to be the husband's property, to do with as he pleased. No amount of begging or pleading would change the fact that the sheriff believed Nora to be Horace's wife.

"I had our marriage annulled!" Nora cried out. Horace came to an abrupt halt.

The sheriff had finished his mutton and tossed the bone to the ground. People in the crowd began to murmur amongst themselves.

"When did you have that done?" he asked as he took a step toward her.

"Months ago," Nora said anxiously as her chest heaved up and down.

The sheriff raised an eyebrow as if he was not sure he should believe her. "Who annulled it?"

"A priest," Nora began. "Father Michael is his name."

"I know of no priest by that name here," the sheriff said.

"He is Father Michael of Dunshire," Nora suddenly felt quite unsteady.

Horace interjected with a laugh. "A foul Scottish priest!"

The sheriff seemed to be mulling the facts over in his mind. A man in the crowd spoke up. "I do not think a Scottish priest can annul an English marriage."

The sheriff turned to face the crowd as if their opinions had any merit to the situation at hand. "I think we should let the earl decide," he told Horace before quickly adding. "He's gone until the morrow. You can put her in the hole until he's made his decision."

Nora felt all hope disappear in the span of one heartbeat. The earl hated all Scots and anything associated with them. He would give no weight to Father Michael's annulment, even if the church were to allow it. He would find Nora guilty simply because she had associated with a Scot.

Her feet felt as though they were cast in iron as Horace led her to the hole. Exhausted, nauseous, and terrified, she had no fight left to give. Her limbs felt as weighted down as her spirits as she reluctantly took the ladder down into the dark hole. Horace pulled the ladder up the moment her feet hit the dirt.

The last vision Nora saw before darkness completely enveloped her was Horace's gleam of victory as he placed the last plank over the entrance.

28

Nora had lost all track of time. The tiny rays of sunshine that had streamed into the hole earlier had disappeared, along with any hope she had that Wee William would come for her.

When she had first entered the hole, she felt along the wall and counted out her steps. She had dug a tiny hole in the dirt floor and slowly made her way around in the dark. Thirty-six steps later she had made her way back to her mark. It was as she figured it to be -- a very small space.

She sat huddled against the cold dirty wall, shivering uncontrollably, thirsty, unsettled, and frightened. Horace knew all too well how much she hated the dark and he used that simple bit of knowledge to punish her. She supposed he was sitting in the inn right now, gloating over the fact that he had found her and brought her back for his idea of justice.

The only satisfaction she could take was the belief that his reputation would precede him and there would not be a woman within three hundred miles that would ever agree to be his wife. She felt as though she were saving innocent women from the same fate she had endured. Sacrificing her life would keep other women safe.

As much as she tried to sleep, her dreams were invaded with images of wolves, satyrs, and Horace's laughing face. He taunted her, called her names, laughed at her fears and weaknesses. There were moments when she questioned her lucidity for it became difficult to separate reality from her dreams.

Her stomach, though devoid of any food or water, still wretched, sometimes violently. Knowing she would most likely be left to die in the hole did not mean she would die without holding on to some of her dignity. With her bare hands she had dug as far as she could and used that space to empty her bladder and to wretch in and tried to stay as far away from it as possible.

Between fits of sleep, she cried. Her heart ached for Wee William. She sent silent prayers up asking the good Lord to let Wee William know she had forgiven him. Aye, he had lied, but she realized now *why*. He had lied because he loved her. William had shown her nothing but kindness and adoration. He respected her, loved her unconditionally. To her core, she knew he would never do anything to hurt her, not intentionally anyway. Nay, he would have done anything he could to protect her.

She longed to feel his arms around her, to listen to his steady breathing as he slept, holding her tightly yet gently. Each morning when they woke to start their day, he oft said he did not want to let her go. William's idea of holding on to her was so far removed from Horace's.

Wee William wanted to hold on to her because he loved her, cherished her. Horace held as much value in Nora as he did his ox. In his mind there was no distinction between the two. He owned Nora and Benny and could do whatever he pleased with either.

She was grateful for the time she had spent with William. He had taught her what true love and adoration felt like. He allowed her to love him as much as he loved her. Their love and devotion to one another was something she could take into the afterlife with her, although it was only a few moments compared to the lifetime she wanted with him.

As she sat holding on to her memories, her heart tearing with each beat, she thought she heard a scratching sound coming from above.

Her first thought was that it was Horace coming to taunt her further, mayhap throw down garbage or a few rats to make her even more miserable.

She held her breath and listened, though it was difficult to hear anything over the blood rushing in her ears. One of the planks was lifted and moonlight streamed in, but only for a moment. A figure soon blocked most of it before she heard a soft whooshing of air and a quiet thud as something landed on the floor. Nora could not move, fearful the object dropped was filled with something she did not want to see.

"Lass," came a familiar voice.

Nay! It couldn't be. Her mind was playing tricks on her. She'd been stuck in the hole for far too long. She'd officially lost her mind and was now lost in some odd hallucination.

"Lass," the voice whispered to her. "'Tis me, David!"

Nora shook her head as if doing so would break the spell of the hallucination.

"Lass, there be water and food wrapped inside the blankets," David called down to her.

It was all too much to hope for. It had to be a dream, hadn't it? Nora reluctantly felt around in the dark until her hands landed on the soft blanket. If she were hallucinating, would she be able to feel the soft blanket under her fingertips? She doubted it.

Jumping to her feet, she clung to the blanket and looked up into the darkness. "Is that really you, David?" she called up to him. Her throat felt sore and scratchy from lack of water and all her crying.

"Aye, lass!"

Nora could hear the significant sound of relief in his voice. She could almost imagine the bright smile that was undoubtedly formed on his face.

"Daniel and a few others are with me. We need ye no' to give up hope, lass. Wee William will be here soon. There are too many English soldiers nearby to get ye out just yet. Can ye hold on for a while?"

She was too relieved and happy to ask how long it might take. As long as she knew they were there, simply waiting for Wee William and more men to arrive, she reckoned she could last for weeks if needed.

For the first time in days, she felt more than just a glimmer of hope. She felt downright giddy!

"Aye, I can David!" She could get through anything knowing her husband was on his way.

"I'm sorry I let ye down, lass," David whispered.

Nora could hear the sincerity and regret in his voice. "It isn't your fault, David, it is mine. I set out to find Horace so that I could run my sgian dubh through his heart."

She could hear David chuckle from above. "I ken ye weren't a Sassenach the first time I met ye! And yer Gaelic be improvin', lass!" he said. "I must go now. Just ken that we're nearby, watchin'. If things get too ugly, we'll no' wait for Wee William. We'll get ye out, I promise."

David replaced the plank before Nora had a chance to thank him.

Although it was dark again, her spirits had been lifted a thousand fold. She sat back against the wall and carefully unwrapped the contents of the blanket. She felt the flagon of water, a loaf of bread that smelled magnificent even in the musty confines of her prison. Further inspection found a hunk of cheese, dried meat that turned out to be venison, and a small pouch filled with ripe berries.

She drank greedily at first, the cold water soothing her scratchy throat. Not knowing how soon before she'd be rescued, she decided to ration out the water and the food. It might be days before Wee William arrived and it might be too risky for David to bring her more supplies.

Nora wrapped the blanket around her body and ate some of the bread and cheese and a few of the berries. Her stomach tried to protest the invasion of food, but she forced herself not to wretch again.

With her thirst sated and her belly as full as it could tolerate, she curled up under the blanket. *William is on his way!* As much as she wanted to shout that news out to the world, she knew better. It might be days from now, but her husband, her true husband, the man who loved her was on his way.

The despair and anguish she had felt only moments ago evaporated like an apparition. She felt happy, elated, and hopeful. This would all be over soon. Wee William was coming for her and soon she would be back in Scotland, back in their little cottage next to Castle Gregor. She would soon be reunited with John and Elise. Nora vowed she would never again leave any of them. And if she must leave, she'd have more sgian dubhs hidden about her person than any man could find.

And she would never again let her temper control her actions.

HORACE COULDN'T RESIST THE URGE TO CHECK ON NORA. SHE'D been in the hole for two days now. He imagined he would find her curled up in a little ball, crying her stupid blue eyes out, trembling and terrified. The image excited him and put a little bounce in his step.

He would go check on Nora then head over to Castle Firth and find Fritz. Fritz would help to alleviate some of his physical needs. The image of his whore of a wife trembling with fear combined with the knowledge of Fritz' expertise at certain things doubled his excitement.

He left the inn and practically skipped his way to the hole. Confusion began to set in as he neared the hole. Something was wrong. The closer he got to the hole, the louder the sound. Angrily, he flipped up the plank and peered down.

She was supposed to be huddled in a ball, terrified, overcome with fear and trepidation. She was *not* supposed to be singing.

"What the bloody hell are you doing Nora?" he blared down at her.

Nora looked up, shielded her eyes with the back of her hand, and smiled.

"Good morning to you, Horace," she said cheerfully. "Did you sleep well?"

This was all wrong. "Why were you singing?" he demanded.

Her smile increased. "Well, I made a decision."

Horace blinked, growing just as irate as he was confused. "What are you talking about?"

Nora giggled. "I decided that I'll not let you win. Aye, I might die a horrible death down here, all alone in the dark. But I'll die knowing that I did nothing wrong and that you are a despicable, perverse man who prefers the company of boys to women. I'll die knowing you'll burn in hell someday. That gives me a good deal of satisfaction and makes me want to sing!"

Horace could only conclude that she had lost her mind. She wasn't *truly* happy—she was insane. It was the only plausible explanation. Oh, she would die in that hole, he was certain of it. Sooner or later, her smile would fade. She could pretend for now not to be worried, not to be fearful. He knew her better than that.

"Bah! You've lost your mind, woman! Sing all you want to. It won't change the fact that I'm up here and you're down there. It's your grave you're singing in." He rolled his eyes and replaced the plank.

As he walked away, Nora began to sing again. He couldn't make out the words, but the sound of her gleeful singing made his ballocks shrink. He cursed at her as he walked toward the castle. *I'll have the last laugh* he swore to himself.

SINGING HELPED TO SOOTHE NORA'S WORRIES AND TO PASS THE time. She hadn't expected to see Horace, but found a good deal of satisfaction in the confusion she saw on his face. It made her feel a bit happier knowing she had irritated and confused him. She was quite sure he had stomped off thinking he would have the last laugh. His ignorance, arrogance, and selfishness was going to be the death of him. A tingling sensation came over her when she thought of him finally dying. She couldn't help herself. Knowing William would eventually arrive and Horace would finally get what was coming to him, brought forth the overwhelming urge to dance happily around the hole.

It won't be long now, she thought happily. William will be here soon. He'll take me home.

Settling down, Nora fell asleep with a smile on her face, happy in the belief that William was on his way. For the first time in many days, she actually dreamt of her cottage and flowers blooming across the Highlands, of her husband and John and Elise.

IT HAD TAKEN WEE WILLIAM AND THEIR GROUP TWO DAYS TO

locate Gillon and Bree. It had taken only moments to extricate her from Gillon's encampment.

Gillon had miscalculated several things. Firstly, he misjudged the amount of time required to make it to Bowie lands. While he thought he was safely ensconced in Bowie territory, he was in fact, camped on Carruthers land. Gillon and his band of fools had missed the mark by nearly thirty miles.

Secondly, he had misjudged his accomplices' fealty. When they had seen the furious Angus McKenna, Wee William, Caelen McDunnah, and Nial McKee along with seventy-five equally furious Highlanders storm into their camp, not one of Gillon's men stood to fight or defend him. Obviously, Gillon Randolph had not earned enough of their respect or admiration that they were willing to lay down their lives for him.

Thirdly, he misjudged his captive's tenacity, intelligence, and determination entirely. Bree McKenna was every bit her father's daughter and she was determined not to be one of Gillon Randolph's victims.

Nial was the first man to dismount and with sword drawn, he demanded to know the whereabouts of Bree McKenna. The young man to whose throat Nial held the edge of his sword shakily told him she was in the tent with Gillon. Nial shoved the terrified young man to the side and bounded to the tent, threw open the flap and stepped inside.

Nial was beyond furious, his face red with anger, every muscle on full alert, ready to do battle if he must, in order to save Bree. He had been fully prepared to kill Gillon Randolph, either with sword or his bare hands, he didn't care which. He had not, however, been prepared for the sight before him.

There was Bree, straddled over a prone, gagged and bound Gillon Randolph. She had a sgian dubh in one hand while her forearm was bearing down on the back of his neck. A blend of relief and admiration washed over Nial.

"I see ye have things well in hand," Nial muttered, as he stood dumbfounded at the entrance of the tent.

Bree had not seen him enter for she had been so focused on making certain Gillon understood that, in no uncertain terms, she would cut off his manly parts before she would ever become his wife. Startled, she raised her head at the sound of Nial's voice. Nial watched as her shoulders sagged in what could only be relief.

She was a vision of beauty as far as he was concerned. Aye, she was covered in dust and dirt, her dress was torn in several places, and her hair had come loose from its braid.

"Well it's about damned time!" she fumed at him, still straddled across Gillon's back. Gillon jerked his own head around to see to whom she was talking. His eyes were wide with fear and Nial wasn't sure if it was his presence that caused it, or the fact that Bree still held her sgian dubh next to his throat. "What the bloody hell took ye so long?" she demanded.

Nial didn't know which he wanted to do more at the moment. Chastise her for getting herself into this mess to begin with, argue with her over her lack of gratitude, or scoop her into his arms and plant a passionate kiss on those lovely lips. He laughed in spite of himself.

"I do apologize, lass, if we took too long. It will no' happen again, I can assure ye that," he said as he crossed his arms over his chest.

Bree climbed off Gillon's back and stood, kicking him once in his side for good measure. Gillon grumbled something indiscernible, but Nial was certain it was nothing that should be said in front of a lady.

Bree rolled her eyes and kicked him again. "Haud yer wheesht ye eejit! I'm still thinkin' on whether or not I should let ye keep yer man parts."

Bree then turned her attention back to Nial. "And what do ye mean *it won't happen again?*" she asked as she returned her sgian dubh to the waist of her dress.

Nial uncrossed his arms and took a step forward. He was about to say something that he never thought he'd say to any woman, let alone Bree McKenna. "Because when ye become me wife, I shall assign guards to watch over ye, all the hours of the day. Save fer when yer with me. Then I shall be the one guardin' ye and keepin' ye out of trouble."

Bree's eyes widened. She was just as surprised to hear Nial speak in such a manner as he was to say the words aloud. She swallowed hard, brushed the wayward strands of hair away again. "Me marry ye? Ye canna be serious!"

Nial nodded his head and took another step forward. Bree could not retreat unless she walked over Gillon.

"Aye, lass, I am serious. I'm goin' to make ye my wife if it's the last thing I do."

Bree laughed nervously. "Well then there be no sense in marryin' ye if ye do no plan on stickin' around afterward. I mean, if marryin' me is the last thing ye do, then why do it?"

Nial took another step toward her, his smile growing larger. "Good, then it will no' be the last thing I do. I'll marry ye."

Bree laughed again with the belief that he could not possibly be serious. Aye, she had grown quite fond of him, what with his broad shoulders, rippling muscles, and those odd colored gray blue eyes of his. Never before had she considered him attractive or anything more than a very good friend. But that had changed somehow, on that day not long ago when she had run into him in the hallway. Something dramatic had happened in that tiny moment of time. It was as though she were looking at him for the very first time.

It had been his braw smile and the twinkling in his eyes when he had looked at her that made her legs feel weak. Aye, she had seen Nial smile many times and had even witnessed the sparkle in his eyes on numerous occasions. Bree could not begin to fathom or understand what exactly had changed in that moment. But something had. Mayhap it was the first time she had really *looked* at him, with her heart as well as her eyes.

"Ye jest, Nial McKee. Ye canna jest about such a serious thing as marryin'."

Nial was close enough now that he could kiss her if he chose to. "I would never jest about such a serious subject as marriage."

Nial knew her heart was beating rapidly, for he could see it in that little spot on the base of her throat. However, he thought his own beat faster. He searched her eyes, looking for some sign that she too might be feeling the way he was feeling. Though there was little light inside the tent, Nial could see that her eyes were moist. His heart skipped a beat or two for he couldn't be certain if it was fear he saw looking back at him or something else.

Bree licked her lips and held her breath for a moment before speaking again. "Yer certain ye want me as a wife?"

Nial nodded his head.

"Has me father warned ye that I can be a handful at times?" she asked as she leaned her head back a bit further in order to see his face more completely. His smile returned and she discovered that it made her toes tingle.

"And has he warned ye that I tend to talk a bit more than most?"

Nial nodded his head again. "I've kent ye fer years, lass. I ken yer faults well."

Bree tilted her head as her brow creased. "Faults? Ye think me talkin' a fault? What other faults do ye find in me Nial McKee?"

Nial reached out and tucked a loose strand of hair behind her ear. "Many," he said as he continued to smile. "Ye talk too much. Ye have a tendency to interfere with other people's lives, like ye did with Aishlinn and Duncan. And ye have a remarkable way of gettin' yerself into trouble." He motioned toward Gillon Randolph who lay still on the floor.

Bree snorted. "Then why on earth do ye want to marry me?"

Nial answered her question with a kiss. Sweetly, tenderly, he pressed his lips to hers as he folded her into his arms. He was relieved as well as elated when Bree returned his kiss and wrapped her hands around his neck.

He pulled away and pressed his forehead to hers. "I want to marry ye because ye are a most beautiful young woman. And, ye be the only woman I ken that could find a way to bind and gag a man much taller and stronger than yerself."

Bree giggled and took a deep breath. "It wasna easy to do. Mayhap ye should keep that in mind in the future. If I ever find the need to do the same to ye, I will."

The mental image of Bree trying to overpower him and wrestle him into submission was a delightful one. He had to restrain the urge and desire to carry her away and find Father Michael.

"Have ye asked me da and mum yet? Fer me hand?"

"No' yet, but I will, if yer agreein' to it."

Bree bit her bottom lip and pretended to think on it. "Aye, I think I'd be agreein' to it."

It was then that Gillon Randolph began to wriggle around and mumble and they noticed that Angus had entered the tent. Bree caught sight of her father as he stood rolling his eyes. "Bloody hell," he mumbled before exiting the tent.

Bree laughed as she gave Nial a hug. "I think da kens our intentions now."

Nial sighed heavily and broke the embrace. "Aye, he's kent fer some time how I feel about ye. He has always denied me. Mayhap now that we're both in agreement, he might finally agree to it."

A very wry smile formed on Bree's lips. "He'll agree to it."

Nial ran a hand through his hair. "How can ye be so certain?"

Bree winked at him. "Do no' fash yerself over it. I can be very convincin' when I need to be."

Nial studied her closely for several long moments before erupting into a fit of laughter. Bree McKenna was a force of nature in her own right. Nial had no doubt whatsoever that she'd be able to convince any man of anything. Either through intense negotiations or physical altercations, whichever she found necessary. The bound Gillon Randolph was all the proof that he needed that Bree was fully capable of taking care of herself. Aye, he'd be very proud to call her his wife.

29

Years later when the story would be told of how angry Wee William had become upon hearing the news that his beloved wife had been taken by her former husband, people would say it was like watching Mount Vesuvius erupt.

His rage lasted only moments, most of it concentrated on the foolish man held in Castle Gregor's dungeon.

Angry. Furious.

His reaction bordered on insanity.

Wee William had returned to Gregor with the hope that after being gone for almost five days, his beautiful wife would have calmed down enough to speak with him. Instead, he discovered she was gone -- taken by Horace Crawford and his brother Donald.

The only thing that kept William from killing anyone was the fact that Tall Thomas and Garret had discovered Nigel lurking inside the keep. They had immediately tossed Nigel into the dungeon and began their interrogation. It took no threats of torture, disembowelment or hanging to get Nigel Crawford to talk. Tall Thomas and Garret didn't even have to ask where Horace had taken Nora. Nigel volunteered everything.

Nigel had, with more than a hint of relief, explained how Horace had found the empty hole in the cellar and had convinced himself that the Highlanders had stolen something of significant value. Nigel told of how Horace had been so angry that he sold everything they owned and set out to find Aishlinn and Nora. He also explained that when Horace learned exactly what the treasures had truly been, he decided to get even by taking Nora back to England.

Nigel's honesty and forthrightness was the only thing that had saved his life. He did not beg to be set free from the dungeon, nor did he beg for mercy. He did however, beg Tall Thomas and Garret to not send him back to England. For when Horace learned that Nigel had spilled his guts and told the Highlanders everything he knew, Horace would kill him. Nigel preferred to spend the rest of his days in a dungeon than have to face his older brother.

"Ye'll no' be havin' to worry about Horace," Garret told him. "Fer when Wee William gets his hands on the whoreson, there will be nothing left fer the wolves or scavengers to feast upon."

Nigel hadn't known true fear or pain until Wee William entered the dank, dark dungeon. Wee William could not have cared less that Nigel had been a model prisoner, had asked for nothing, or that he freely offered as much information as he could. Nay, Nigel was just as guilty as Horace for what had happened to Nora. Each of the three Crawford brothers would pay the price for taking Nora.

Wee William stood for the shortest of moments before Nigel's cell. Silently, Wee William fumed, embracing the rage that had consumed him. Without a word or introduction, Wee William next proceeded to beat the living hell out of Nigel Crawford. It took five men to pull Wee William off the battered, bloody Englishman.

Wee William had learned that David, Daniel, Phillip and a handful of others had set off to follow Horace. He had also been told that John had followed after them. The events had unfolded in less than an hour after Wee William had set off to help find Bree and as yet, none had returned.

What gave the men around Wee William pause was the fact that he displayed no outbursts, did not attack any tables, and did not thunder around the keep threatening the loss of anyone's life or limbs.

Wee William was quiet and that was something his friends were unaccustomed to witnessing.

But none made the mistake in believing his silence meant he was not angry. Nay, they could tell by the pulse throbbing in his forehead, the way he clenched his fists and jaw, and by the look of utter outrage in his eyes that the man had surpassed anger and fury. Rowan remarked to Black Richard that a new word would have to be created in order to describe just how furious Wee William of Dunshire truly was.

Wee William took no time in having a fresh horse readied for his use. He asked for no one's help or aid in retrieving his wife from the hands of Horace Crawford. He didn't bother to pack provisions, extra weapons, or even a change of clothes. After learning the truth and circumstances surrounding his wife's disappearance, he mounted his horse and left. With or without help, he was going to get his wife back.

Word spread rapidly throughout the keep that Wee William had left alone to find his wife. In no time at all provisions were packed and men were gathered in order to help their friend and fellow warrior.

They had to ride like the devil in order to catch up with him. When Wee William heard the thundering of horses approaching from behind, he paused only long enough to allow them to catch up. He gave no magnanimous words of gratitude regarding their presence. He merely nodded his head and continued his ride across the Highlands in search of his wife.

ANGER WAS NOT THE ONLY THING THAT FUELED WEE WILLIAM'S determination to find his wife. Anguish and guilt consumed him heart and soul, like a demonic flame that could not be extinguished. The ordeal he was certain his wife was suffering was entirely his fault. If by some act of God she were to survive whatever it was that Horace was putting her through, Wee William prayed fervently that she would not be interminably scarred by it.

He could not think of the possibility that she was dead. When that image was conjured, it was all he could do not to slice his own wrists. Had it not been for the knowledge that Nora would want him to raise Elise and John, he would have taken his own life.

Wee William was grateful that Angus, Rowan, Black Richard, as well as Caelen McDunnah and the other men were with him on this hard ride toward England. He knew he would need their silent strength to get through whatever his future held. The longer they rode without any sign of his wife, the bleaker his future seemed. He did not want to imagine his life without Nora. It was too heart wrenching a thing to imagine. He needed her, as much as he needed water or food. Nora was his life, his everything. Without her, he was nothing.

They took the route they assumed Horace would have taken. The steady rain they were riding through had washed away any traces that might have shown they were on the right course.

Not one man questioned Wee William's direction or the relentlessness with which he pushed forward. They stopped only long enough to rest their horses. While the others would doze at those brief stops, Wee William could not. There would be no rest or peace until he found his wife. Dead or alive, he would not rest until he found her. He would bring her home.

30

They had found no traces of Nora. As the journey dumped them back onto English soil Wee William could only hope that not finding any sign of his wife meant that she still lived.

They were not far from Castle Firth when they stumbled upon David, Daniel, John and the other men who had joined them. Wee William jumped from his horse and thundered through the forest toward the little band of men who had been hiding there for days.

He was relieved to find John was with them. When Wee William had first learned that the boy had left to follow David and the others, he had worried that the boy would have become lost, or might have stumbled into a situation that would have gotten him killed. He had no doubt that Nora would never forgive him if anything happened to John.

Daniel and David stood side by side, with John nearby. The brothers looked absolutely terrified when they saw Wee William approaching. John's expression was unreadable.

David held his palms up, as if that alone could stop the desperate and furious giant.

"She lives!" David shouted, knowing those two simple words were the only thing keeping him from certain death.

Wee William came to an abrupt halt, tilted his head and for the first time in days, he spoke. "Where?"

He was relieved to learn his wife was alive. Now, if he could learn she was unharmed, he might be able to breathe a sigh of relief.

David knew it was no time to pause or breathe easily. "Penrith," he managed to blurt out. How much information Wee William was ready to learn, the young David could not be certain.

"*Where* in Penrith?" Wee William asked as Angus, Rowan and Findley approached. The other riders remained mounted and drew their horses closer in order to hear the conversation.

David and Daniel cast furtive glances at each other before turning to Wee William.

"She is well, Wee William, I promise ye," Daniel said.

"Where in Firth is she?" Wee William demanded as his mind raced toward the endless possibilities.

"The new Earl, he refused to honor the Scottish annulment, Wee William. Horace still claims her as his wife." David was attempting to avoid telling Wee William the exact location of his wife.

Wee William advanced. "You tell me where my wife is now, or I swear David that I will kill you with me bare hands." He didn't give a damn whether or not the new Earl of Penrith cared to acknowledge a Scottish annulment or not. Nora was Wee William's woman, his wife, the only reason he took one breath after another.

Daniel stepped in between David and the furious Wee William. "Wee William," he said as calmly as he could under the circumstances. "Nora is well, but it is important that ye understand the situation we be dealin' with."

Wee William stopped, folded his arms across his chest and with a nod of his head, bid Daniel to continue.

"We followed them all the way here. We would have stole Nora away ourselves, but there is a regiment of about one hundred and fifty English soldiers spread throughout Castle Firth and the village. We dared not try to get her out with just the ten of us. We've been makin' our way into the village at night, giving her food and water. She be a strong lass, Wee William. You'd be verra proud of how well she's been holdin' up."

Wee William's brow drew into a thick line of confusion. "Holdin' up from what?"

This was the moment David had been dreading the most. He swallowed hard and shifted his weight from one foot to the other. "Horace accused her of being an adulteress and a bigamist. The sheriff let him decide her punishment. They put her in the hole near the center of the village. It's like an oubliette."

Wee William's heart plummeted to his feet. He knew his wife must be terrified. He knew all too well how she feared the dark and small spaces. His patience, tenuous at best, was quickly deteriorating.

Angus had been listening quietly. "So she is well, in an oubliette in the center of town," Angus said by way of both clarifying and assessing the situation at hand. "And there be a regiment of English soldiers around as well."

Daniel and David gave quick nods of their heads.

John finally stepped forward and stood in front of Daniel and David. "Wee William," John called out.

Wee William stopped and looked down at the young boy. "This isn't your fault," John began. "Nora left the keep to find Horace so she could kill him. Unfortunately, he found her first."

Although Wee William thought John's attempt to assuage any guilt he might harbor, deep within himself he knew this was entirely all his fault. Had he killed Horace months ago they would not be in this current predicament. Wee William chose not to respond to John. Now was not the time to have the argument over who was at fault.

"Well, then," Angus said as he looked around at the men and rubbed his hands together as if he anticipated something wonderful was about to happen. "Ye've assessed the situation properly, lads."

"Wee William!" Angus called out to him.

Wee William turned toward Angus.

"What say we get that bonny wife of yers back," Angus said with a devious smile. "I say she's been on English soil long enough, aye?"

Wee William stood quietly for a moment before his lips turned upward. His wife was alive, and according to Daniel and David, she was well. He would lay aside his guilt for the time being. There would be time for guilt after he had his wife safely back in Scotland.

Angus drew Wee William and the other men near as they made plans to rescue Nora and finally seek the retribution that had been long overdue for Horace Crawford.

NORA COULDN'T IMAGINE WHAT WAS TAKING HER HUSBAND SO LONG. She had been stuck in the blasted hole for days. David had promised her that William was on his way when he had visited her again last night to replenish her food and water supply. He had reassured her that it would not be long now.

Nora angrily asked him what *his* definition of "not long" was. Either he couldn't or wouldn't answer her question. Instead, he begged her to remain steadfast and strong. *It won't be long.*

When David had first appeared he had lifted her spirits immeasurably. She had danced around her little prison, hummed and sang to herself, and mentally made plans for her return to Gregor. He had informed her that there was a regiment of English soldiers occupying the village. It was far too dangerous for him and his small band of men to rescue her. They simply must wait for their own reinforcements.

Now she fumed and paced and cursed her husband, along with David and Daniel and everyone else she could think of. She had gone from blissfully ecstatic to sullen and angry. She'd lost the urge to laugh and sing and had returned to bouts of crying and fretting.

It should not be taking him this long. Foolish man! Does he not understand how upsetting this is? I'd like to see him spend hours stuck in a rotten hole, wearing the same clothes for a fortnight! Sleeping in dirt, having people who used to call you "friend" come now to call you whore and adulteress. I'd like to see how long he would last under these conditions!

Her anger would soon turn to worry. But what if he can't come? What if he were injured while trying to find Bree? Something must have happened to him, otherwise, he would have been here by now. What if he's been gravely wounded? Who is taking care of him? Will he live? And if he dies, how long before word reaches David and Daniel?

So back and forth she went between bouts of anger and worry as the hours stretched on. The longer she remained in the hole, the angrier she grew with herself. It was not like her to fret and worry to the point of vomiting.

Nay, she was a planner, a thinker, a doer. Aye, she may worry over situations, but she usually managed to come up with a plan or solution. Though it was true that most of her plans failed, at least she could think of *something* to do.

Now she was a muddled mess and was unable to think clearly. No matter how hard she tried, she could not think of a way to extricate herself out of her current predicament.

Though David had brought her more food, she found she could not eat. Food, blended with the worry over her husband and her fate, turned her stomach. Everything tasted foul and smelled like the damp and musty restraints of her prison.

She mulled over David's promise that if things were to get *ugly* they'd not wait for William; they would rescue her without him. Nora snorted indignantly and wondered how much uglier things would need to get before she was rescued from this dark, black place.

THROUGH A DRUNKEN STUPOR, HORACE CRAWFORD ASSUMED THE rumbling sound he heard in the distance was thunder. It had been raining steadily for two days so the sound of thunder did not surprise him.

As he sat at a table in a dark corner of the inn, he smiled as he conjured up the image of rain seeping into Nora's grave. If starvation and freezing nights didn't do her in, then mayhap she'd drown. The image brought only a small amount of relief to his frustrated, black soul.

Horace looked around the empty inn. It was not quite the noon hour and aside from the old innkeeper, he was the only one there. Donald still slept in a room above stairs, having drunk himself stupid the night before. Apparently Donald was angry that they'd left Nigel behind in Scotland and thus, refused to speak to Horace. Donald's silence didn't bother him in the least. Horace was too angry with the lot life had given him of late to worry over either of his brothers. As far as he was concerned, they could rot in hell with Nora.

He had sold everything he owned in order to go to Scotland. Now, he was left with nothing to his name but a few coins and the clothes on his back. No farm, no home, and no treasures.

When he had first learned that the *treasures* the Scots had stolen were nothing more than meaningless baubles and trinkets, he had never felt more the fool. It was all for naught. His only comfort came with believing that Nora would die soon.

He blamed his current predicament on everyone from his father to his stepmother to Aishlinn and Nora. As he drank, he mused how he should have sold Aishlinn to slave traders in the north. He could have earned quite a pretty penny for the stupid girl. And he should have chosen his wife a bit more carefully.

The thunder in the distance drew nearer. *Good,* he thought to himself. He lifted his tankard as if to cheer some creature that sat invisible before him. *May the grave the stupid bitch sings in be beset with a deluge of rain!* He laughed aloud which caused the innkeeper to eye him curiously. Horace cared not what anyone else thought of his outburst.

He drained the last of his ale and slammed the empty tankard down on the table and ran a hand across his face. One of the first things he had done when he had returned to England was to shave and cut his hair. Every time he caught the reflection of his long hair and bearded face, it reminded him of Scotland and all that had been cruelly stolen from him. He was glad the reminders were gone.

Horace turned toward the innkeeper to call for another tankard of ale when he noticed the innkeeper had stepped toward the door of the inn. The old man stood in the open doorway, his attention drawn to something up the street. The sound of thunder had grown quite loud. Horace assumed it had been the storm that had drawn the innkeeper's attention. But when he saw shock on the old man's face, he realized it had to be more than lightning or thunder that had gained the man's attention.

Horace pushed himself away from the table and staggered toward the door. Impatiently he shoved the old man aside and took a step out to find out what the bloody hell was going on. He was at first, confused by what he saw. His current state of inebriation did not help. When it finally dawned on him what was happening, he could feel the dread and fear clear to his fingers and toes.

Damned bloody Scots!

They were pounding toward him and leading the pack was the damned giant that all of Scotland seemed to be enamored with. There were hundreds of them.

It did not take long to surmise why they were here.

Nora.

He would kill her before he let the Scots steal her away again.

NORA WAS SOAKED TO THE BONE FROM THE RAIN THAT HAD SEEPED in through the dirt walls and the wood planks above her. Her teeth chattered incessantly, her fingers were stiff, and her entire body ached. Certainly Daniel and David would take her away soon, for she couldn't imagine her current conditions improving. Things were ugly and she could not see them getting better any time soon.

Her dress clung to her skin and the blanket felt as heavy as lead from all the rain. Puddles had formed throughout the small prison. If she had figured correctly, it had been close to a fortnight since she'd last bathed, eaten a good meal or slept in a warm bed. She imagined she smelled and looked as awful as she felt.

Nora tried walking around the tiny area, bouncing from one foot to another, rubbing her hands over her arms to keep warm. Her efforts failed miserably, but she knew she had to keep her spirits up. Tonight, she was certain, would be the night that Daniel and David would rescue her from this horrid place. When they came later to give her more food and water, she would demand being removed no matter how many English soldiers might be milling about. She simply could not take any more. She hadn't the strength or will left to suffer through another day in this dark hellhole.

She leaned her shoulder against the wall, fearful of sitting on the waterlogged ground. She let her mind drift to visions of warm, dry places where sunshine, clean clothes, and hot meals were abundant. She would take at least two warm baths each and every day. She would have candles lit all through the night even while she slept. Never again would she be in total darkness.

It was difficult to keep standing or to remain awake. She had to get out of here and soon for she knew she would not survive another night. Death would claim her before the sun rose again on the morrow.

As she leaned against the wall, she thought she felt the earth begin to shake around her. Terrified that the walls were collapsing in from all the rain, she jumped away and stood in the middle of the room. Water and mud seeped in through her already waterlogged boots as the earth continued to shake and the planks above rattled. Never in her life had she heard or felt thunder of such magnitude. It drew nearer and nearer, vibrating the walls and the earth where she stood.

The sound was so tremendous that it drowned out the sound of her hammering heart. There was nowhere to hide from it or from the chunks of dirt that fell all around her. This was it. Her end. Her death. She was going to die under a wall of dirt and mud.

Just as she resigned herself to her fate, the thunder came to an unexpected halt. She stood with her arms out, bracing herself for the earth to come crashing down around her. Moments later, the planks overhead were lifted and thrown aside and what little light the clouds hadn't blocked came streaming through the opening.

Either she had lost her mind or a promise had just been kept.

WEE WILLIAM FELT HIS HEART PLUNGE TO HIS FEET WHEN HE SAW her there. Standing below him, covered from head to toe in dirt and mud, soaked, her teeth chattering, her hair matted to her head, was his beautiful wife. Seeing Nora alive, albeit in less than perfect condition, nearly knocked the wind from his lungs. She had been put through hell, but at least she was alive.

When she fell to the floor in a sodden heap, he was tempted to forgo the ladder and jump in after her. But within moments, Rowan was lowering a ladder down into the darkness. The rest of his men had fanned out, acting as a barrier to anyone dumb enough to try to stop Wee William from getting to his wife.

Just as he was beginning to lower himself down into the hole, a voice called out his name.

"Wee William!" John called out. "Behind you!"

Wee William spun around, drawing his sword from its sheath as Rowan did the same. Coming toward them with his own sword drawn was Horace Crawford.

It was then that Horace noticed John, standing just a few steps away. Horace had reached John before the lad had a chance to draw his own sword. In the blink of an eye, Horace grabbed John around his neck and pulled him into his chest, using the boy as a shield.

"If you do not want to see this boy die, you will walk away from that hole!" Horace yelled at Wee William and Rowan. Both men froze in place and stared at Horace.

John struggled, tried loosening the tight grip Horace had around him. His struggle to free himself angered Horace. He tightened his hold. "Settle down you little brat or I'll kill you before I kill your sister!"

John quieted himself and began to breathe in through his nose and out through his mouth as Wee William had taught him to do on the training fields. One of the lessons Wee William had taught was how to clear your thoughts and steady your breathing in order to assess any situation with a calmer mind.

"Let the boy go, Crawford," Wee William said calmly.

"Nay," Horace said shaking his head and pressing the sword against John's chest. "I don't believe I'll do that. If you want him to live, you'll do as I tell you."

"I strongly encourage ye to listen to the man, Horace," Rowan said coolly.

"Why would I want to listen to a filthy Scot?" Horace barked.

"It be fer yer own good that I warn ye to heed him. Let the lad go and we might let ye live to see another day," Rowan took a step sideways.

Wee William climbed off the ladder and quietly assessed the situation. With a nod of his head, he could order his men to kill Horace.

But Horace had his sword pressed against John's side. He might stab the boy before anyone could kill him. If any harm came to John, he knew Nora would never forgive him.

Horace Crawford did not see the dagger coming. Naively unaware of the fact that John had been training with the best warriors in all of Scotland, Horace had not been prepared for the boy's assault.

As Horace had been arguing with Rowan and making threats he could not possibly keep, John had been stealthily removing the small dagger from his belt. Curving his fingers around the hilt with the blade pointed down, John lifted his hand ever so slightly and thrust back and upward with all his might. The moment John felt the blade tearing through Horace's skin, he pushed himself forward and headed toward Rowan and Wee William.

Horace reeled backward, clutching his side, unable to believe that the boy had just stabbed him. The blade had only grazed his skin, though it did begin to bleed considerably. As John scurried toward Rowan, Horace reflexively chased after him as he drew his sword over his head, ready to slice off the boy's head.

In the end, it was Horace's arrogance and over-confidence that killed him. That combined with Wee William's intimidating speed and strength as he thrust his sword through Horace Crawford's stomach. Horace spoke no final words as blood gurgled up his throat and out of his mouth.

The sickening rasp of metal sucking through skin, flesh, and muscle when Wee William pulled his sword from Horace broke the deathly silence that had fallen around them. Horace Crawford slumped to his knees before keeling over, unable even to clutch his hands against his wounds.

He died alone, just as Aishlinn and Nora had warned him he would.

John had turned as pale as milk, his eyes wide, staring at the sight of Horace Crawford as he died in a thick pool of blood. John had never seen a man killed before. This was not fun and games, this wasn't he and his friends playing as warriors fighting against evil. This was real life. Or real death, depending on one's perspective.

Wee William wiped Horace's blood from his sword by running it back and forth across Horace's legs. One of his men stepped forward and offered him a dirty cloth so that he could more fully clean the blood from it. Wee William waved him away with his hand as he sheathed his sword. He'd worry about cleaning it later. For now, he had to get to his wife.

As Wee William climbed down the ladder to his wife, Rowan stayed above with John, who continued to stare at Horace's body.

Thinking the lad felt remorse or guilt or worry over what had just taken place, Rowan placed a hand on John's shoulder. "Ye did good, lad, with yer dagger. Ye should be verra proud that ye didna let fear get the better of ye. Do no' worry or feel guilt over the death of Horace Crawford."

John had only been half listening to Rowan. It was his statement about feeling guilt that broke his quiet contemplation. John blinked and tore his gaze away from Horace to look Rowan in the eye.

"I carry no worry or guilt over his death, Rowan. Horace Crawford was a mean son of a whore and the world is a better place without him."

John took a deep breath as he knelt down and began to clean his dagger using the water from a sizable puddle. He would lose no more sleep over Horace Crawford.

31

The stench of vomit, musty air, and damp earth assaulted Wee William's senses. Infuriated with the harsh treatment shown his wife, he dropped to his knees beside her and lifted her head gently onto his lap. He ran his hands across her arms and legs, looking for signs of broken bones or bruises. The relief at finding her in one piece, unharmed save for filthy and soaked clothes, he allowed a sigh of relief to escape through his lips.

Nora trembled and shook as he lifted her into his arms and carried her up the ladder. Rowan carefully took Nora from Wee William's arms only so that he could climb freely. John stood anxiously next to Rowan.

"Is she alive?" John asked with a trembling lip.

Rowan offered him a slight smile. "Aye, she is lad. Cold and soaked to the bone though, but we'll remedy that shortly. To yer horse now lad, and be quick about it."

John fought back tears of relief before running off to gather his horse.

Black Richard hurried to the small group, pulling Wee William's horse along behind him. "How is she?" he asked apprehensively.

Wee William answered as he mounted his horse. "She fainted when she saw me and has yet to wake," he answered curtly. He leaned over and took Nora from Rowan's arms and settled her on his lap. Black Richard handed up a blanket that Wee William wrapped around his wife.

As he settled his wife in, he took in his surroundings. His men still encircled the area but none of the villagers had yet made any attempt at stopping them. Nor had anyone stepped forward to tend to Horace. Wee William knew that the serene atmosphere could change in the blink of an eye.

"Mount up, men. We'll meet Angus and the others at Castle Firth and then be gone from this stinkin' place!"

Wee William tapped his feet against the flanks of his horse urging him forward. Many of his men were still mounted, their senses on full alert, scanning the crowd of villagers that had formed for any sign of trouble. They offered a safe barrier as they parted to let Wee William ride through.

In short order, the three hundred Highlanders that had stormed through the town less than a quarter of an hour ago were now leaving. They left in the same thunderous manner as they had arrived.

Wee William led the way out of the village and down the road that led to Castle Firth. He clung to his wife, praying he had reached her in time, praying that she would soon wake. Nora continued to shake but had yet to open her eyes. Frequently, he would look down at her lying limp in his arms as he sped down the road. His own eyes began to fill with tears of joy and regret.

Soon they were riding past the gates of Castle Firth where Angus, Duncan and Findley and four hundred other Highlanders had surrounded the castle. They were taking no chances with the English soldiers that were within those walls.

Angus and the others had surrounded the place an hour ago and thus far, only one man had come to the gate to make inquiry to their presence. Angus had responded by telling the young soldier to deliver a message to the new earl of Penrith. It was a simple message. *We have four hundred men surrounding your castle, three hundred more within in the village, and another four hundred waitin' patiently in the forest to the west. If one soldier so much as peeks his head out a window, a rain of hell and fury will ensue, the likes of which the earl has never witnessed before.*

Obviously the earl took Angus at his word for not another person had been seen since Angus had given his warning.

Once Wee William felt they were far enough away from Penrith and Firth, he led his horse into a dense part of the forest. Rowan and Black Richard followed him in, gave him a tunic, woolens, and clean blankets then left Wee William to tend to his wife.

Tenderly and with great care, Wee William peeled away the layers of his wife's dirty clothes. Goosebumps appeared the moment the mist hit her skin, but still, she did not move nor make a sound. Quickly, he dried her skin with one of the blankets as best he could and pulled the tunic over her head. Next, he covered her legs with the woolens. So large they were and so wee she was, that he was able to pull them up to the middle of her thighs.

Once he had her in fresh, dry clothing, he wrapped her in both blankets, rubbing warmth into her arms and legs with the palms of his hands. Even with dry clothes and warm blankets, she shook and trembled and grew paler as the moments slowly crawled by.

"Nora," he whispered her name as he held her close. Mayhap he had not arrived in time. Mayhap she had slipped into a sleep from which she would never wake. It was killing him slowly, moment by agonizing moment that she did not wake.

"*Mo bhean álainn,*" he whispered softly as he pressed a kiss to her forehead.

Her skin was as cold as ice and just as pale. There were dark circles under her eyes, dirt under her fingernails and scrapes across her knuckles. The image of his wife trying to claw her way out of the deep hole tore through his heart.

"*Mo bhean álainn,*" he repeated. "Please, open your eyes for me," he pleaded, he begged.

Tears of anguish and regret formed, threatening to spill. Honestly, he could not remember the last time he cried. He had to have been a boy. But cry he did. Big, large tears fell from his hazel eyes, down his cheeks, leaving trails through his dust covered skin.

He cried until his body shook, so overcome with grief, anguish, regret, guilt, and sorrow. Aye, he was holding his wife in his arms, holding her tightly against his chest, but it wasn't enough. He desperately needed to look into her eyes, to see all the love and adoration that she had, at one time, felt for him. He needed to hear the sound of her voice, telling him that all would be well and that she would be fine.

The steady rain had turned to a fine mist as Wee William of Dunshire held the love of his life close to his heart, rocking back and forth under the canopy of trees. Back and forth, he cradled Nora in his arms, begged her, and pleaded with her to not leave him alone in this world.

When his pleas went unanswered, he looked upward, sobbing like a bairn, looking to God for hope, direction, and help. He prayed openly, uninhibited and desperate, that God would take his life and spare Nora's.

Nora deserved better than to die here, on English soil after all that she had endured these past many days. Nora was all that was good and right with the world. She was a bright light in an otherwise dark world. She was gentle and kind and showed everyone nothing but compassion and generosity.

Nora was his life, the reason he took one breath after another, and why his heart continued to beat. She was his only reason for living. He cried out to God for Him to please show his wife some grace and mercy. He cried until he was spent and certain he could not shed another tear. Nora was slowly slipping away from him, he could feel it in the way her body slowly stopped trembling and her breathing grew shallow.

He had no idea how much time had passed as he begged and made deals with God. Soon, Nora had stopped shaking altogether.

He pulled her limp body away so that he might see her face. He brushed away loose strands of her dark hair and tenderly caressed her cheek with the backs of his fingers. She was the most beautiful woman that he had ever seen, even as she teetered near death.

Just when he thought he had shed all the tears that he owned, they began to fall again, though not nearly as torrential as earlier. This time, they fell away from his face, dripping off the end of his chin. He continued to caress Nora's cheek and to pray.

Wee William whispered soothing words, speaking in the Gaelic. Quite some time passed as he rocked steadily and spoke his words of love to Nora. He spoke them not so much for her, but for himself. If she were going to die this day, then he would feel better knowing he had shared what was in his heart.

The mist had slowly evaporated, leaving the air heavy and humid. Soon the sun peeped through the gray clouds just as it began its late afternoon descent to the west.

Wee William pressed his lips against Nora's forehead again, closed his eyes and whispered softly against her skin. "*Le do thoil nach dtéann, Is breá liom tú." Please, do not go, I love you.*

It was then that Nora took a deep, slow breath and tried to speak.

"William." The sound of her weak, ragged voice tore through his heart. Elated though he was to finally hear her speak, his heart warned him that these were her last words.

"Wheesht, lass," he murmured against her forehead. "I am so sorry, Nora." He pressed another tender kiss against her forehead.

"William," she tried to speak more forcefully but her throat and mouth were far too dry. "Water," she managed to scratch out.

Wee William searched for the flagon of water, found it lying on the ground next to his legs and hurriedly opened it. Nora took a mouthful and swallowed slowly before taking another drink. When she had her fill, she wiped her mouth against Wee William's shirt. She sighed contentedly and snuggled against him.

"Do I dream husband, or are you truly here?" she asked him sleepily.

He choked back his tears and tried to remain as calm as he could. She was dying and he'd be damned if he'd make her last moments on this earth painful. "Aye, lass, I am here."

"Well, it's about time," she mumbled against his chest.

Wee William shook his head and tried to find some humor in her words. He hurt too much and could not find it within himself to laugh. "I am so sorry, Nora."

Nora tried opening her eyes again. The bright light of the sun stung. "Is that the sun I see?"

Wee William nodded his head and murmured aye, it was.

"It feels good. So very warm. Like you."

He could not speak, could not find the right words to respond. He simply held her close and choked back the pain.

"I dreamt about you William. All the while I was in that hole. I wish we had not fought." She took another deep breath before letting it out slowly. "It feels good to be out of there. I knew you would come for me."

Wee William swallowed back the bile that was forming in his throat. *But I did no' get to ye in time,* he thought.

Nora struggled to sit up, but Wee William would not allow it. "Rest now, lass."

"What happened? Did you find Horace?"

Och! Why must her last thoughts be of Horace? He supposed she would find some comfort in knowing that finally, the son of a whore had been dealt with properly. "Aye," he whispered. "He burns in hell as we speak lass."

Nora tilted her head up and opened her eyes. She was trying to read his face, to see if he told the truth or if by chance he was lying about that again. "You swear it? You do not lie just to make me feel better?"

Wee William gave a shake of his head. "Nay, I do no' lie, I swear it. I killed him meself. His blood still lingers upon me sword. Ye'll no' need to worry about him ever again." He could give her the peace of mind she needed before death claimed her. That was the least he could do for her.

"So I am a widow?"

Wee William chuckled softly. She still worried whether or not they were married properly. "Lass, I told ye the truth. I had Father Michael annul yer marriage to Horace. We were married proper."

Nora's brow creased as she scrutinized her husband. "I think I would feel better if Father Michael married us again."

His chest tightened painfully. He was certain she would not live through the afternoon, let alone long enough to return to Gregor for another ceremony. The fact that she still wanted to be married to him lifted his spirits. Wanting to make her last moments as comfortable and beautiful as possible, he agreed. "Aye, we can do that, lass. Anything ye want."

Nora closed her eyes and snuggled against his chest again. "Thank you William. Please, take me home now so that we can marry again."

He remained silent, rubbing her back with his hand. Several moments of silence passed.

"William?"

"Aye lass?"

"Can we please leave now?"

Wee William chuckled softly again. Even as she lay dying she could bring a smile to his face. "Why are ye in such a hurry to return home?"

Nora sighed. "It is very important to me William, that we marry again."

Wee William drew her away from his chest and stared down at her. "Why be it so important?"

She sighed again before her lips began to curve upward ever so slightly. "Because I don't want our babe born a bastard."

Wee William blinked back his tears and gave his wife a fond, loving smile. *Bairns. Even now she thinks of bairns.* "Wheesht lass, ye need to rest. Now is no' the time to be thinkin' of bairns."

Nora opened her eyes and lifted her head and smiled at him. "Well, better now than in seven months when I'm telling you to fetch Isobel."

He supposed it would not be long now before death claimed his beautiful wife for she was now delirious. He would have given her as many bairns as she wanted. It pained him to think she would never have the chance to carry a child or to be a mother.

"William, what on earth is the matter with you?" She struggled to sit up but his hold on her was too tight.

How could he tell her that she was dying? He couldn't have choked the words out if someone had put a dagger to his throat.

Wee William had been so distraught with thinking she was dying in his arms that he had not noticed the color had returned to her cheeks or that her voice had grown stronger. Nora tried to wriggle out of his firm hold. Exasperated, she gave up.

"William, what is wrong?" She began to fret and worry that something had happened to Elise or John and he didn't have the courage to tell her.

"Has something happened to Elise? To John?" She began to

struggle against his strong arms again. Frustrated, she punched him in his shoulder with her fist.

"Lass, ye must save yer energy!" Wee William admonished her.

Nora was as confused by her husband as she had ever been. His response over learning she was carrying his babe was not what she had expected. Of course, she couldn't be completely certain until they returned to Gregor and Isobel had the opportunity to examine her.

She had missed her last two courses and she had been throwing up for days. At first, she thought it had been the stress of being taken from her family, her husband and her home, that had brought on the nausea. However, at some point, while still being held as Horace's prisoner, she had figured out that it was quite possibly more than just stress and worry. She had started feeling quite unwell days before Horace stole her away.

Wee William finally let loose his hold and allowed her to sit. The expression he wore was quite baffling. Nora was certain he had been crying for his eyes were red and puffy, and tiny white trails lined his cheeks. He looked as though someone had just died. The only thing she could think of was her earlier supposition that something had happened to either John or Elise. Panic set in as she scrambled to her feet.

"William, you must tell me what is wrong, this very moment!" She felt dizzy and lightheaded when she stood. Had Wee William not reached out and caught her, she would have fallen to the ground.

"Nora, ye are no' well! Ye must lie back down now, and rest!" It was then that he finally noticed her rosy cheeks. Certainly a woman who was dying would not have rosy cheeks. And she wouldn't be able to stand up, let alone yell at him, would she?

Wee William held her at arm's length, a thousand different thoughts and emotions running through his head and his heart. So many that he was unable to grasp a single one. He appraised his wife, taking the time to look her up and down, still uncertain that he could believe what his eyes were showing him.

"Nora?" he said her name disbelievingly. "How? I -- ye --" He was quite unable to form any kind of sentence.

Nora stared back at him from shaky legs and a muddled head.

"William, please, tell me what is the matter. Has something happened to Elise or John? To Aishlinn?"

"Nay, they are all well," he answered with a quivering voice. He blinked and shook his head as if it would help to clear his mind and focus better on his wife.

"Then why do you look as though someone has just died?" she asked. She gave him no time to answer as a sudden, even more horrifying thought flashed in her mind.

"It is the babe," she began. "You do not want the babe? I thought you wanted lots and lots of babes, William. That's it, isn't it? You are upset that I want to marry again. You're upset that I carry your babe. I can't believe this, William! We talked about this, even before we married!"

Awareness of what his wife was trying to tell him hit him with as much force as a wall of bricks falling on his head. He felt his legs begin to wobble and his head began to spin out of control. She was not dying and she was carrying his babe. His babe. He was going to be a father.

He held on to his wife's shoulders so that he wouldn't collapse. Nora was going to be fine, praise God! And he was going to be a father.

Wee William took several steadying breaths as his wife continued to talk. She was warning him that it was his fault she was with child to begin with.

"You cannot join with your wife two or three times a day, every day, and not expect a babe to be the result of it! I do not care one whit William, if you are happy about this or not! You will marry me again. My child will not be born a bastard because of, well, whatever it is that is going on in that thick, Scottish, man head of yours!"

There was no way to contain the overwhelming sense of joy. He threw his head back and laughed loudly. He pulled her into his chest and began to kiss her cheeks, her nose, her forehead and her lips.

"Nora, I am sorry," he told her between kisses and chuckles. "I thought ye were dyin', ye were so cold and pale and shakin'. I didna think ye'd survive this day lass. Now, here ye stand before me, tellin' me ye carry me babe. Nothin' lass, could make me happier!"

Nora's shoulders slumped with relief. In the back of her mind she heard the echo of Aishlinn's words, explaining that Highlanders were good honorable men, a little stupid and at times, and slightly tetched. Nora realized Aishlinn was correct in her description of Highlanders.

Nora smiled brightly as her husband smothered her with kisses, checked her over again from head to toe to make certain she was in fact quite well. He prattled on about how happy and proud he was and how much he loved her. His hazel eyes sparkled and twinkled in the late afternoon sun and she noticed that it must have been days since he had last shaved.

Wee William of Dunshire was a very honorable, funny, and handsome man. He was a giant of a man, a good man who was going to make a very good father to their children.

Nora continued to smile and only half listened to him as he retrieved their horse and promised he would have her home soon and she could bathe and eat and sleep in their big, warm bed. She took note of the twinkle in his eye and knew exactly where that last thought had taken him.

She made her own quiet plans as he mounted his horse and lifted her up to settle on his lap. When they returned to their little cottage, she'd like to spend the next week alone with her husband. It had been quite some time since they'd loved one another.

Nora tried to listen to him, but her mind flooded with the memory of the day Wee William had come into her life. It felt like ages had passed since they'd taken that first journey from Penrith to Scotland. She recollected how drastically her life had changed in these past months.

"And do no' worry if it be a girl child ye have, I'll love her just as much as I would a son. And do no' worry that the babe will be too big, like me. Me mum will tell ye that I was a verra wee babe. So wee in fact that they worried that I'd no' live to see me first birthday." He gave her a gentle hug as he urged the horse forward.

Nora had to suppress the urge to laugh aloud as he continued to talk about their babe.

Aye, he may be a little dumb and more than just slightly tetched. But he's mine and he loves me and I'm his woman.

EPILOGUE

EIGHT MONTHS LATER

Until the moment he saw his babe for the very first time, Wee William of Dunshire was wholeheartedly unprepared for the love a father feels for his babe. That unconditional, amazing, and strong bond increased a thousand fold when he set his eyes upon the *second* babe, right before he fell into the chair next to his wife's bed. God's teeth!

Two babes. One each. And they were very tiny, just as he had once been.

Isobel and Aishlinn had helped his wife bring his two beautiful babes into the world. Unfortunately for Nora, she had not had as easy a time as Aishlinn had experienced. Nay, it took Nora two full days to birth her first babe, a son, then surprisingly not long after that, his sister.

His beautiful wife now lay in their bed, smiling as if it had been the easiest thing in the world to do. Wee William knew better. Nora had not cried out in agony, hadn't cursed him to the devil and back again, nor had she otherwise fussed. Throughout it all, she displayed a quiet strength, not, he remarked, unlike a Highland warrior in battle. It wasn't until the very end, when it was time to push, that she made more than just a slight moan. When he had heard that blood-curdling cry come from his wife, he felt the blood rush from his head. It was almost too much for his heart to bear.

Now Wee William held his son and daughter in his arms as he sat on the bed next to his wife. Isobel had reassured him at least a dozen times that Nora was doing very well, as were his babes. He could not get over just how wee and tiny they looked or felt in his arms.

His son began to fuss and cry while his daughter slept on as if she didn't have a care in the world. Gently, Wee William handed the boy over to Nora. The babe quieted the moment he latched on to his mother's breast.

"I knew that if I had a boy, he would have an appetite like his father's," Nora smiled down at her son and caressed his cheek.

Life was a wonder at times. One day you believe you have nothing to call your own, and before you know it, you have a family. *Family*, Wee William mused, was the most important thing a man could have. It was more precious than gold or silver. Nay, a man couldn't put a price on the value of a family.

So much had taken place in the past year. Most of it was for the better. The rest of it was heartbreakingly sad.

The seven clans had come together in a formidable union, even though Gillon Randolph had done his level best to see that it didn't happen. Of course, he hadn't come up with the idea of his own accord. He'd been deceived and in the end, the deception was more than the young man could bear.

Gillon had been duped by his blood father, deceived into believing falsehoods and unimaginable lies. Part of Wee William felt sorry for Gillon Randolph. Gillon had put his belief in the man who had raped his mother and was long believed to be dead, only to come back a year ago and claim otherwise.

After learning the truth, the *real* truth, Gillon Randolph had been so overwrought with grief, anger, and betrayal that he took his own life. It was James Randolph who had found his son hanging from the rafters in his bedchamber just three short days after learning the truth about the man whose blood ran through his veins.

Apparently, Gillon could not stand knowing that Randall Bowie had lied, that Randall wasn't the man he had portrayed himself to be.

He ended his life without leaving a letter of explanation. One could only assume that it was guilt that had led him to it. Overcome with his own grief, James Randolph swore he would kill Randall Bowie as soon as he was found. To date, Randall Bowie was still out there, hiding only heaven knew where. Wee William prayed that James Randolph would soon be able to avenge his son's death. Gillon may have hung himself, but as far as most were concerned, Randall Bowie might just as well have killed the boy by his own hands, for the blame lay with him.

Rowan had married the beautiful Kate Carruthers and they were now living quite happily at Castle *Áit na Síochána*, a little more than a week's ride from MacDougall lands. Though for years Rowan had been quite reluctant to set a date for him and Kate to marry, once he had set eyes upon the beautiful woman, all his worries faded away rapidly.

Findley had written months ago, announcing that Maggy had given birth to a healthy, beautiful baby girl. In his letter, Findley had informed Wee William that he was in the process of building four trebuchets and having a moat installed around their home.

A soft knock on their chamber room door broke Wee William's train of thought. He smiled down at his wife, kissed the top of her head, thanked God once again for all the blessings He had bestowed on him and bid whomever entry.

Elise bounced in, excited that she was an aunt at the ripe old age of seven. John followed behind, with his arms crossed over his chest, looking every bit the Highlander with a dagger in his belt and the MacDougall plaid draped across his chest.

Not long ago John had informed Nora and Wee William that he had decided Scotland wasn't such a bad place after all. Witnessing the way his former villagers had treated Nora last summer had left a very bitter taste in his mouth. John vowed never to return to England. Scotland was now his home.

Wee William watched quietly as Elise carefully climbed into the bed and placed herself directly between him and Nora. John stood next to Wee William and looked quite amazed by his niece and nephew.

"What are you going to name them?" Elise asked.

Nora and Wee William glanced at each other. There were many names to choose from and they had decided to wait until they saw their babe before naming him or her. Now that they had two, the choices had doubled.

"Well," Nora said as she looked adoringly at her husband. "I would like to name the boy William John."

Wee William and John each looked very pleased with that choice. "I'd be verra honored," John said. Nora giggled when she heard the faint Scottish brogue that had begun to form in John's speech.

"And me daughter," Wee William said as he looked down at the sweet little bundle in his arms. "She should have a name to go with her beauty. Siusan Elise I believe will work. Siusan is Gaelic for lily or beautiful, dependin' who ye ask. And I do believe she be as delicate as a lily and just as beautiful." He pressed a gentle kiss to his daughter's forehead before looking to his wife.

"What say ye, wife?" Wee William asked with a broad smile.

Nora could never say no to that braw, handsome smile of his. "Aye, I think that is a very fine name, William."

So the little family sat looking in awe at the wee, tiny babes.

And never was a man more proud of his family than Wee William of Dunshire.

A SAMPLE- MCKENNA'S HONOR

An old adage declares there is no honor among thieves. The same can be said of traitors. Traitors often hide in the open, in plain sight. The truth is there for people who choose to see it, for those who are determined to see things as they are and not as they wish them to be.

In reality, traitors are nothing more than pretenders. Master manipulators. Actors in a play in which only they know who is who and what is what.

The people around them are but an audience, often seeing only what they *wish* to see.

When a traitor performs, openly defending the weak, speaking only with highest regard for his king and country and displaying an unequaled façade of honor, well, who would question his fealty? The traitor reveals only what he *wishes* others to see and only what he knows they wish to believe.

All the while the traitor silently laughs at the folly he has created, taking great pleasure in the absurdity of the entire situation.

And if he is extremely careful the world will never know who or what he *truly* is.

However, as is often the case with thieves, traitors, and ne'er-do-wells, fate steps in at the most unexpected times. It rips away the heavy curtain of subterfuge and duplicity, to openly display to the world not what it wishes to see, but what it, in fact, *must* see.

Such inaugurations to the truth are often painful and traumatic, leaving the newly inaugurated feeling stunned, stupefied and bitter. For some, the only means of survival is outright denial. They shun the truth, cursing it, preferring instead to live in denial. Mayhap because they love the traitor so much, it is easy to justify the traitor's behavior. Or, they may not wish to believe they could have been so easily duped.

But as in all good plays, there are subtle twists and turns. Some are quite obvious, others, not so much. Mayhap the truth isn't always what it seems. Mayhap there is far more to it than anyone realizes.

What then, motivates a man? A man like Angus McKenna who has spent his life defending the defenseless, offering hope to the hopeless, lifting up the weak? Honorable. Honest. Steadfast. A leader of men. A man loyal to king and country. A man above reproach. This is the man Angus McKenna's people see, the man other leaders see, the man the world sees.

Ever since the day he took his oath as chief of the Clan MacDougall and made the promise to uphold and protect his clan above all other things, Angus McKenna put his family and his clan first. Each decision he made since that fateful day in 1331 was made with only one thought in mind: how will it affect his family and his clan?

Nothing mattered but the safety and wellbeing of his people. Not his own comfort, his own desires nor his own needs could be taken into consideration when making decisions that would directly affect his people.

What could have made Angus McKenna don a red and black plaid and turn against his king? His country? How could a man like Angus McKenna do such a thing? What could be of such a value that he would plot to murder his king and to forge a pact with the English? A pact that would cause the fall of his country and put it squarely into the hands of the very people he has spent his entire life fighting against.

Gold? Silver? Power? Something more?

Time and experience reveal that things are not always as they appear.

ONE

Edinburgh, Scotland, Summer 1347

"ANGUS MCKENNA, YE STAND BEFORE THIS TRIBUNAL TODAY, accused of crimes against our king and the country of Scotland," the under-sheriff read from the document he held in his thin, trembling hands. He paused, looking toward the dais where the leader of the tribunal, the Sheriff of Edinburgh, sat.

The under-sheriff was a scrawny man, with bloodshot eyes and pale skin. With dark circles under his bloodshot eyes, he looked as though he had not slept in days. He stood in direct contrast to the sheriff, who was a rotund, portly man.

After a heavy sigh and a wave of a hand from the sheriff, the under-sheriff continued. His dull eyes darted about the room, looking everywhere but at Angus McKenna.

Coward, Angus thought to himself. *He does no' have the courage to look me in the eye.* Angus found the man's demeanor amusing.

"How do ye plead to these charges?" the under-sheriff asked. Angus noted the slight tremble in the man's voice, as if he were not only afraid to ask the question, but also to hear Angus' answer.

Angus stood tall and proud, ignoring the fact that his hands and feet were shackled. He looked the sheriff straight in the eyes when he answered.

"Guilty."

His reply was loud and firm. He was determined to remain that way, no matter what the outcome might be. Admittedly, he *had* done all the things of which he was accused. There was no denying the accusations let alone the charges. He *had* conspired against his king, his country.

Angus did not care for the arrogant sheriff, what with his fancy ways, false airs and his unearned pride. Phillip Lindsay was a haughty fool, with a mean streak as long as a summer day in the Highlands. It was difficult for Angus to believe the man was the son of Carlich Lindsay, his long-time friend and ally.

The under-sheriff's eye began to twitch, as he looked first at Angus and then to Phillip. He seemed to shrink, to draw himself inward as if he were afraid the floor beneath his feet would open up and swallow him whole. The tall scrawny man waited for the sheriff to say something.

Phillip Lindsay sitting with his head resting against his pudgy index finger seemed unmoved by Angus' answer. If he took any joy in the matter, it did not show. Indifferent and mayhap a bit disgusted. Whether with Angus or the proceedings was difficult for him to ascertain. *No matter*, Angus thought to himself. It also did not matter how he pleaded to the charges. Phillip Lindsay would have found him guilty anyway regardless of any claim of innocence Angus might have made.

Before either the sheriff or under-sheriff could speak, Duncan McEwan, Angus' son-in-law spoke up. His shackles rattled as he took a step forward to stand next to Angus. Although the man was covered in dirt and grime, his blonde hair hanging in filthy strings about his face, his blue eyes still held the look of a proud Highland warrior. He stood straight and tall, proud, and dignified. The fool was as stubborn as Angus, something he had learned no doubt from watching Angus all these years.

"I plead guilty as well," Duncan said with more than just a hint of pride in his voice.

The under-sheriff was startled by Duncan's voice as it boomed through the room. His eyes blinked rapidly for a moment before he found the courage to speak. "Ye need to wait yer turn, Duncan McEwan."

Duncan tilted his blonde head to the side and smiled deviously at the skinny man in charge of keeping him and Angus in chains. "Why?"

Duncan asked. "The charges be the same fer me as fer Angus. I simply be savin' ye time and breath."

"Silence," Phillip Lindsay ordered in a calm voice. "Ye'll get yer turn soon enough, ye traitor."

Before Duncan could respond to the insult, Angus pulled tight on the shackles to keep the young man in place and from making a deadly mistake. "Hold, son," he whispered firmly.

Duncan pursed his lips together and drew his shoulders back. His dark blue eyes flickered with silent understanding. He gave a nod of affirmation before turning back to the under-sheriff.

"Ye both are accused of crimes against the king, against the great country of Scotland. Ye planned and plotted with the English to murder our king. Ye've both admitted to such." Phillip Lindsay spoke from the dais, his voice carried through the half-empty room. One would have thought throngs of people would be in attendance this day, considering the charges and the circumstances. Mayhap it was the rain that kept the usual anxious, excited onlookers away. Angus did not think it was the rain that kept people away. Nay, it was something more, something he could not quite put his mind to. Those few men in attendance were drawn to Phillip Lindsay's deep voice and turned their attention to him.

Phillip continued to stare at Angus, looking ashamed to call Angus a Scot. *So be it,* Angus thought as he straightened his back and lifted his head high. He would not let a man like Phillip Lindsay make him feel regretful, ashamed or humiliated.

Phillip Lindsay's upper lip curled slightly, as if he were standing too near a pile of horse dung. After several long moments, he let out a sigh of disgust and sat upright in his ornately carved chair.

Angus did not believe for one moment that Phillip Lindsay was actually mulling over the charges. Nor did he fight with his conscience over the sentence he should mete out to Angus or Duncan. Nay, 'twas all nothing more than a show for the few men sitting on the benches as witnesses. 'Twas nothing more than play-acting, and the sheriff was the bard, a teller of stories.

"I hereby sentence ye both to death. One week from today, ye shall be taken to Stirling, where ye will both be hanged by yer necks until dead," he declared to those observing the tribunal. "Get the traitors out of me sight," he ordered the under-sheriff.

Reluctantly, almost solemnly, the under-sheriff led Angus and Duncan out of the dark room. Three of his men were waiting outside. Once in the hallway, the trio surrounded Angus and Duncan and led them out of the building and into the courtyard.

It had been days since Angus and Duncan had seen the sun. From the looks of the gloomy sky and the steady rain that fell, it would be even longer before they would see it again.

Though a number of people huddled in the rain, none would look at Angus or Duncan. Angus wondered if it was fear that kept their eyes cast to the ground or mayhap and much worse, *shame.*

It was of his own doing. He *had* shamed his people, his family, and his reputation. There was no denying this. No one, save mayhap for the young man chained to him, would understand the reasons for what he had done. The choice had been his to make three years past and made it he had.

The only guilt Angus felt at the moment was the fact that Duncan was here with him. Duncan was his adopted son as well as his son-in-law. Duncan was just a boy when his family had been killed by a band of English soldiers who had attacked his village. Only three boys had survived the ordeal, two of which were Angus' nephews by blood. The boys had come to live with him and Isobel and not long after, they had adopted all three lads.

Angus and Isobel had adopted several children over the years, but together, they had only one flesh and blood daughter. Angus did, however, have another daughter whom he had long thought dead, along with her beautiful mum. Through circumstances not of his choosing, he did not learn of her existence until three years ago and then not until after Duncan and Aishlinn had fallen hopelessly in love with one another.

The young man did not deserve to be here for he was no more a traitor in this macabre mess Angus had gotten into than Mother Mary. 'Twas Duncan's own stubbornness that brought him here and nothing more.

Soon they came to the entrance to the dungeon. When the under-sheriff opened the heavy wooden door, the smell of filth, death and despair assaulted their senses. The skinny man grabbed a lit torch from the brace on the wall and led the way down the filthy, damp stone stairs. Through a maze of twists and turns, they made their way to the bowels of the dungeon. They passed numerous cells filled with all sorts of lost souls. Men, and aye, even a few women, who had lost all hope long ago.

Some were thieves, some murderers, and some whose only guilt was being poor and uneducated. Compassion for the poor and uneducated tugged at Angus' heart. It was through no fault of their own that they were here. If Angus had had any control over the current situation, he'd have done what he could to free them and send them to Gregor, to give them a chance at a somewhat decent life.

Nay, 'twas not to be. Not today. Nor at any time in the foreseeable future.

He could not help them any more than he could help himself at the moment and the thought pulled at his heart.

Once Angus and Duncan stepped into their cell, the door was closed behind them. Even though they were given a private cell and not tossed in with the murderers, both men knew they were not necessarily safe from harm.

While the under-sheriff appeared both afraid and sympathetic, Angus knew the other guards held no such feelings toward them. And with all that had taken place since the battle at Neville's Cross last October, it was sometimes difficult to tell who was friend and who was foe.

For three long years, Angus had been playing the role of spy and traitor. He had played it so well that the lines had begun to blur. It had been a very fine line he had walked, a very fine line indeed.

And after the events at Neville's Cross, Angus knew that *no one* could be trusted.

TWO

ANGUS HANGS AT DAWN.

No matter how many times Nial McKee read the missive he held in his hand, he could not grasp the reality of it. Surreal. Unbelievable.

Angus McKenna, one of the most honorable men he'd ever known, his own father-in-law for the sake of Christ. And he had not only been accused of treason and crimes against their king, he had admitted to them!

Why? Why would the most respected and revered chief of one of the mightiest clans in Scotland do such a thing?

Nial ran a hand through his short brown hair, tossed the missive onto his desk and finally looked up at Caelen McDunnah, the man who had brought him the news.

Caelen had been Nial's best friend for as long as he could remember. To anyone who did not know the two men well, their friendship was a curious one, for no two men could be more dissimilar.

Where Nial was short and stocky, with short-cropped light brown hair and gray blue eyes, Caelen was tall and built like a wall of stone. He wore his nearly black hair long, with braids on either side of his temples, and his dark brown eyes, rarely, if ever, sparkled. Where Nial's body was relatively free of scars, a rough, jagged scar ran from Caelen's forehead, down the left side of his face, and ended a few inches under his left armpit.

Nial knew it should have been *his* face and body marred by that scar, not Caelen's.

Their friendship had begun not long before the Battle of Berwick in 1333. They'd been very young men, eager to prove to themselves and to the world their abilities on the battlefield. Both men had come close to dying at Berwick. Much blood -- a good portion of it belonging to Caelen -- along with their youthful exuberance and immature lust for fighting was left on that marshy battlefield.

Since that day, Nial had done everything he could to avoid fighting. Nay, he was no coward, for he would fight to his own death if the circumstances called for it. He had fought in too many battles to count. But whenever possible, he would give diplomacy a chance before drawing his sword.

The same could not be said for Caelen. The man enjoyed a good fight. It was often said that he would sometimes start an argument for the sole purpose of brawling. Whether it was boredom or some twisted, inner desire to test fate and death, one couldn't be certain. For whatever reason, Caelen enjoyed fighting.

"I couldna believe it meself when I first read it," Caelen said from the opposite side of Nial's desk. Nial found it difficult at the moment to ascertain what Caelen might truly be thinking. Nial was one of the very few people who could read Caelen's moods and sometimes thoughts, regardless of any outward expression. But today, Caelen's thoughts were indiscernible.

Nial's principal worry however, was his wife, Bree, and how she would take the news of her father's incarceration and the charges leveled against him. *This is going to kill Bree,* he thought to himself.

"Where is Duncan in all of this?" Nial asked, his voice sharp and full of concern.

Caelen cleared his throat and crossed well-muscled arms over his broad chest and leaned against the fireplace mantle. "Sittin' right next to his treasonous father-in-law."

Nial's eyes widened with surprise and shock. It was bad enough that his father-in-law sat in the dungeon in Edinburgh. Caelen knew the two men as well as Nial. He was astonished to hear Caelen refer to either man as a traitor. "Certainly ye dunna believe Angus a traitor?"

Caelen cocked his head as he chewed on the inside of his cheek. "He's admitted to it, Nial. Both have."

Nial's eyes turned to small slits. "I do no' believe it. I will no' believe it until I speak to them." *How in the name of God am I goin' to tell Bree?*

Angus and Duncan. Accused of treason. That either man would admit to such a thing would be laughable, were they not both sitting in a dungeon in Edinburgh, waiting to be hanged. Nial had known these men most of his life. Never, not once in all that time had either of them done anything, said anything, or otherwise acted in any manner that would make anyone question their loyalty to Scotland or her king.

"Where are Isobel and Aishlinn?" Nial asked as he tried to make sense of the news.

"That be a good question," Caelen began. "I was hopin' they were here."

More confusion knitted on Nial's brow. "Nay, we've not seen any of them in many months." Clarity began to dawn as he studied his friend more closely. There was something in Caelen's countenance and his voice that gave Nial pause. "Ye dunna ken where they are?" It was more a statement than a question.

"Nay, we do no' ken where they be. It seems they disappeared the same night that the sheriff's men came fer Angus and Duncan. The babes be missin' too." Caelen looked pained to tell Nial that last bit of news.

"Disappeared?" Unease and worry began to double. His stomach suddenly felt heavy, filled with the dread of having to explain all of this to his sweet wife. *Bree.*

Caelen remained silent for a time, allowing Nial time to come to terms with the news that two of his in-laws were admitted traitors and their female counterparts, along with his nephews were missing.

With a scrutinizing gaze, pursed lips, and furrowed brow, Nial tried to read Caelen's face. What exactly *wasn't* he telling him? He could not quite put his finger on it, but there *was* something hidden, something Caelen was deliberately keeping from him.

The men watched each other closely for several long moments. The only sound in the room came from the crackling fire and the soft rain as it fell against the shutters of the keep.

Nial hoped for some sign of what his friend might be thinking. It suddenly dawned on him that there was a strong possibility that Caelen worried that Nial too, might be less than loyal to their king. "Ye think me a traitor as well? Is that why ye be here Caelen?" He made no attempts to hide his anger or his disgust. "Ye ken I be no more a traitor than ye!"

"What of Angus' admission?" Caelen asked. His voice was calm. Holding not even the slightest hint as to what he was thinking or feeling.

Nial let out an exasperated sigh. "What of it?" he barked. "There must be a reason fer him to admit to such a thing." Nial would never believe Angus or Duncan was a traitor.

"Each has admitted to it, Nial. The question be *why*? Be it the truth, or something more?"

In his heart, Nial knew there could be no truth to the accusations. He turned to gaze out the window behind his desk. Dawn was just beginning to break beyond the horizon. Green as far as his eye could see save for the ewes and their lambs that dotted the summer grass. On this rainy day, the sheep looked like gray clouds that had fallen to the earth.

Below stairs, the keep was slowly coming to life. Soon the younger maids would begin to light the fires in the gathering room and the kitchen staff would begin preparing the morning meal. Within the hour, the many inhabitants of the keep would begin scurrying about with their daily duties.

The early morning hours had always been Nial's favorite time of day. He loved waking up and pulling Bree into his arms and holding her close to his chest. Sometimes, if he woke early enough, he would have time to show her just how much he adored and cherished her before their son woke and demanded her full and undivided attention.

He would not relish waking her this morn. Nay, he would let her sleep until Jamie woke. Nial imagined it would be some time before they slept in blissful, untroubled, contented sleep again.

Bree was just four doors away from where he now stood. Their seven-month-old son Jamie was fast asleep in his cradle just steps away from their bed. Nial wished he could climb back into bed with his wife and forget that Caelen had just delivered him such dire news.

"I tell you, there has to be a reason, but I dunnae what it be," Nial said, still trying to come to terms with the news.

Caelen straightened himself and came to stand before Nial's desk. "What can ye think of that would get men like Angus McKenna and Duncan McEwan to admit to treason? If it be not the truth, then what?"

Nial thought on the question for a time, his lips pursed together as a hard line formed above his brows. There could be only one reason, other than the truth, that would elicit Angus' confession.

"Isobel," Nial murmured. Isobel was Angus' wife, Bree's mum, and the love of Angus McKenna's life.

"Aishlinn, Bree," Caelen offered, "his grandchildren." He waited patiently for his friend Nial to join his own way of thinking.

Nial turned to face Caelen. Only a moment passed before realization began to sink in. Angus and Duncan were protecting their wives and families. Nothing else made sense. Nial noticed a twinkle of sorts present in Caelen's deep brown eyes. For those who did not know the man well, they might have thought it something malevolent, but Nial knew better. Relief enveloped Nial as he came to the sudden conclusion that Caelen did not think Angus McKenna a traitor any more than Nial did.

"Ye do no' think Angus a traitor," Nial said.

Caelen smiled and shook his head. "No more than I think ye be."

Suddenly, Nial felt hopeful and encouraged. Caelen's twinkling eyes said enough. There might be hope for Angus and Duncan after all. Nial smiled, his spirits lifting considerably. But it was short-lived.

Aye, Caelen may well have a plan, something as yet unspoken, that might, just *might,* help the two men he admired most in life. But he still had to break the news to Bree. He knew it would be one of the most difficult conversations of his life.

NIAL TOOK A DEEP BREATH AND STEELED HIMSELF FOR HIS WIFE'S reaction to the news that her father was an admitted traitor. Her reaction was not what he had expected. They had been married for a year and a half and he knew there was still much he needed to learn about the woman who was his sole reason for living.

He had expected her to be outraged and appalled that anyone would accuse her father of such misdeeds. He fully expected her to stomp about their bedchamber, furious, and demanding action. And if Nial wouldn't put the call out to bring their warriors to arms, she would do it herself.

Instead, his strong, beautiful wife sat in a chair beside the fireplace watching their son Jamie as he suckled at her breast. She seemed unmoved by the news. Her calm demeanor, her quiet façade scared the hell out of him. Aye, she may have responded in a quiet and dignified manner, but Nial felt certain she was quietly plotting the deaths of the person or persons who had accused her father and Duncan of such atrocities.

Bree smiled proudly at Jamie as she spoke to her husband. "And what do we intend to do about it?" she asked without looking up.

Nial stood speechless for a moment. He supposed she was keeping her anger in check for fear of upsetting their babe.

"Caelen waits fer me below stairs," he began. "We do no' know yet who is behind this. They canna find Isobel or Aishlinn and the babes."

Bree's head shot up at that piece of news. "What do ye mean they canna find them?"

"They went missin' the same night they came to take Angus and Duncan away," Nial told her as he bent to one knee beside her. He ran a hand over his son's dark locks. Under normal circumstances he would have felt a tad jealous that his son was enjoying that part of Bree that Nial found pleasure with as well.

Bree reached out and gently laid a hand on Nial's arm. She needed his reassurance that all would be well. Although she was worried for her father and Duncan, her stomach drew into knots with worry over where Isobel and Aishlinn were. Who knew where they might be and what they were going through. She did her best to chase those terrifying thoughts away. She knew she'd be no good to them, or anyone else, if she could not keep herself together.

"Nial, please tell me what ye believe is happenin'," she asked softly.

"I do no' believe yer da, or Duncan, are traitors. There must be a reason why they would make such admissions. I can only assume it has something to do with the fact that Isobel and Aishlinn are missin'." He took a deep breath and turned to face his wife.

Bree's beautiful green eyes were missing their usual sparkle. They were filled with worry and questions Nial could not answer.

"I want ye to take Jamie and go to Findley and Maggy's," Nial told her. He stopped her before she could protest. "Bree, within the hour I will be leavin' with Caelen for Edinburgh. I canna help Angus or Duncan if I must worry over ye. If me guess is right, someone has Isobel and Aishlinn and are usin' them against Angus and Duncan. I canna let anyone get to ye and Jamie." His voice was soft, yet firm. If he had to tie her up and drag her to Maggy and Findley's, he would.

Nial could see his wife contemplating his argument. After a time, she finally nodded her head in agreement. "I suppose yer right," she said. Maggy and Findley's home was much closer to Stirling than the McKee keep and from there, she might be able to do more to help her parents and the rest of her family. But she kept that line of thinking to herself. If Nial caught even an inkling of what she might be thinking, he would probably tie her up and put a dozen guards around her.

Nial breathed a sigh of relief and caressed his wife's cheek before giving her a tender kiss on her forehead. "I will send Ellen up to help ye pack. I've men readyin' themselves to take ye to Maggy's. If ye leave soon, ye can be in Stirling within three days.

Bree smiled up at her husband and gave his hand a gentle squeeze. "When are they set to hang?" she asked over the lump in her throat.

"If our information is correct, they're plannin' on takin' them to Stirling fer the hangin'. I'm told they'll be leavin' Edinburgh in five days' time. Hopefully, we can figure out what the bloody hell has happened before then and get this all sorted out."

"Has anyone talked to Robert? Has anyone appealed to him?" Bree asked. If anyone could stop her father and Duncan from hanging, it was Robert Stewart, High Steward of Scotland. With King David's capture by the English at Neville's Cross, Robert Stewart was leading their country. Bree knew he was the one and only man at the moment who could help her father and Duncan.

"I dunnae. I've only just been told of what happened. I'll ken more when we get to Edinburgh. I believe Wee William is now on his way to get an audience with Robert Stewart as we speak."

Purchase McKenna's Honor Here

ALSO BY SUZAN TISDALE

The Clan MacDougall Series

Laiden's Daughter

Findley's Lass

Wee William's Woman

McKenna's Honor

The Clan Graham Series

Rowan's Lady

Frederick's Queen

The Mackintoshes and McLarens Series

Ian's Rose

The Bowie Bride

Rodrick the Bold

Brogan's Promise

The Clan McDunnah Series

A Murmur of Providence

A Whisper of Fate

A Breath of Promise

Moirra's Heart Series

Stealing Moirra's Heart

Saving Moirra's Heart

Stand Alone Novels

Isle of the Blessed

Forever Her Champion

The Edge of Forever

Arriving in 2018:

Black Richard's Heart

The Brides of the Clan MacDougall

(A Sweet Series)

Aishlinn

Maggy (arriving 2018)

Nora (arriving 2018)

Coming Soon:

The MacAllens and Randalls

ABOUT THE AUTHOR

USA Today Bestselling Author, storyteller and cheeky wench, SUZAN TISDALE lives in the Midwest with her verra handsome carpenter husband. Her children have all left the nest. Her pets consist of dust bunnies and a dozen poodle-sized groundhogs – all of which run as free and unrestrained as the voices in her head.

For the latest news about upcoming books and events, subscribe to Suzan's newsletter here.

Get text messages on new releases! **Text CheekyWenchUS** to **24587**

Keep Up To Date
www.suzantisdale.com
suzan@suzantisdale.com

Made in the USA
Columbia, SC
26 May 2021

38562671R00255